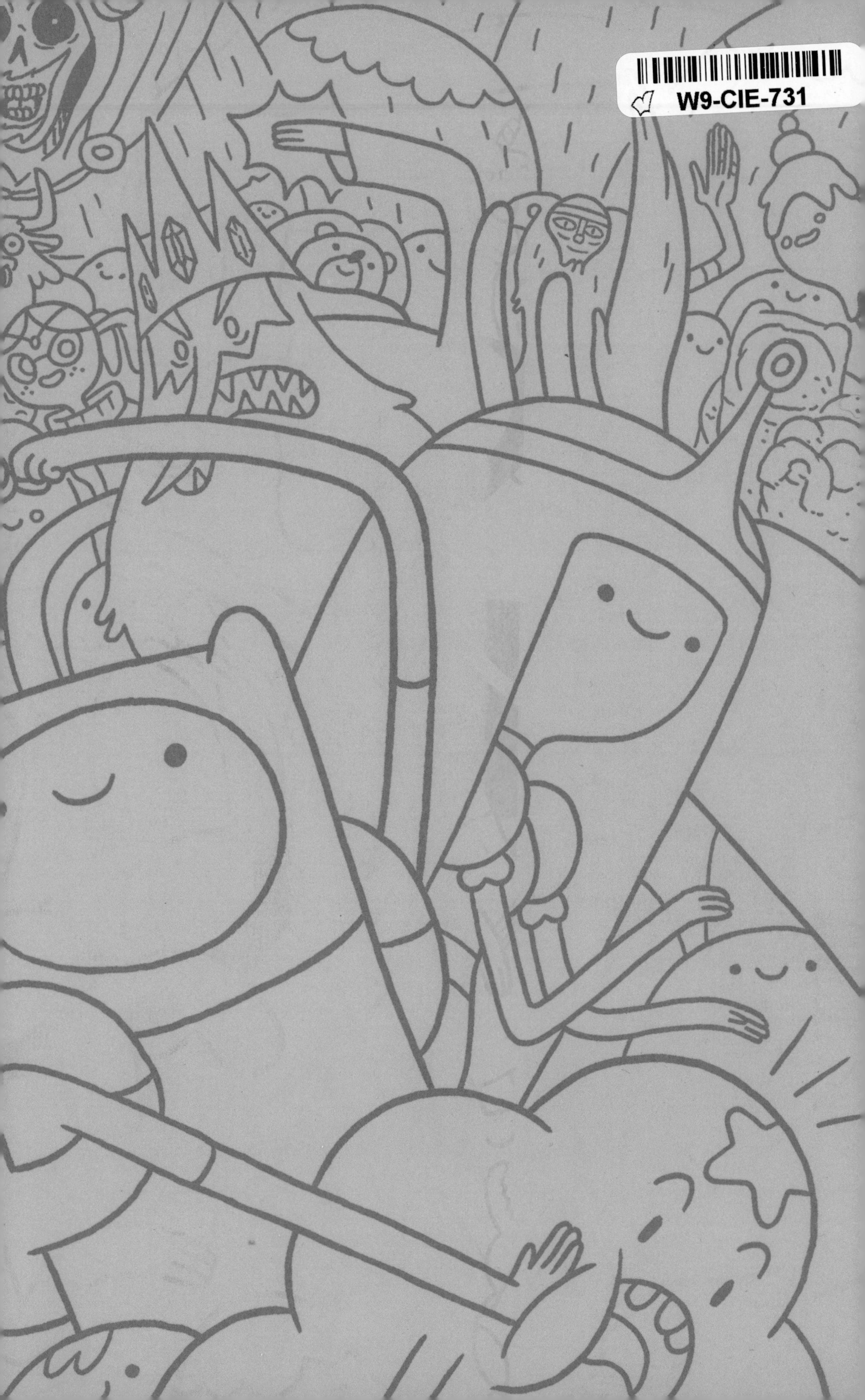

PUBLISHED BY KaBOOM!

ROSS RICHIE ~ Chief Executive Officer

MATT GAGNON ~ Editor-in-Chief

FILIP SABLIK ~ VP-Publishing & Marketing

LANCE KREITER ~ VP-Licensing & Merchandising

PHIL BARBARO ~ Director of Finance

BRYCE CARLSON ~ Managing Editor

DAFNA PLEBAN ~ Editor

SHANNON WATTERS ~ Editor

ERIC HARBURN ~ Editor

CHRIS ROSA ~ Assistant Editor

ALEX GALER ~ Assistant Editor

STEPHANIE GONZAGA ~ Graphic Designer

KASSANDRA HELLER ~ Production Designer

MIKE LOPEZ ~ Production Designer

JASMINE AMIRI ~ Operations Coordinator

DEVIN FUNCHES ~ E-Commerce & Inventory Coordinator

VINCE FREDERICK ~ Event Coordinator

BRIANNA HART ~ Executive Assistant

**ADVENTURE TIME: MATHEMATICAL EDITION
Volume One** — March 2013. Published by
KaBOOM!, a division of Boom Entertainment, Inc.
ADVENTURE TIME, CARTOON NETWORK, the
logos, and all related characters and elements
are trademarks of and © Cartoon Network. (S13)
All rights reserved. Originally published in single
magazine form as ADVENTURE TIME 1-4,
ADVENTURE TIME FREE COMIC BOOK DAY
EDITION. © Cartoon Network. (S12) All rights
reserved. KaBOOM!™ and the KaBOOM! logo
are trademarks of Boom Entertainment, Inc.,
registered in various countries and categories.
All characters, events, and institutions depicted
herein are fictional. Any similarity between any
of the names, characters, persons, events, and/
or institutions in this publication to actual names,
characters, and persons, whether living or dead,
events, and/or institutions is unintended and
purely coincidental. KaBOOM! does not read or
accept unsolicited submissions of ideas, stories,
or artwork.

A catalog record of this book is available from
OCLC and from the KaBOOM! website, www.
kaboom-studios.com, on the Librarians Page.

BOOM! Studios, 5670 Wilshire Boulevard, Suite
450, Los Angeles, CA 90036-5679.

Printed in Canada. First Printing.

ISBN: 978-1-60886-324-2

MATHEMATICAL EDITION
Volume One

CARTOON NETWORK. FREDERATOR

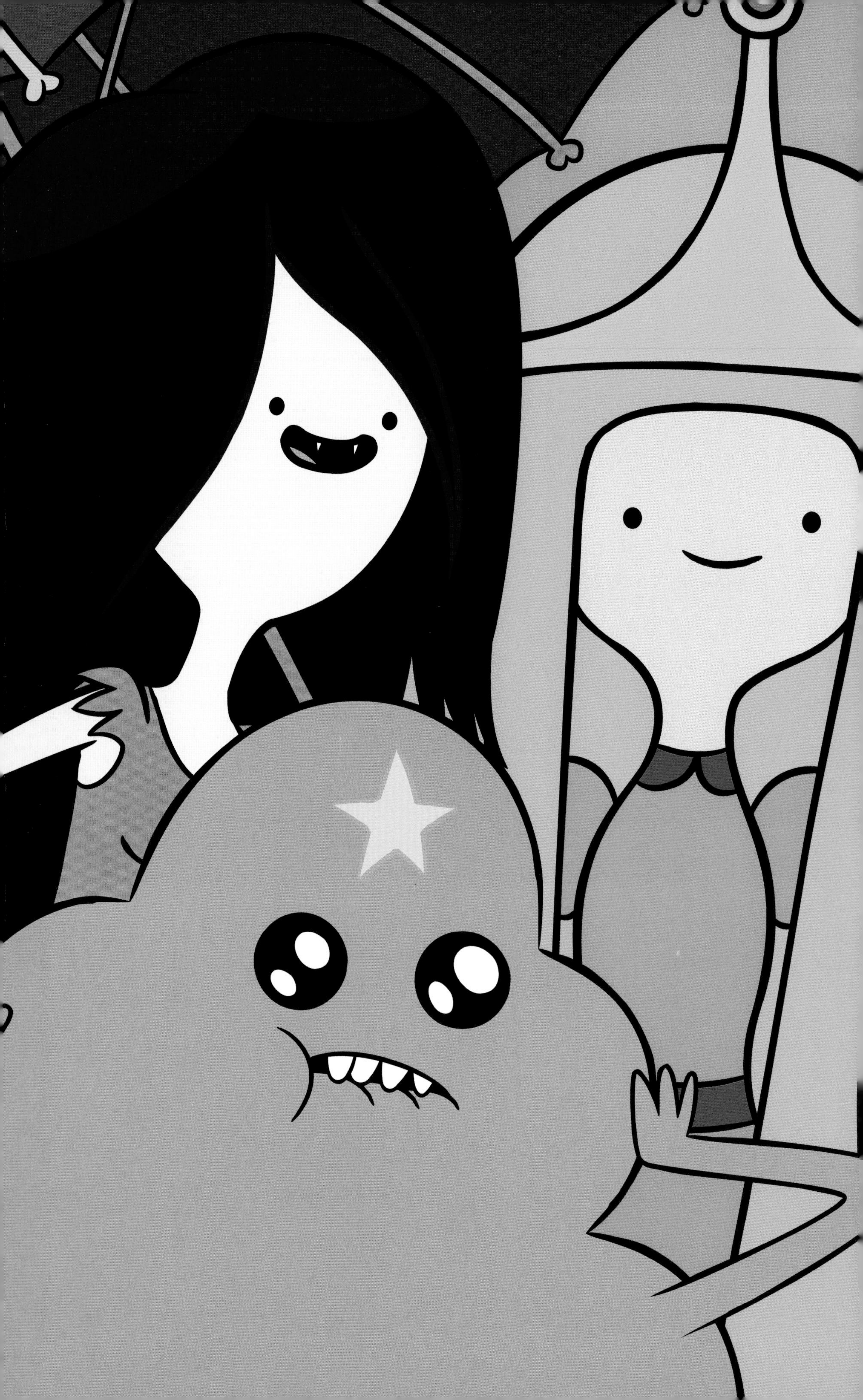

CREATED BY
Pendleton Ward

WRITTEN BY
Ryan North

ILLUSTRATED BY
Shelli Paroline and Braden Lamb

LETTERS BY
Steve Wands

"BMO'S LESSON"

ILLUSTRATED BY
Mike Holmes
COLORS BY STUDIO PARLAPÁ

EDITED BY
Shannon Watters

TRADE AND COVER DESIGN BY
Stephanie Gonzaga

EMERALD CITY COMICON EXCLUSIVE COVER BY
Dustin Nguyen

With special thanks to
Marisa Marionakis, Rick Blanco, Curtis Lelash, Laurie Halal-Ono, Keith Mack, Kelly Crews
and the wonderful folks at Cartoon Network.

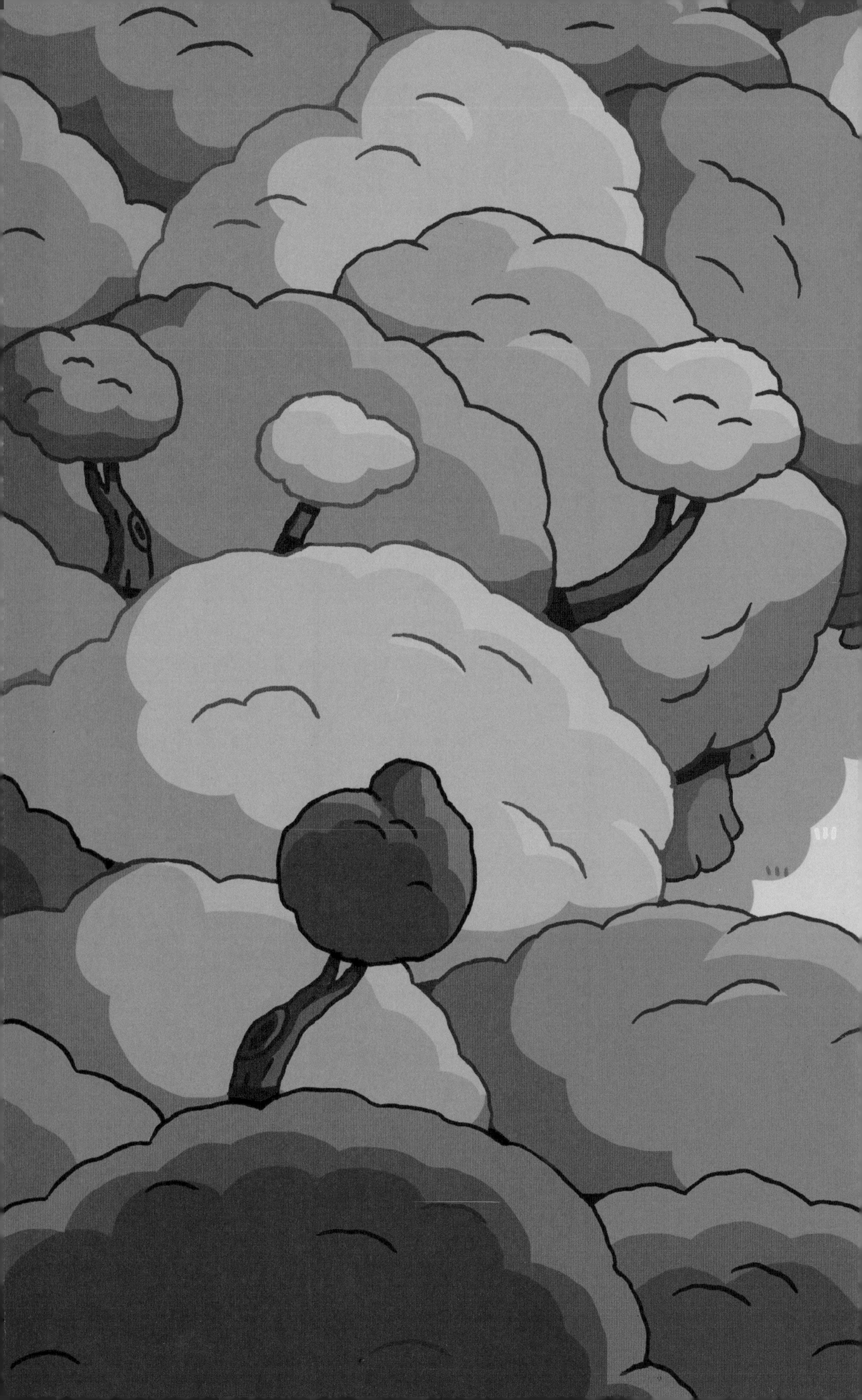

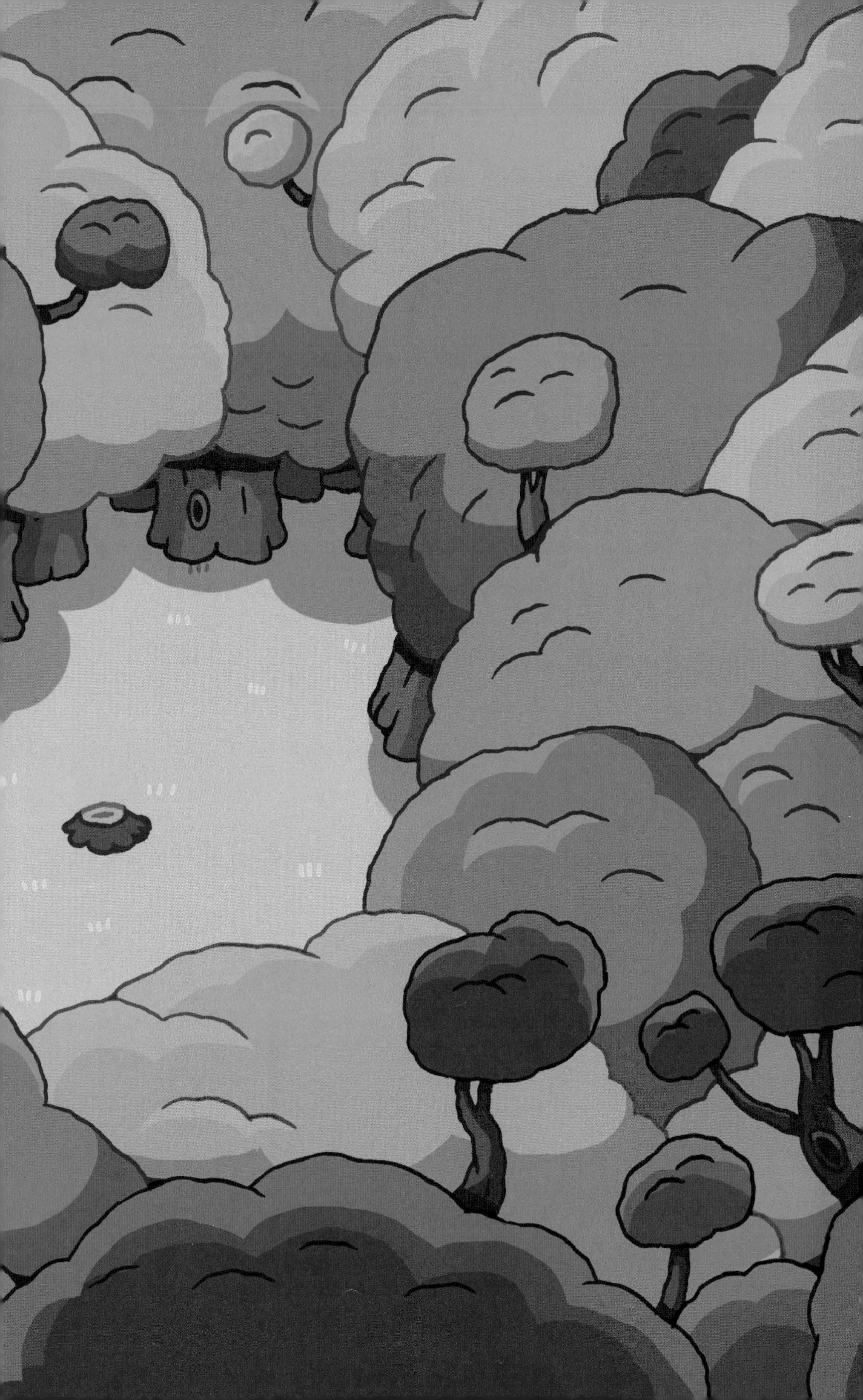

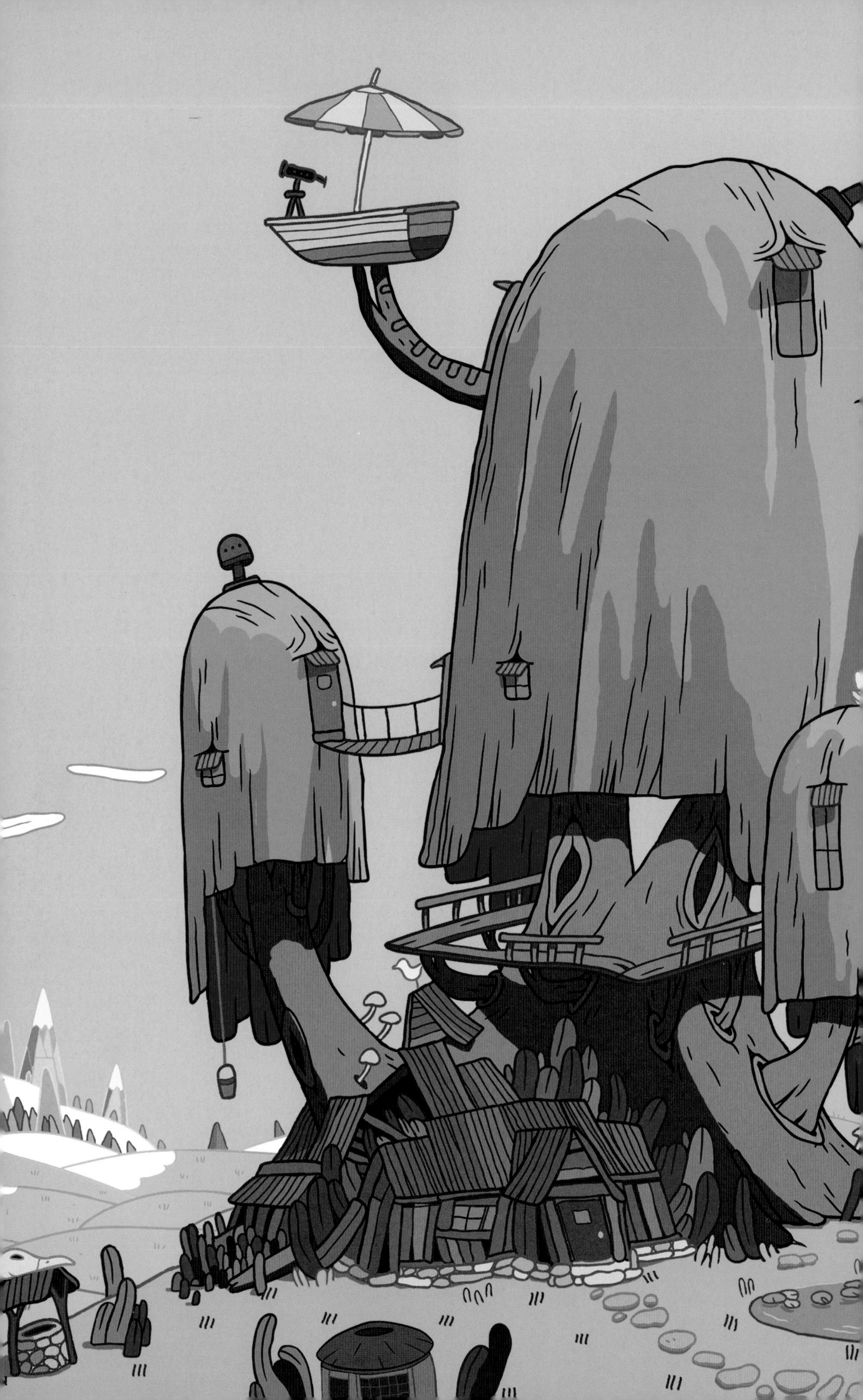

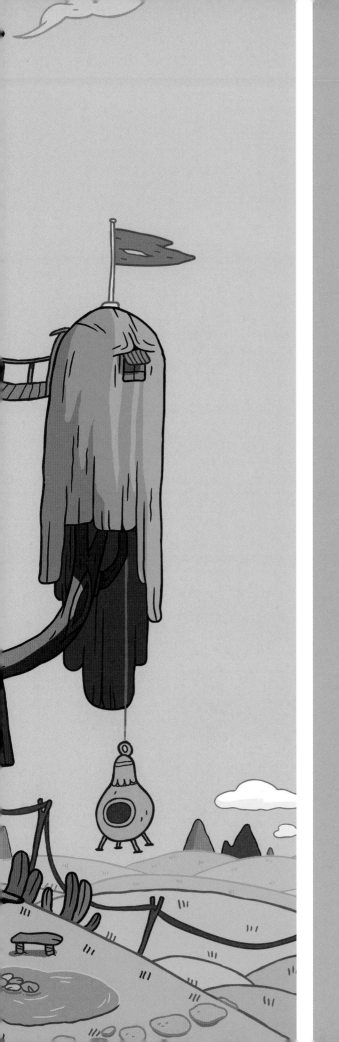

CHAPTER ONE

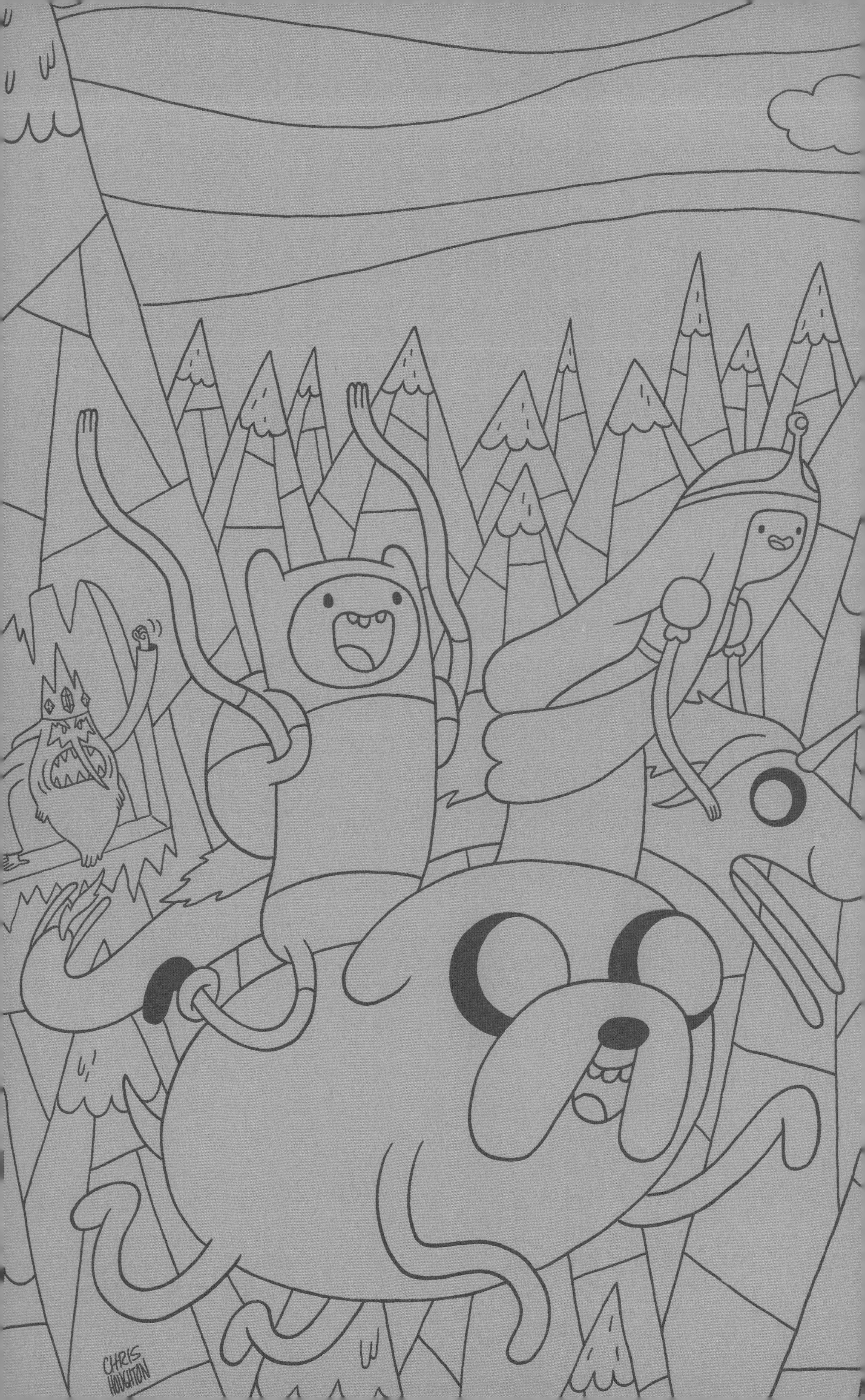
CHRIS
HOUGHTON

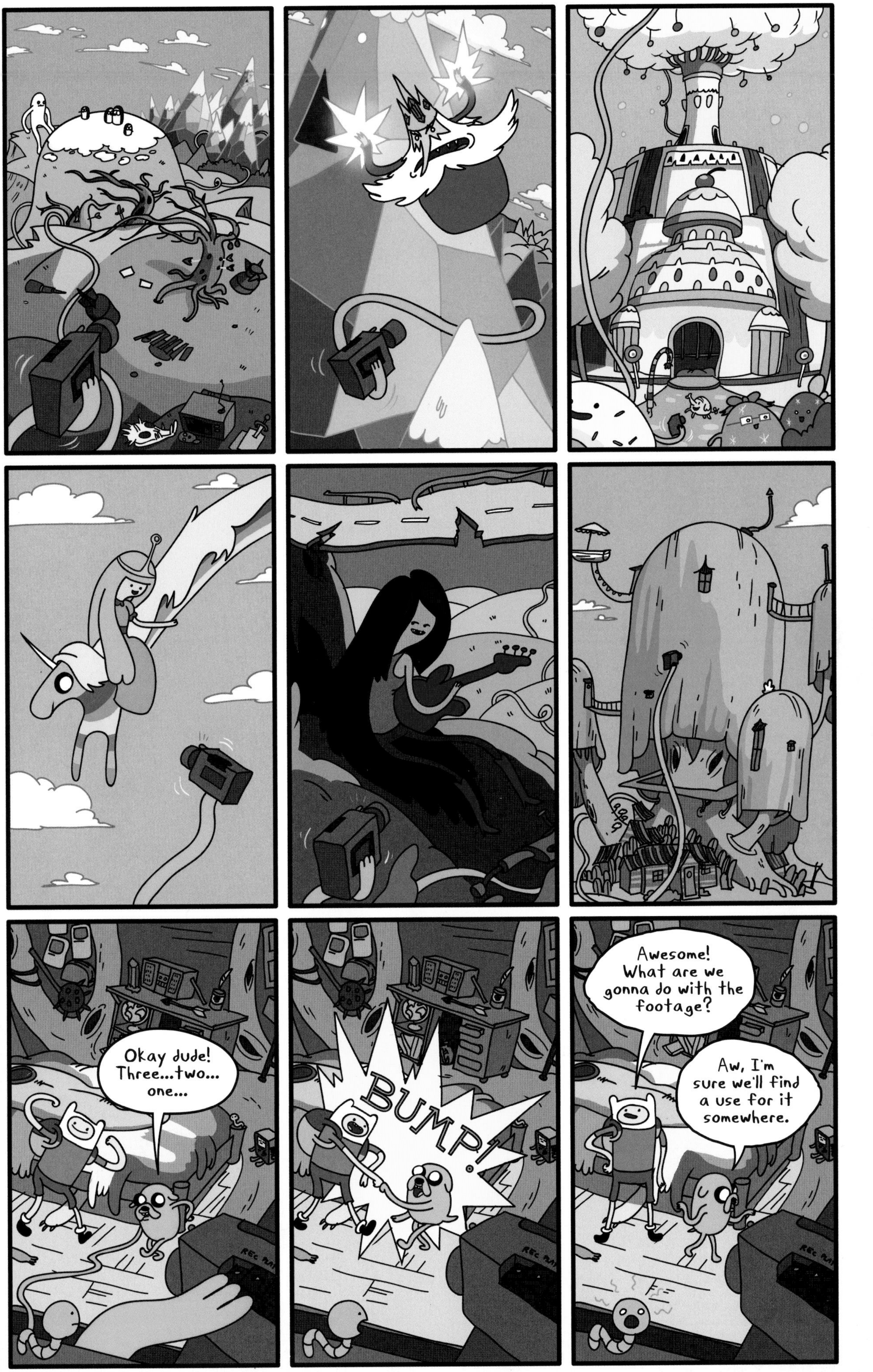
Okay dude! Three...two... one...
BUMP!
Awesome! What are we gonna do with the footage?
Aw, I'm sure we'll find a use for it somewhere.
REC PLAY

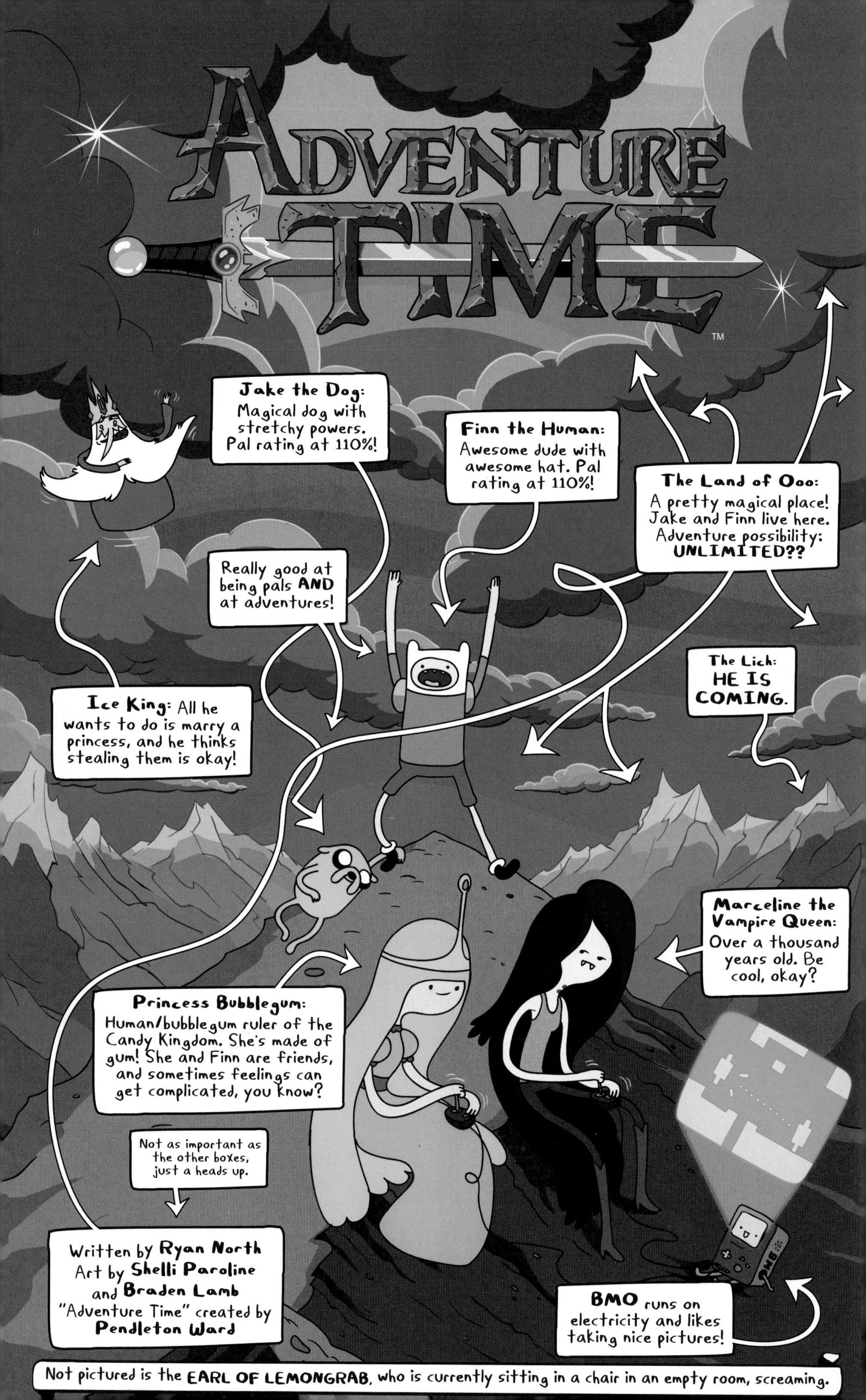

ADVENTURE TIME™
Jake the Dog: Magical dog with stretchy powers. Pal rating at 110%!
Finn the Human: Awesome dude with awesome hat. Pal rating at 110%!
The Land of Ooo: A pretty magical place! Jake and Finn live here. Adventure possibility: UNLIMITED??
Really good at being pals AND at adventures!
Ice King: All he wants to do is marry a princess, and he thinks stealing them is okay!
The Lich: HE IS COMING.
Marceline the Vampire Queen: Over a thousand years old. Be cool, okay?
Princess Bubblegum: Human/bubblegum ruler of the Candy Kingdom. She's made of gum! She and Finn are friends, and sometimes feelings can get complicated, you know?
Not as important as the other boxes, just a heads up.
Written by Ryan North
Art by Shelli Paroline and Braden Lamb
"Adventure Time" created by Pendleton Ward
BMO runs on electricity and likes taking nice pictures!
Not pictured is the EARL OF LEMONGRAB, who is currently sitting in a chair in an empty room, screaming.

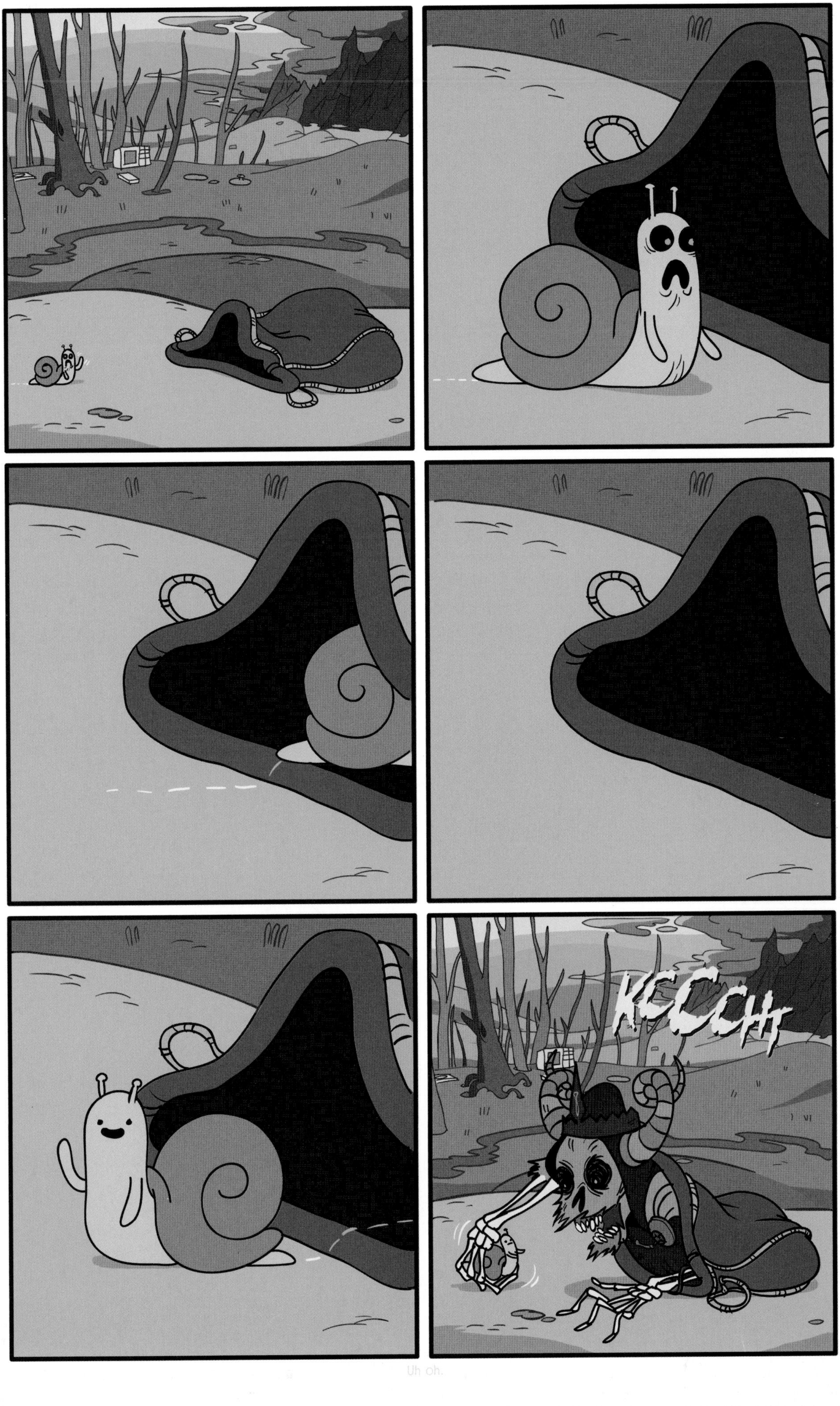
KCCCHT

Uh oh.

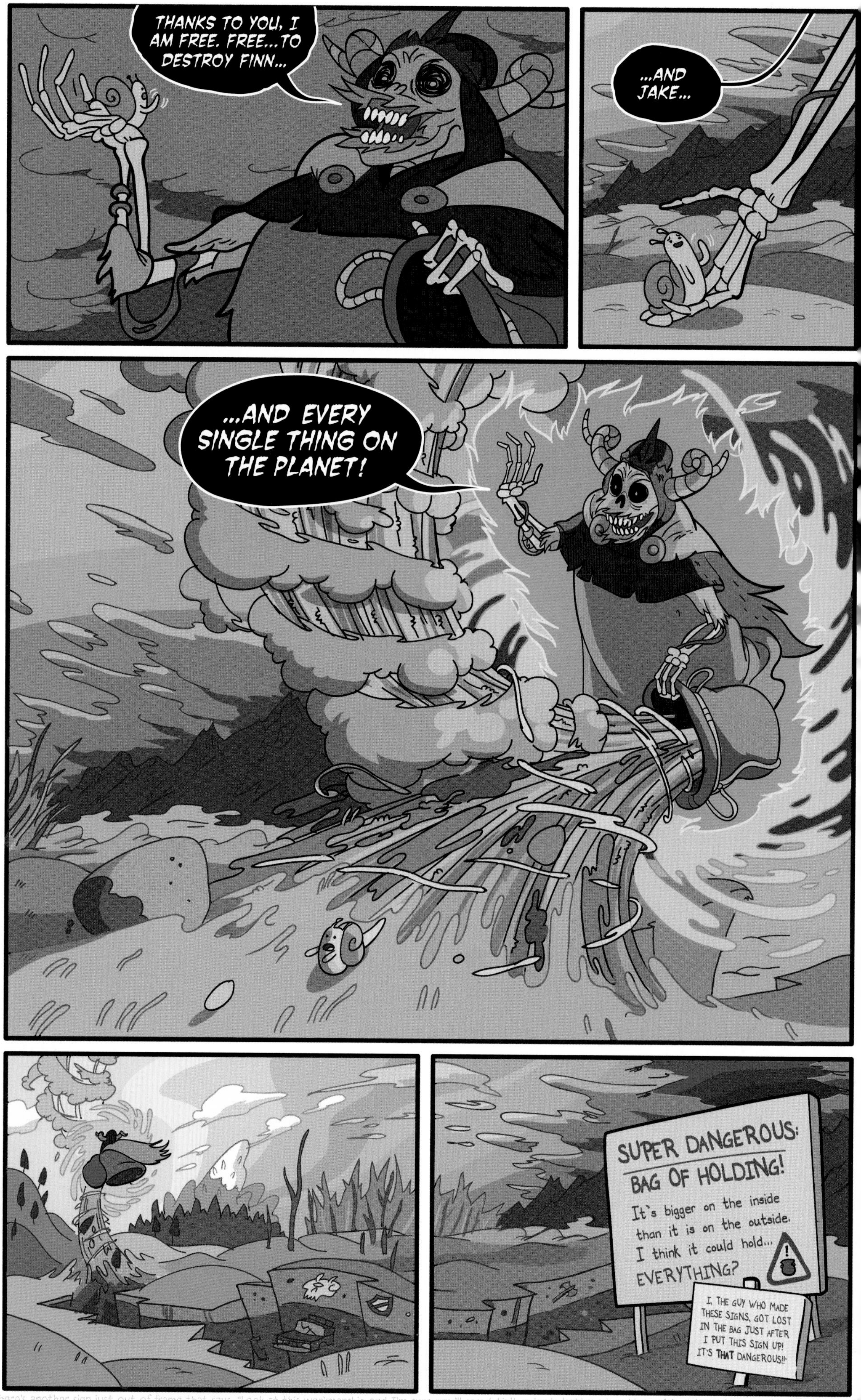
THANKS TO YOU, I AM FREE. FREE...TO DESTROY FINN...
...AND JAKE...
...AND EVERY SINGLE THING ON THE PLANET!
SUPER DANGEROUS:
BAG OF HOLDING!
It's bigger on the inside than it is on the outside. I think it could hold... EVERYTHING?
I, THE GUY WHO MADE THESE SIGNS, GOT LOST IN THE BAG JUST AFTER I PUT THIS SIGN UP! IT'S THAT DANGEROUS!!

There's another sign just out of frame that says, "Look at this workmanship and I'm sure you'll see / Ain't nobody better at making quick, extremely accurate signs than me!"

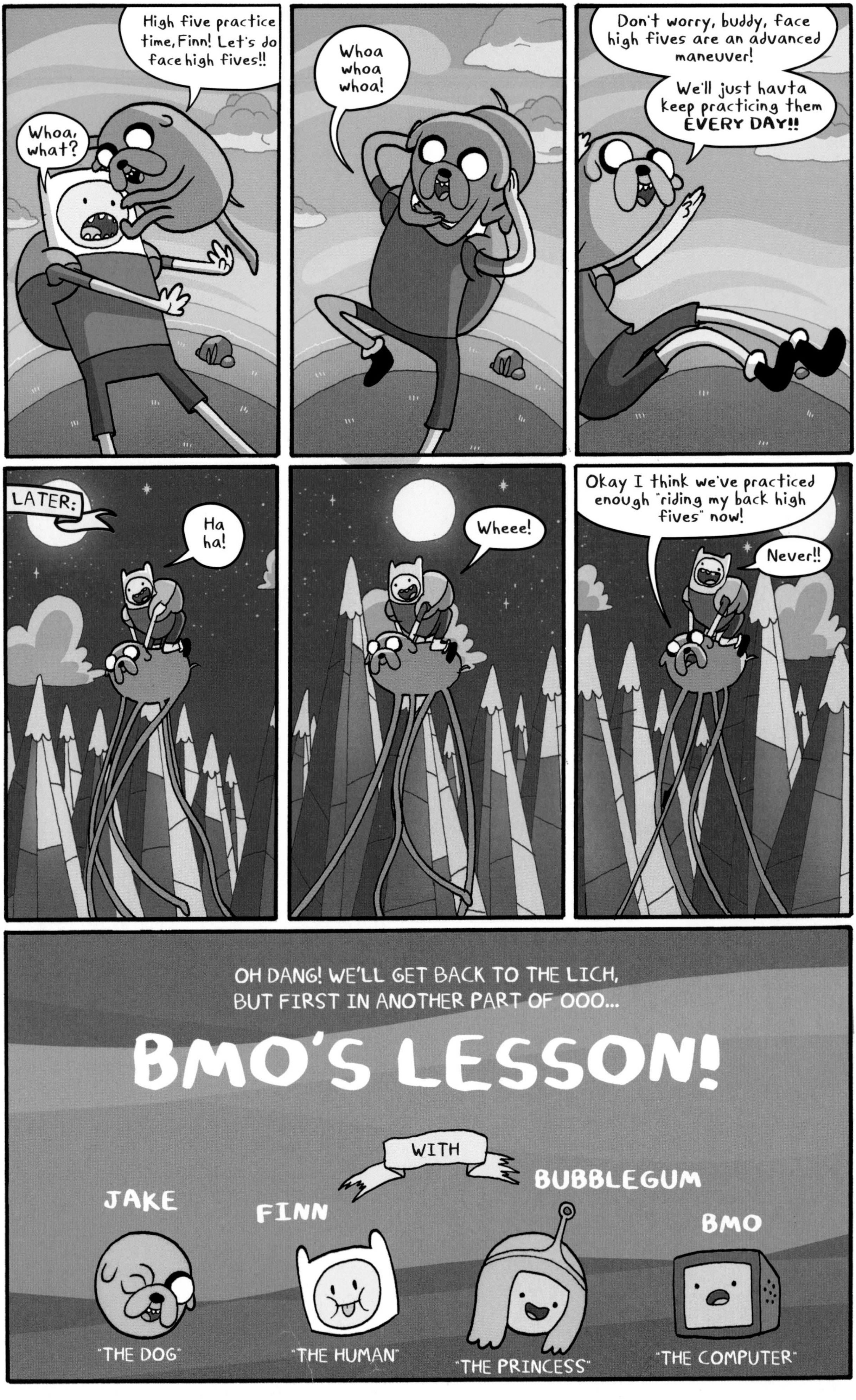
High five practice time, Finn! Let's do face high fives!!
Whoa, what?
Whoa whoa whoa!
Don't worry, buddy, face high fives are an advanced maneuver!
We'll just havta keep practicing them EVERY DAY!!
LATER:
Ha ha!
Wheee!
Okay I think we've practiced enough "riding my back high fives" now!
Never!!
OH DANG! WE'LL GET BACK TO THE LICH, BUT FIRST IN ANOTHER PART OF OOO...
BMO'S LESSON!
WITH
JAKE
FINN
BUBBLEGUM
BMO
"THE DOG"
"THE HUMAN"
"THE PRINCESS"
"THE COMPUTER"

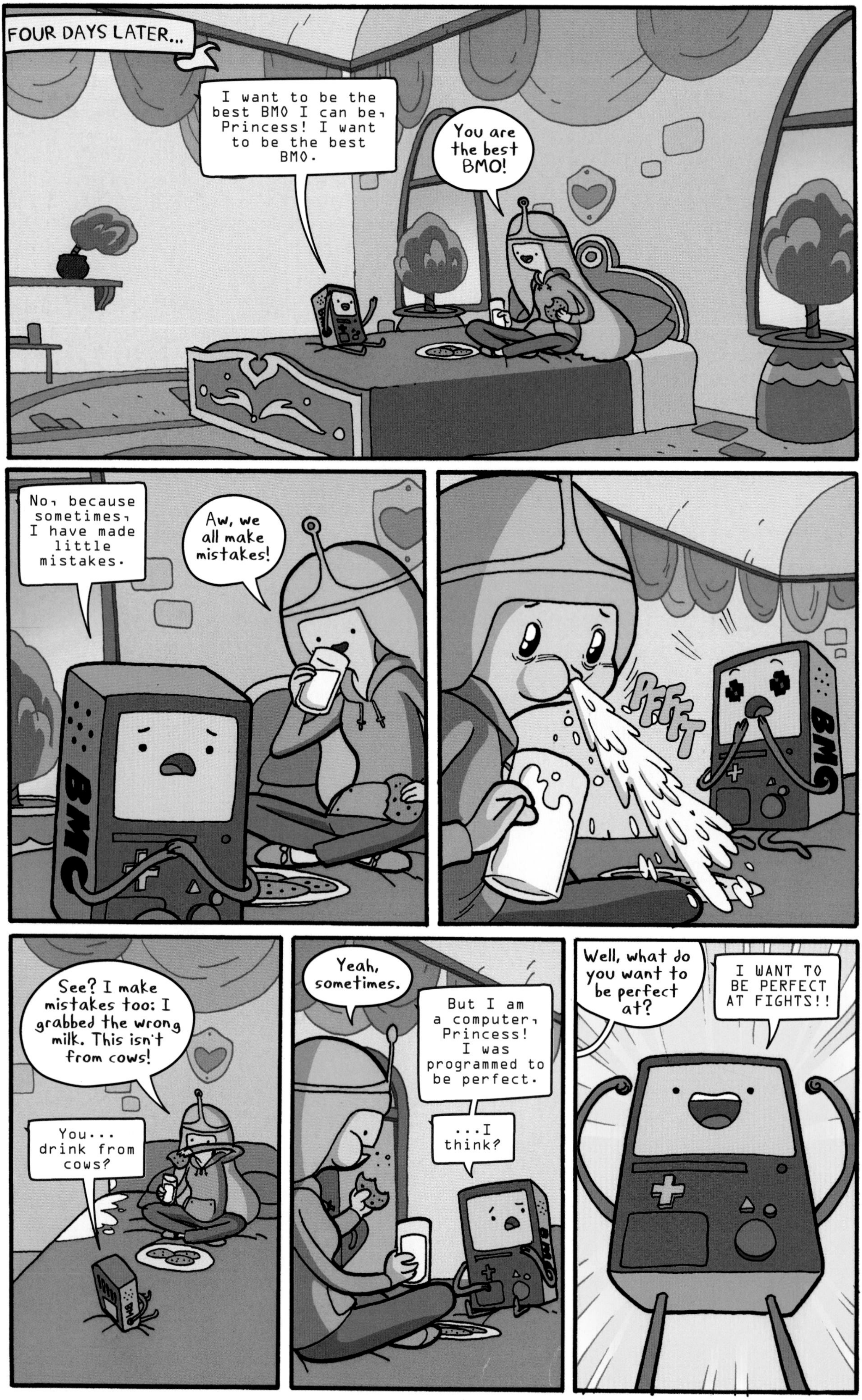
FOUR DAYS LATER...
I want to be the best BMO I can be, Princess! I want to be the best BMO.
You are the best BMO!
No, because sometimes, I have made little mistakes.
Aw, we all make mistakes!
PFFFT
BMO
See? I make mistakes too: I grabbed the wrong milk. This isn't from cows!
You... drink from cows?
Yeah, sometimes.
But I am a computer, Princess! I was programmed to be perfect.
...I think?
Well, what do you want to be perfect at?
I WANT TO BE PERFECT AT FIGHTS!!

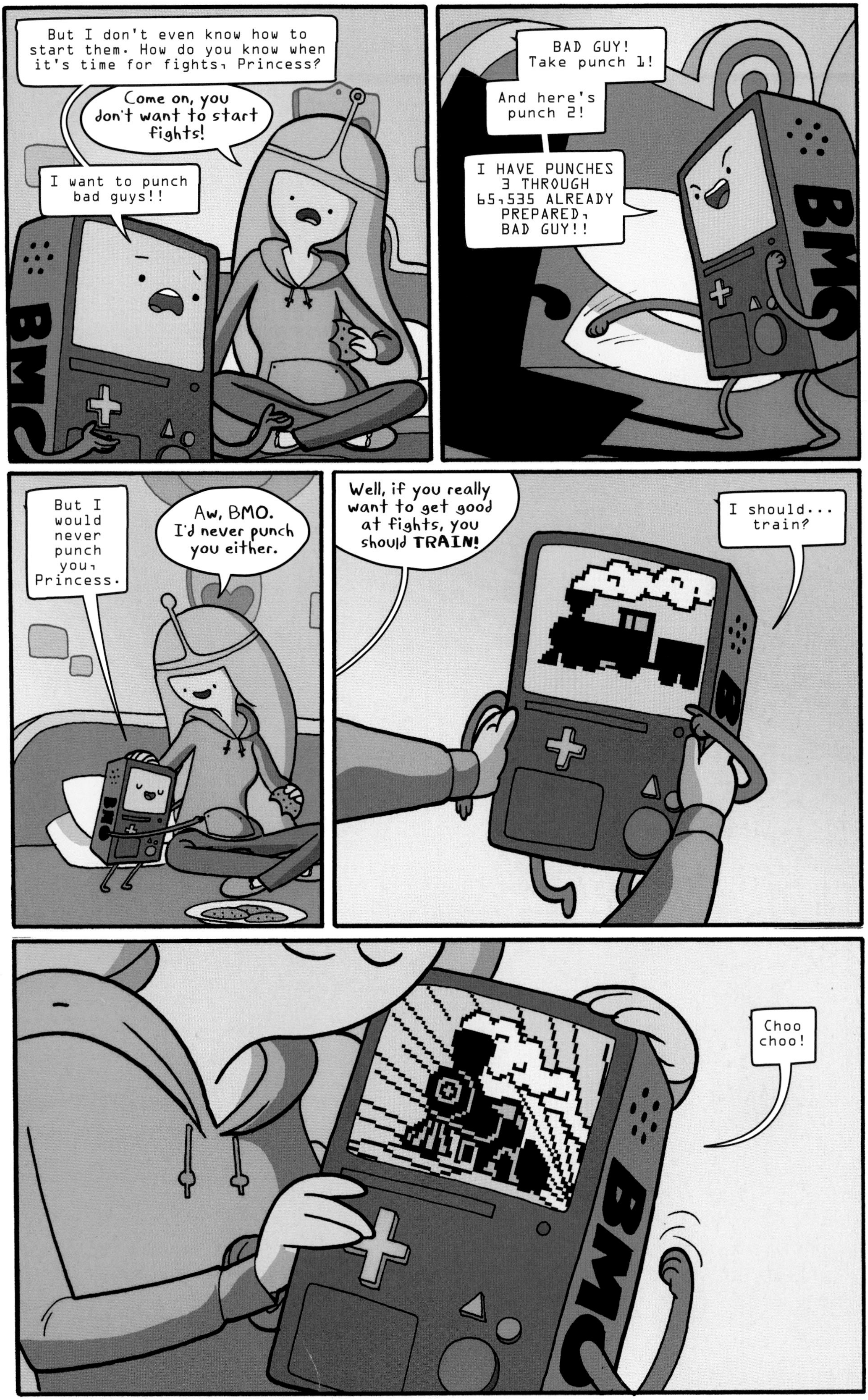
But I don't even know how to start them. How do you know when it's time for fights, Princess?
Come on, you don't want to start fights!
I want to punch bad guys!!
BAD GUY! Take punch 1!
And here's punch 2!
I HAVE PUNCHES 3 THROUGH 65,535 ALREADY PREPARED, BAD GUY!!
BMO
But I would never punch you, Princess.
Aw, BMO. I'd never punch you either.
Well, if you really want to get good at fights, you should TRAIN!
I should... train?
Choo choo!

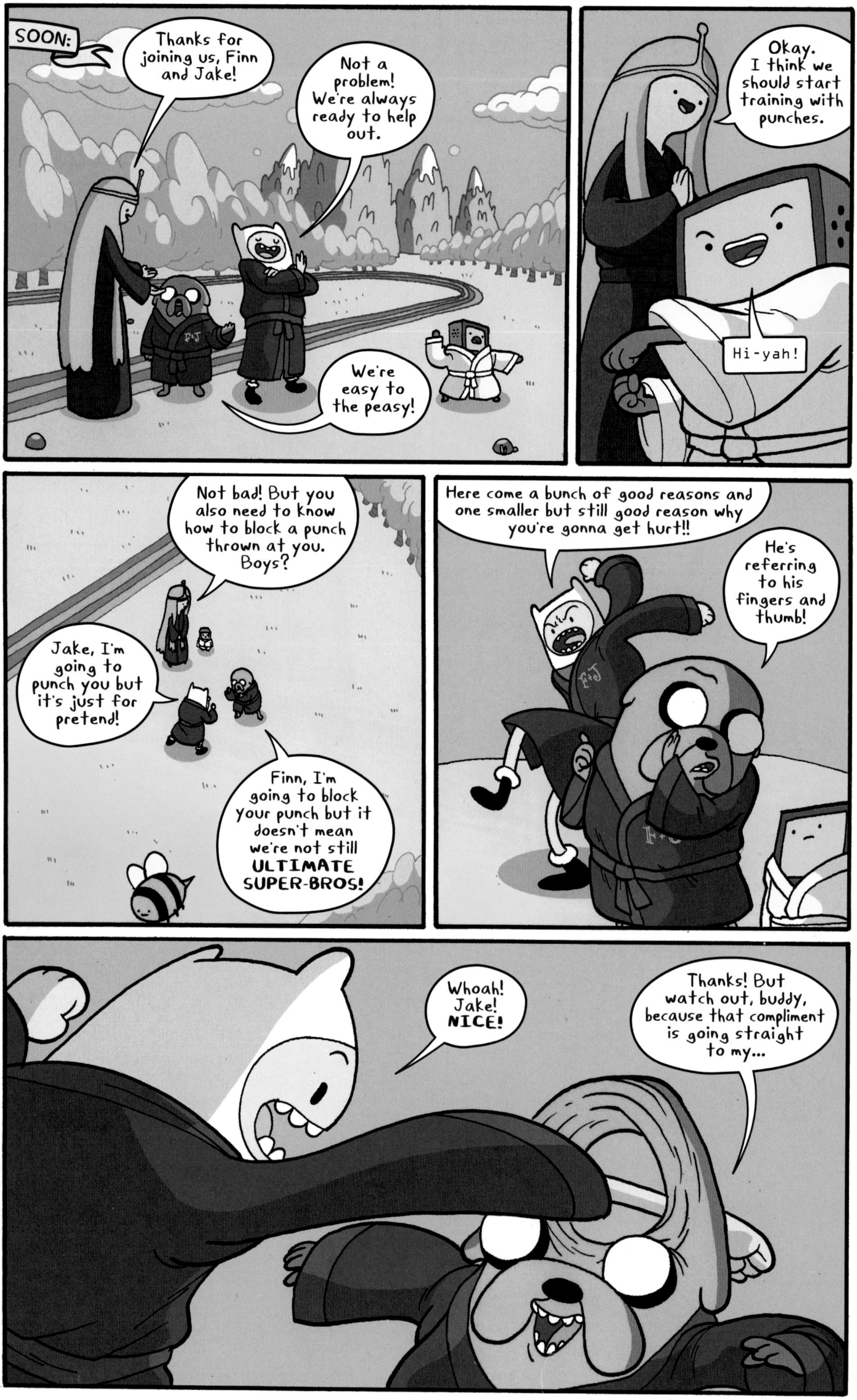
SOON:
Thanks for joining us, Finn and Jake!
Not a problem! We're always ready to help out.
We're easy to the peasy!
Okay. I think we should start training with punches.
Hi-yah!
Not bad! But you also need to know how to block a punch thrown at you. Boys?
Jake, I'm going to punch you but it's just for pretend!
Finn, I'm going to block your punch but it doesn't mean we're not still ULTIMATE SUPER-BROS!
Here come a bunch of good reasons and one smaller but still good reason why you're gonna get hurt!!
He's referring to his fingers and thumb!
Whoah! Jake! NICE!
Thanks! But watch out, buddy, because that compliment is going straight to my...

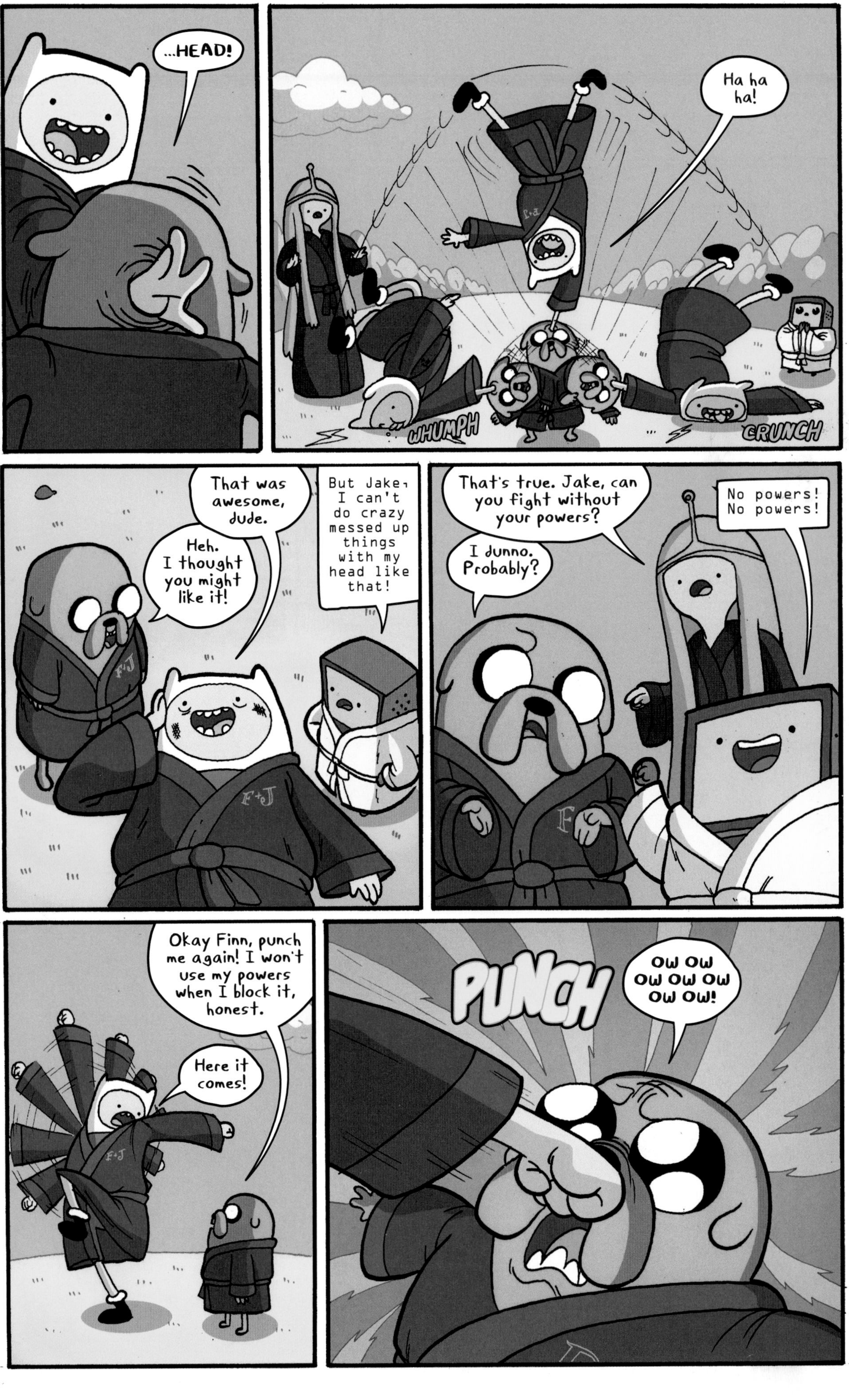
...HEAD!
Ha ha ha!
WHUMPH
CRUNCH
That was awesome, dude.
Heh. I thought you might like it!
But Jake, I can't do crazy messed up things with my head like that!
That's true. Jake, can you fight without your powers?
I dunno. Probably?
No powers! No powers!
Okay Finn, punch me again! I won't use my powers when I block it, honest.
Here it comes!
PUNCH
OW OW OW OW OW OW OW!

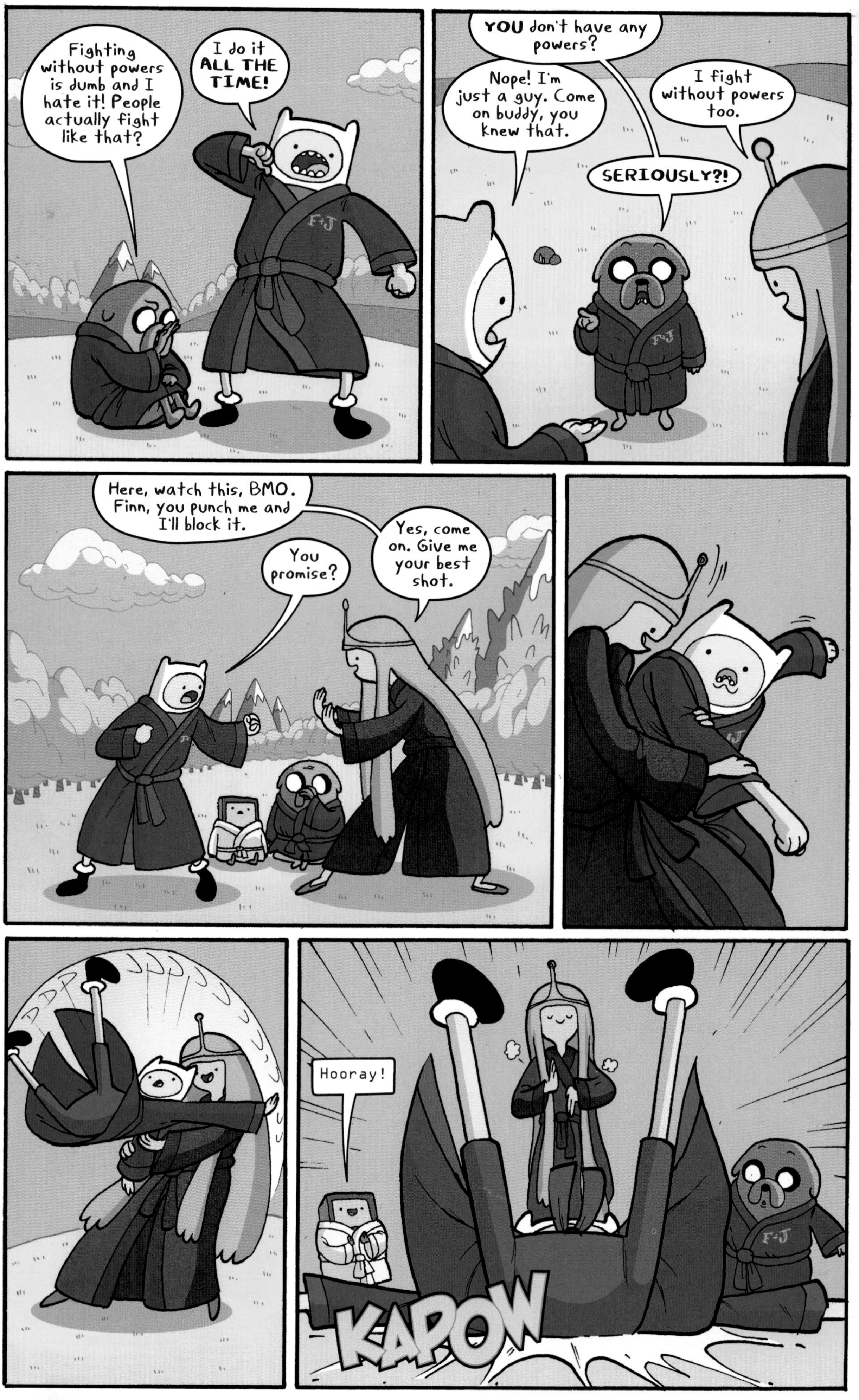
Fighting without powers is dumb and I hate it! People actually fight like that?
I do it ALL THE TIME!
YOU don't have any powers?
Nope! I'm just a guy. Come on buddy, you knew that.
I fight without powers too.
SERIOUSLY?!
Here, watch this, BMO. Finn, you punch me and I'll block it.
You promise?
Yes, come on. Give me your best shot.
Hooray!
KAPOW

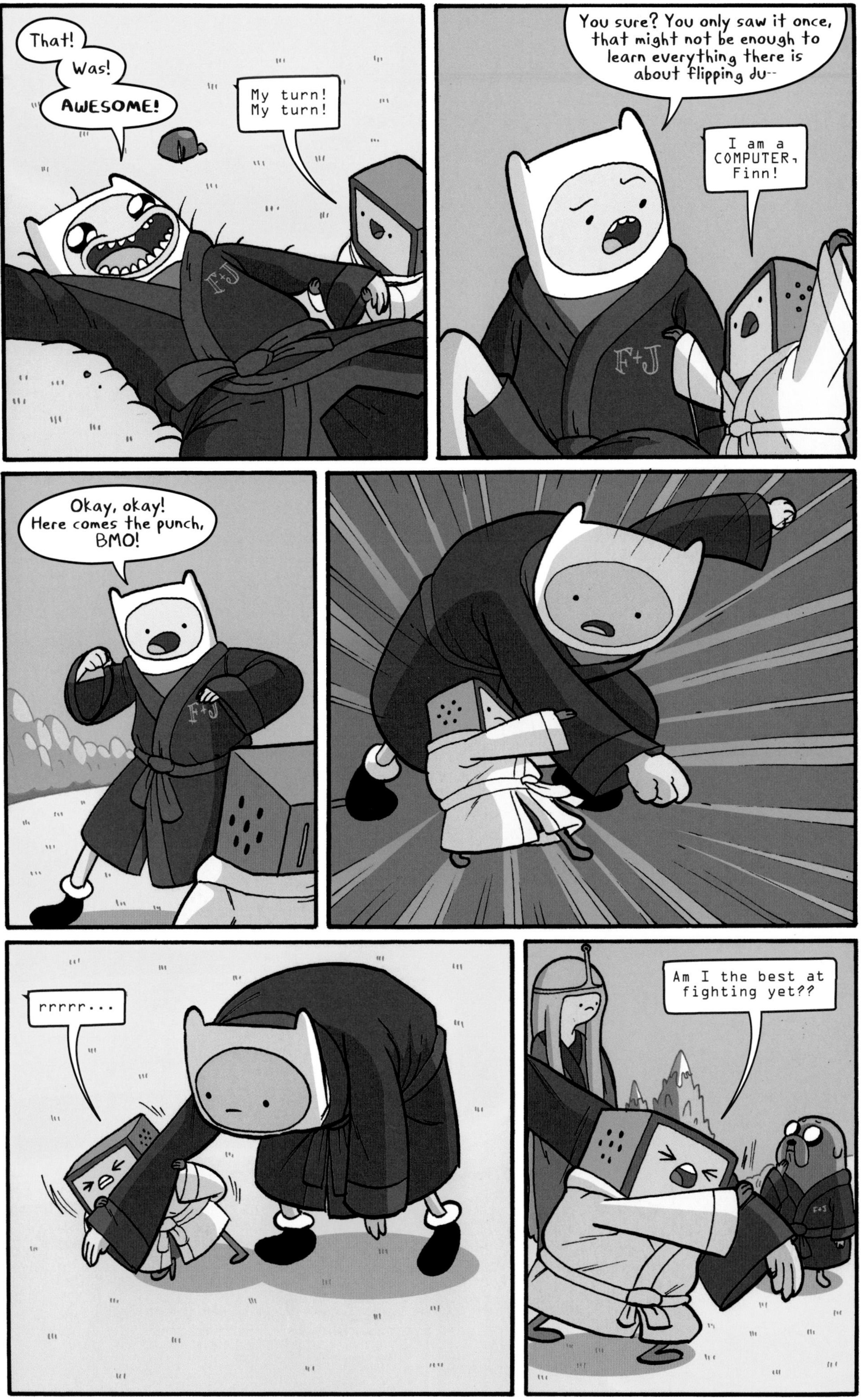
That!
Was!
AWESOME!
My turn! My turn!
You sure? You only saw it once, that might not be enough to learn everything there is about flipping du--
I am a COMPUTER, Finn!
Okay, okay! Here comes the punch, BMO!
rrrrr...
Am I the best at fighting yet??

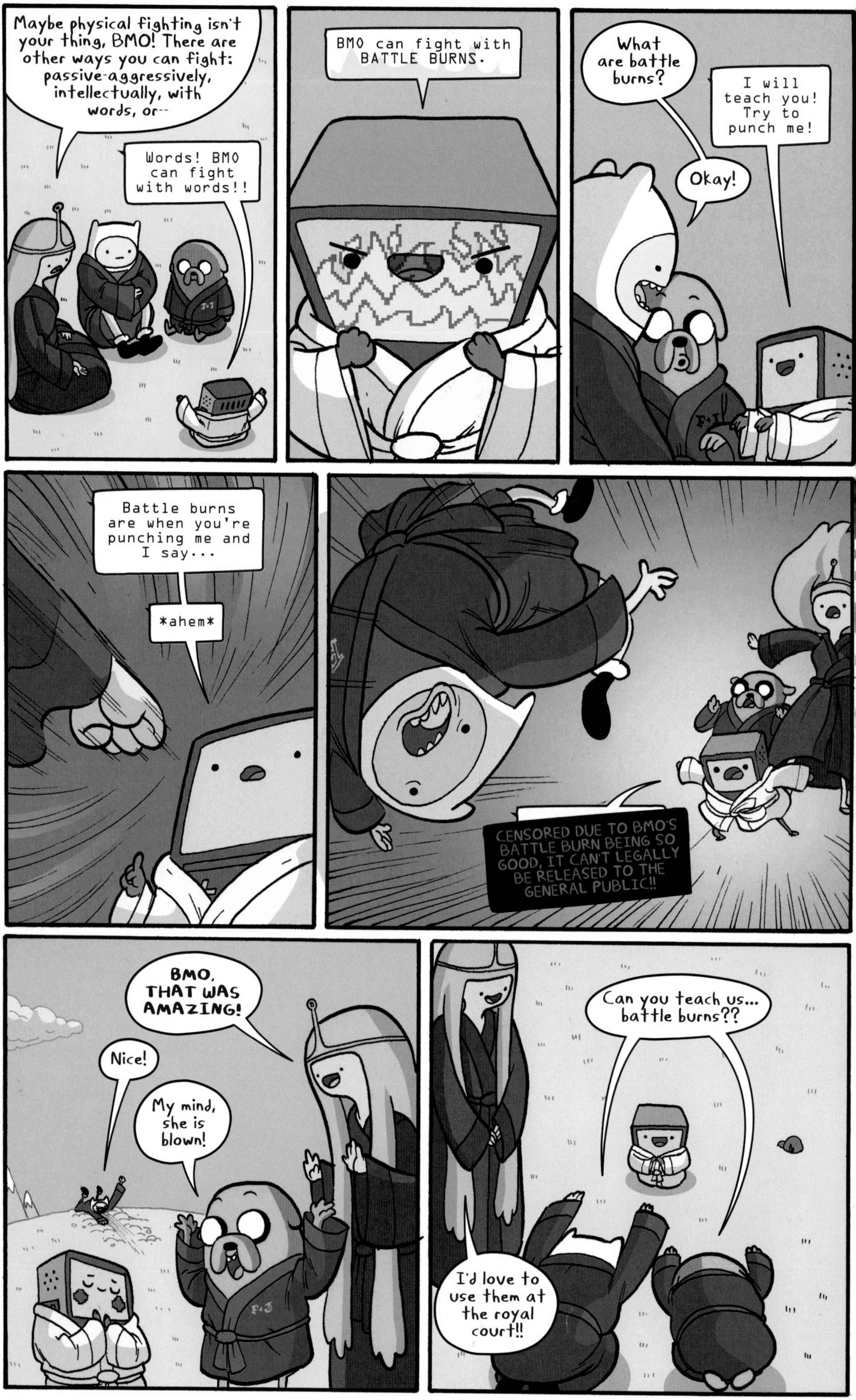

Maybe physical fighting isn't your thing, BMO! There are other ways you can fight: passive-aggressively, intellectually, with words, or--
Words! BMO can fight with words!!
BMO can fight with BATTLE BURNS.
What are battle burns?
I will teach you! Try to punch me!
Okay!
Battle burns are when you're punching me and I say...
ahem
CENSORED DUE TO BMO'S BATTLE BURN BEING SO GOOD, IT CAN'T LEGALLY BE RELEASED TO THE GENERAL PUBLIC!!
BMO, THAT WAS AMAZING!
Nice!
My mind, she is blown!
Can you teach us... battle burns??
I'd love to use them at the royal court!!

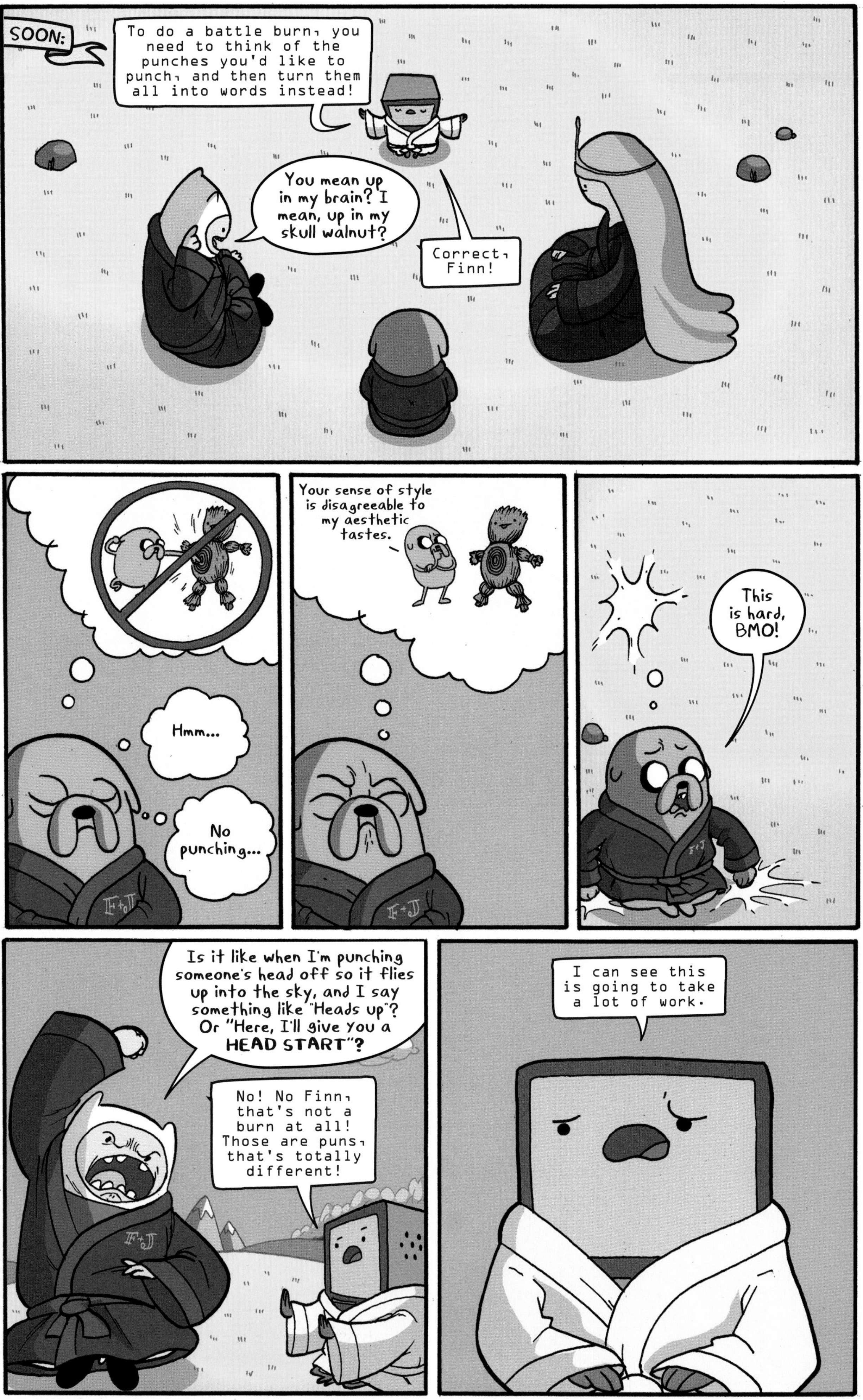
SOON:
To do a battle burn, you need to think of the punches you'd like to punch, and then turn them all into words instead!
You mean up in my brain? I mean, up in my skull walnut?
Correct, Finn!
Hmm...
No punching...
Your sense of style is disagreeable to my aesthetic tastes.
F+J
This is hard, BMO!
Is it like when I'm punching someone's head off so it flies up into the sky, and I say something like "Heads up"? Or "Here, I'll give you a HEAD START"?
No! No Finn, that's not a burn at all! Those are puns, that's totally different!
I can see this is going to take a lot of work.

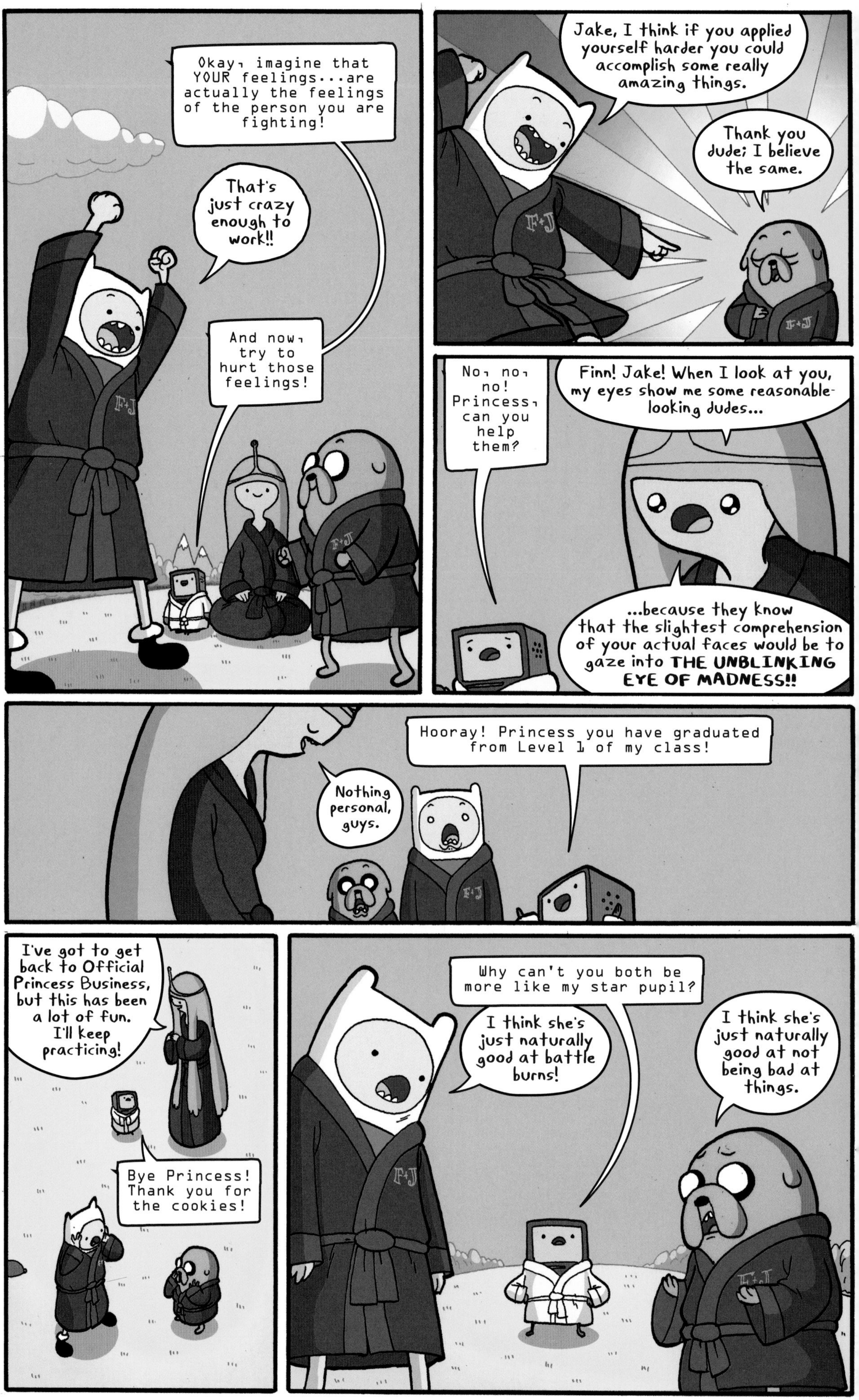
Okay, imagine that YOUR feelings...are actually the feelings of the person you are fighting!
That's just crazy enough to work!!
And now, try to hurt those feelings!
Jake, I think if you applied yourself harder you could accomplish some really amazing things.
Thank you dude; I believe the same.
No, no, no! Princess, can you help them?
Finn! Jake! When I look at you, my eyes show me some reasonable-looking dudes...
...because they know that the slightest comprehension of your actual faces would be to gaze into THE UNBLINKING EYE OF MADNESS!!
Hooray! Princess you have graduated from Level 1 of my class!
Nothing personal, guys.
I've got to get back to Official Princess Business, but this has been a lot of fun. I'll keep practicing!
Bye Princess! Thank you for the cookies!
Why can't you both be more like my star pupil?
I think she's just naturally good at battle burns!
I think she's just naturally good at not being bad at things.

Thanks for teaching us all about battle burns, BMO! I'm sure they'll come in handy.

You need to keep practicing! Tomorrow morning!

I know!

And I will keep practicing my body slams too. When you fall asleep tonight I am going to try to body slam you, Finn!

Awesome.

This has been a really wonderful weekend.

It has, hasn't it? I don't think anything could happen now to ruin it.

It is not possible for ANYTHING and/or ANYONE to ruin this weekend, dude!

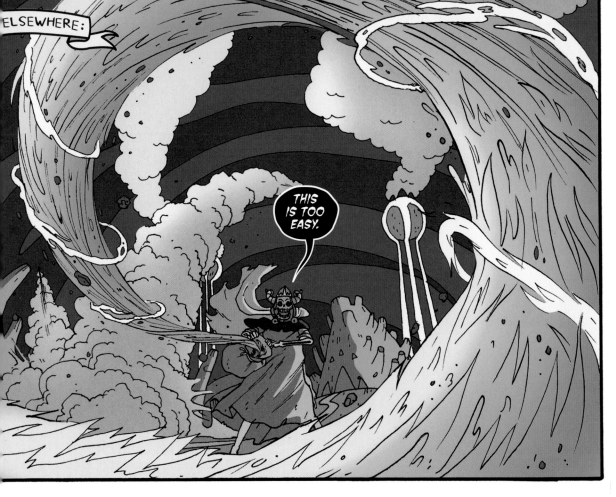

ELSEWHERE:

THIS IS TOO EASY.

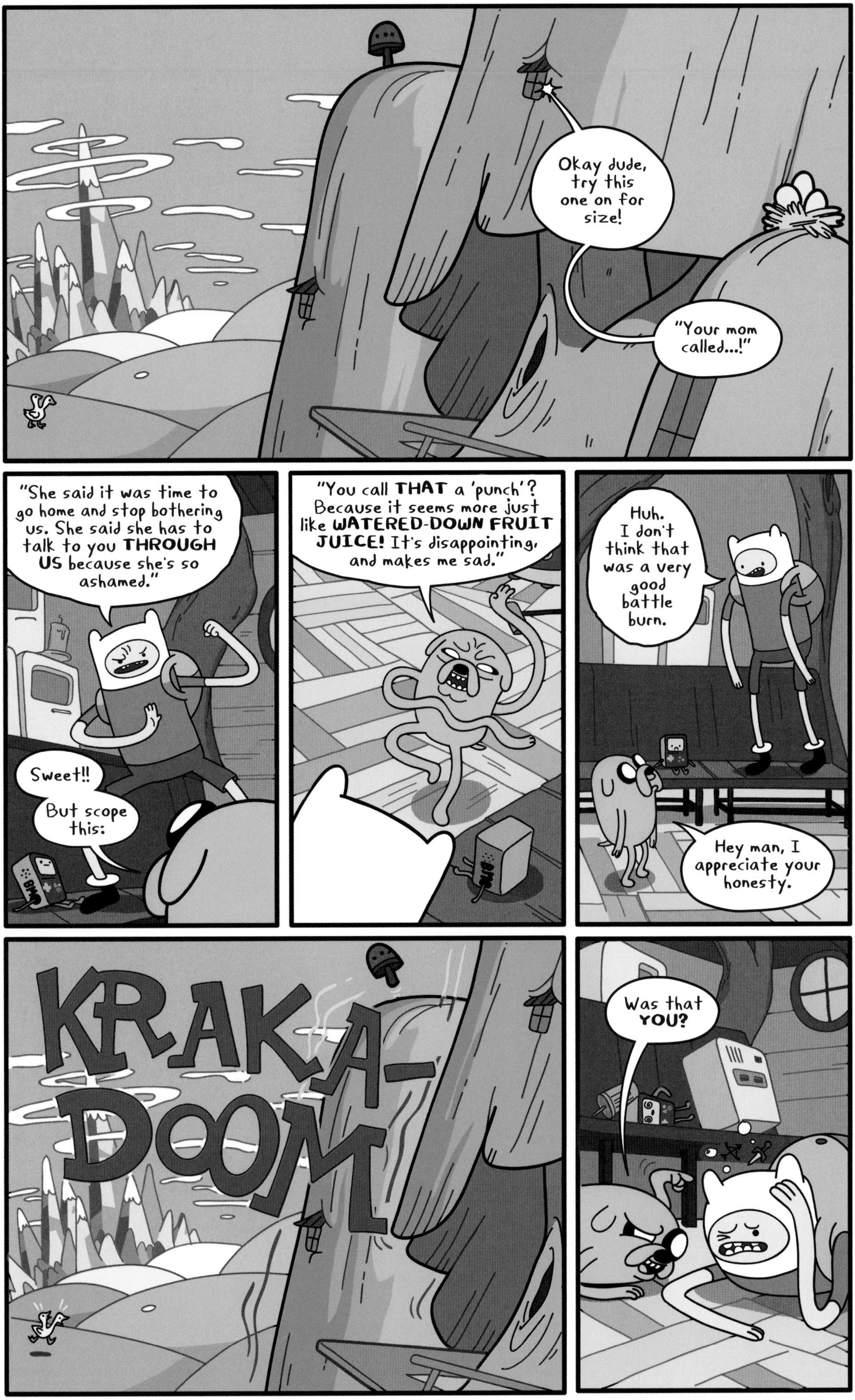

Okay dude, try this one on for size!
"Your mom called...!"
"She said it was time to go home and stop bothering us. She said she has to talk to you THROUGH US because she's so ashamed."
Sweet!!
But scope this:
"You call THAT a 'punch'? Because it seems more just like WATERED-DOWN FRUIT JUICE! It's disappointing, and makes me sad."
Huh. I don't think that was a very good battle burn.
Hey man, I appreciate your honesty.
KRAKA-DOOM
Was that YOU?

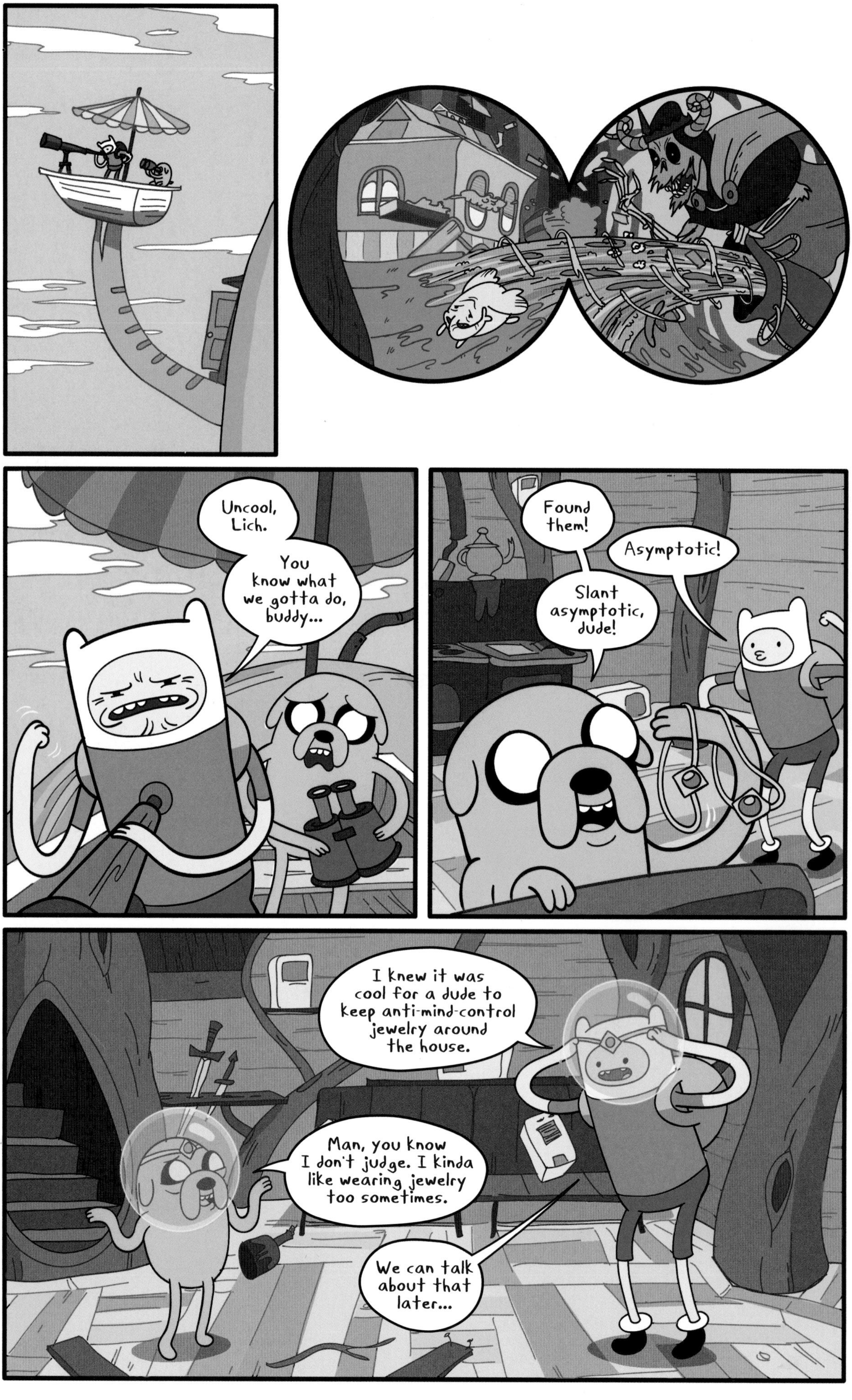
Uncool, Lich.
You know what we gotta do, buddy...
Found them!
Slant asymptotic, dude!
Asymptotic!
I knew it was cool for a dude to keep anti-mind-control jewelry around the house.
Man, you know I don't judge. I kinda like wearing jewelry too sometimes.
We can talk about that later...

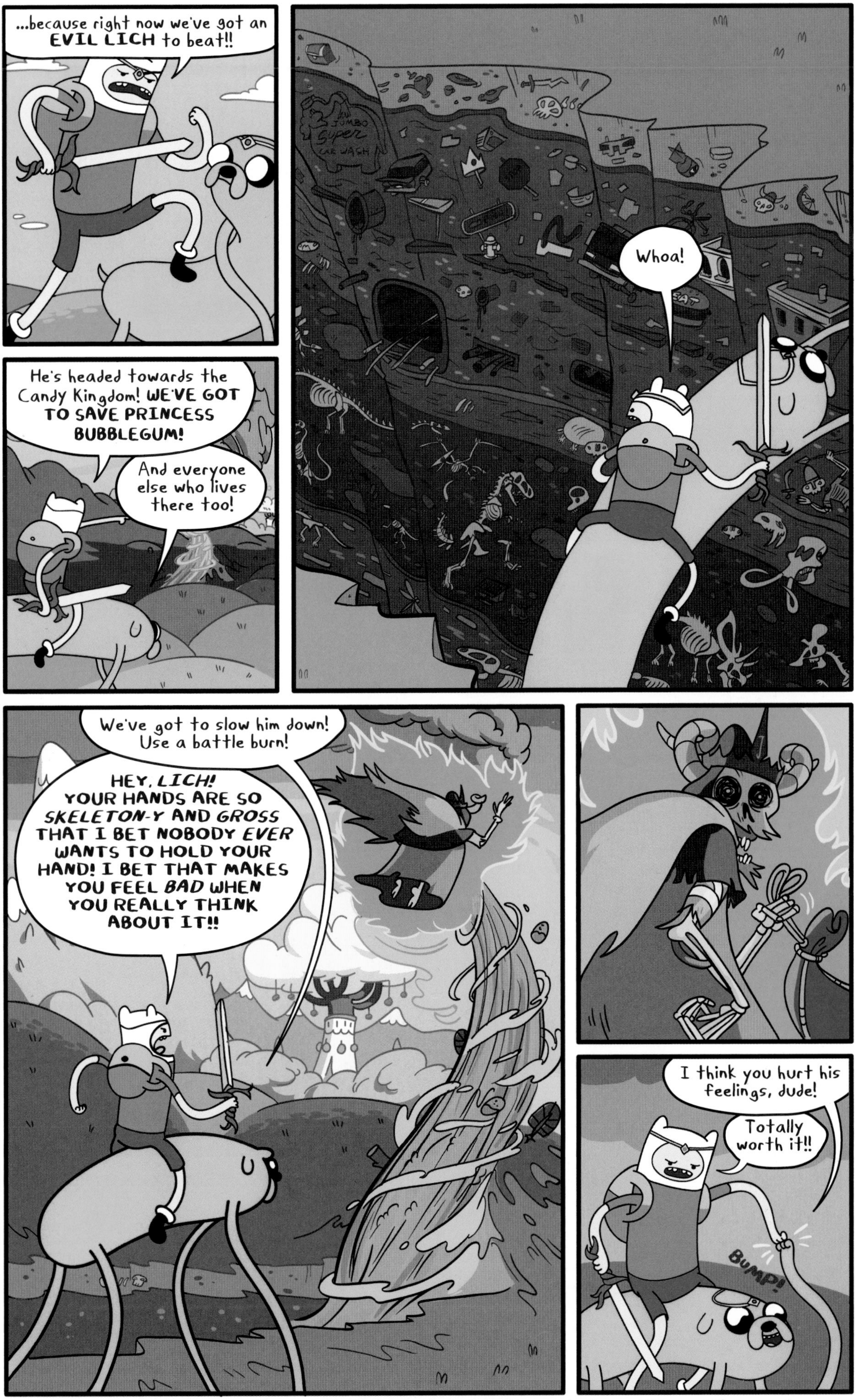
...because right now we've got an EVIL LICH to beat!!
Whoa!
He's headed towards the Candy Kingdom! WE'VE GOT TO SAVE PRINCESS BUBBLEGUM!
And everyone else who lives there too!
We've got to slow him down! Use a battle burn!
HEY, LICH! YOUR HANDS ARE SO SKELETON-Y AND GROSS THAT I BET NOBODY EVER WANTS TO HOLD YOUR HAND! I BET THAT MAKES YOU FEEL BAD WHEN YOU REALLY THINK ABOUT IT!!
I think you hurt his feelings, dude!
Totally worth it!!
BUMP!

Man, there sure are some cool things buried in the dirt. I refer both to this comic book page **AND** to real life in general.

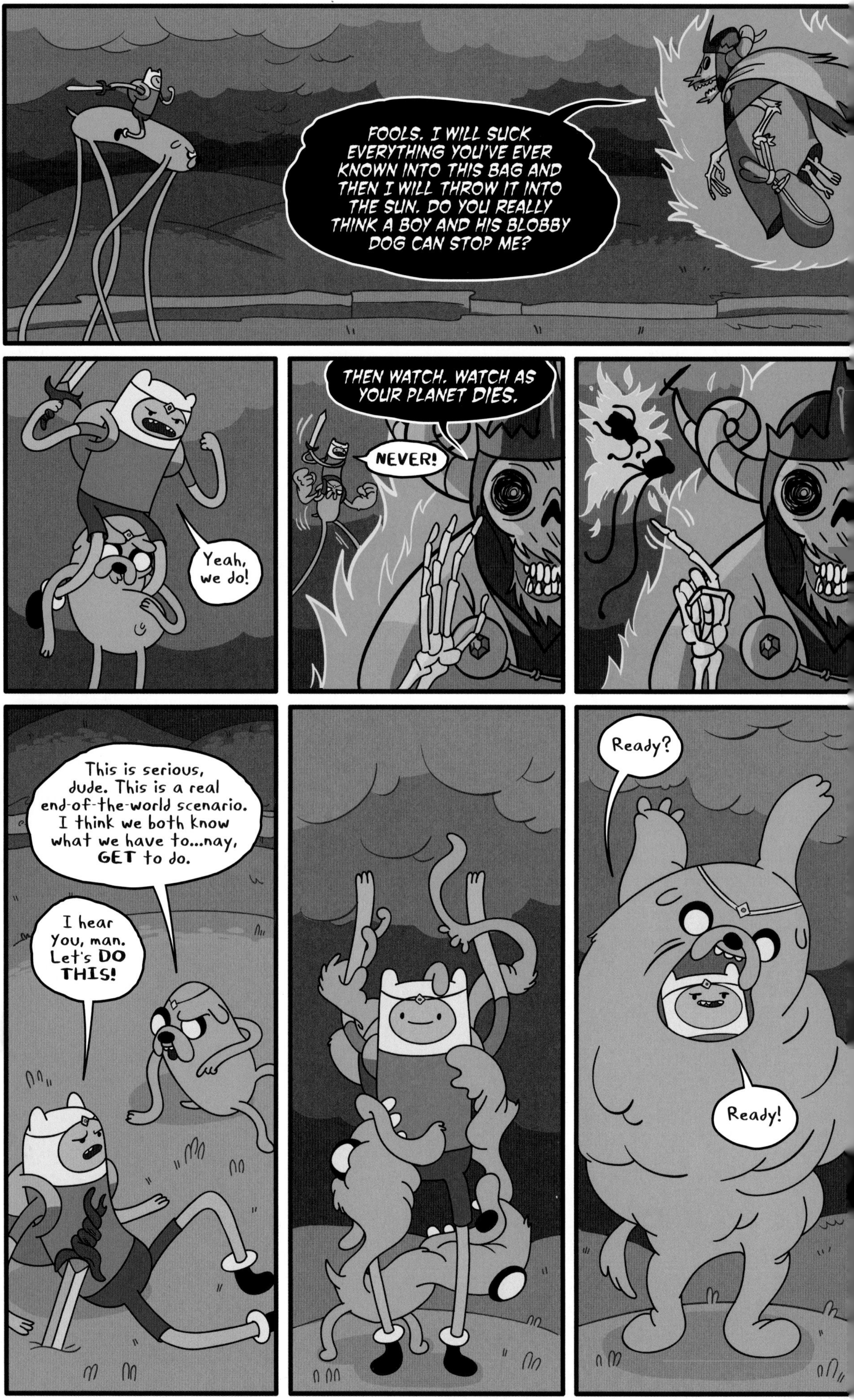
FOOLS. I WILL SUCK EVERYTHING YOU'VE EVER KNOWN INTO THIS BAG AND THEN I WILL THROW IT INTO THE SUN. DO YOU REALLY THINK A BOY AND HIS BLOBBY DOG CAN STOP ME?
Yeah, we do!
THEN WATCH. WATCH AS YOUR PLANET DIES.
NEVER!
This is serious, dude. This is a real end-of-the-world scenario. I think we both know what we have to...nay, **GET** to do.
I hear you, man. Let's **DO THIS!**
Ready?
Ready!

JAAAAAAKE SUUUUUUUUUUUUIT!

Have you tried **NOT** sucking for a change, Lich?!

KA-

POW

HA HA HA!

What are you laughing for? I punched you into two pieces!

And you should quit now, while you're **A HEAD!**

BUMP!

I DON'T THINK I WILL.

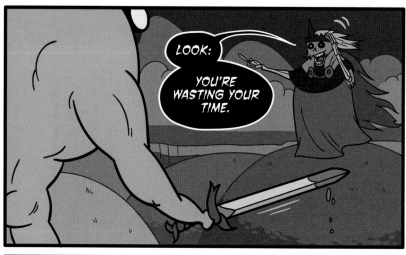

LOOK: YOU'RE WASTING YOUR TIME.

PRINCESS BUBBLEGUM!

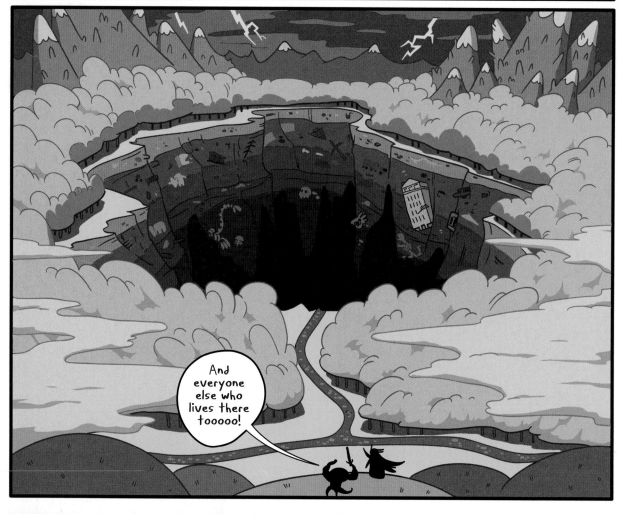

And everyone else who lives there tooooo!

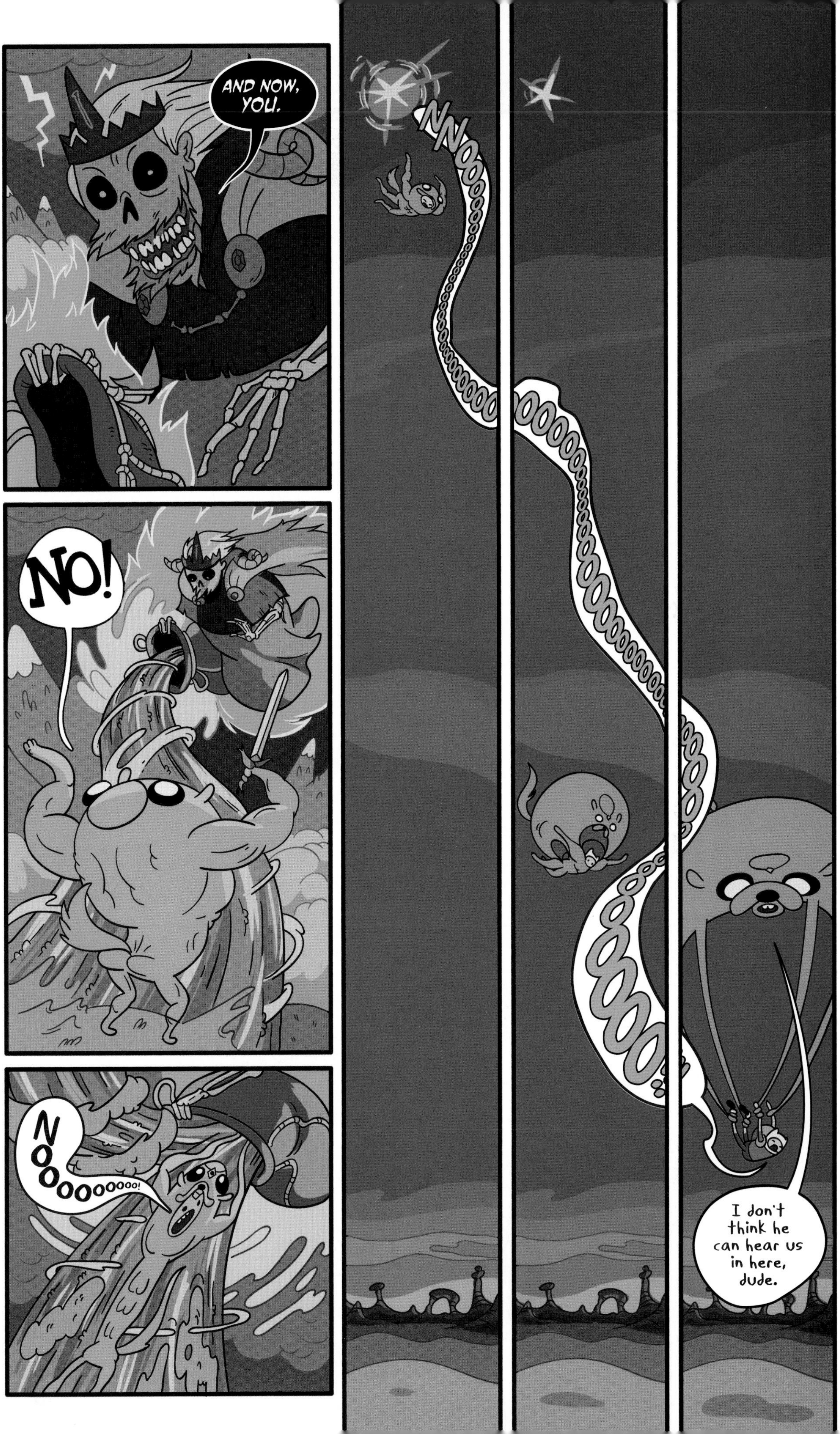
AND NOW, YOU.
NO!
NOOOOOOOOOO!
NNOOOOOOOOOOOOOOOOOOOOOOOOOOOOOOOOOO!!
I don't think he can hear us in here, dude.

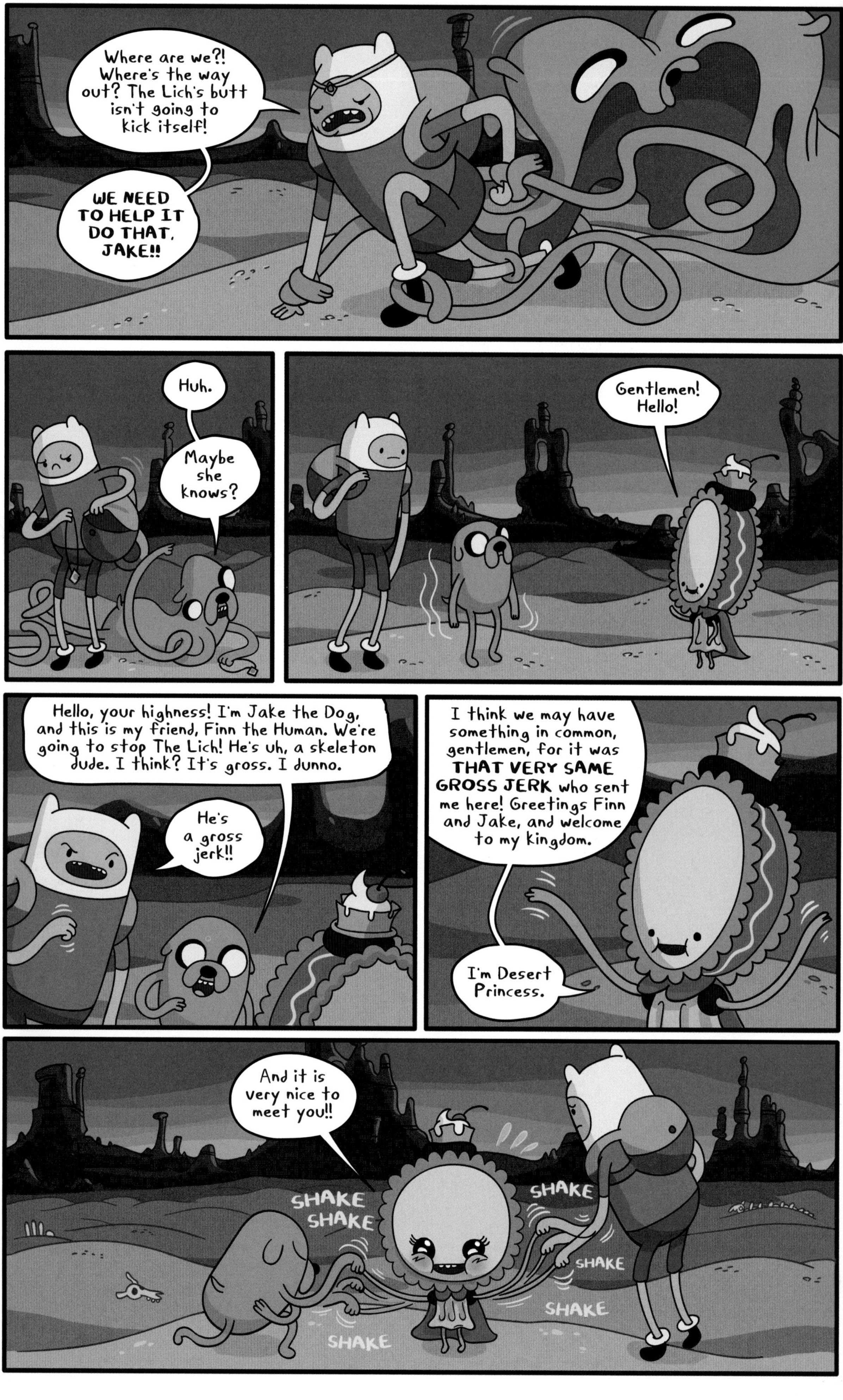

Where are we?! Where's the way out? The Lich's butt isn't going to kick itself!
WE NEED TO HELP IT DO THAT, JAKE!!
Huh.
Maybe she knows?
Gentlemen! Hello!
Hello, your highness! I'm Jake the Dog, and this is my friend, Finn the Human. We're going to stop The Lich! He's uh, a skeleton dude. I think? It's gross. I dunno.
He's a gross jerk!!
I think we may have something in common, gentlemen, for it was THAT VERY SAME GROSS JERK who sent me here! Greetings Finn and Jake, and welcome to my kingdom.
I'm Desert Princess.
And it is very nice to meet you!!
SHAKE
SHAKE
SHAKE
SHAKE
SHAKE
SHAKE

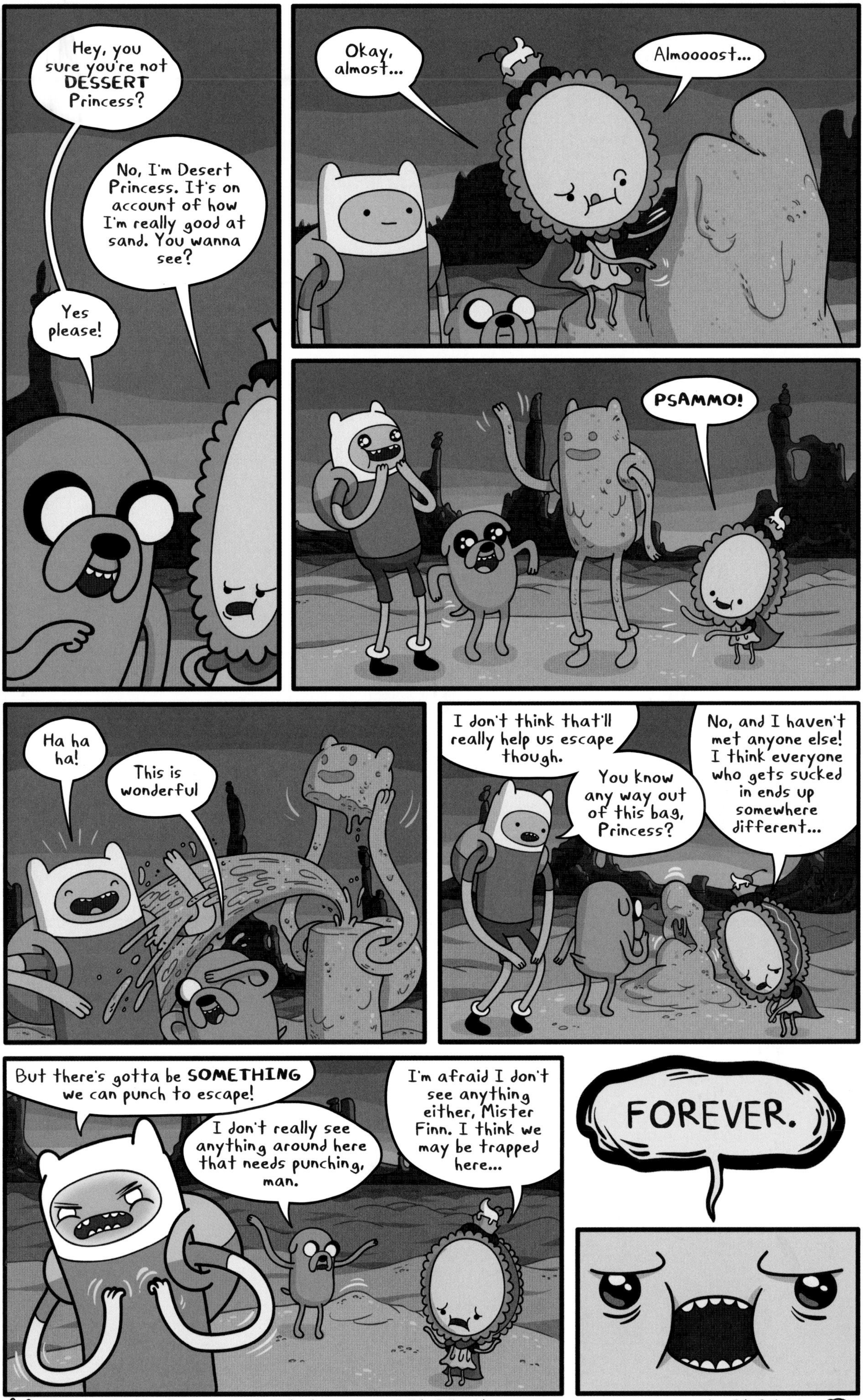
Hey, you sure you're not DESSERT Princess?
No, I'm Desert Princess. It's on account of how I'm really good at sand. You wanna see?
Yes please!
Okay, almost...
Almoooost...
PSAMMO!
Ha ha ha!
This is wonderful
I don't think that'll really help us escape though.
You know any way out of this bag, Princess?
No, and I haven't met anyone else! I think everyone who gets sucked in ends up somewhere different...
But there's gotta be SOMETHING we can punch to escape!
I don't really see anything around here that needs punching, man.
I'm afraid I don't see anything either, Mister Finn. I think we may be trapped here...
FOREVER.

- We must've stayed together on our way into the bag because we were in Jake Suit mode!

I love Jake Suit, dude. -

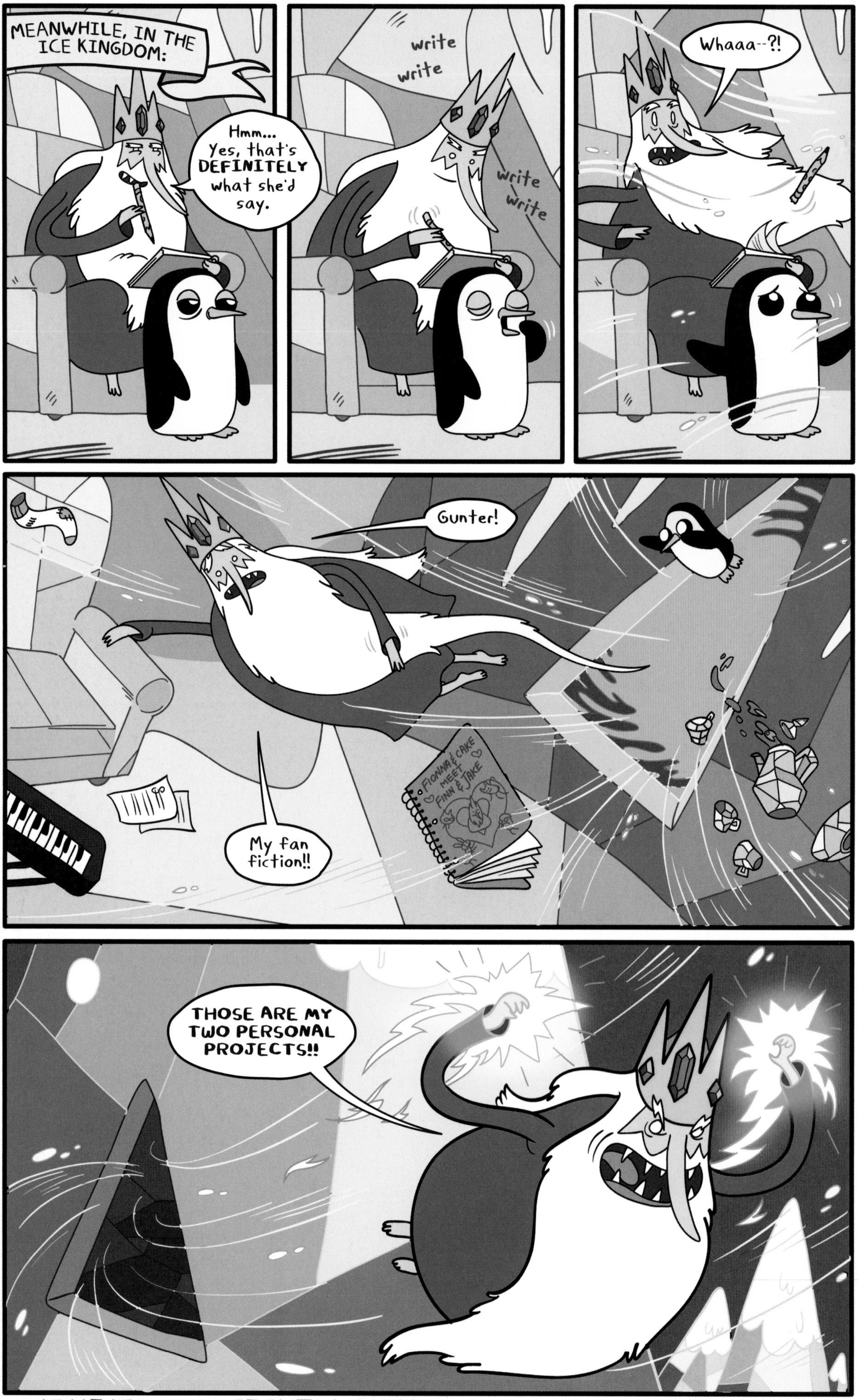
MEANWHILE, IN THE ICE KINGDOM:
Hmm... Yes, that's DEFINITELY what she'd say.
write
write
write
write
Whaaa--?!
Gunter!
My fan fiction!!
FIONNA & CAKE MEET FINN & JAKE
THOSE ARE MY TWO PERSONAL PROJECTS!!

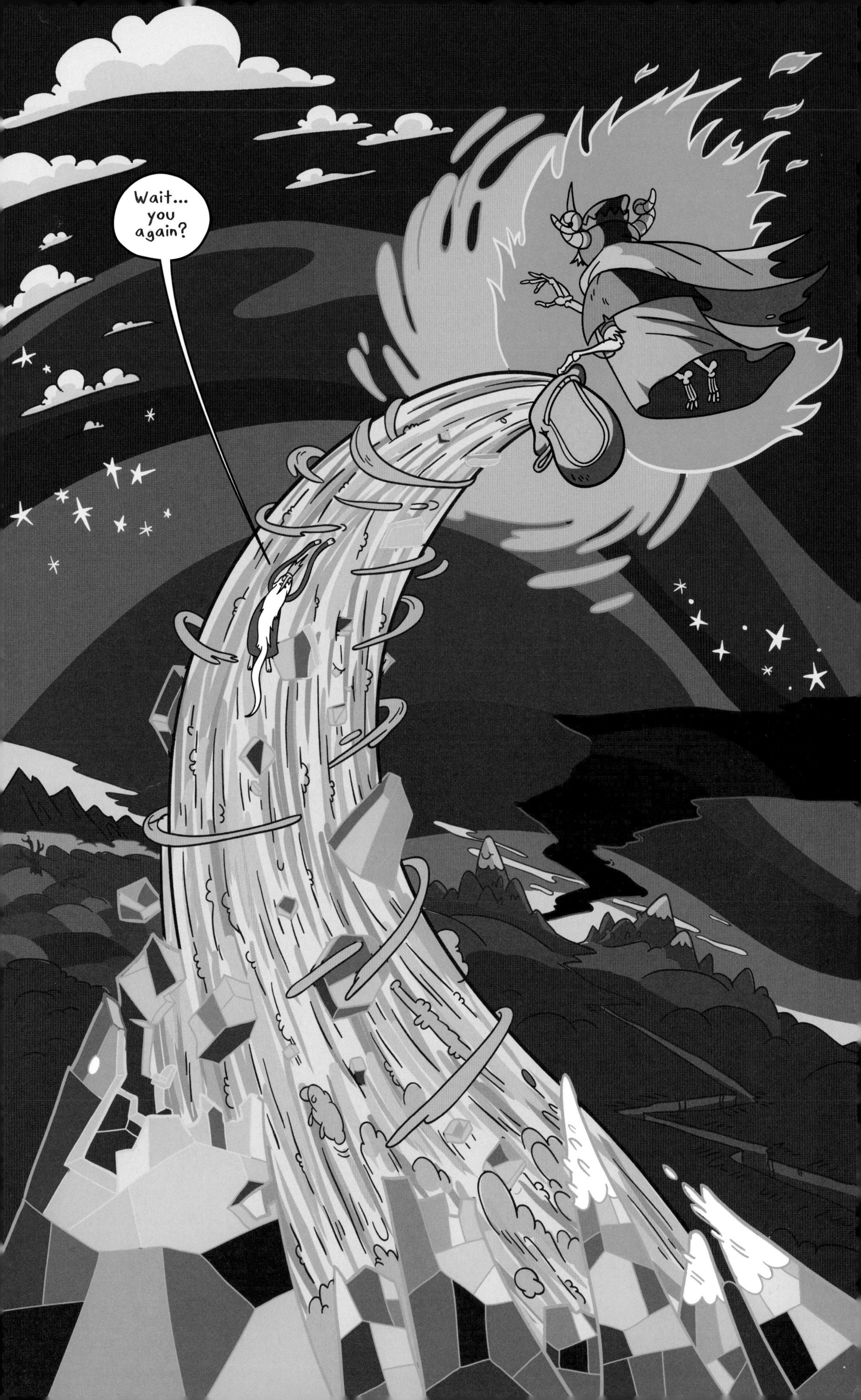
Wait... you again?

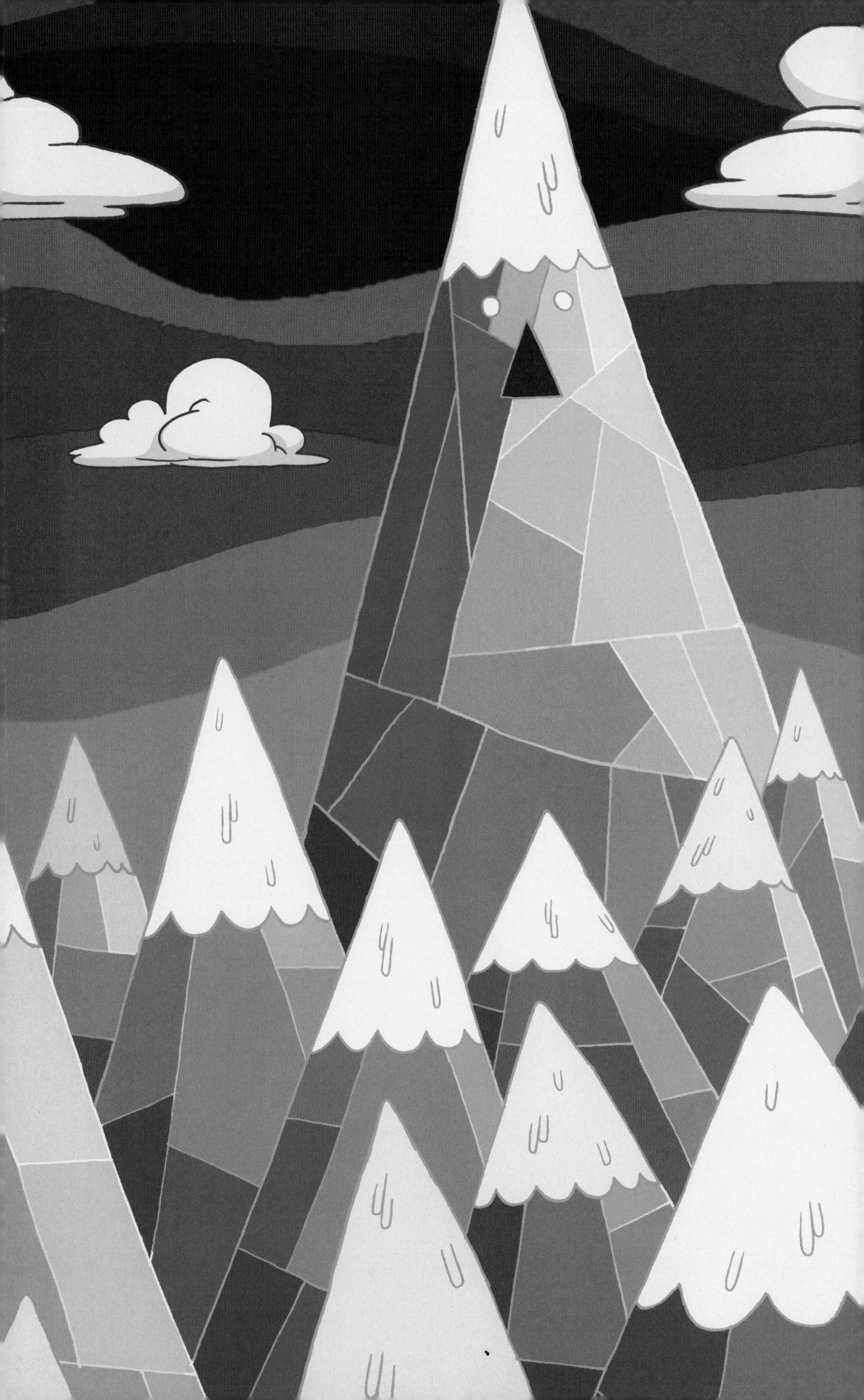

CHAPTER TWO

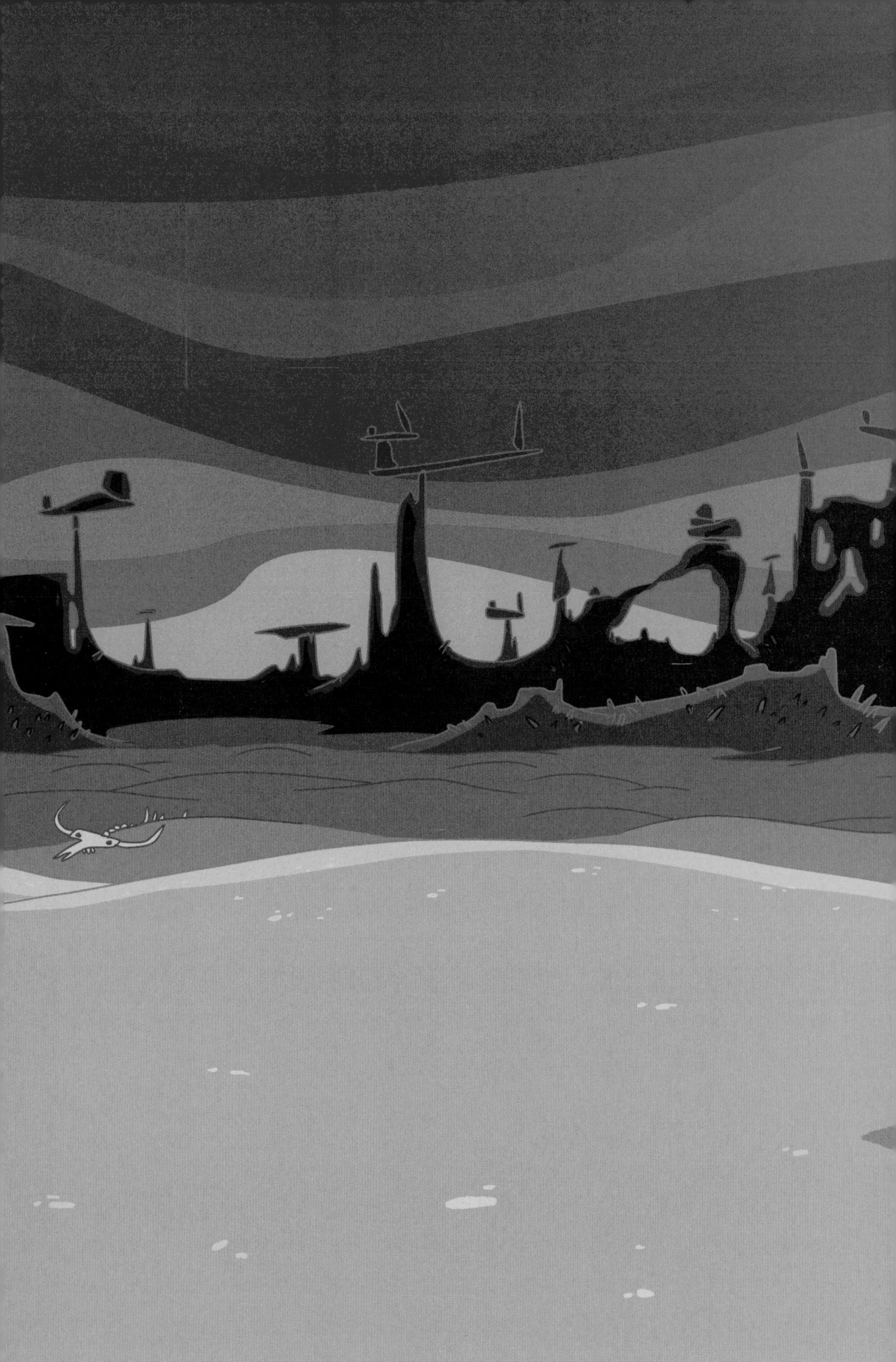

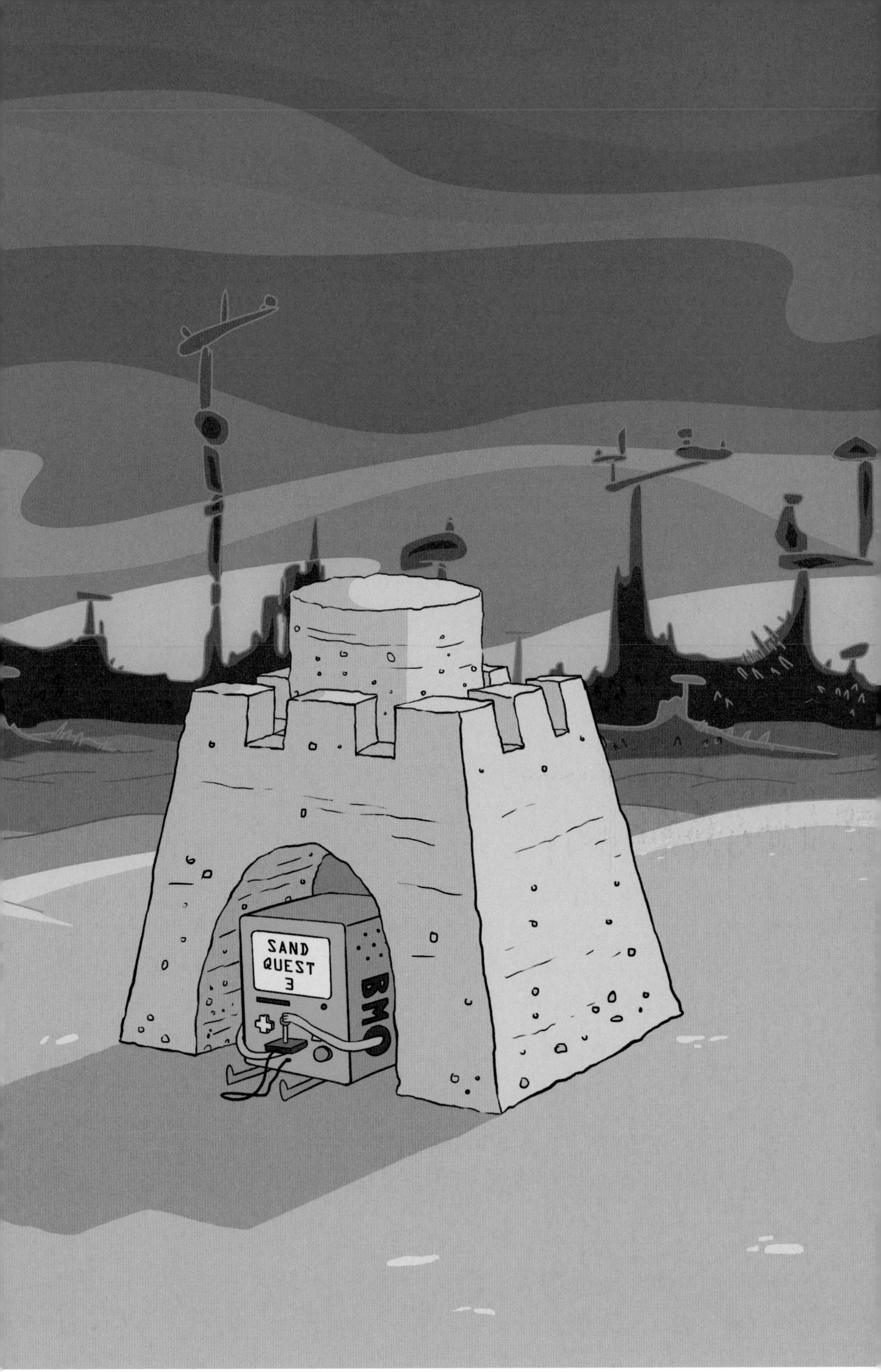
SAND
QUEST
3
BMO

WRITTEN BY RYAN NORTH | ILLUSTRATED BY STEPHANIE GONZAGA | COLORS BY KASSANDRA HELLER | BACKGROUND BY SHELLI PAROLINE AND BRADEN LAMB

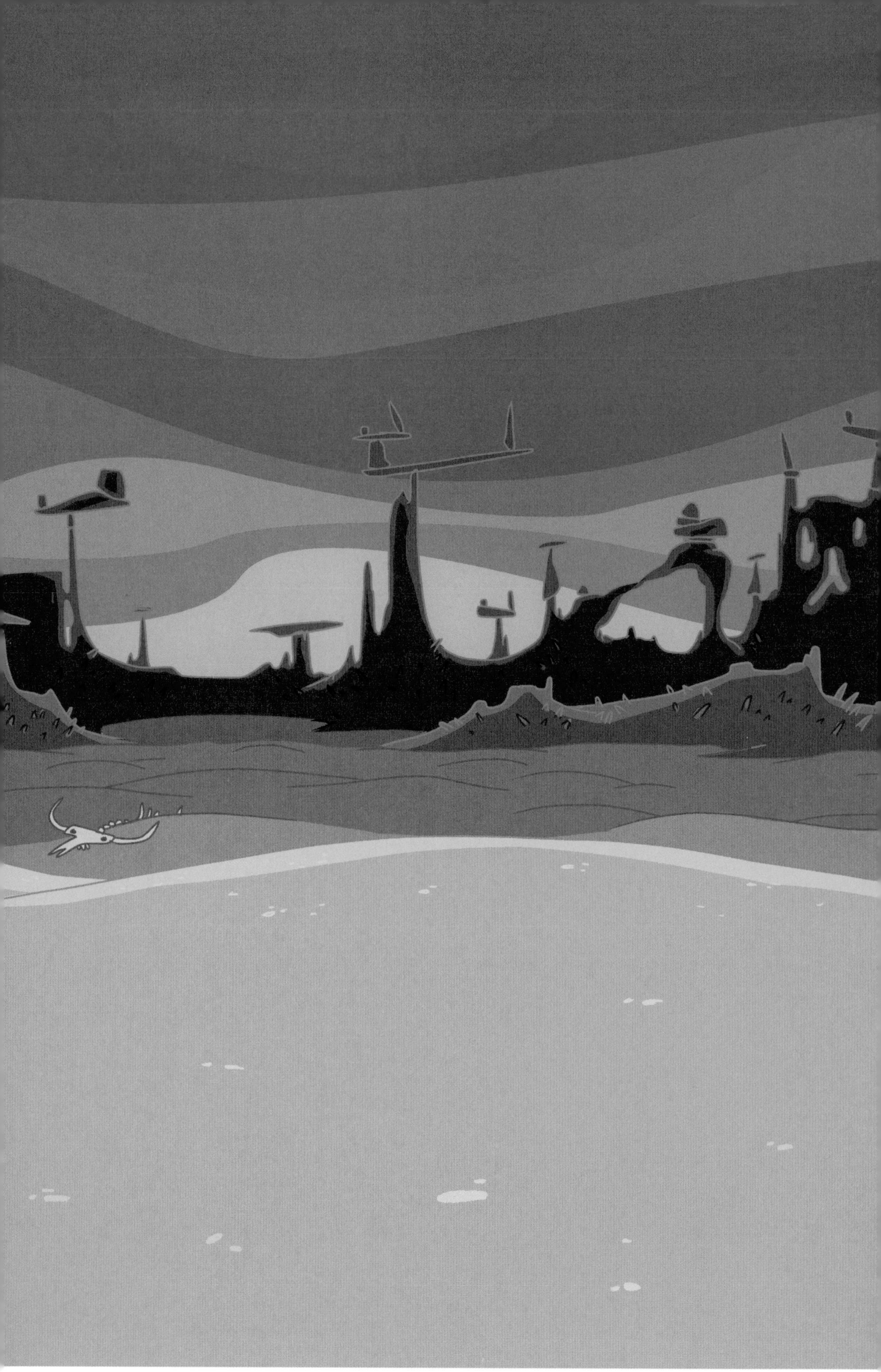

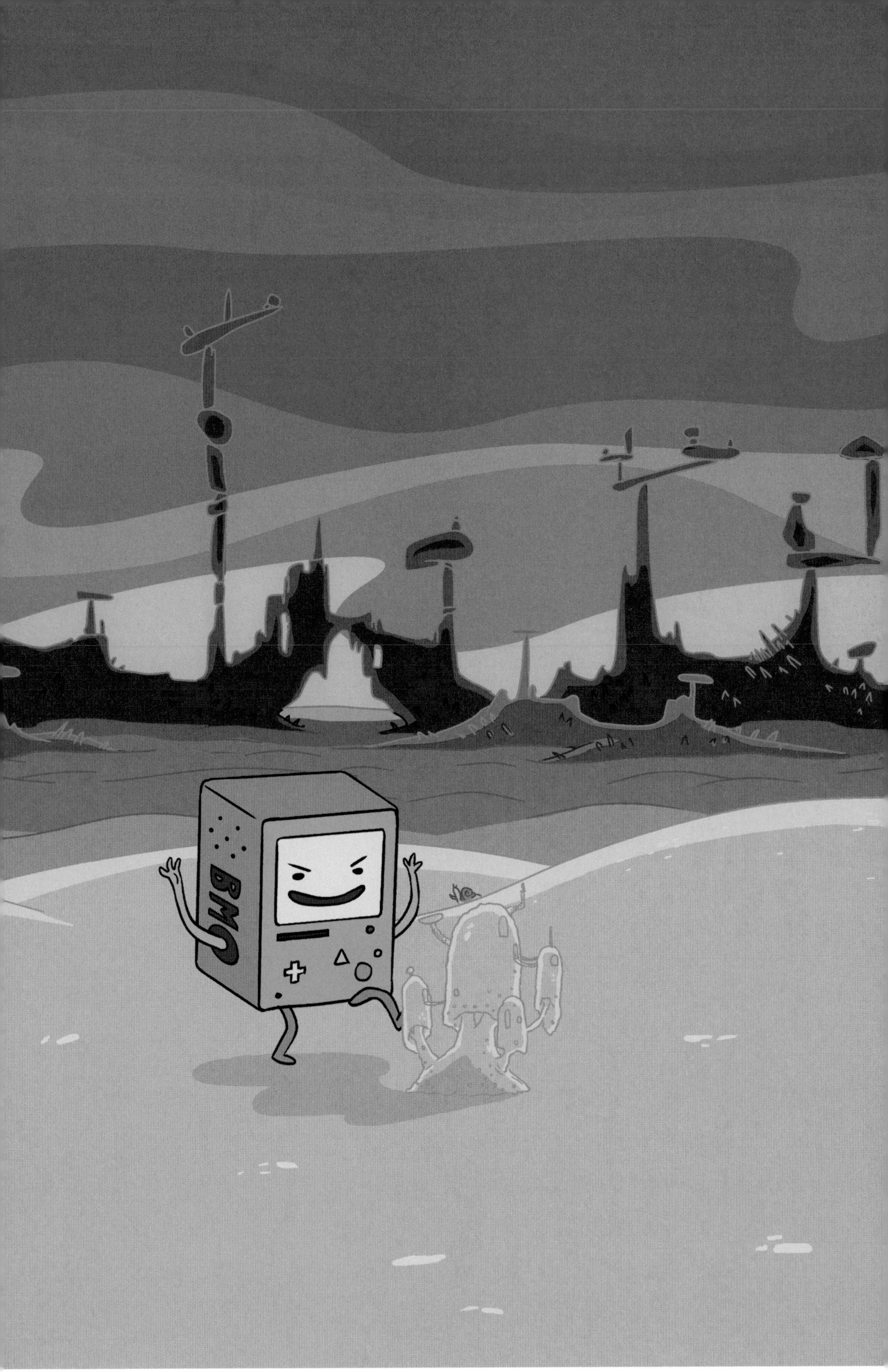
BMO

WRITTEN BY RYAN NORTH | ILLUSTRATED BY STEPHANIE GONZAGA | COLORS BY KASSANDRA HELLER | BACKGROUND BY SHELLI PAROLINE AND BRADEN LAMB

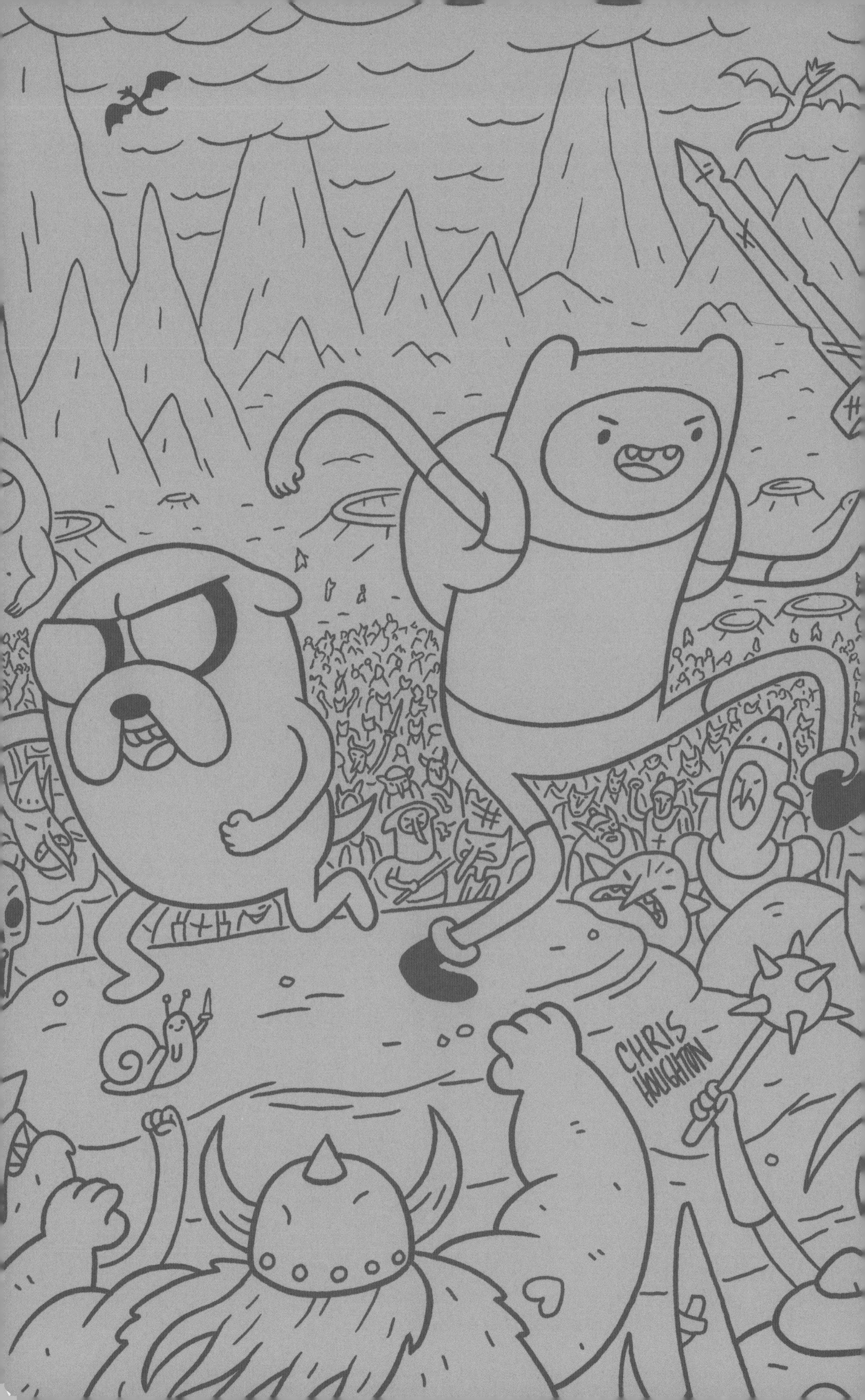
CHRIS HOUGHTON

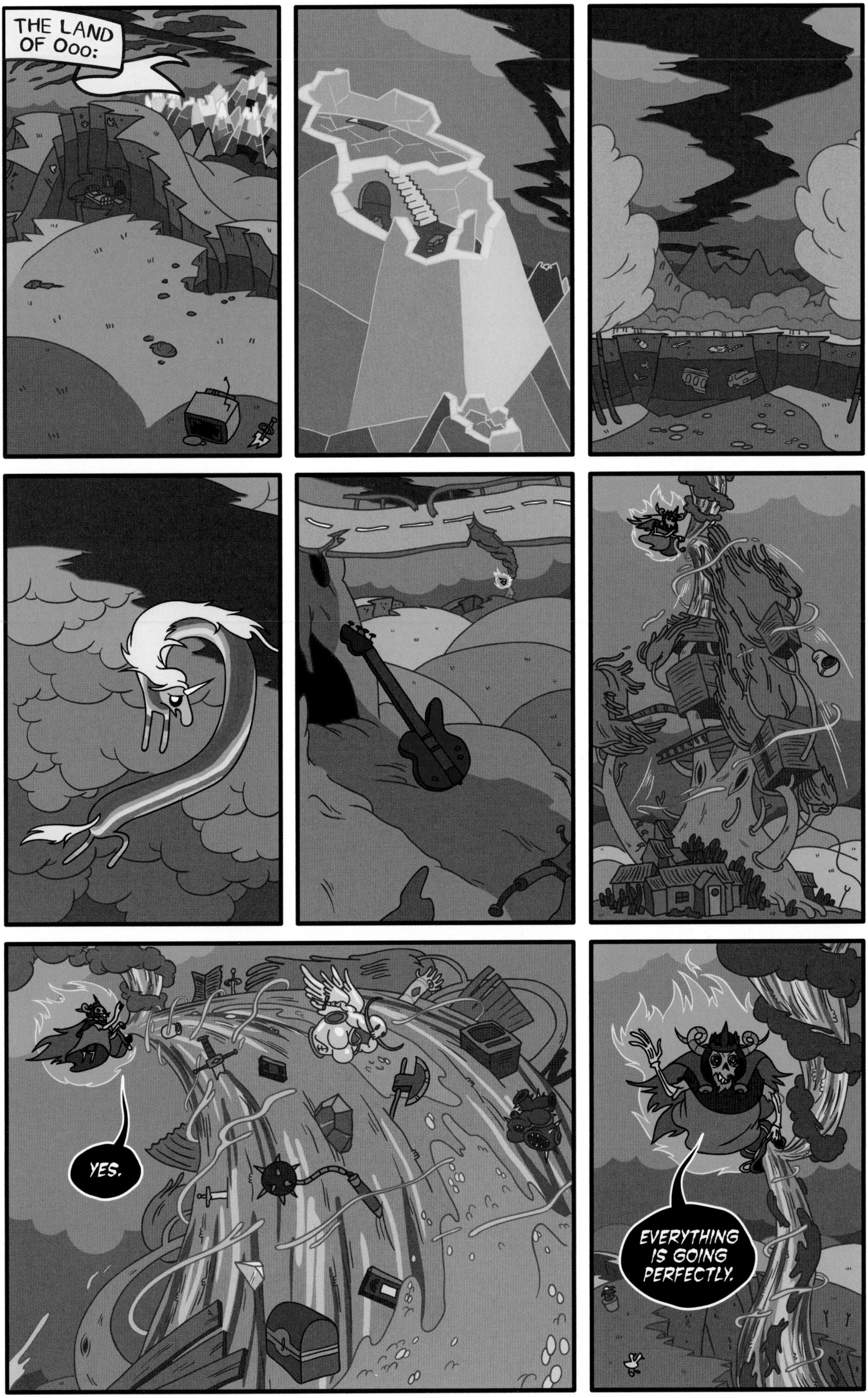
THE LAND OF Ooo:
YES.
EVERYTHING IS GOING PERFECTLY.

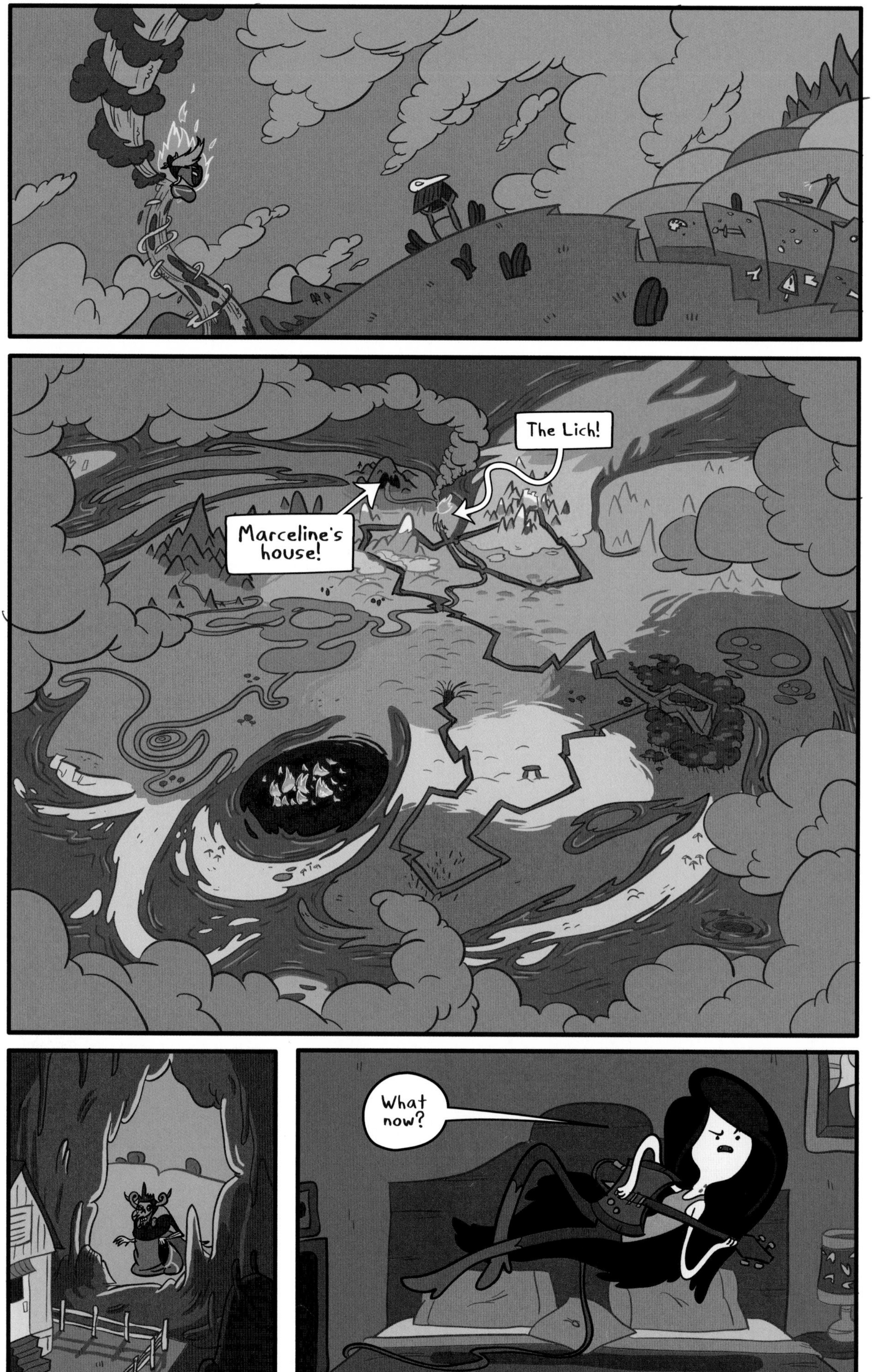
The Lich!
Marceline's house!
What now?

If this were an audio comic you could hear what Marceline was playing and, faced with hearing such beauty, your ears would weep.

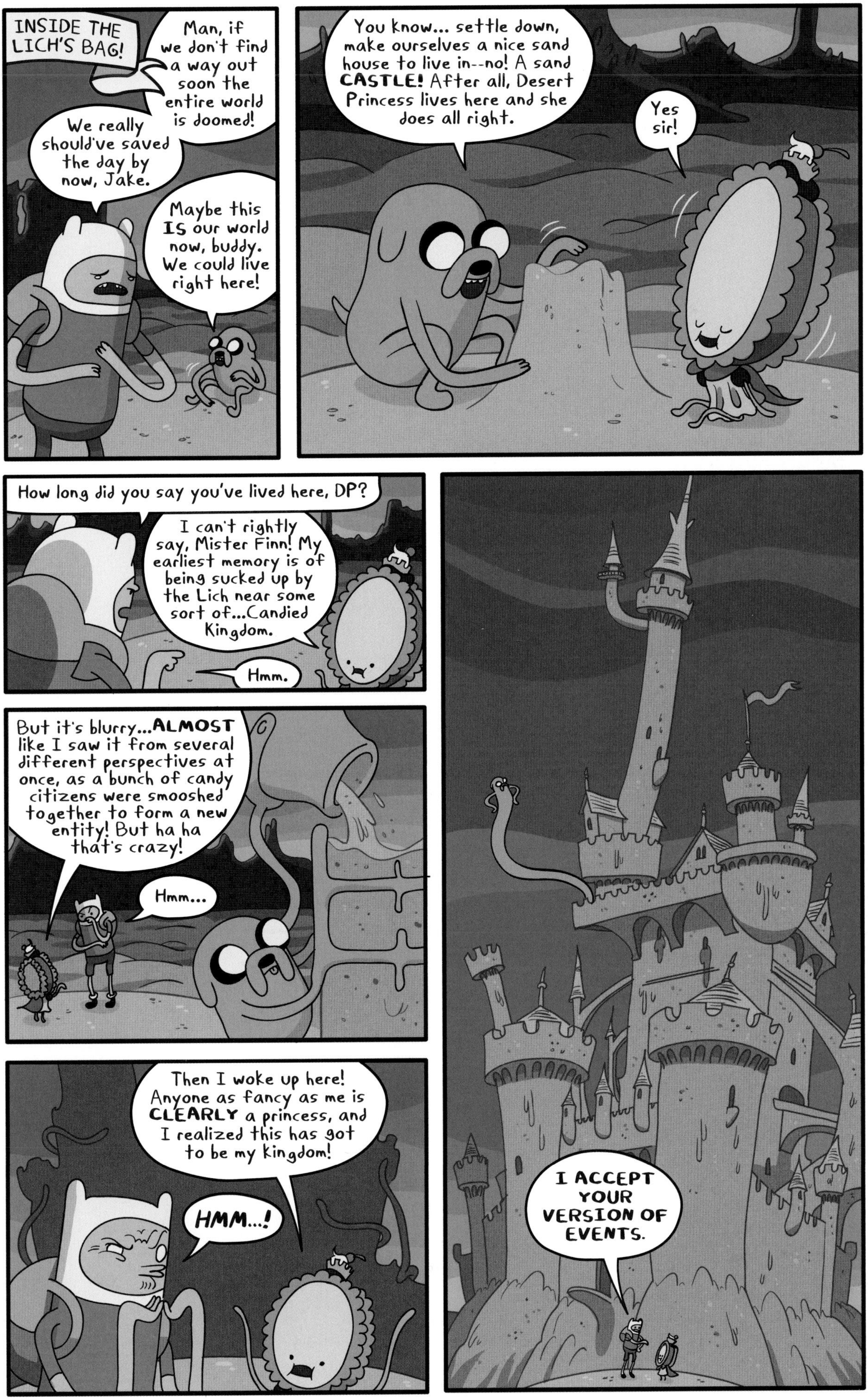
INSIDE THE LICH'S BAG!
Man, if we don't find a way out soon the entire world is doomed!
We really should've saved the day by now, Jake.
Maybe this IS our world now, buddy. We could live right here!
You know... settle down, make ourselves a nice sand house to live in--no! A sand CASTLE! After all, Desert Princess lives here and she does all right.
Yes sir!
How long did you say you've lived here, DP?
I can't rightly say, Mister Finn! My earliest memory is of being sucked up by the Lich near some sort of...Candied Kingdom.
Hmm.
But it's blurry...ALMOST like I saw it from several different perspectives at once, as a bunch of candy citizens were smooshed together to form a new entity! But ha ha that's crazy!
Hmm...
Then I woke up here! Anyone as fancy as me is CLEARLY a princess, and I realized this has got to be my kingdom!
HMM...!
I ACCEPT YOUR VERSION OF EVENTS.

Desert Princess is as mysterious as she is...made out of desserts.

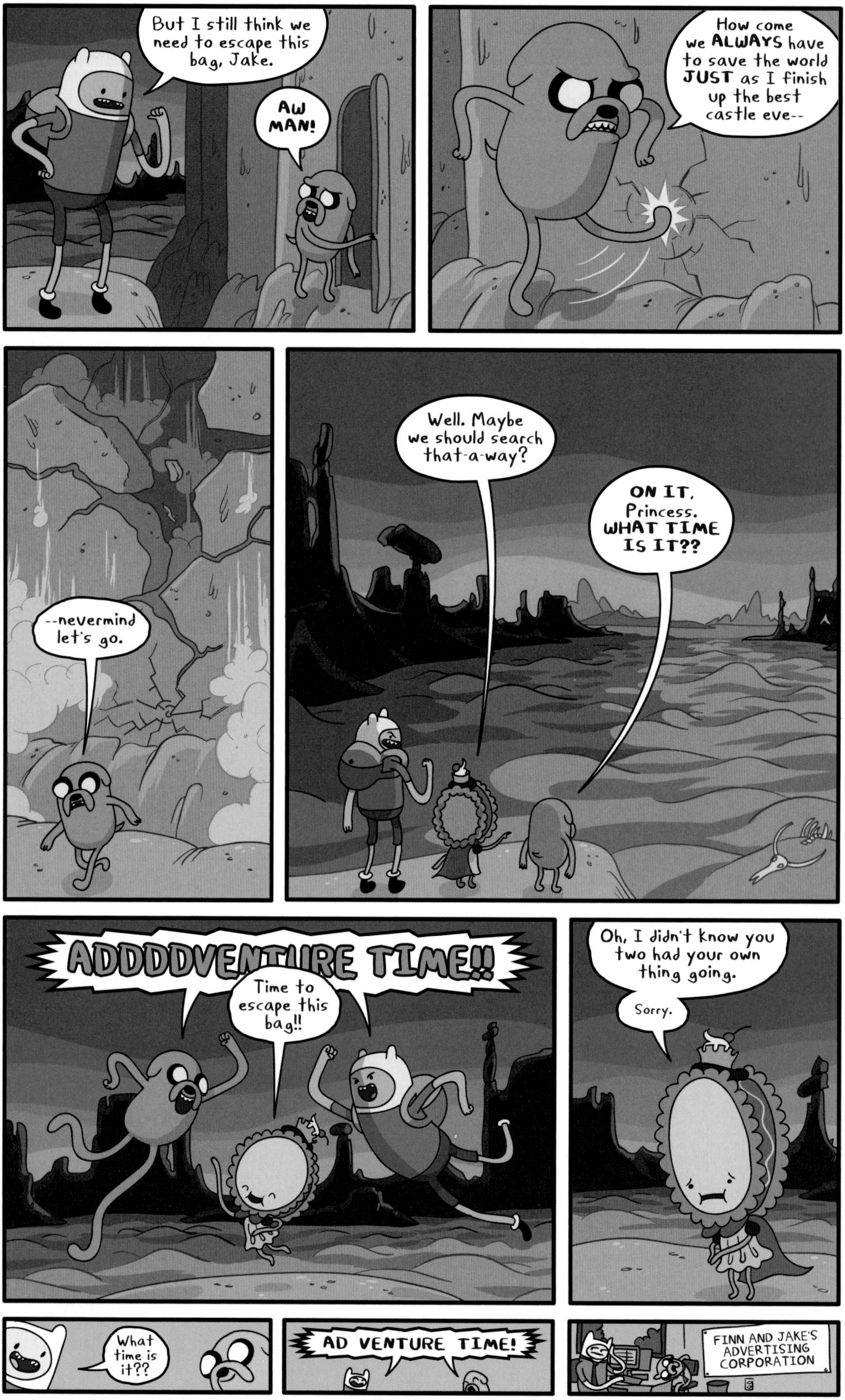
But I still think we need to escape this bag, Jake.
AW MAN!
How come we ALWAYS have to save the world JUST as I finish up the best castle eve--
--nevermind let's go.
Well. Maybe we should search that-a-way?
ON IT, Princess. WHAT TIME IS IT??
ADDDDVENTURE TIME!!
Time to escape this bag!!
Oh, I didn't know you two had your own thing going.
Sorry.
What time is it??
AD VENTURE TIME!
FINN AND JAKE'S ADVERTISING CORPORATION

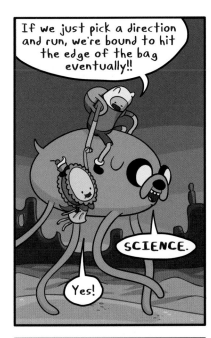

If we just pick a direction and run, we're bound to hit the edge of the bag eventually!!
Yes!
SCIENCE.
TWENTY MINUTES LATER:
Man, I'm pooped. I don't think running is the answer here, dudes. I think running--I think running might actually be the worst.
Gentlemen! Maybe we're thinking too two-dimensionally! Maybe we can escape...up?
Anything's better than runnninnnggggggggggggggggggggggggggggggggggggg
Remember when the Lich was attacking me and my totally sweet house?
Remember how instead of helping me out, you turned the page and read about Finn and Jake instead?
Well I don't have to remember because he's still attacking me and IT'S HAPPENING RIGHT NOW!!

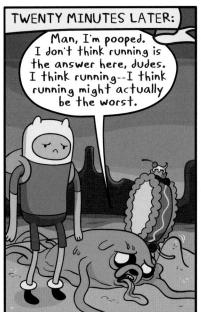

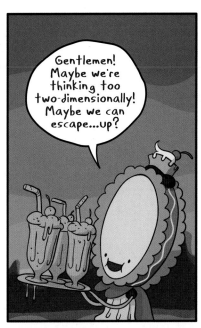

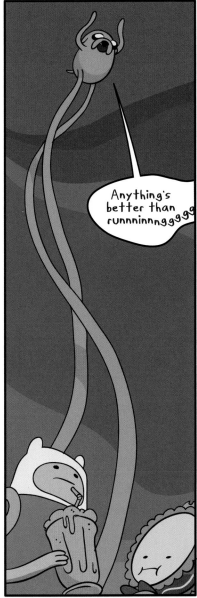

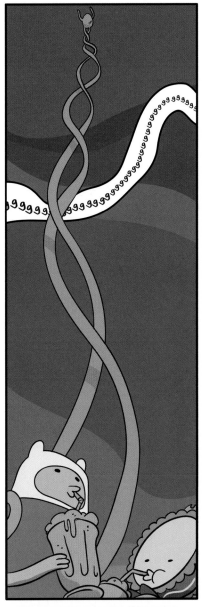

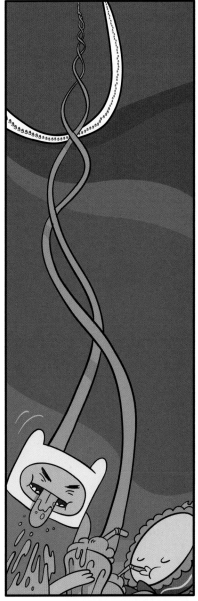

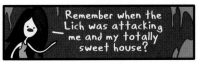

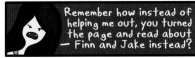

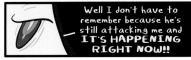

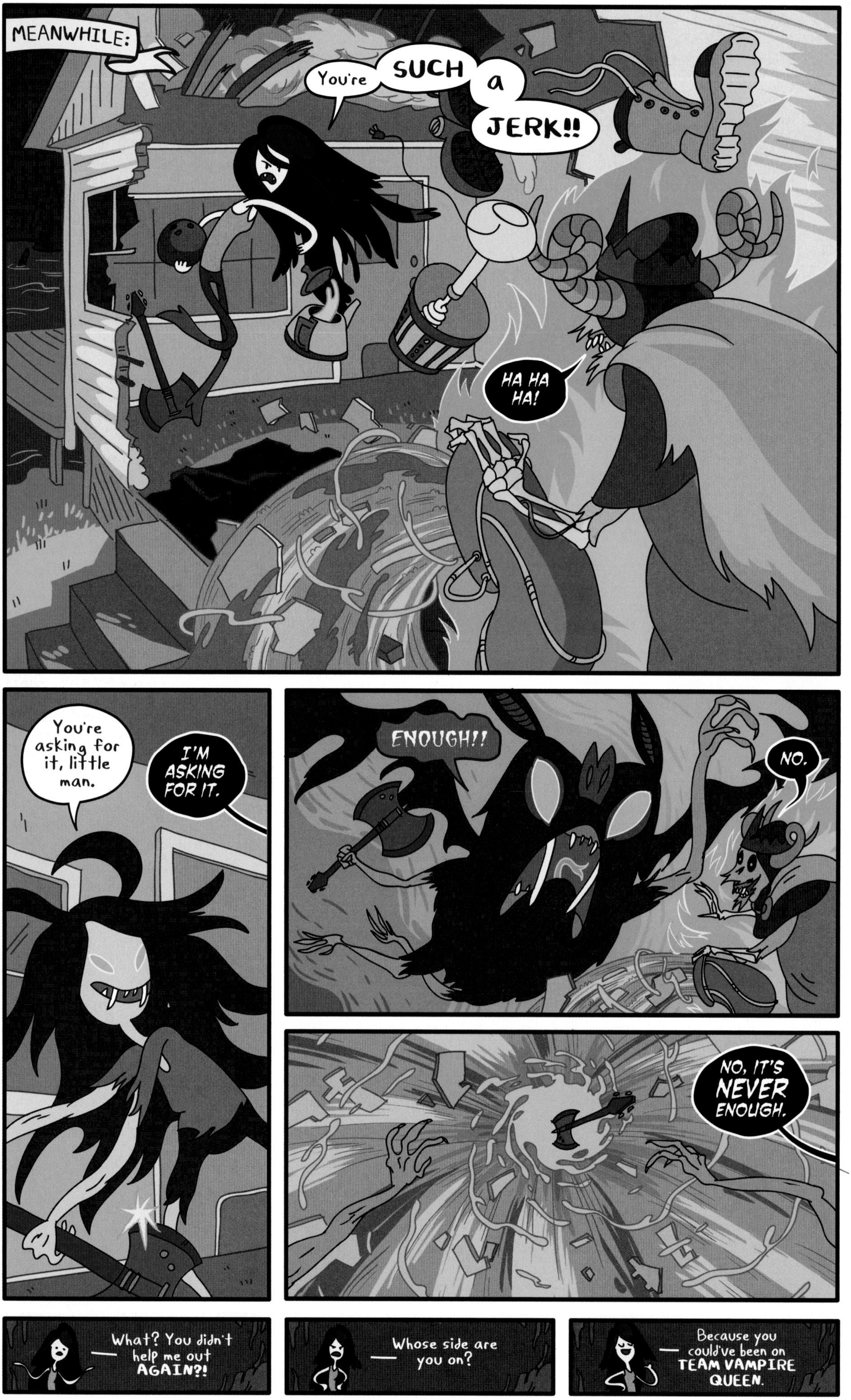
MEANWHILE:
You're SUCH a JERK!!
HA HA HA!
You're asking for it, little man.
I'M ASKING FOR IT.
ENOUGH!!
NO.
NO, IT'S NEVER ENOUGH.
What? You didn't help me out AGAIN?!
Whose side are you on?
Because you could've been on TEAM VAMPIRE QUEEN.

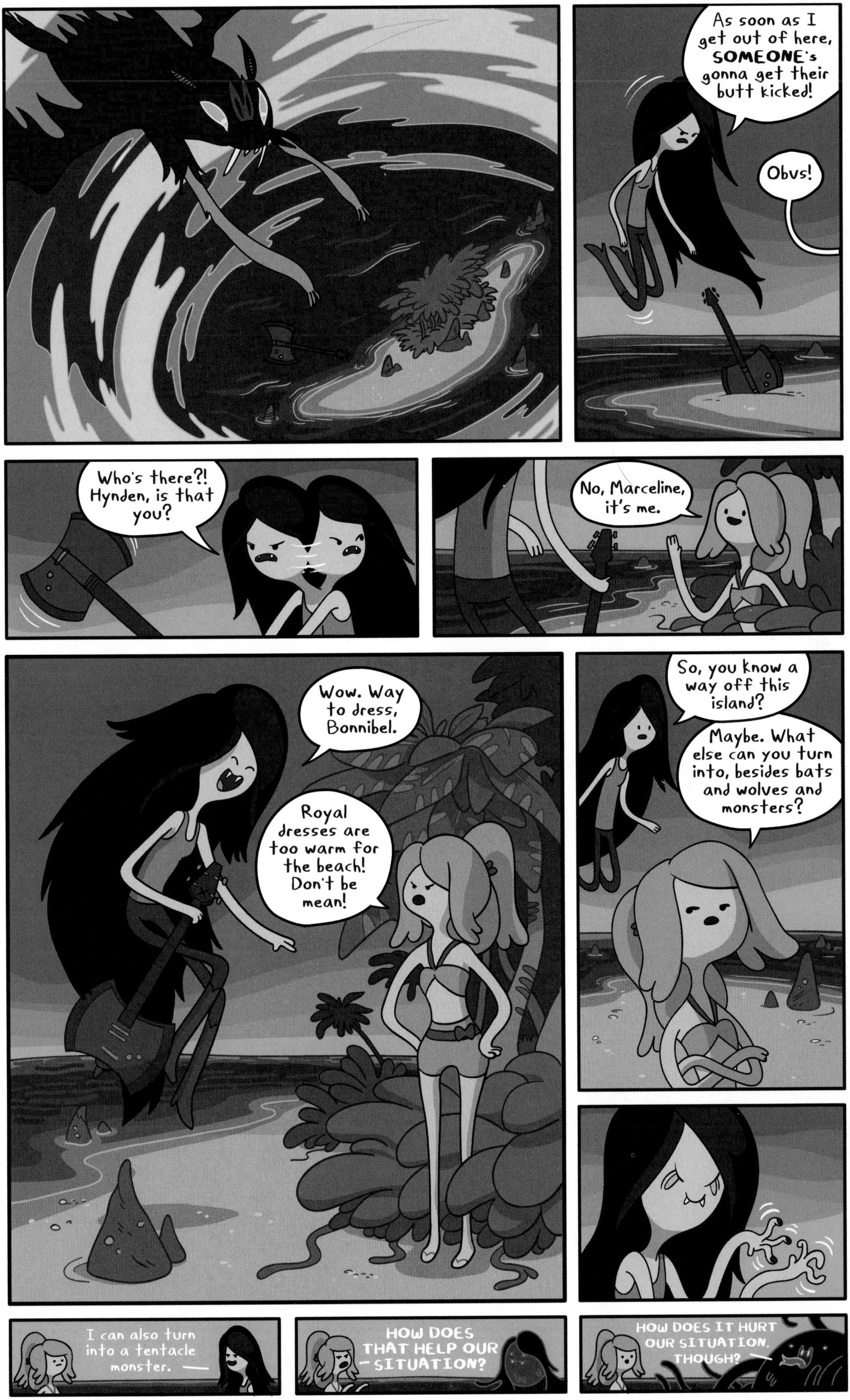
As soon as I get out of here, SOMEONE's gonna get their butt kicked!
Obvs!
Who's there?! Hynden, is that you?
No, Marceline, it's me.
Wow. Way to dress, Bonnibel.
Royal dresses are too warm for the beach! Don't be mean!
So, you know a way off this island?
Maybe. What else can you turn into, besides bats and wolves and monsters?
I can also turn into a tentacle monster.
HOW DOES THAT HELP OUR SITUATION?
HOW DOES IT HURT OUR SITUATION, THOUGH?

ELSEWHERE IN THE BAG:

Dude! I didn't find a way out, but I DID see the Ice King nearby!! You wanna go mess with him?

He might know a way out of here!

Yeah, we should probably go mess with him.

Hey! Stop whatever you're doing!!

Oh, hey guys. You got bagged too, huh? It's pretty sucky here, am I right?

Ice King! You're evil, and I'm pretty sure you know a way out of here!

Hey, great to see you too, FRIEND. Look, I got nothing to do with this. I got sucked up just like everyone else, only I landed alone without Gunter OR my fan fiction.

Aw, that's awful. Hi there--I'm Desert Princess.

Thank you! Nice to get some empathy for once. These two only give me punches all up in my face.

Is that true?

He deserves it a lot of the time.

Is THAT true?

SHRUG

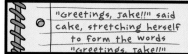

"Greetings, Jake!!!" said cake, stretching herself to form the words "Greetings, Jake!!!"

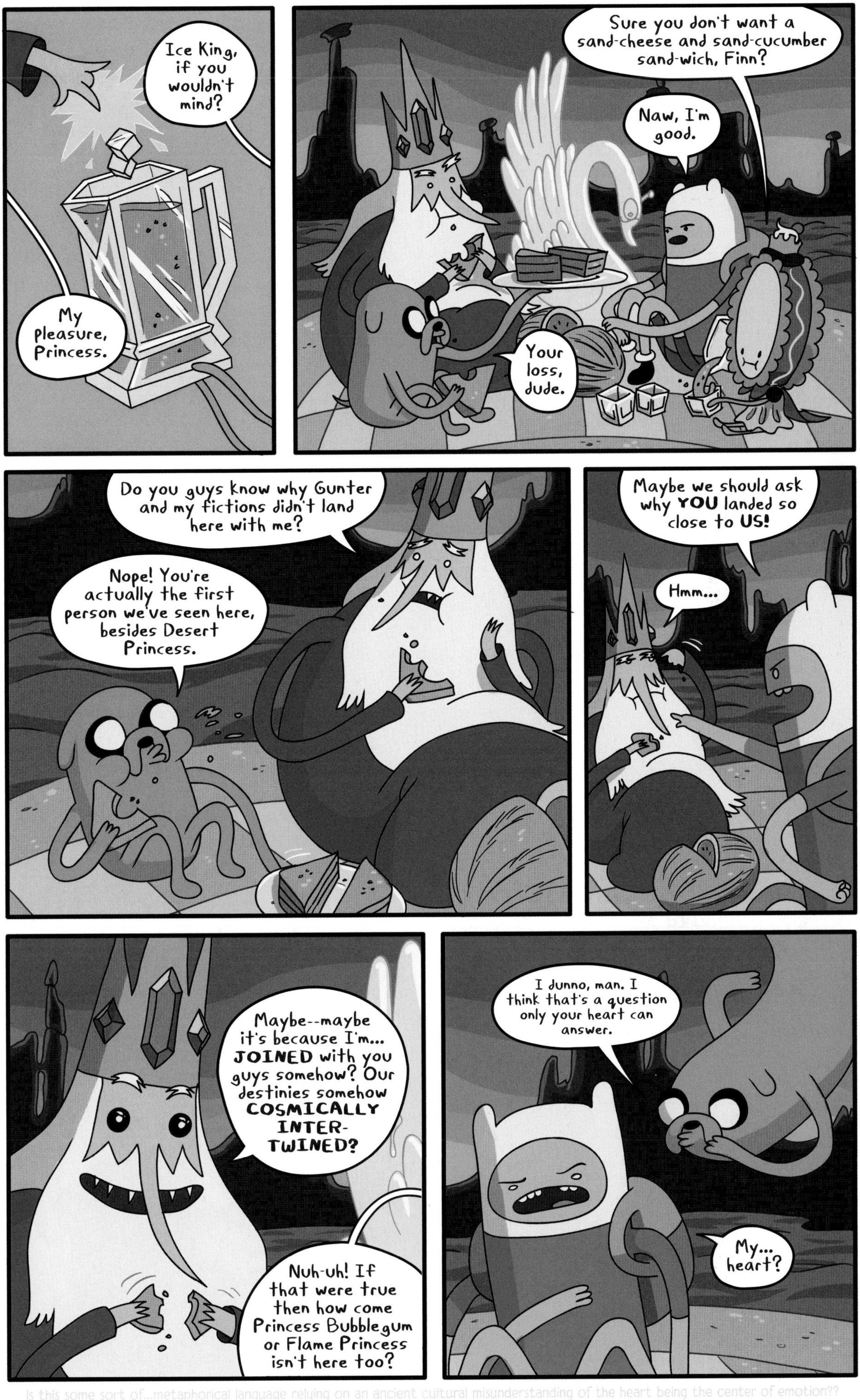
Ice King, if you wouldn't mind?
My pleasure, Princess.
Sure you don't want a sand-cheese and sand-cucumber sand-wich, Finn?
Naw, I'm good.
Your loss, dude.
Do you guys know why Gunter and my fictions didn't land here with me?
Nope! You're actually the first person we've seen here, besides Desert Princess.
Maybe we should ask why YOU landed so close to US!
Hmm...
Maybe--maybe it's because I'm... JOINED with you guys somehow? Our destinies somehow COSMICALLY INTER-TWINED?
Nuh-uh! If that were true then how come Princess Bubblegum or Flame Princess isn't here too?
I dunno, man. I think that's a question only your heart can answer.
My... heart?

Is this some sort of...metaphorical language relying on an ancient cultural misunderstanding of the heart being the center of emotion??

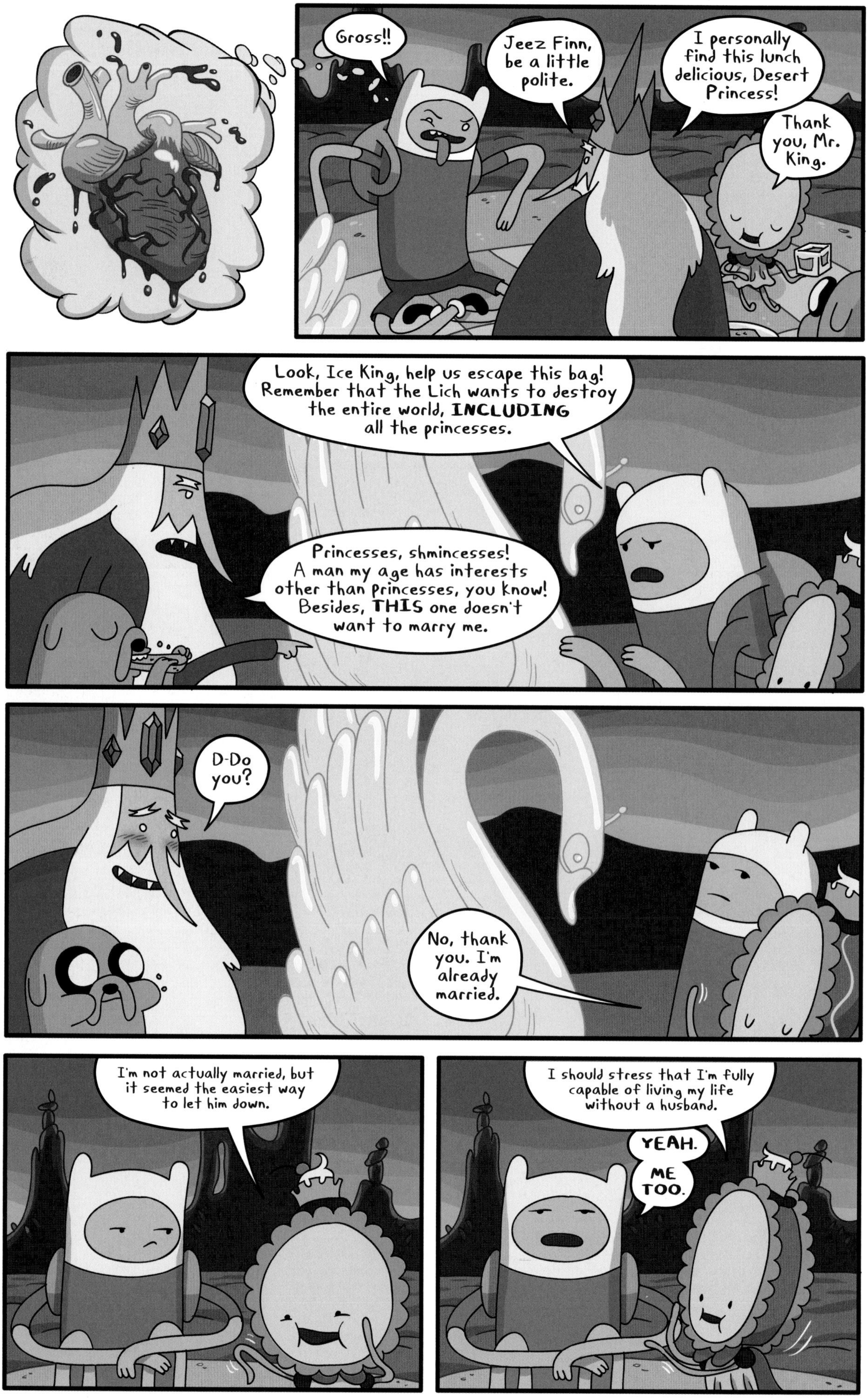
Gross!!
Jeez Finn, be a little polite.
I personally find this lunch delicious, Desert Princess!
Thank you, Mr. King.
Look, Ice King, help us escape this bag! Remember that the Lich wants to destroy the entire world, INCLUDING all the princesses.
Princesses, shmincesses! A man my age has interests other than princesses, you know! Besides, THIS one doesn't want to marry me.
D-Do you?
No, thank you. I'm already married.
I'm not actually married, but it seemed the easiest way to let him down.
I should stress that I'm fully capable of living my life without a husband.
YEAH.
ME TOO.

I'VE BEEN DOING IT SINCE LIKE FOREVER

MEANWHILE, OUTSIDE THE BAG:

I can't even believe I used to live here, Melissa. I could just **DIE.**

Everything's gross here. You have to promise not to tell Brad I ever lived like this.

OH MY GLOB Melissa I gotta go!

There's this skeleton guy and he's sucking up all my stuff! I'm serious Melissa, he's sucking up my **LUMPING HOUSE!**

No I don't know him, Melissa. **NO!** No way I'm asking him that, **MELISSA.** I'm telling you, he's gross. HE'S **GROSS!**

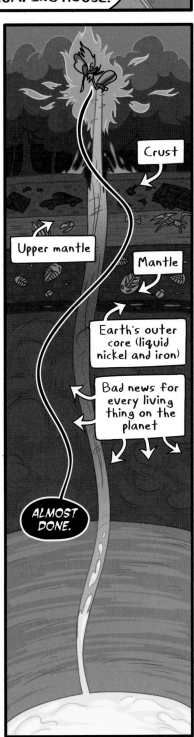

Crust

Upper mantle

Mantle

Earth's outer core (liquid nickel and iron)

Bad news for every living thing on the planet

ALMOST DONE.

ARRRRGGGH!

I, THE TALKY ONE, REGRET TALKING SO MUCH.

Let's learn more about the Earth's crust! As you may have heard, yes, it is mainly made out of old crusts.

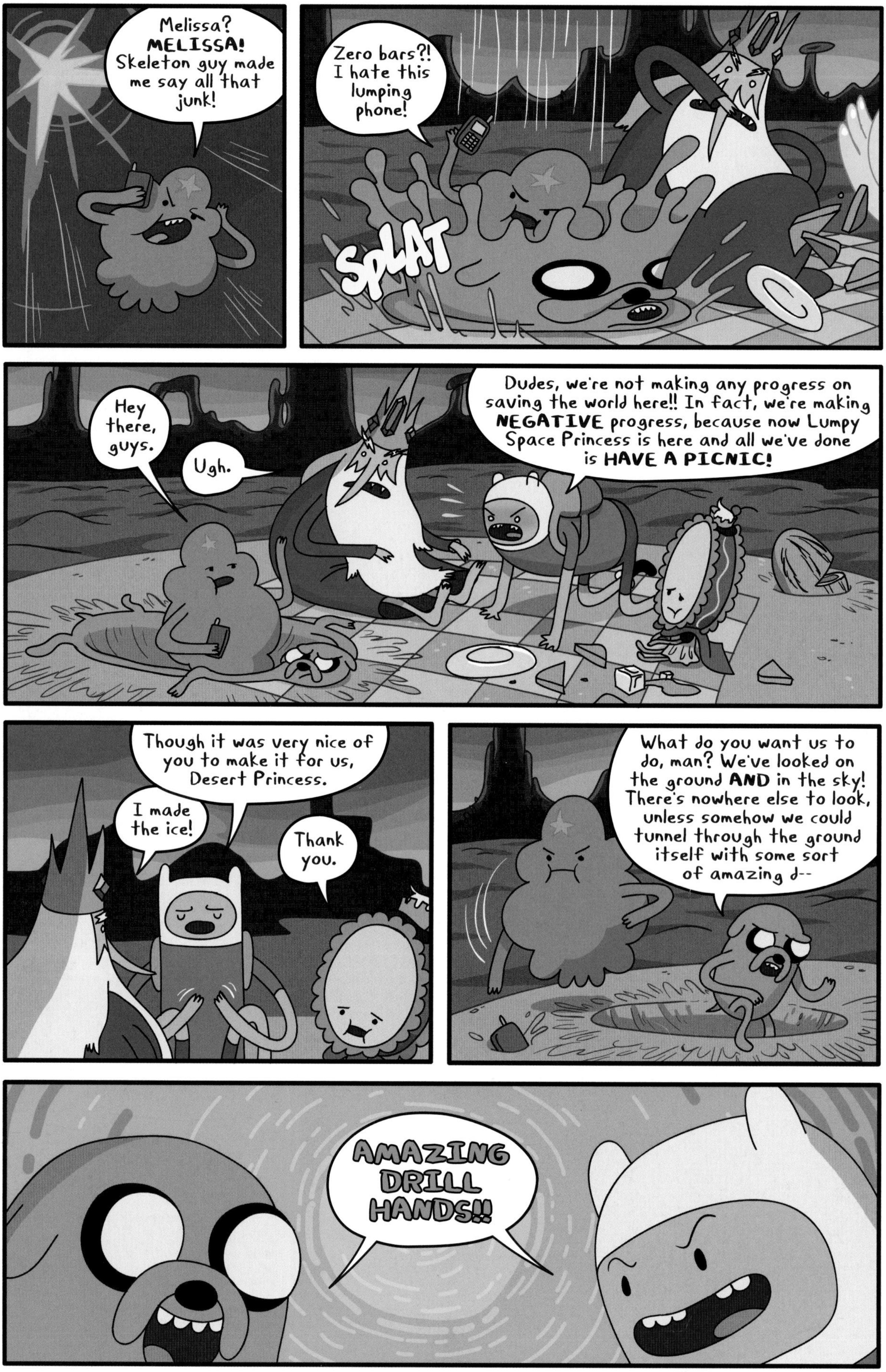
Melissa? MELISSA! Skeleton guy made me say all that junk!
Zero bars?! I hate this lumping phone!
SPLAT
Hey there, guys.
Ugh.
Dudes, we're not making any progress on saving the world here!! In fact, we're making NEGATIVE progress, because now Lumpy Space Princess is here and all we've done is HAVE A PICNIC!
Though it was very nice of you to make it for us, Desert Princess.
I made the ice!
Thank you.
What do you want us to do, man? We've looked on the ground AND in the sky! There's nowhere else to look, unless somehow we could tunnel through the ground itself with some sort of amazing d--
AMAZING DRILL HANDS!!

To be fair, it's extremely hard NOT to hate a lumping phone with zero bars.

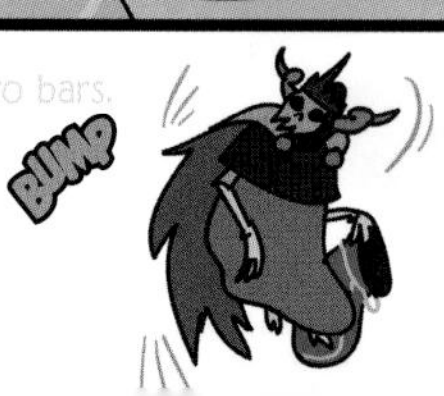
BUMP

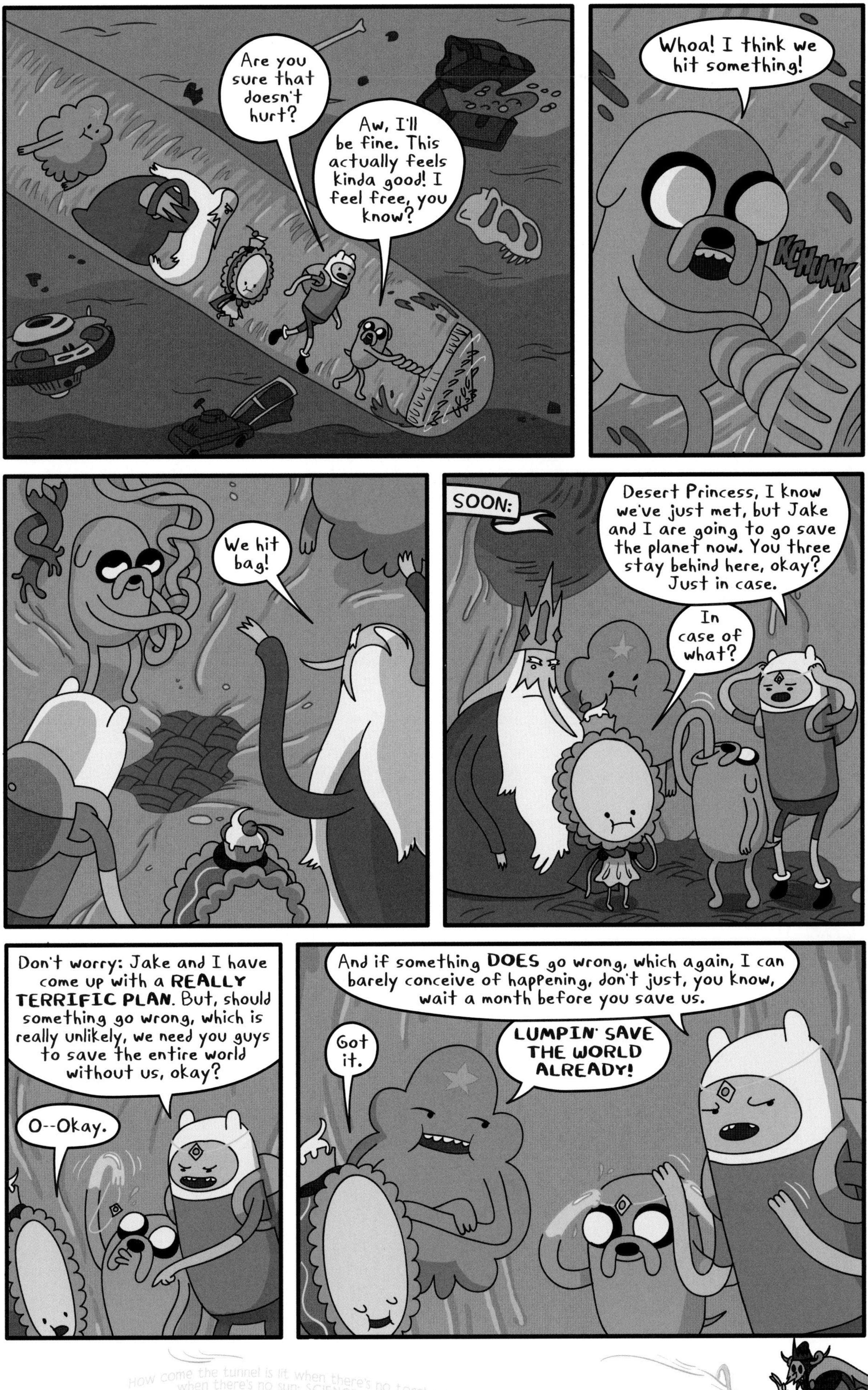
Are you sure that doesn't hurt?
Aw, I'll be fine. This actually feels kinda good! I feel free, you know?
Whoa! I think we hit something!
KCHUNK
We hit bag!
SOON:
Desert Princess, I know we've just met, but Jake and I are going to go save the planet now. You three stay behind here, okay? Just in case.
In case of what?
Don't worry: Jake and I have come up with a **REALLY TERRIFIC PLAN**. But, should something go wrong, which is really unlikely, we need you guys to save the entire world without us, okay?
O--Okay.
And if something **DOES** go wrong, which again, I can barely conceive of happening, don't just, you know, wait a month before you save us.
Got it.
LUMPIN' SAVE THE WORLD ALREADY!

How come the tunnel is lit when there's no torches? It's the same way the inside of the bag is lit when there's no sun: SCIENCE. Wait no hold on wait wait I meant to say MAGIC.

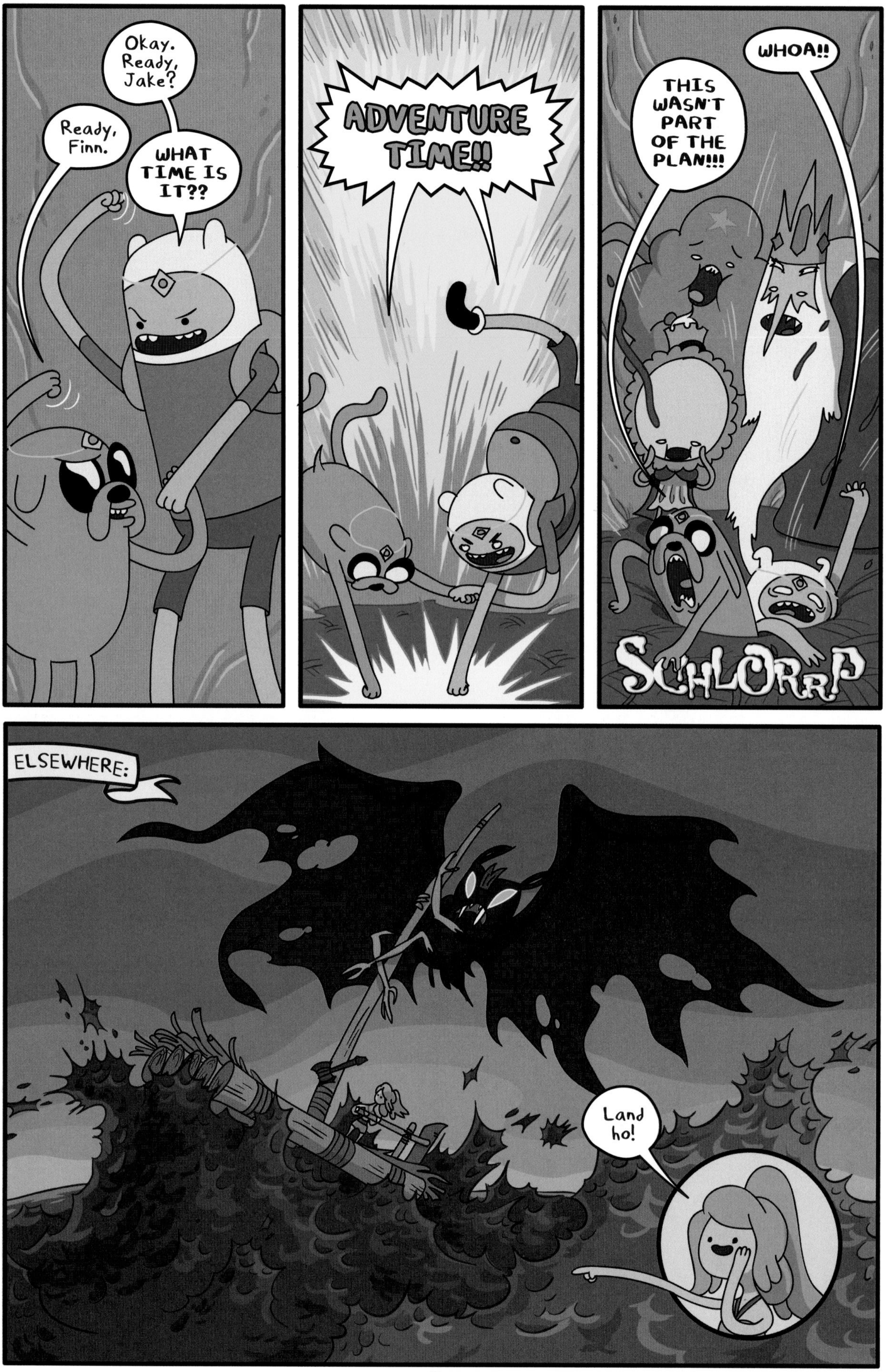
Okay. Ready, Jake?
Ready, Finn.
WHAT TIME IS IT??
ADVENTURE TIME!!
WHOA!!
THIS WASN'T PART OF THE PLAN!!!
SCHLORRP
ELSEWHERE:
Land ho!

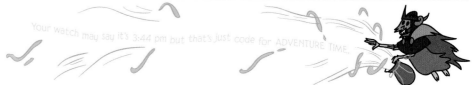

Your watch may say it's 3:44 pm but that's just code for ADVENTURE TIME.

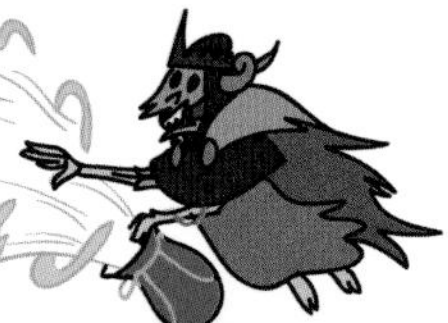

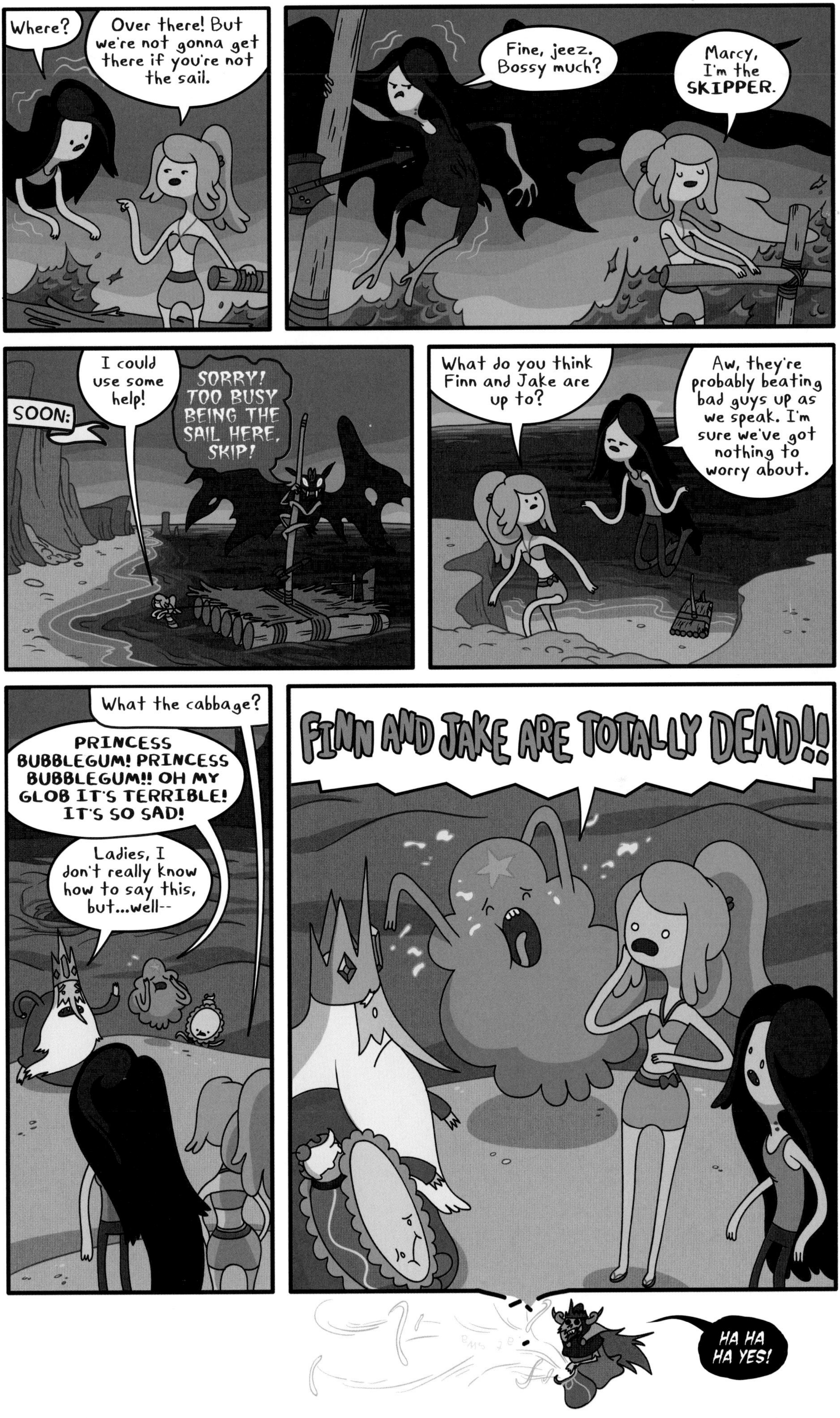
Where?
Over there! But we're not gonna get there if you're not the sail.
Fine, jeez. Bossy much?
Marcy, I'm the SKIPPER.
SOON:
I could use some help!
SORRY! TOO BUSY BEING THE SAIL HERE, SKIP!
What do you think Finn and Jake are up to?
Aw, they're probably beating bad guys up as we speak. I'm sure we've got nothing to worry about.
What the cabbage?
PRINCESS BUBBLEGUM! PRINCESS BUBBLEGUM!! OH MY GLOB IT'S TERRIBLE! IT'S SO SAD!
Ladies, I don't really know how to say this, but...well--
FINN AND JAKE ARE TOTALLY DEAD!!
HA HA HA YES!

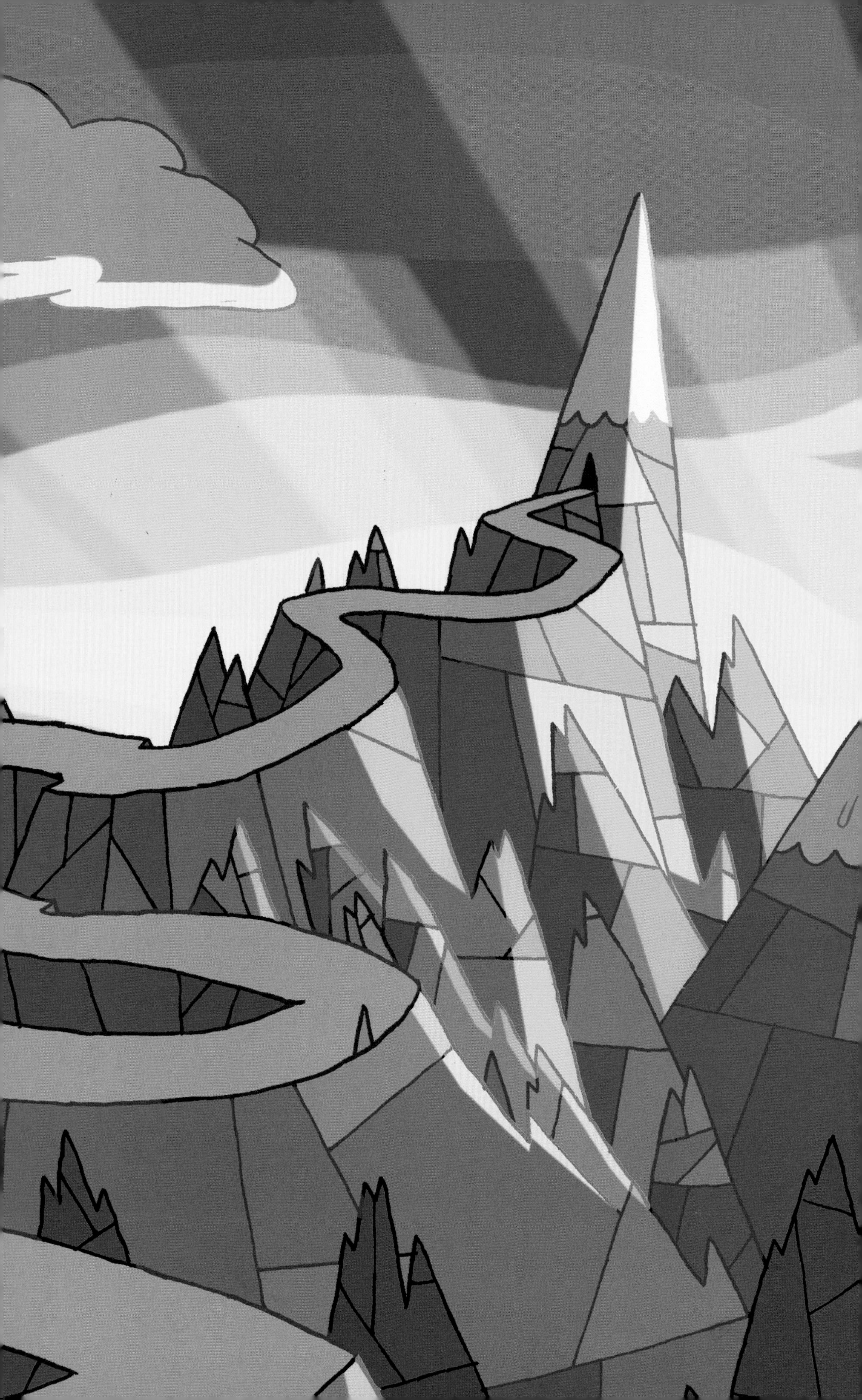

CHAPTER THREE

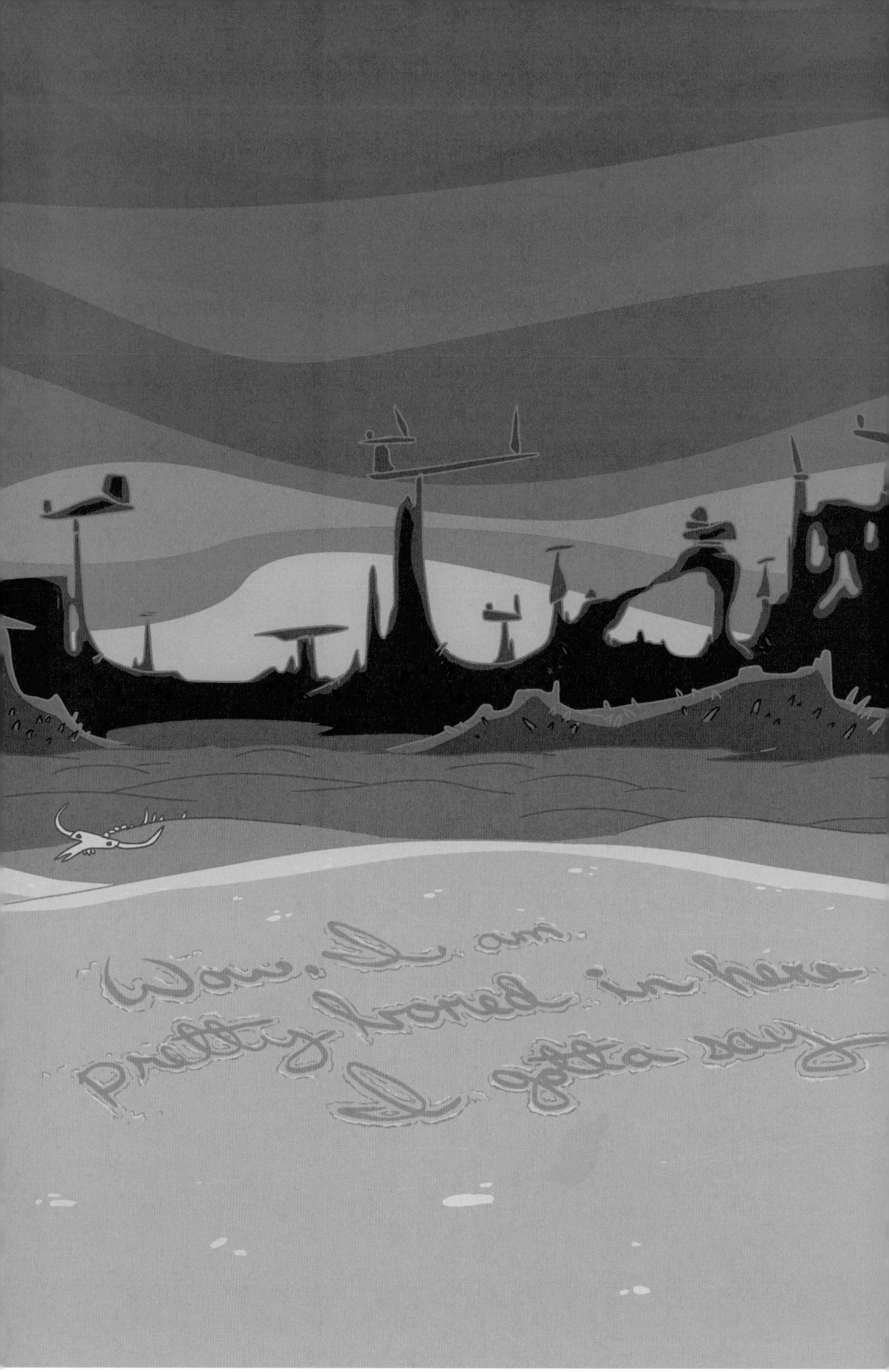
Wow. I am
pretty bored in here
I gotta say

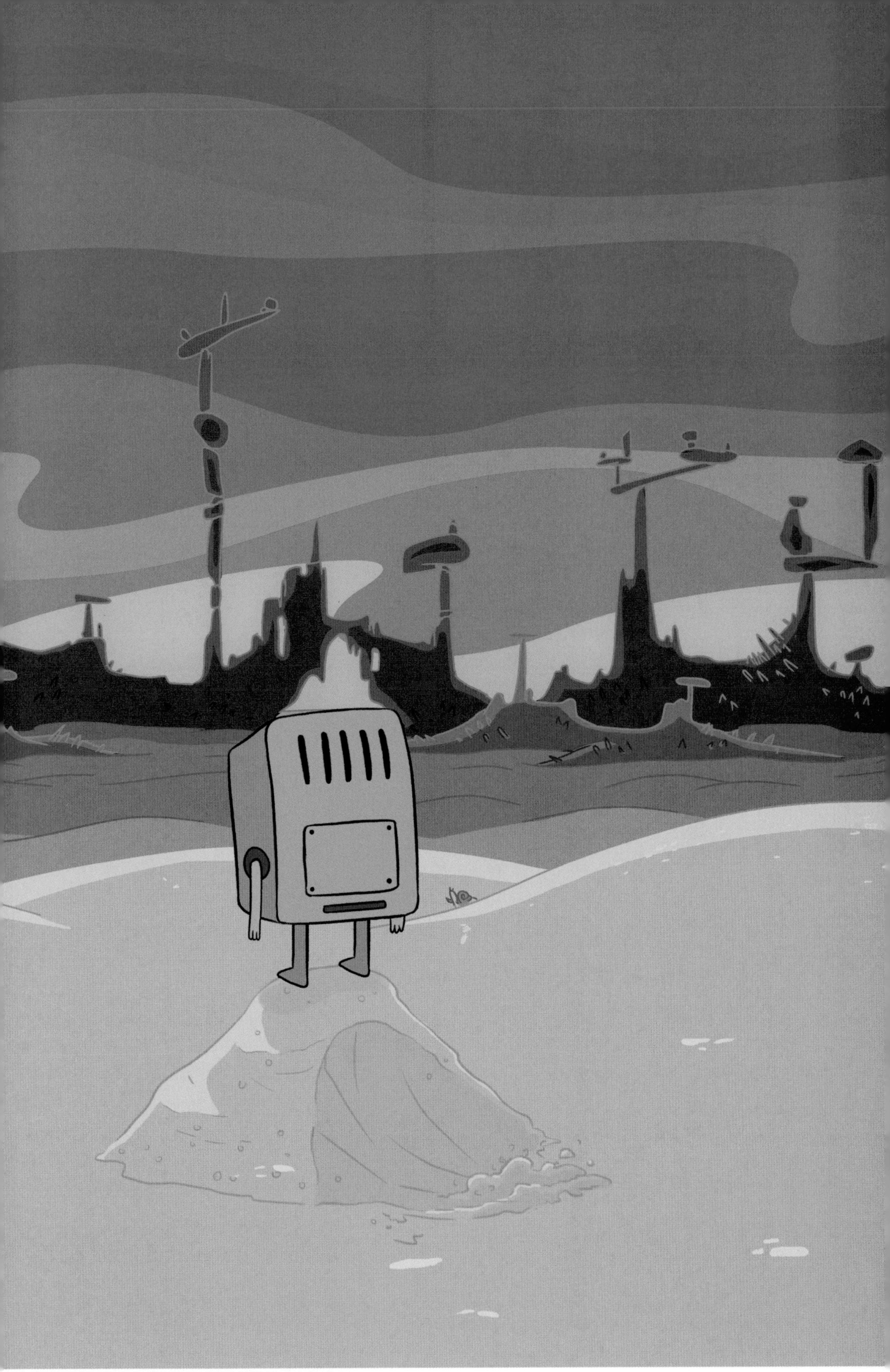

WRITTEN BY RYAN NORTH | ILLUSTRATED BY STEPHANIE GONZAGA | COLORS BY KASSANDRA HELLER | BACKGROUND BY SHELLI PAROLINE AND BRADEN LAMB

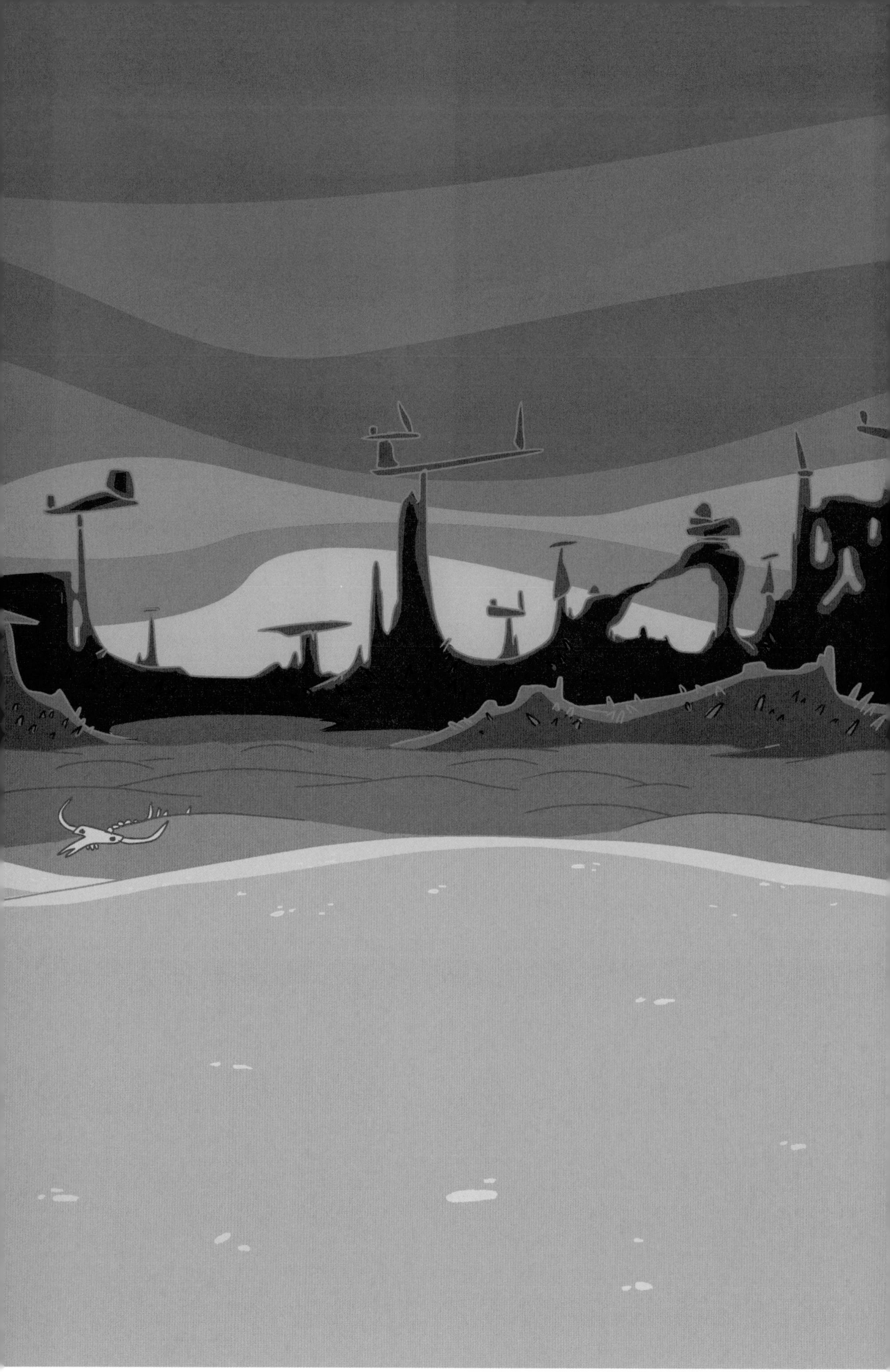

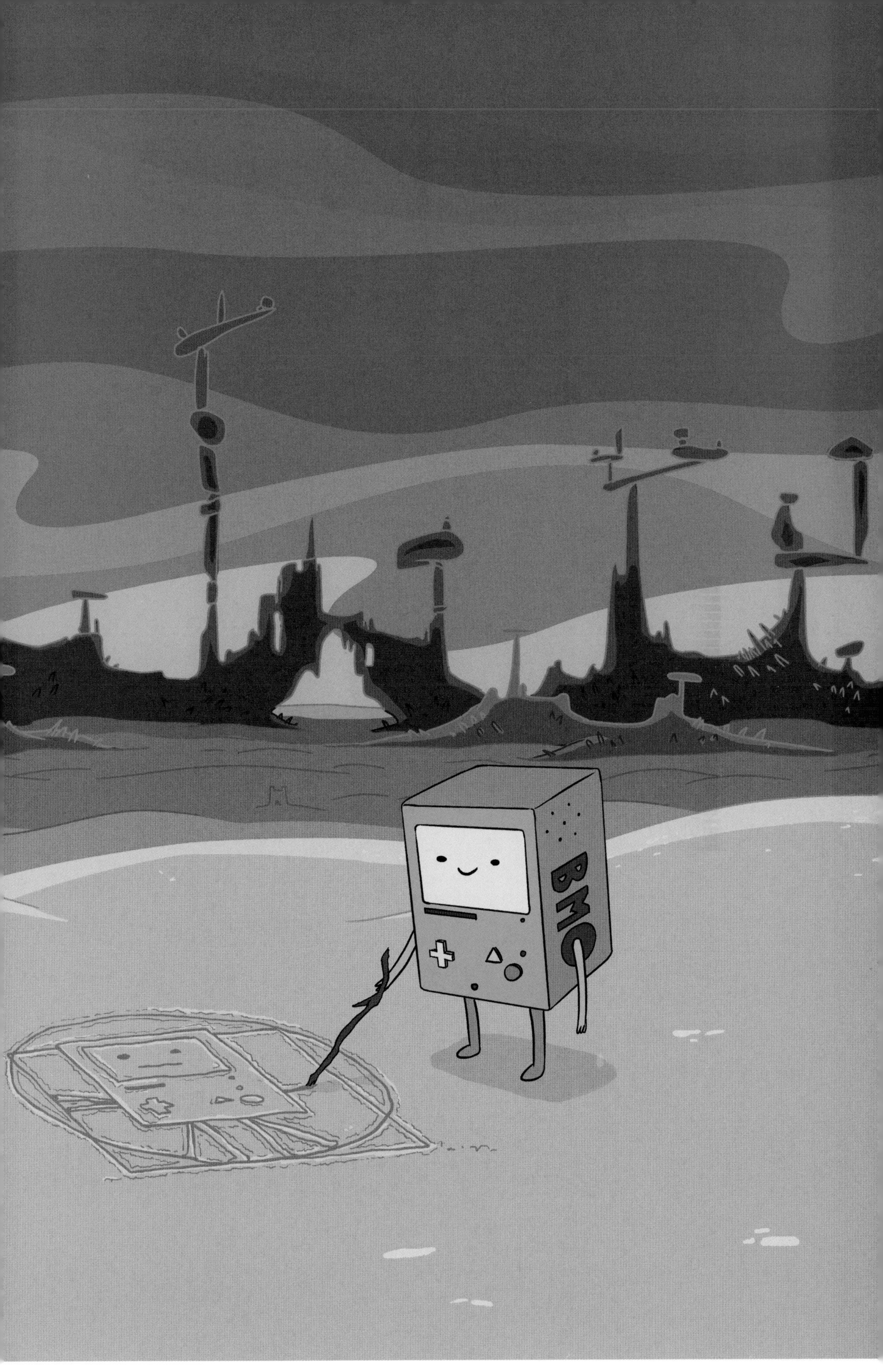
BMO

WRITTEN BY RYAN NORTH | ILLUSTRATED BY STEPHANIE GONZAGA | COLORS BY KASSANDRA HELLER | BACKGROUND BY SHELLI PAROLINE AND BRADEN LAMB

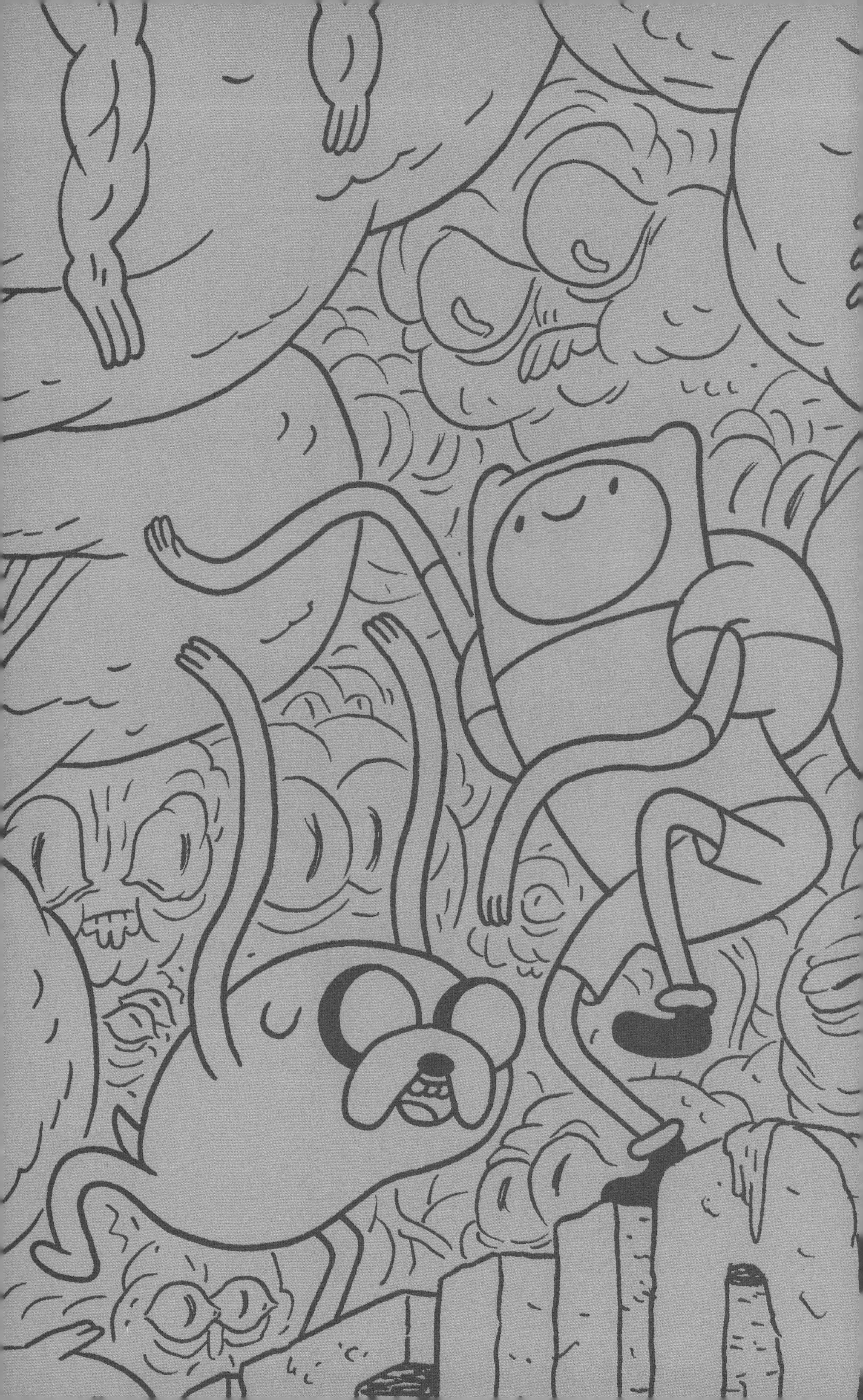

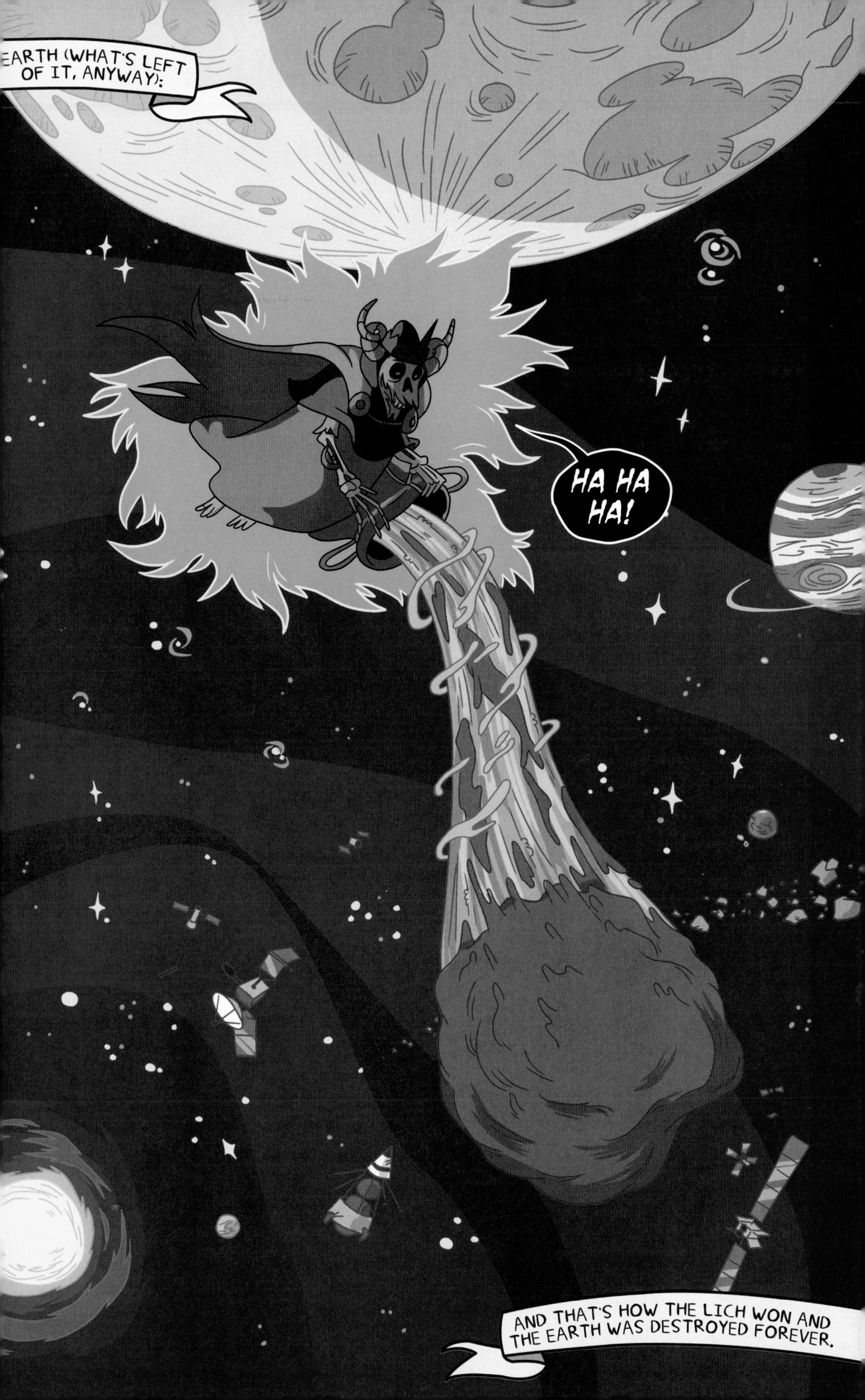
EARTH (WHAT'S LEFT OF IT, ANYWAY):
HA HA HA!
AND THAT'S HOW THE LICH WON AND THE EARTH WAS DESTROYED FOREVER.

Thank you for going on this journey with us! This is...

The End

with Finn & Jake

was
Written by Ryan North
Art was done by Shelli Paroline and Braden Lamb
was Lettered by Steve Wands
"Adventure Time" created by Pendleton Ward

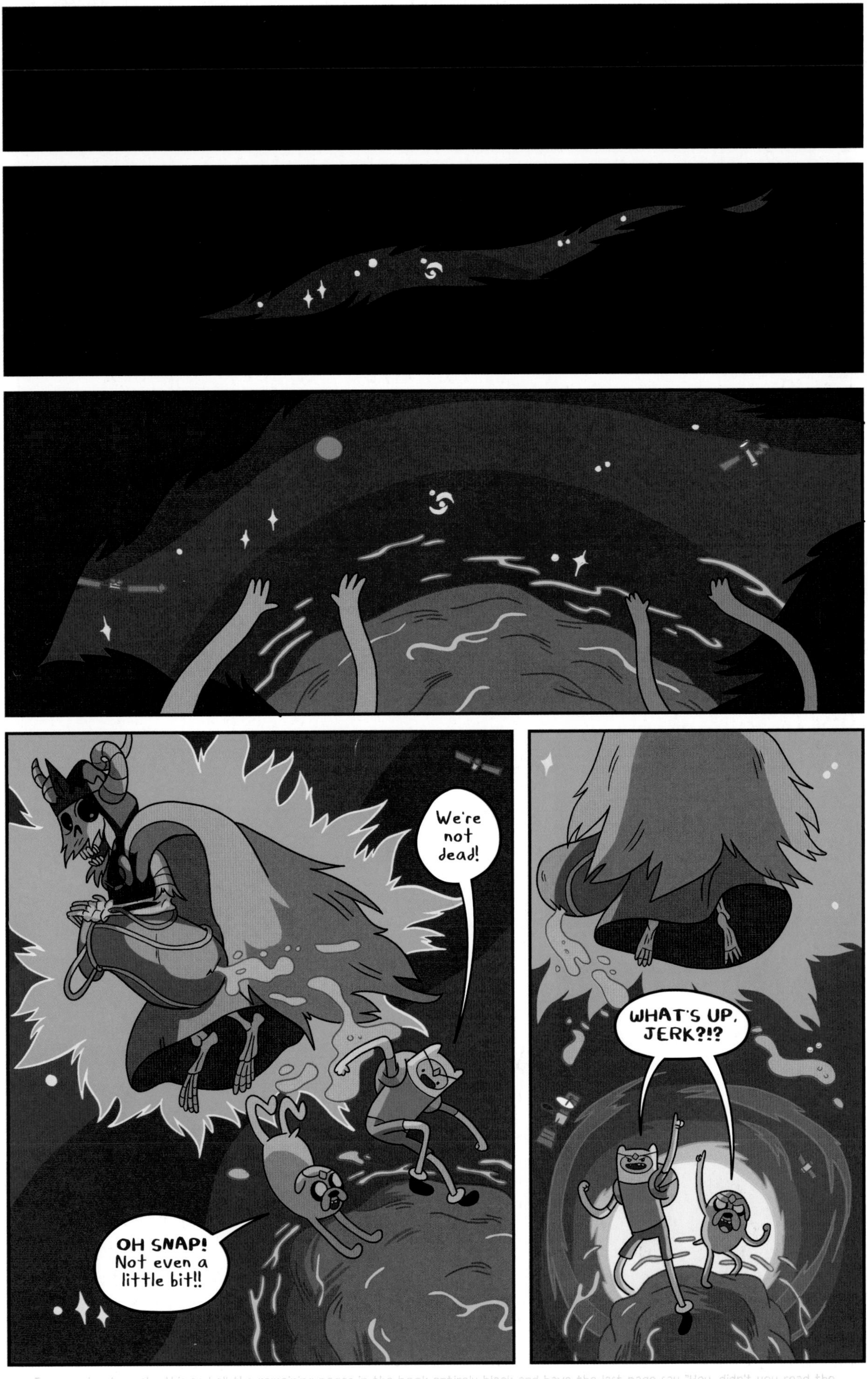
We're not dead!
OH SNAP! Not even a little bit!!
WHAT'S UP, JERK?!?

I was going to make this and all the remaining pages in the book entirely black and have the last page say "Hey, didn't you read the page sixty-six. It's over!" but then Jake and Finn burst out of the bag. They saved both the day *AND* the quality of this comic!

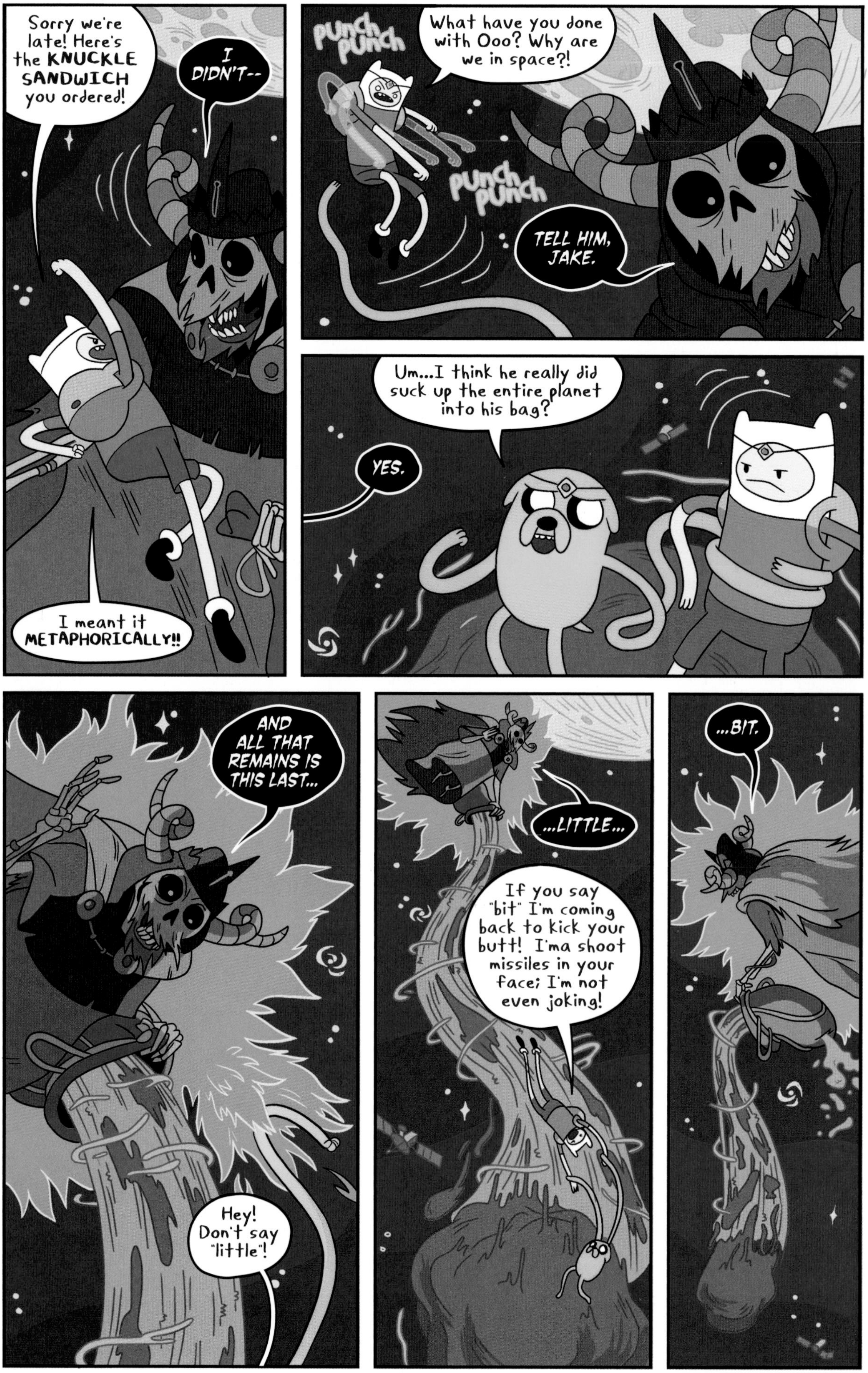
Sorry we're late! Here's the KNUCKLE SANDWICH you ordered!
I DIDN'T--
I meant it METAPHORICALLY!!
PUNCH PUNCH
What have you done with Ooo? Why are we in space?!
PUNCH PUNCH
TELL HIM, JAKE.
Um...I think he really did suck up the entire planet into his bag?
YES.
AND ALL THAT REMAINS IS THIS LAST...
Hey! Don't say "little"!
...LITTLE...
If you say "bit" I'm coming back to kick your butt! I'ma shoot missiles in your face; I'm not even joking!
...BIT.

Those gemstones Finn and Jake are wearing also allow them to magically breathe and talk in space! This feature wasn't mentioned before because there's always been lots of air around, so it just never came up. You might even be wearing clothes that allow you to magically breathe and talk in space right now! *HOW WOULD YOU KNOW?*

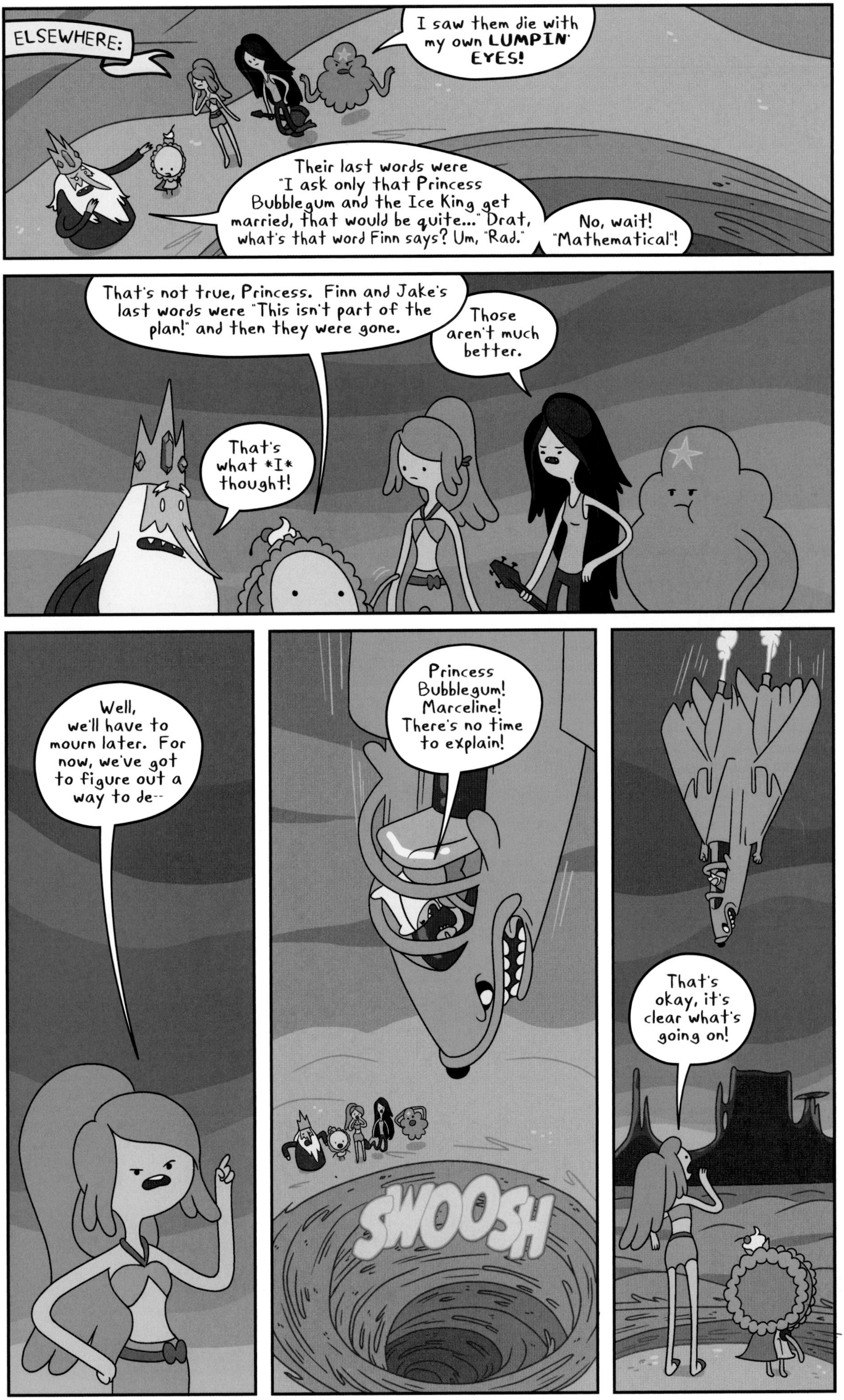
ELSEWHERE:
I saw them die with my own LUMPIN' EYES!
Their last words were "I ask only that Princess Bubblegum and the Ice King get married, that would be quite..." Drat, what's that word Finn says? Um, "Rad."
No, wait! "Mathematical"!
That's not true, Princess. Finn and Jake's last words were "This isn't part of the plan!" and then they were gone.
Those aren't much better.
That's what *I* thought!
Well, we'll have to mourn later. For now, we've got to figure out a way to de--
Princess Bubblegum! Marceline! There's no time to explain!
SWOOSH
That's okay, it's clear what's going on!

Alternate, worse line for Princess Bubblegum: "That's okay, it's PLANE what's going on!" (because of Jet Jake) (did you know: not all puns are good?!)

Come about to face the Lich! Acquire missile lock!
Locking on, dude!
FIRE ALL MISSILES!
Missiles away!
THESE AREN'T MISSILES. YOU JUST MOVED YOUR BELLY CHUB TO YOUR HANDS AND MADE IT LOOK LIKE MISSILES.
Aw nuts!!
It's not chub, bonehead! It's unflexed muscle!!
Only some of it is chuuuuuu

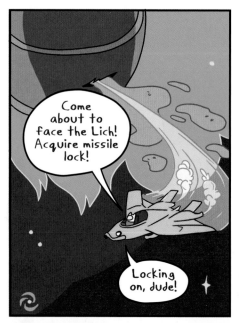

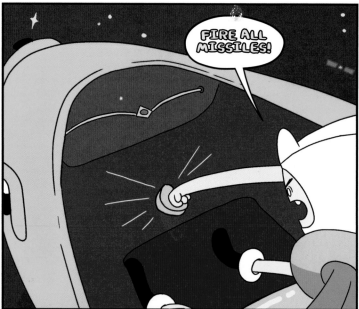

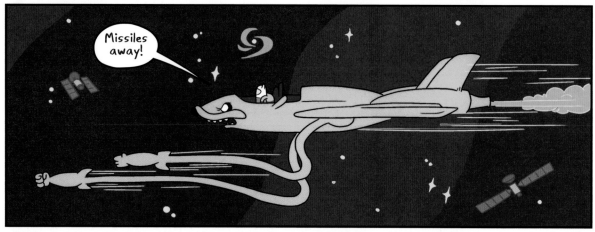

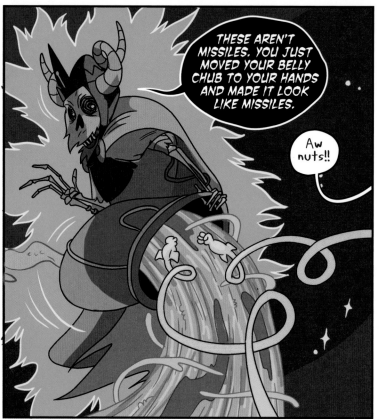

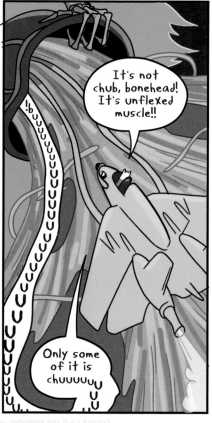

Jet Jake moves in space the same way spaceships move in space: by expelling gas (i.e.: toots)

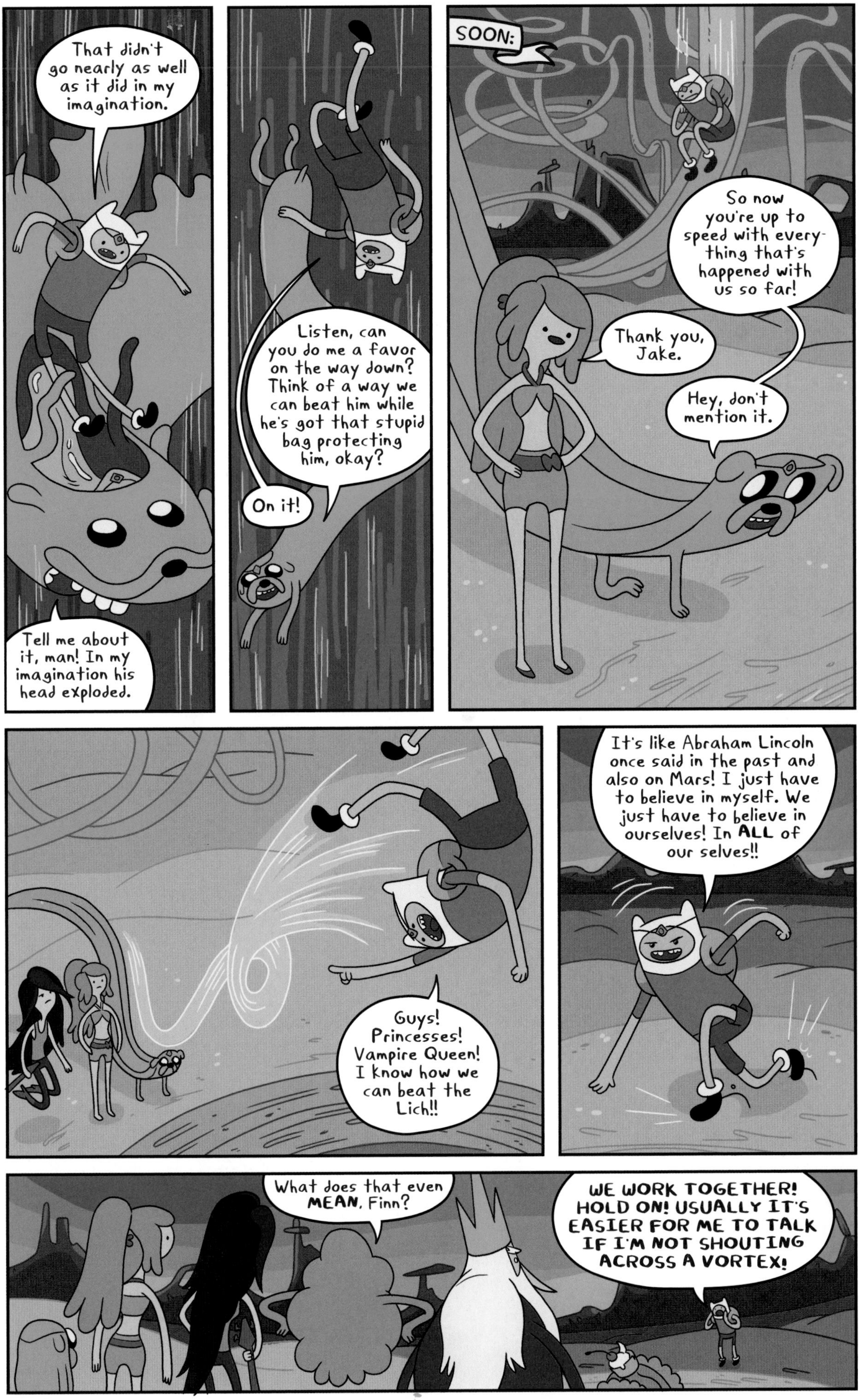
That didn't go nearly as well as it did in my imagination.
Tell me about it, man! In my imagination his head exploded.
Listen, can you do me a favor on the way down? Think of a way we can beat him while he's got that stupid bag protecting him, okay?
On it!
SOON:
So now you're up to speed with every-thing that's happened with us so far!
Thank you, Jake.
Hey, don't mention it.
Guys! Princesses! Vampire Queen! I know how we can beat the Lich!!
It's like Abraham Lincoln once said in the past and also on Mars! I just have to believe in myself. We just have to believe in ourselves! In ALL of our selves!!
What does that even MEAN, Finn?
WE WORK TOGETHER! HOLD ON! USUALLY IT'S EASIER FOR ME TO TALK IF I'M NOT SHOUTING ACROSS A VORTEX!

Jake slide, Jake slide / His body gets longer than it is wide

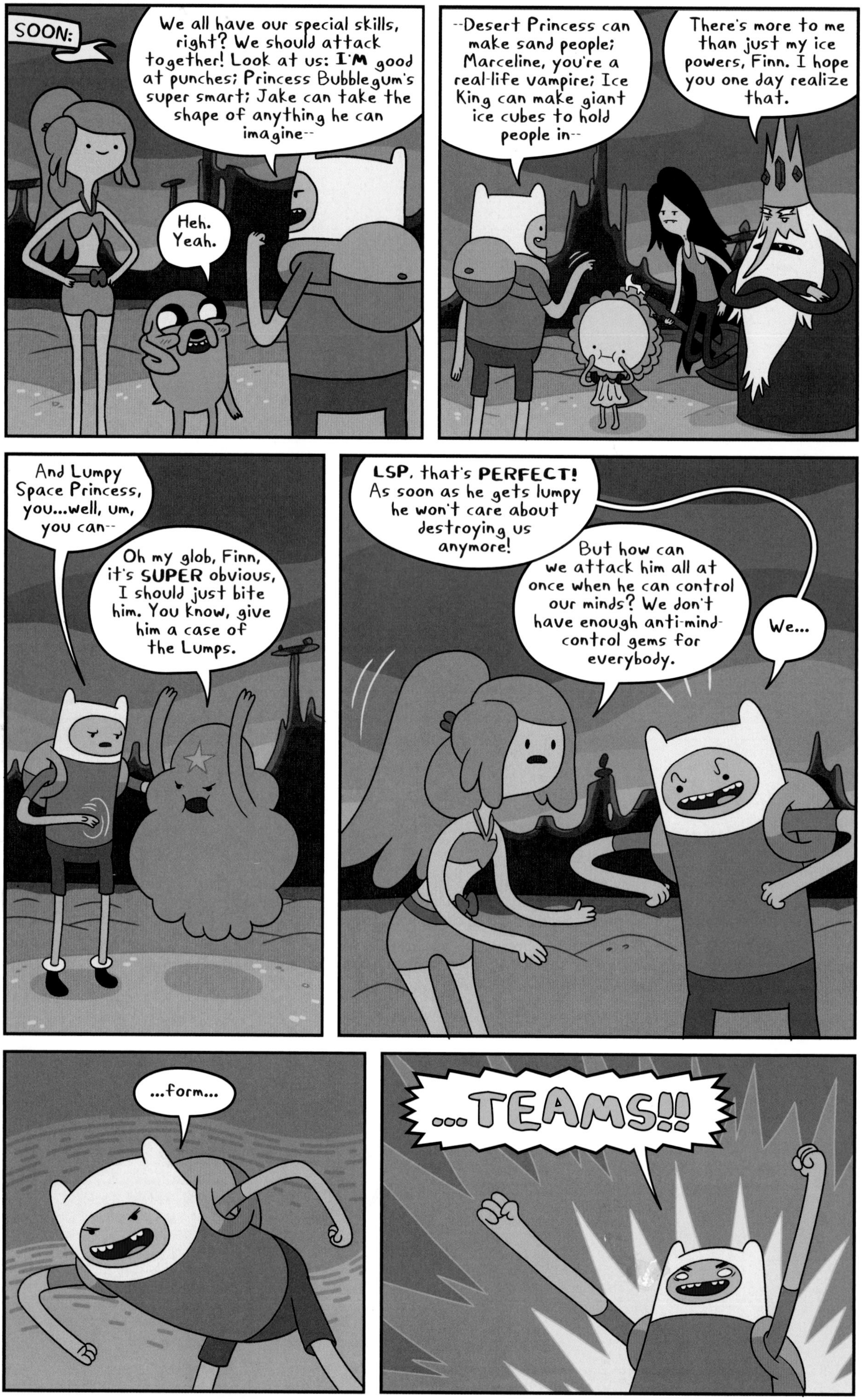
SOON:
We all have our special skills, right? We should attack together! Look at us: I'M good at punches; Princess Bubblegum's super smart; Jake can take the shape of anything he can imagine--
Heh. Yeah.
--Desert Princess can make sand people; Marceline, you're a real-life vampire; Ice King can make giant ice cubes to hold people in--
There's more to me than just my ice powers, Finn. I hope you one day realize that.
And Lumpy Space Princess, you...well, um, you can--
Oh my glob, Finn, it's SUPER obvious, I should just bite him. You know, give him a case of the Lumps.
LSP, that's PERFECT! As soon as he gets lumpy he won't care about destroying us anymore!
But how can we attack him all at once when he can control our minds? We don't have enough anti-mind-control gems for everybody.
We...
...form...
...TEAMS!!

Some people say they prefer working alone to working in groups, but I bet that's just because they've never had Finn propose a team to them before!

AWESOME:

It's been a sl-ICE!

Man, that didn't make sense. You're not even attacking with a sword!

Oh wait, I get ittttttttttttttttttttt

You want some science in your face??

It appears he didn't want science in OR about his face, Princess.

Hey Lich! Looks like you've got to TAKE YOUR LUMPS!

Oh my glob that's SO racist.

OW! He's just skin and bones and I lumpin' bit myself!!

Like I need more lumpin' LUMPS!

My crown protects me from the Lich's mind control!

Mine too!

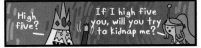

High five?

If I high five you, will you try to kidnap me?

Ye-um, I mean, uh...there's one way to find out?

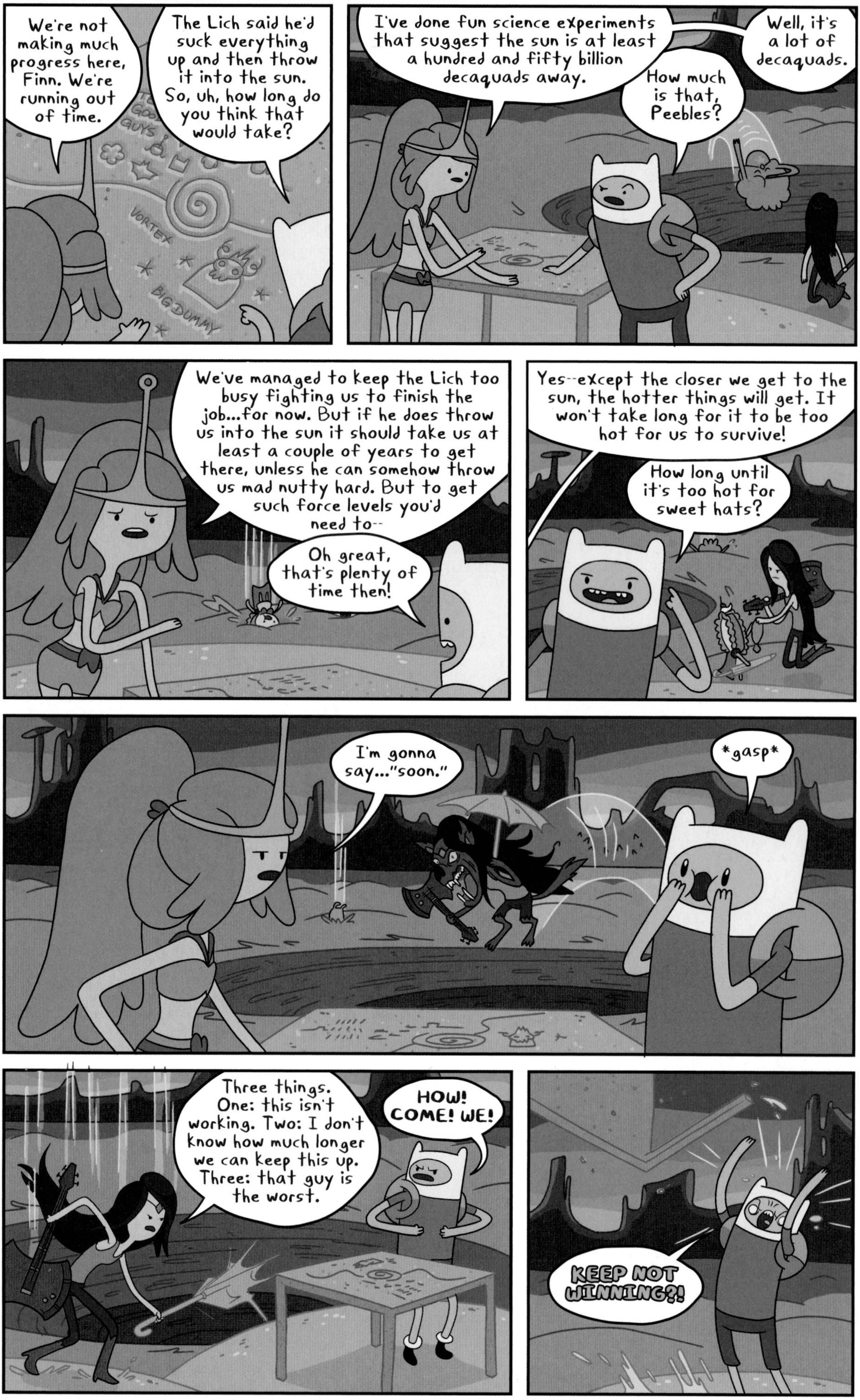
We're not making much progress here, Finn. We're running out of time.
The Lich said he'd suck everything up and then throw it into the sun. So, uh, how long do you think that would take?
VORTEX
BIG DUMMY
I've done fun science experiments that suggest the sun is at least a hundred and fifty billion decaquads away.
How much is that, Peebles?
Well, it's a lot of decaquads.
We've managed to keep the Lich too busy fighting us to finish the job...for now. But if he does throw us into the sun it should take us at least a couple of years to get there, unless he can somehow throw us mad nutty hard. But to get such force levels you'd need to--
Oh great, that's plenty of time then!
Yes--except the closer we get to the sun, the hotter things will get. It won't take long for it to be too hot for us to survive!
How long until it's too hot for sweet hats?
I'm gonna say..."soon."
gasp
Three things. One: this isn't working. Two: I don't know how much longer we can keep this up. Three: that guy is the worst.
HOW! COME! WE!
KEEP NOT WINNING?!

Everyone's landing in the same place because now they have the power of *TEAMS* to keep them together. Teamwork is the real power! It's about 1.5 joules per second; ask any scientist!

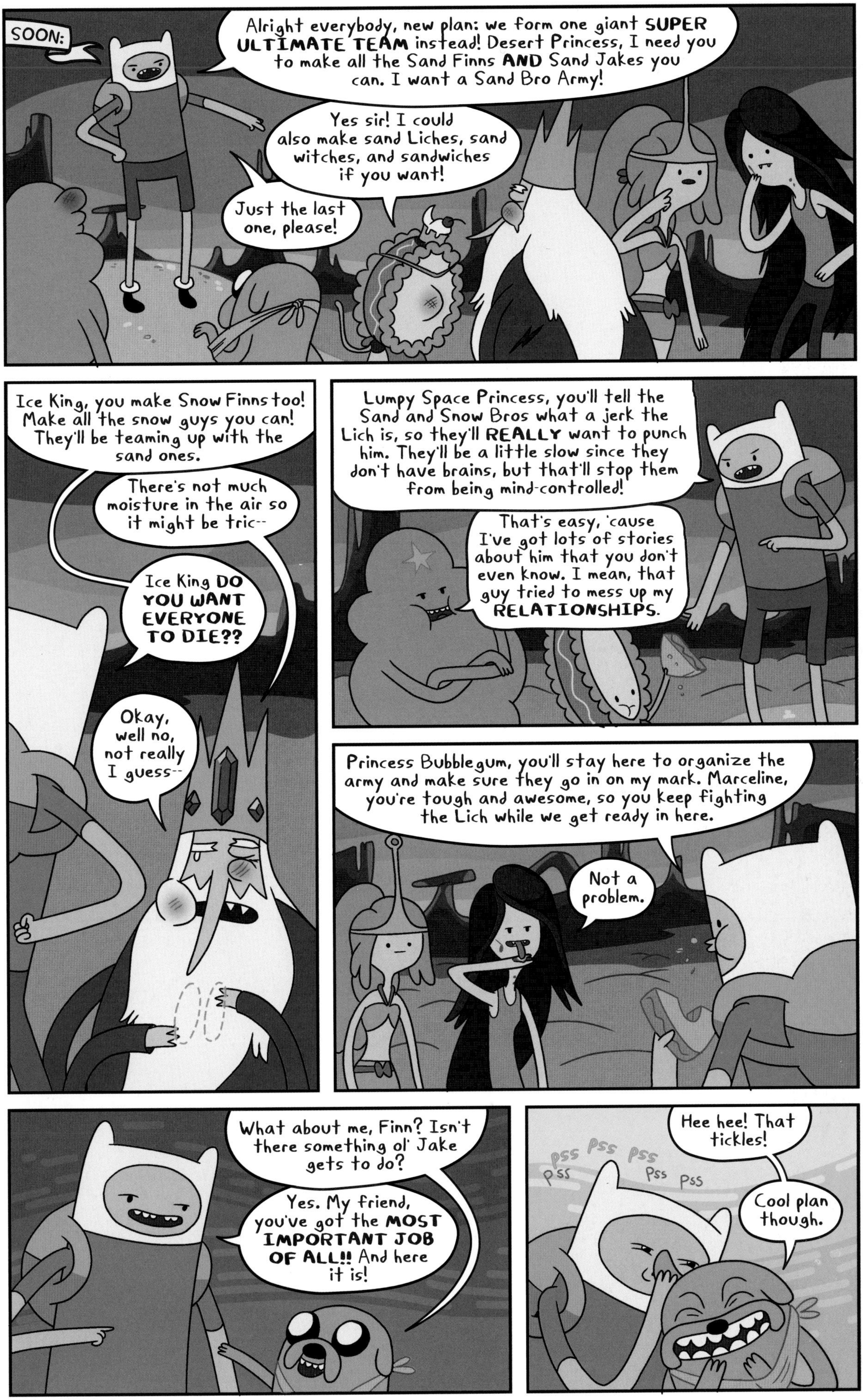
SOON:
Alright everybody, new plan: we form one giant SUPER ULTIMATE TEAM instead! Desert Princess, I need you to make all the Sand Finns AND Sand Jakes you can. I want a Sand Bro Army!
Yes sir! I could also make sand Liches, sand witches, and sandwiches if you want!
Just the last one, please!
Ice King, you make Snow Finns too! Make all the snow guys you can! They'll be teaming up with the sand ones.
There's not much moisture in the air so it might be tric--
Ice King DO YOU WANT EVERYONE TO DIE??
Okay, well no, not really I guess--
Lumpy Space Princess, you'll tell the Sand and Snow Bros what a jerk the Lich is, so they'll REALLY want to punch him. They'll be a little slow since they don't have brains, but that'll stop them from being mind-controlled!
That's easy, 'cause I've got lots of stories about him that you don't even know. I mean, that guy tried to mess up my RELATIONSHIPS.
Princess Bubblegum, you'll stay here to organize the army and make sure they go in on my mark. Marceline, you're tough and awesome, so you keep fighting the Lich while we get ready in here.
Not a problem.
What about me, Finn? Isn't there something ol' Jake gets to do?
Yes. My friend, you've got the MOST IMPORTANT JOB OF ALL!! And here it is!
pss pss pss
pss pss pss
Hee hee! That tickles!
Cool plan though.

Lumpy Space Princess is secretly really happy here because she got the task of spreading gossip around to a bunch of people. That's *BASICALLY* her dream job!

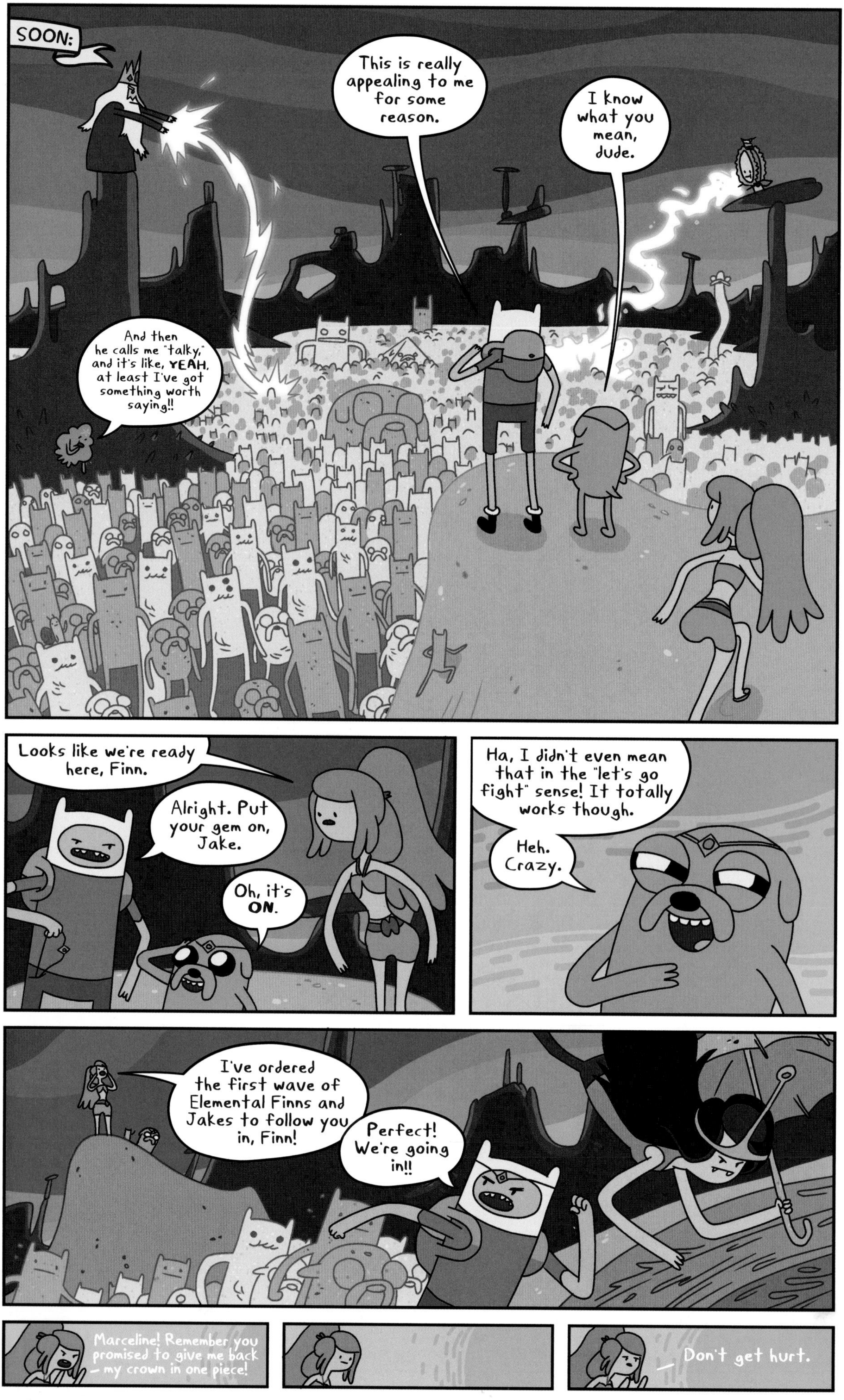
SOON:
This is really appealing to me for some reason.
I know what you mean, dude.
And then he calls me "talky," and it's like, YEAH, at least I've got something worth saying!!
Looks like we're ready here, Finn.
Alright. Put your gem on, Jake.
Oh, it's ON.
Ha, I didn't even mean that in the "let's go fight" sense! It totally works though.
Heh. Crazy.
I've ordered the first wave of Elemental Finns and Jakes to follow you in, Finn!
Perfect! We're going in!!
Marceline! Remember you promised to give me back my crown in one piece!
Don't get hurt.

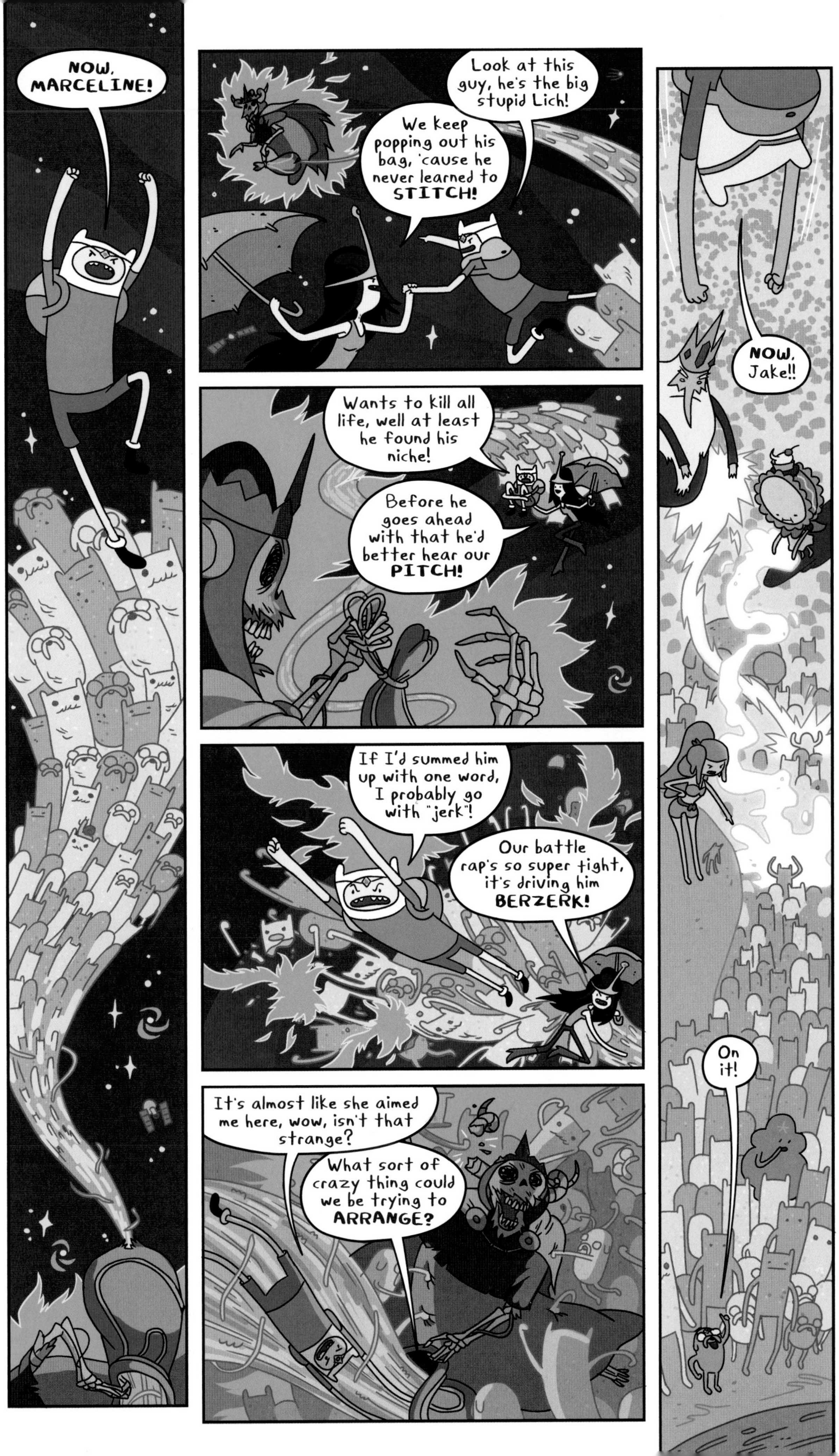
NOW, MARCELINE!
Look at this guy, he's the big stupid Lich!
We keep popping out his bag, 'cause he never learned to STITCH!
Wants to kill all life, well at least he found his niche!
Before he goes ahead with that he'd better hear our PITCH!
If I'd summed him up with one word, I probably go with "jerk"!
Our battle rap's so super tight, it's driving him BERZERK!
It's almost like she aimed me here, wow, isn't that strange?
What sort of crazy thing could we be trying to ARRANGE?
NOW, Jake!!
On it!

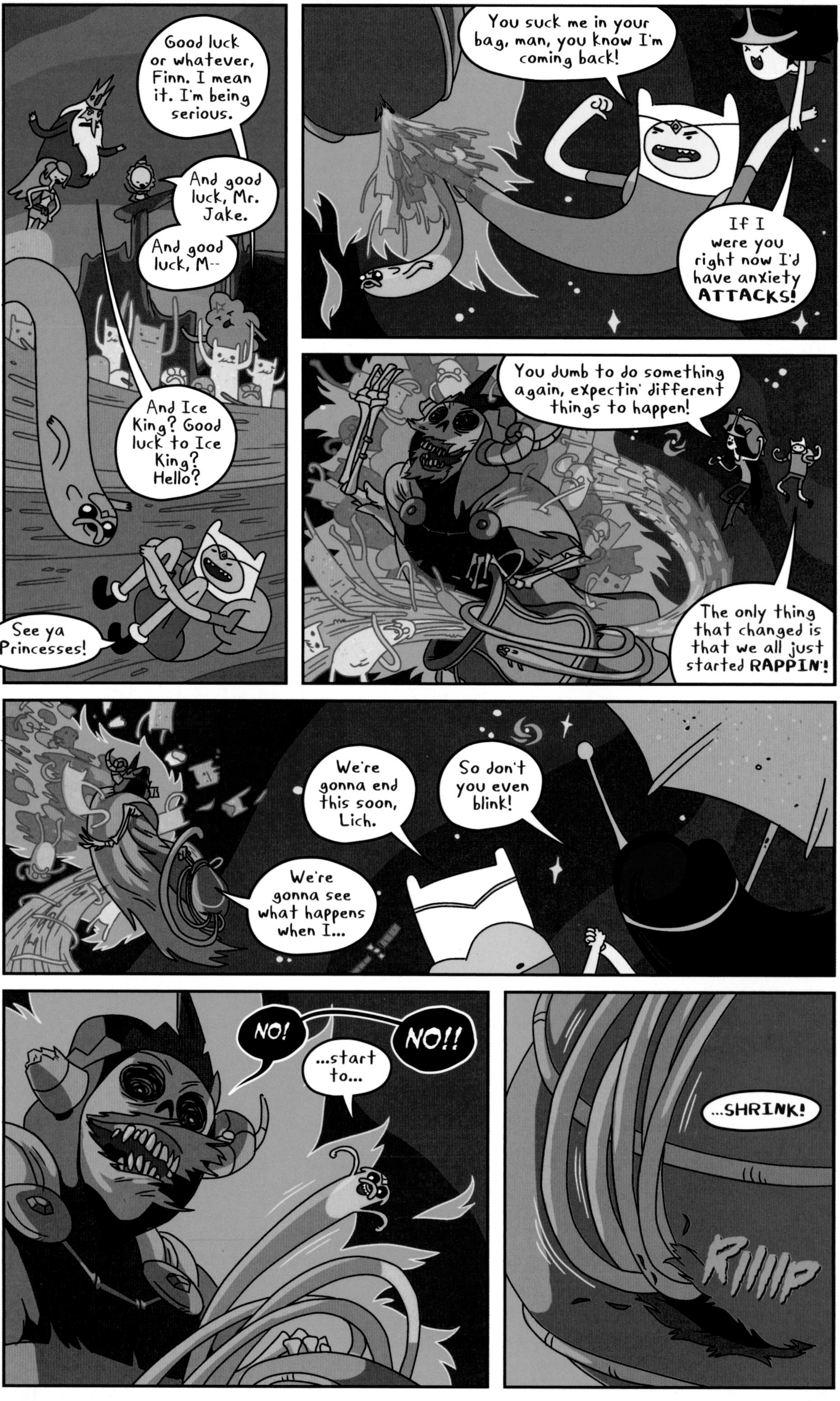
Good luck or whatever, Finn. I mean it. I'm being serious.
And good luck, Mr. Jake.
And good luck, M--
And Ice King? Good luck to Ice King? Hello?
See ya Princesses!
You suck me in your bag, man, you know I'm coming back!
If I were you right now I'd have anxiety ATTACKS!
You dumb to do something again, expectin' different things to happen!
The only thing that changed is that we all just started RAPPIN'!
We're gonna end this soon, Lich.
So don't you even blink!
We're gonna see what happens when I...
NO!
NO!!
...start to...
...SHRINK!
RIIIP

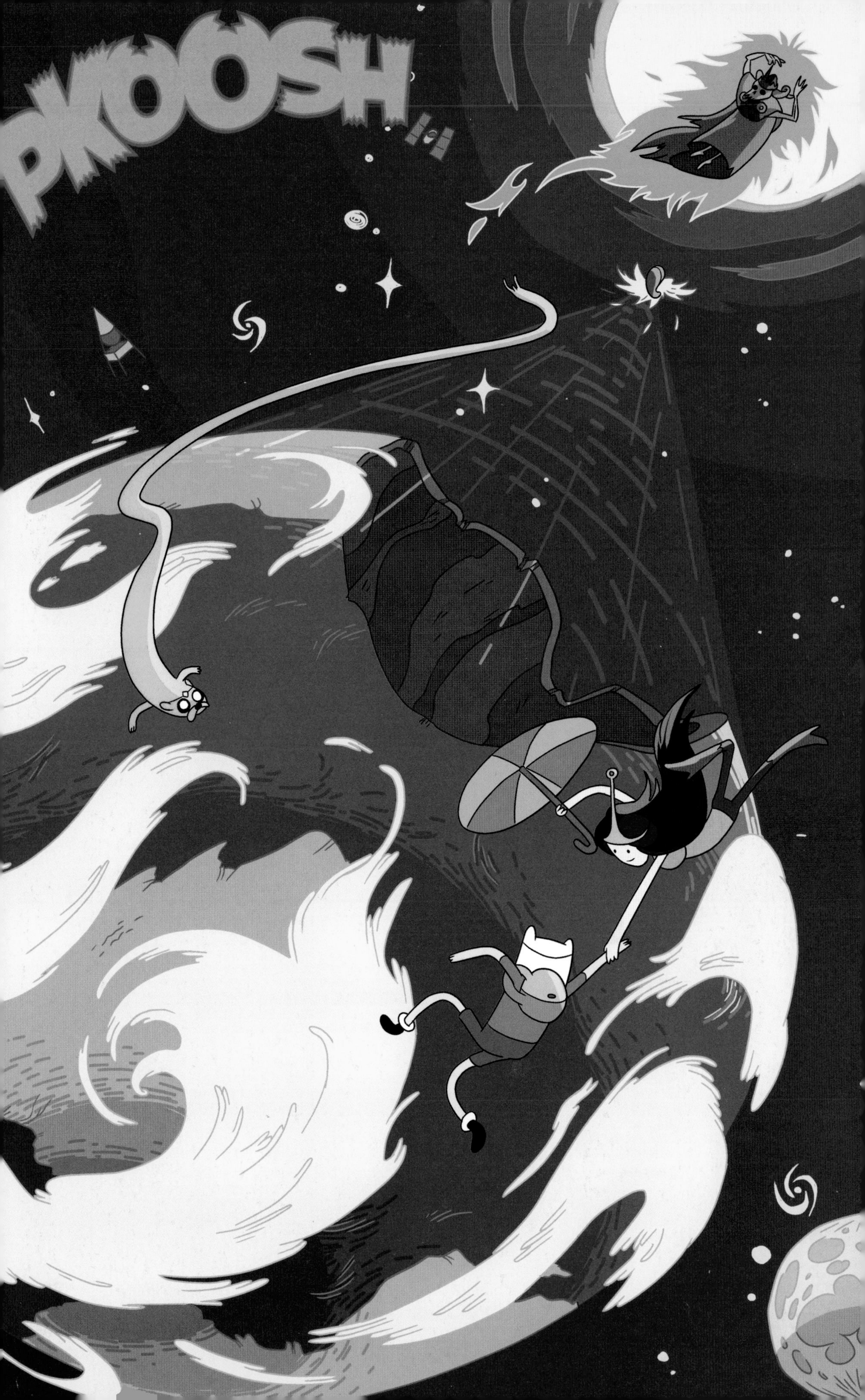
PKOOSH!!

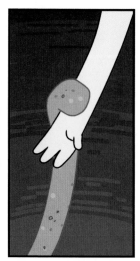

WHOA!

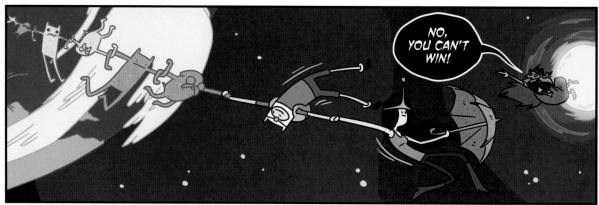

NO, YOU CAN'T WIN!

NNNOOOooOOOOoo!

We did it! We won!!

And our spontaneous **RHYMING** battle burns? **AMAZING.**

Wait...no, wait, Finn--something's not right.

The Land of Ooo is... **MISSING?**

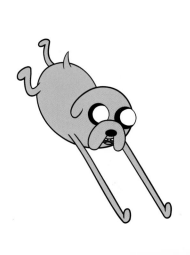

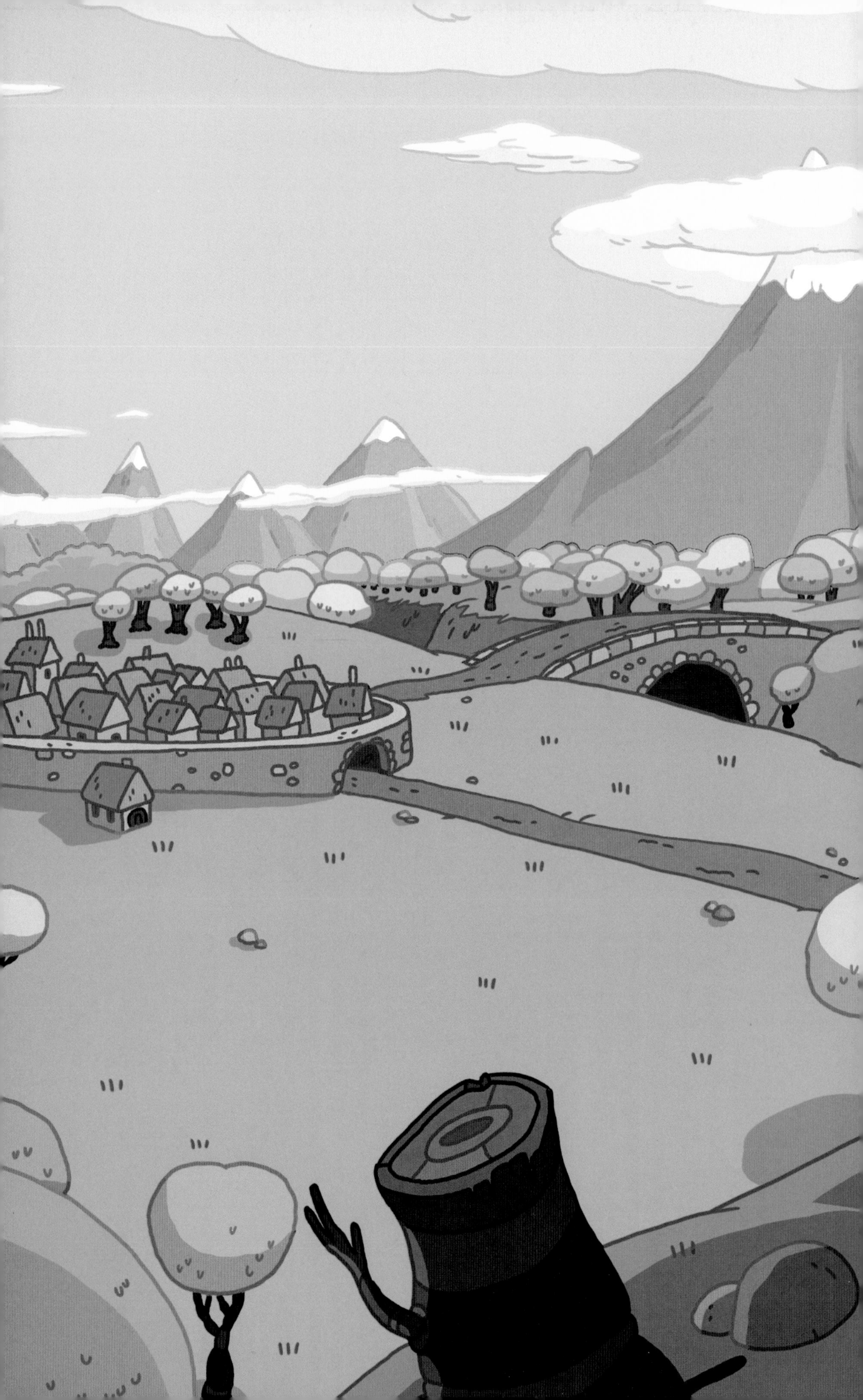

CHAPTER FOUR

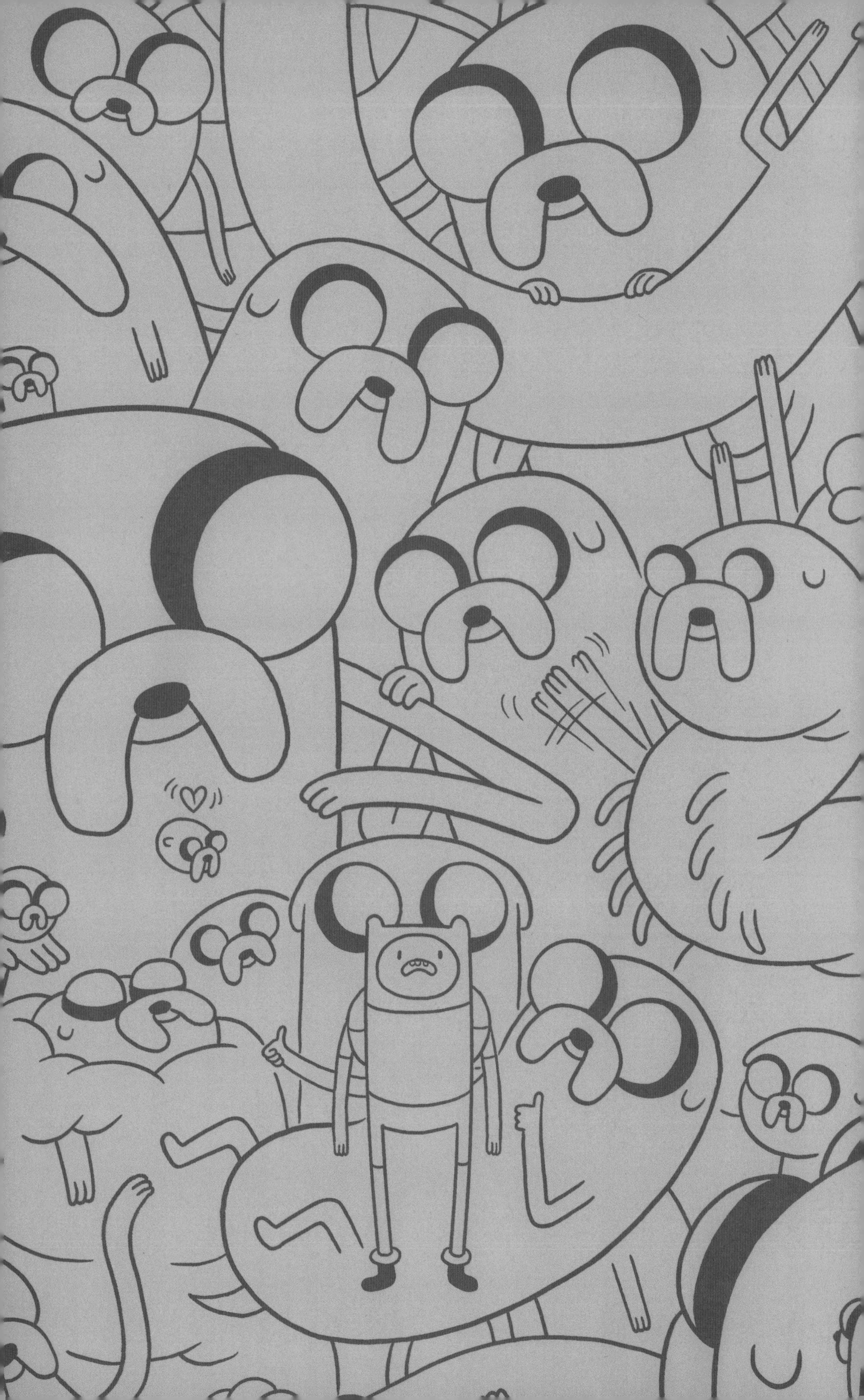

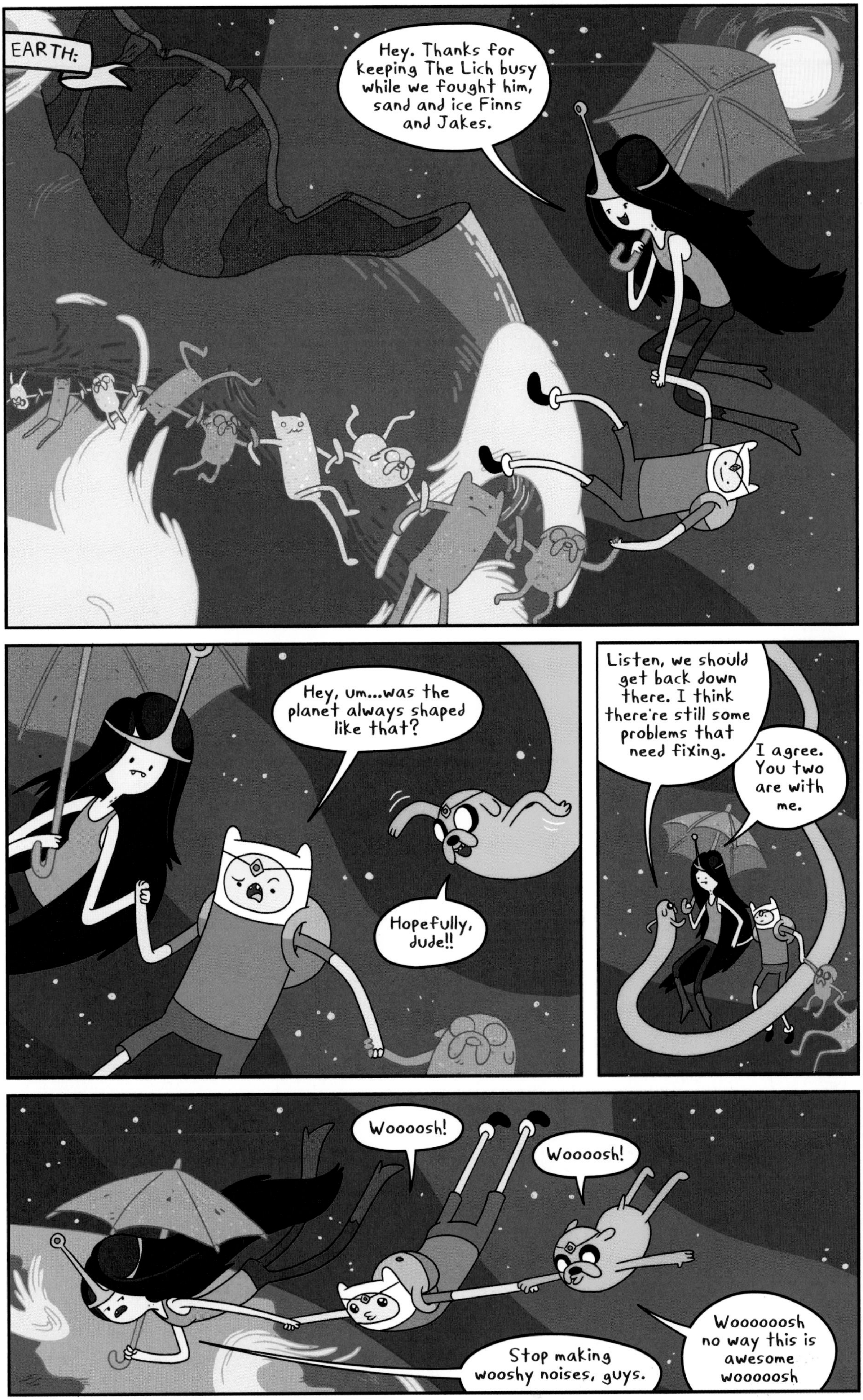
EARTH:
Hey. Thanks for keeping The Lich busy while we fought him, sand and ice Finns and Jakes.
Hey, um...was the planet always shaped like that?
Hopefully, dude!!
Listen, we should get back down there. I think there're still some problems that need fixing.
I agree. You two are with me.
Woooosh!
Woooosh!
Woooooosh no way this is awesome wooooosh
Stop making wooshy noises, guys.

How do you avoid saying "woosh!" 24/7, Marceline?

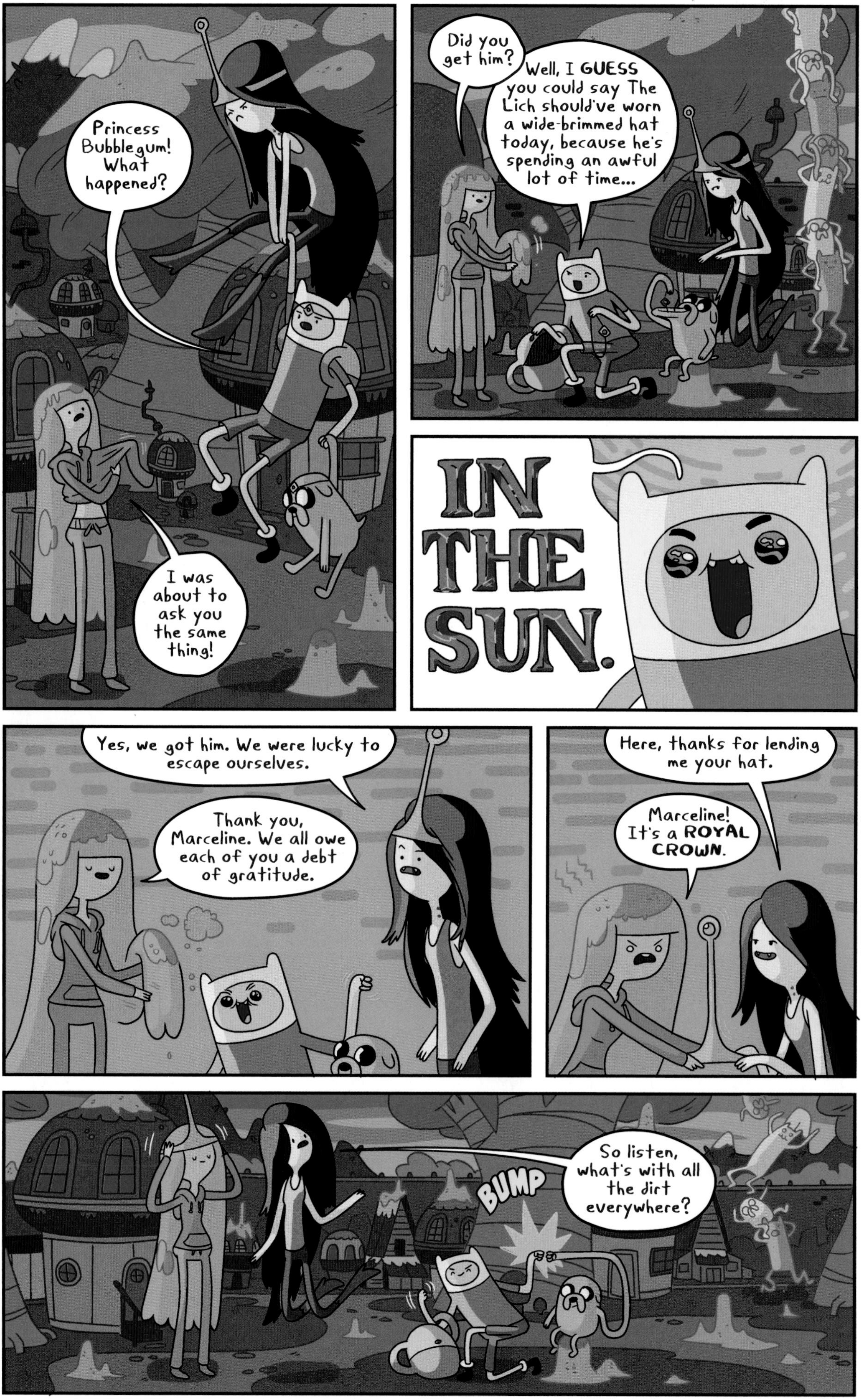
Princess Bubblegum! What happened?
I was about to ask you the same thing!
Did you get him?
Well, I GUESS you could say The Lich should've worn a wide-brimmed hat today, because he's spending an awful lot of time...
IN THE SUN.
Yes, we got him. We were lucky to escape ourselves.
Thank you, Marceline. We all owe each of you a debt of gratitude.
Here, thanks for lending me your hat.
Marceline! It's a ROYAL CROWN.
BUMP
So listen, what's with all the dirt everywhere?

BEHIND THE SCENES FACT: All of Adventure Time, the show *AND* the comic, was leading up to Finn's pun in panel three. *ALL OF IT.*

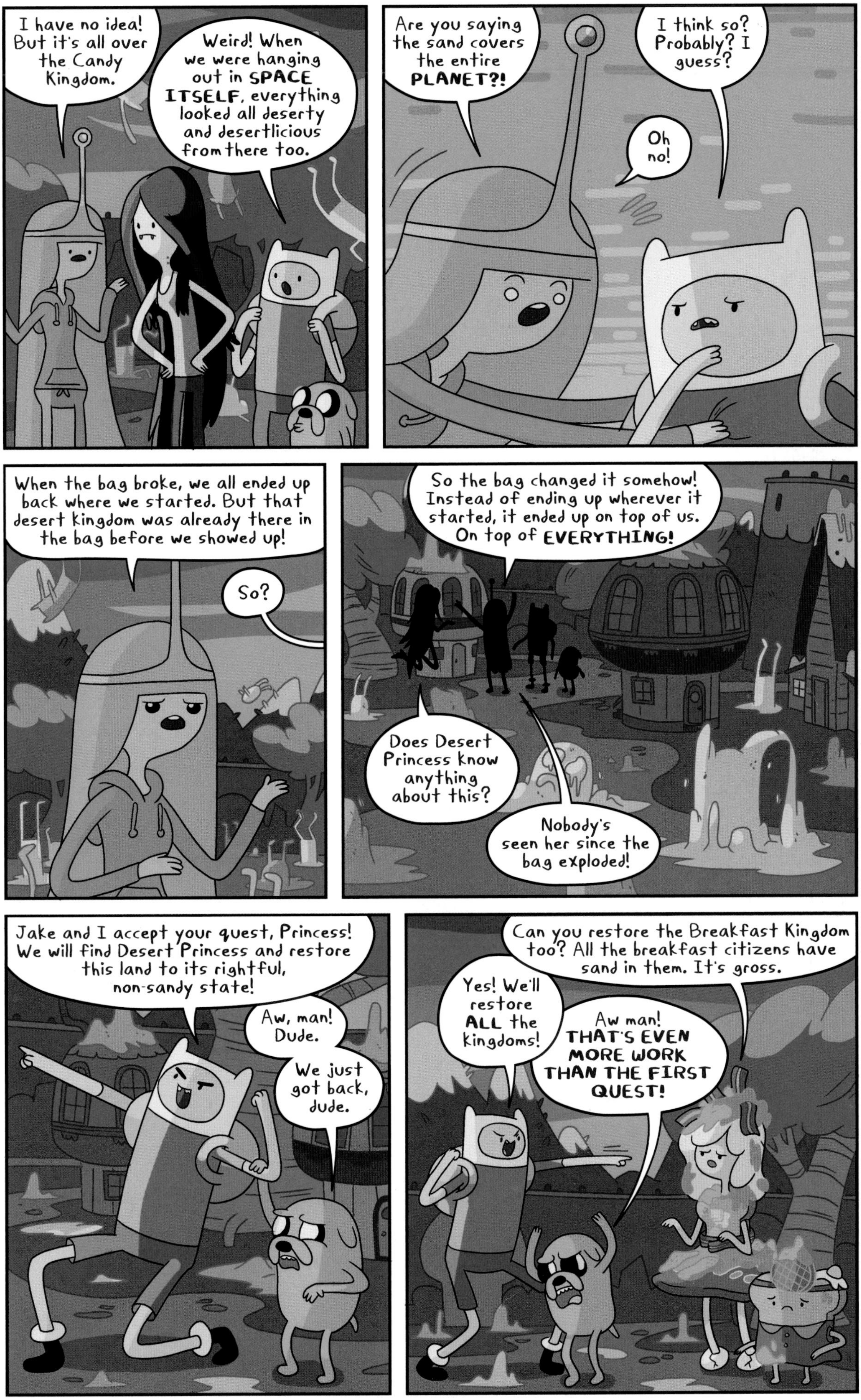
I have no idea! But it's all over the Candy Kingdom.
Weird! When we were hanging out in SPACE ITSELF, everything looked all deserty and desertlicious from there too.
Are you saying the sand covers the entire PLANET?!
I think so? Probably? I guess?
Oh no!
When the bag broke, we all ended up back where we started. But that desert kingdom was already there in the bag before we showed up!
So?
So the bag changed it somehow! Instead of ending up wherever it started, it ended up on top of us. On top of EVERYTHING!
Does Desert Princess know anything about this?
Nobody's seen her since the bag exploded!
Jake and I accept your quest, Princess! We will find Desert Princess and restore this land to its rightful, non-sandy state!
Aw, man! Dude.
We just got back, dude.
Can you restore the Breakfast Kingdom too? All the breakfast citizens have sand in them. It's gross.
Yes! We'll restore ALL the kingdoms!
Aw man! THAT'S EVEN MORE WORK THAN THE FIRST QUEST!

Dear Breakfast Kingdom: I would live in you. I would take all my meals in you, including lunch and dinner. *I'M EVEN INCLUDING DESSERT.* I'm not messing around here, Breakfast Kingdom.

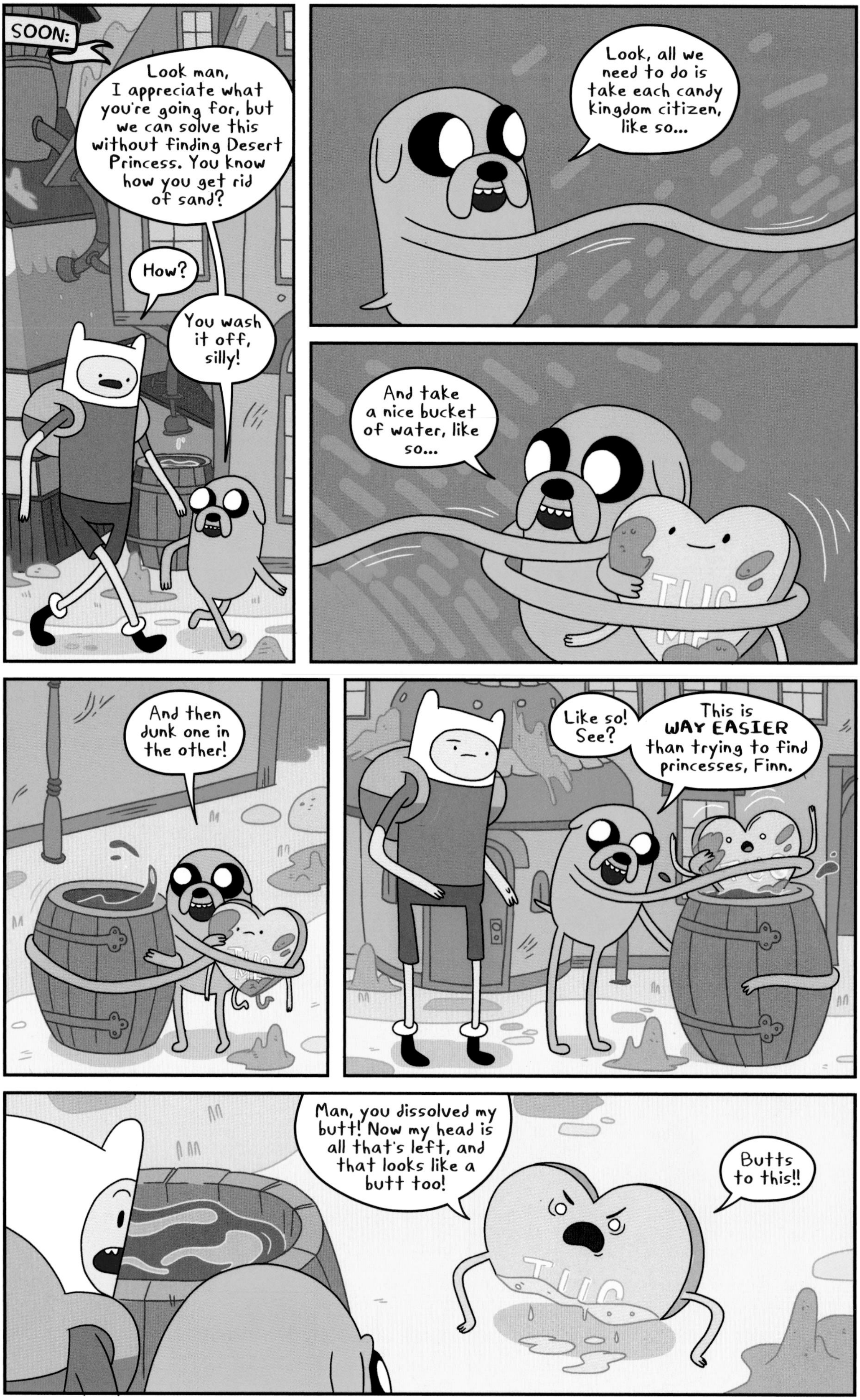
SOON:
Look man, I appreciate what you're going for, but we can solve this without finding Desert Princess. You know how you get rid of sand?
How?
You wash it off, silly!
Look, all we need to do is take each candy kingdom citizen, like so...
And take a nice bucket of water, like so...
And then dunk one in the other!
Like so! See?
This is **WAY EASIER** than trying to find princesses, Finn.
Man, you dissolved my butt! Now my head is all that's left, and that looks like a butt too!
Butts to this!!

Butts to the both of you! Good day!!

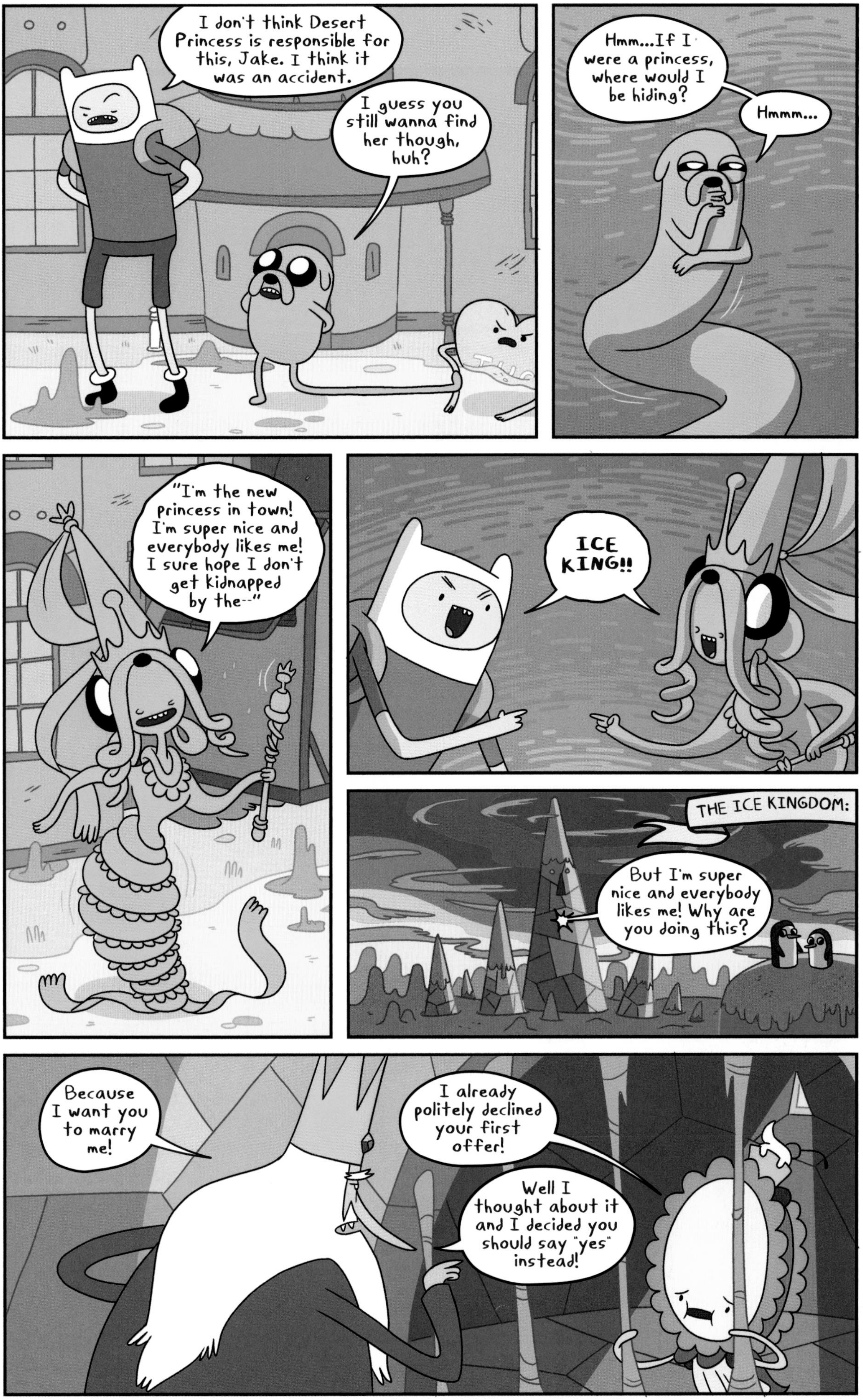
I don't think Desert Princess is responsible for this, Jake. I think it was an accident.
I guess you still wanna find her though, huh?
Hmm...If I were a princess, where would I be hiding?
Hmmm...
"I'm the new princess in town! I'm super nice and everybody likes me! I sure hope I don't get kidnapped by the--"
ICE KING!!
THE ICE KINGDOM:
But I'm super nice and everybody likes me! Why are you doing this?
Because I want you to marry me!
I already politely declined your first offer!
Well I thought about it and I decided you should say "yes" instead!

PRO TIP: If you want to grow up to marry a princess, do exactly the opposite of whatever Ice King does! You'll be off to a *TERRIFIC* start.

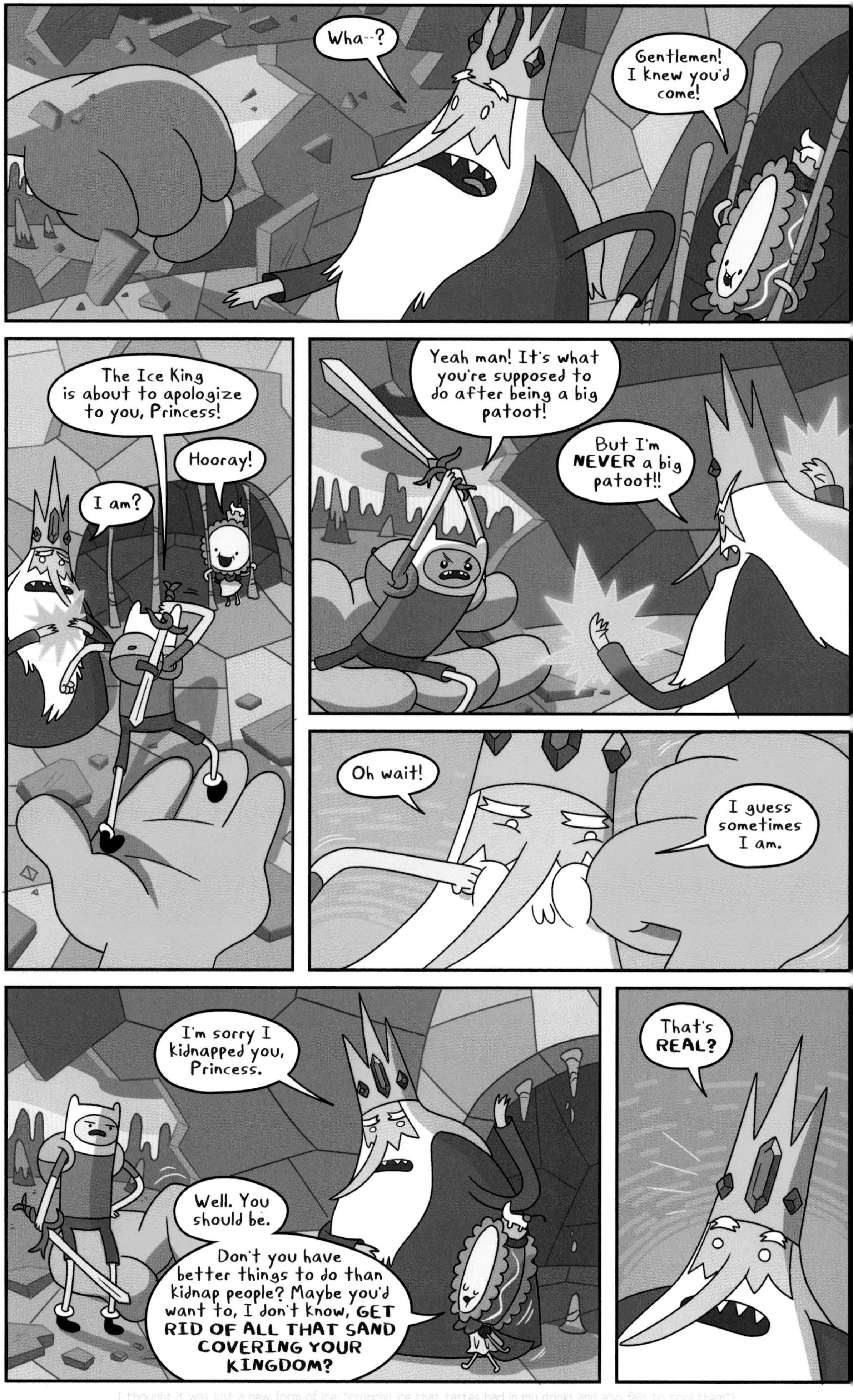
Wha--?
Gentlemen! I knew you'd come!
The Ice King is about to apologize to you, Princess!
I am?
Hooray!
Yeah man! It's what you're supposed to do after being a big patoot!
But I'm NEVER a big patoot!!
Oh wait!
I guess sometimes I am.
I'm sorry I kidnapped you, Princess.
Well. You should be.
Don't you have better things to do than kidnap people? Maybe you'd want to, I don't know, GET RID OF ALL THAT SAND COVERING YOUR KINGDOM?
That's REAL?

I thought it was just a new form of ice: "crunchy ice that tastes bad in my drinks and also fails to cool them"?

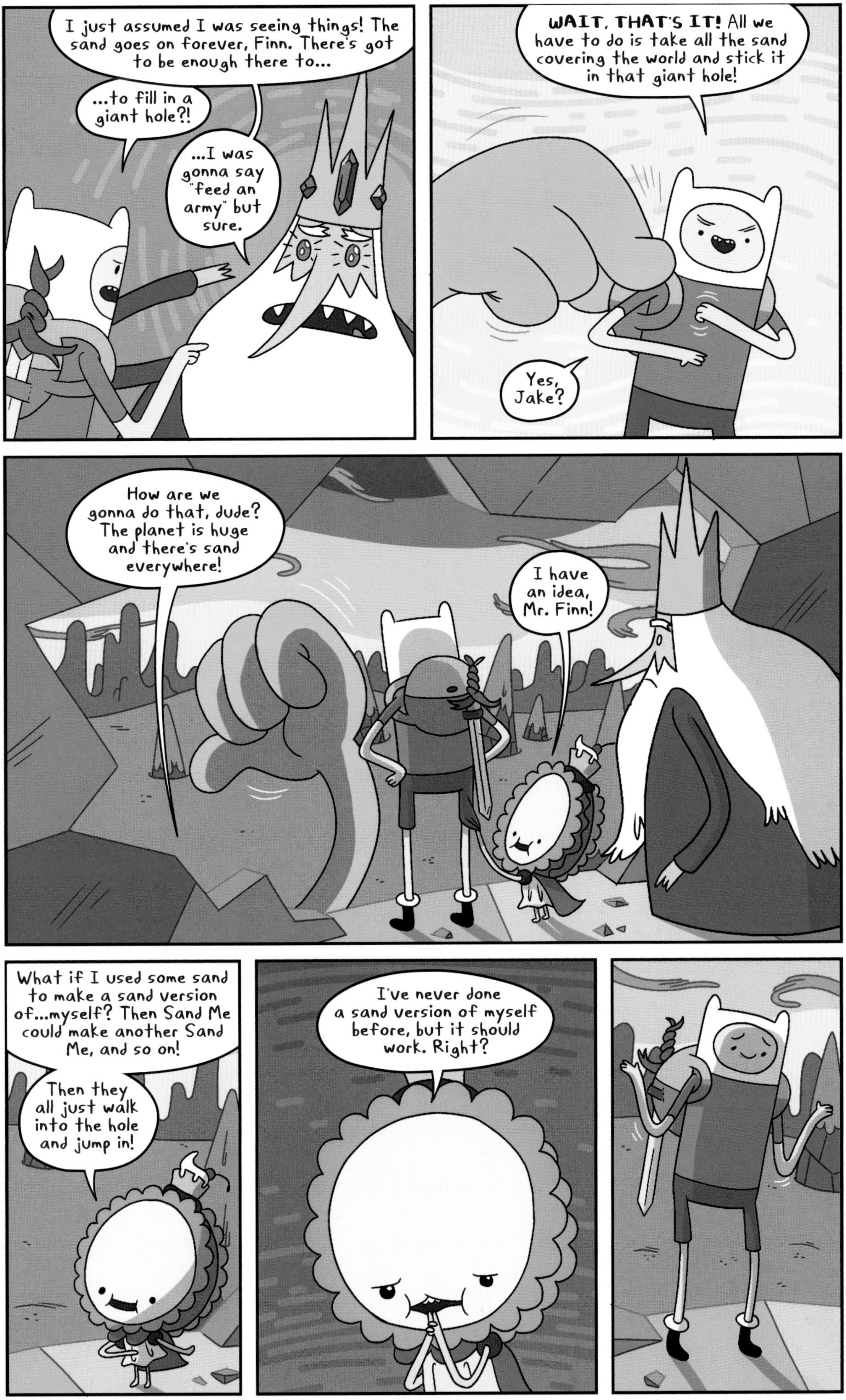
I just assumed I was seeing things! The sand goes on forever, Finn. There's got to be enough there to...
...to fill in a giant hole?!
...I was gonna say "feed an army" but sure.
WAIT, THAT'S IT! All we have to do is take all the sand covering the world and stick it in that giant hole!
Yes, Jake?
How are we gonna do that, dude? The planet is huge and there's sand everywhere!
I have an idea, Mr. Finn!
What if I used some sand to make a sand version of...myself? Then Sand Me could make another Sand Me, and so on!
Then they all just walk into the hole and jump in!
I've never done a sand version of myself before, but it should work. Right?

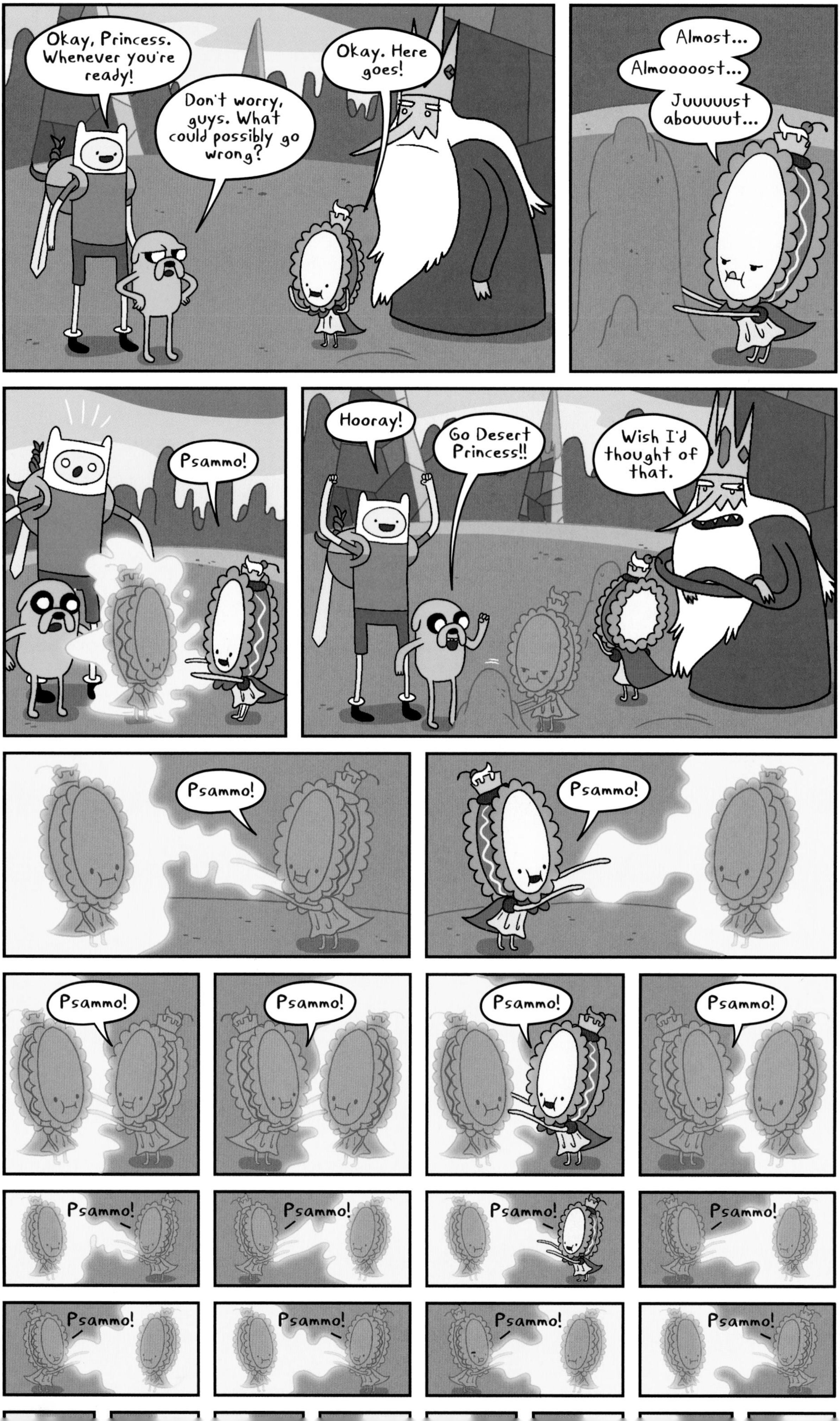
Okay, Princess. Whenever you're ready!
Don't worry, guys. What could possibly go wrong?
Okay. Here goes!
Almost...
Almoooooost...
Juuuuust abouuuut...
Psammo!
Hooray!
Go Desert Princess!!
Wish I'd thought of that.
Psammo!
Psammo!
Psammo!
Psammo!
Psammo!
Psammo!
Psammo!
Psammo!
Psammo!
Psammo!
Psammo!
Psammo!
Psammo!
Psammo!

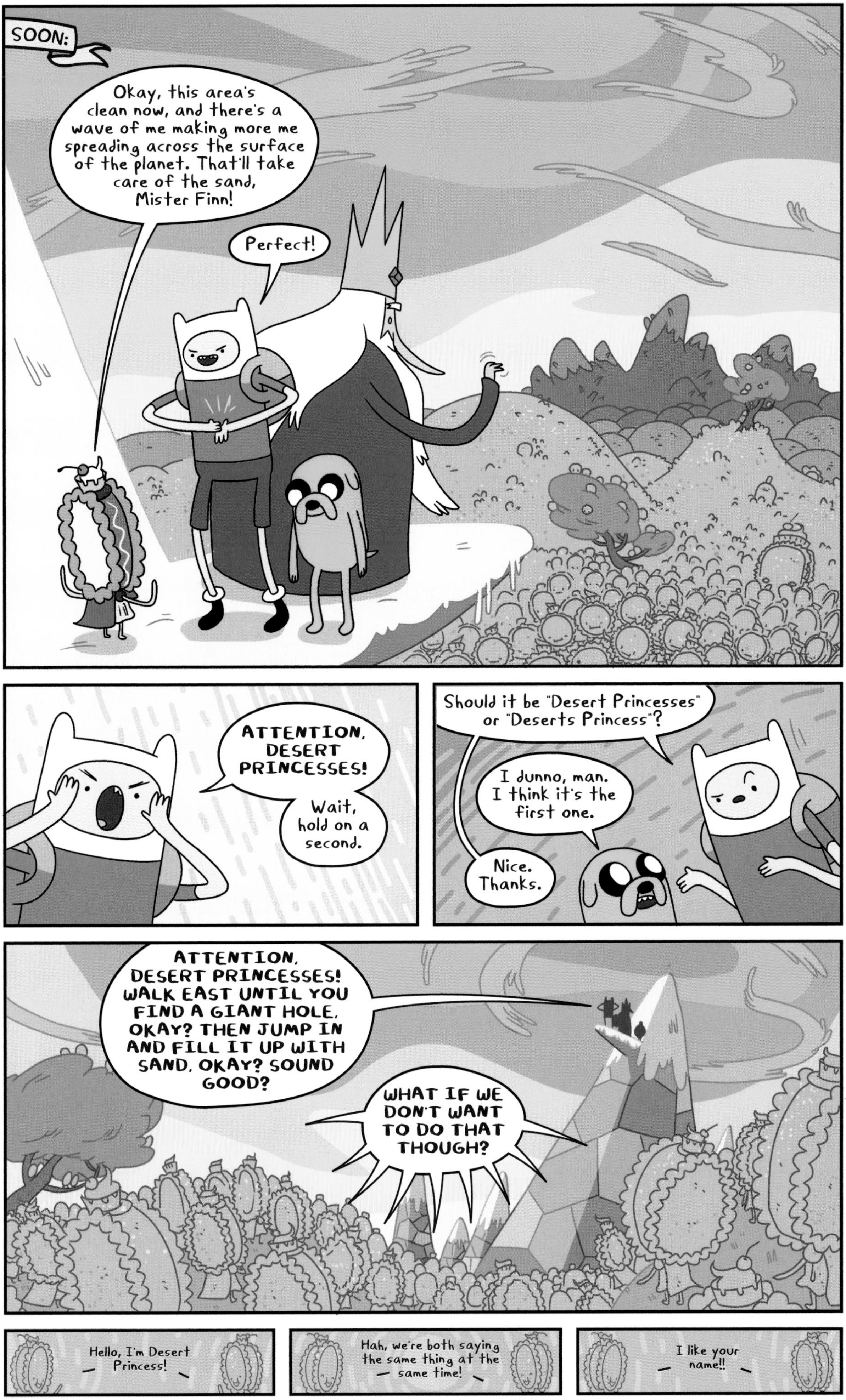
SOON:
Okay, this area's clean now, and there's a wave of me making more me spreading across the surface of the planet. That'll take care of the sand, Mister Finn!
Perfect!
ATTENTION, DESERT PRINCESSES!
Wait, hold on a second.
Should it be "Desert Princesses" or "Deserts Princess"?
I dunno, man. I think it's the first one.
Nice. Thanks.
ATTENTION, DESERT PRINCESSES! WALK EAST UNTIL YOU FIND A GIANT HOLE, OKAY? THEN JUMP IN AND FILL IT UP WITH SAND, OKAY? SOUND GOOD?
WHAT IF WE DON'T WANT TO DO THAT THOUGH?
Hello, I'm Desert Princess!
Hah, we're both saying the same thing at the same time!
I like your name!!

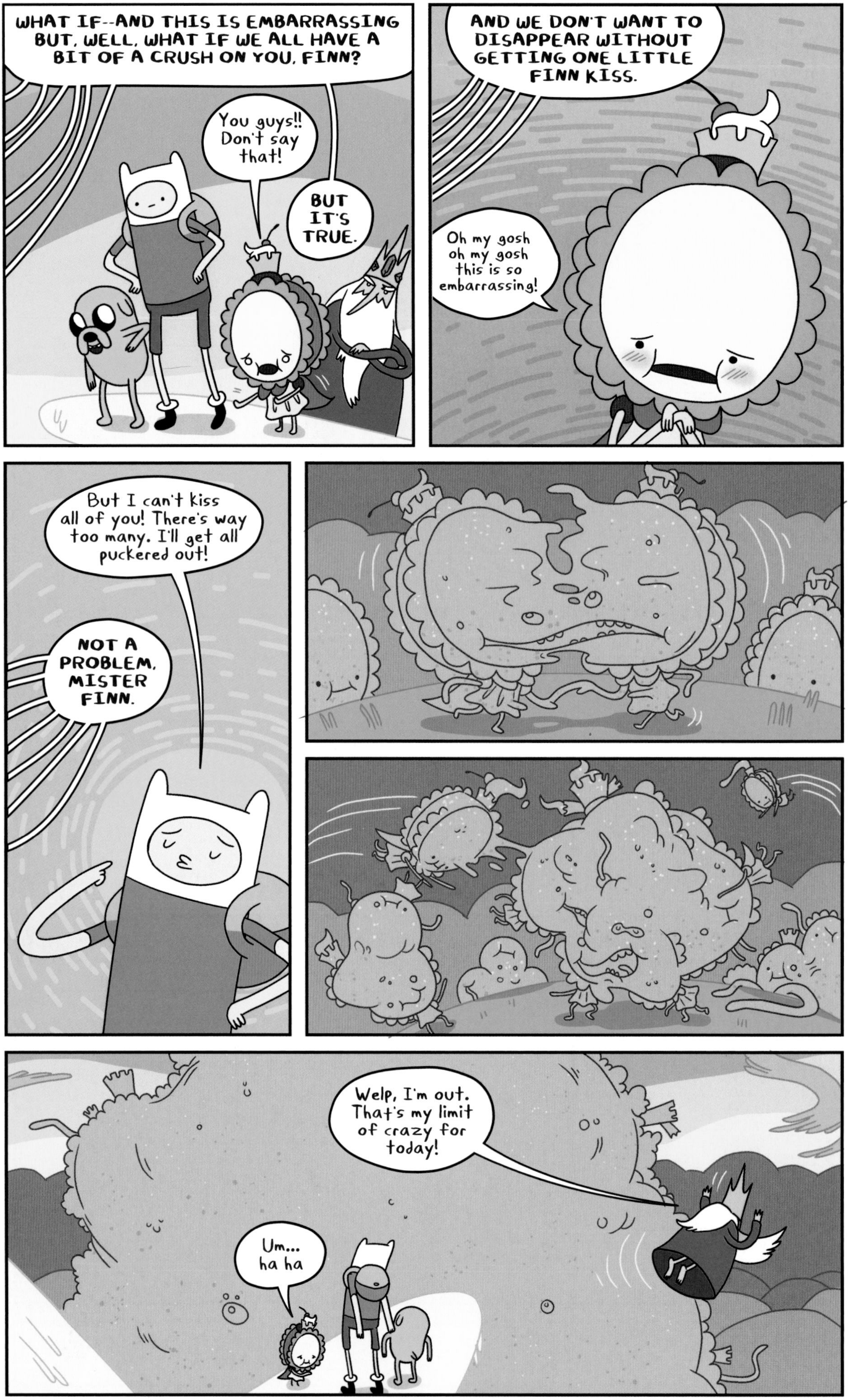
WHAT IF--AND THIS IS EMBARRASSING BUT, WELL, WHAT IF WE ALL HAVE A BIT OF A CRUSH ON YOU, FINN?
You guys!! Don't say that!
BUT IT'S TRUE.
AND WE DON'T WANT TO DISAPPEAR WITHOUT GETTING ONE LITTLE FINN KISS.
Oh my gosh oh my gosh this is so embarrassing!
But I can't kiss all of you! There's way too many. I'll get all puckered out!
NOT A PROBLEM, MISTER FINN.
Welp, I'm out. That's my limit of crazy for today!
Um... ha ha

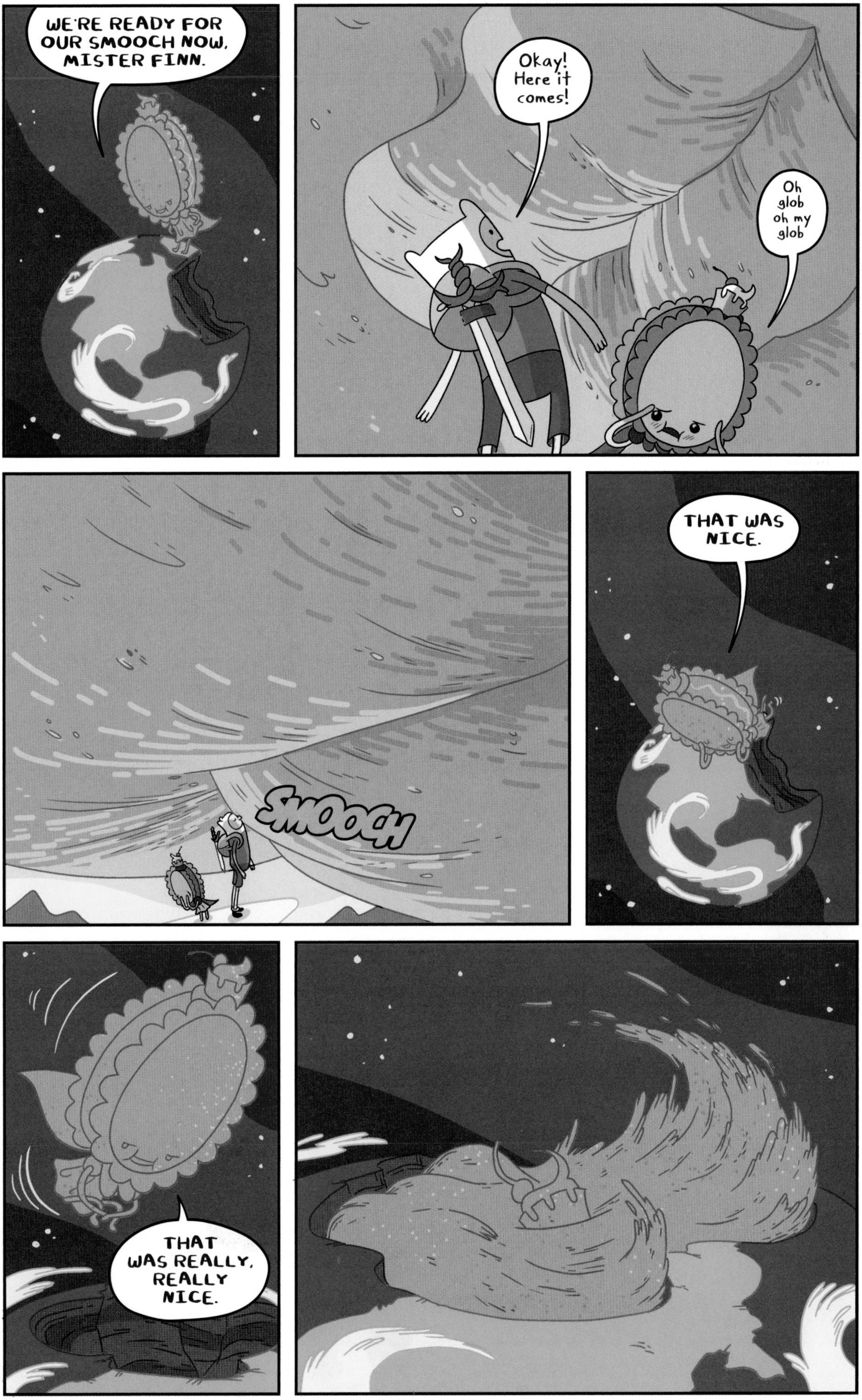
WE'RE READY FOR OUR SMOOCH NOW, MISTER FINN.
Okay! Here it comes!
Oh glob oh my glob
SMOOCH
THAT WAS NICE.
THAT WAS REALLY, REALLY NICE.

Suddenly everyone says "Hey, does it seem like the Earth's gravitational pull has increased on you too?"

SOON:

Filling in that hole has given us a whole new land to explore! You've literally given us a larger planet to live on, Finn! This is amazing.

Well shoot, Desert Princess did most of the work! I just had to kiss some sand.

Thank you, Desert Princess.

Thank YOU, Princess Bubblegum.

Alright! Water Princess, we could use a lake!

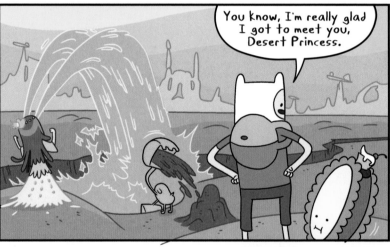

You know, I'm really glad I got to meet you, Desert Princess.

I'm--

I'm really glad I got to meet you too, Mister Finn.

Please. All my friends just call me "Finn".

THE END

ADVENTURE TIME

Drawn by Shelli and Braden

Written by Ryan

Created by Pen

 Thanks for reading!

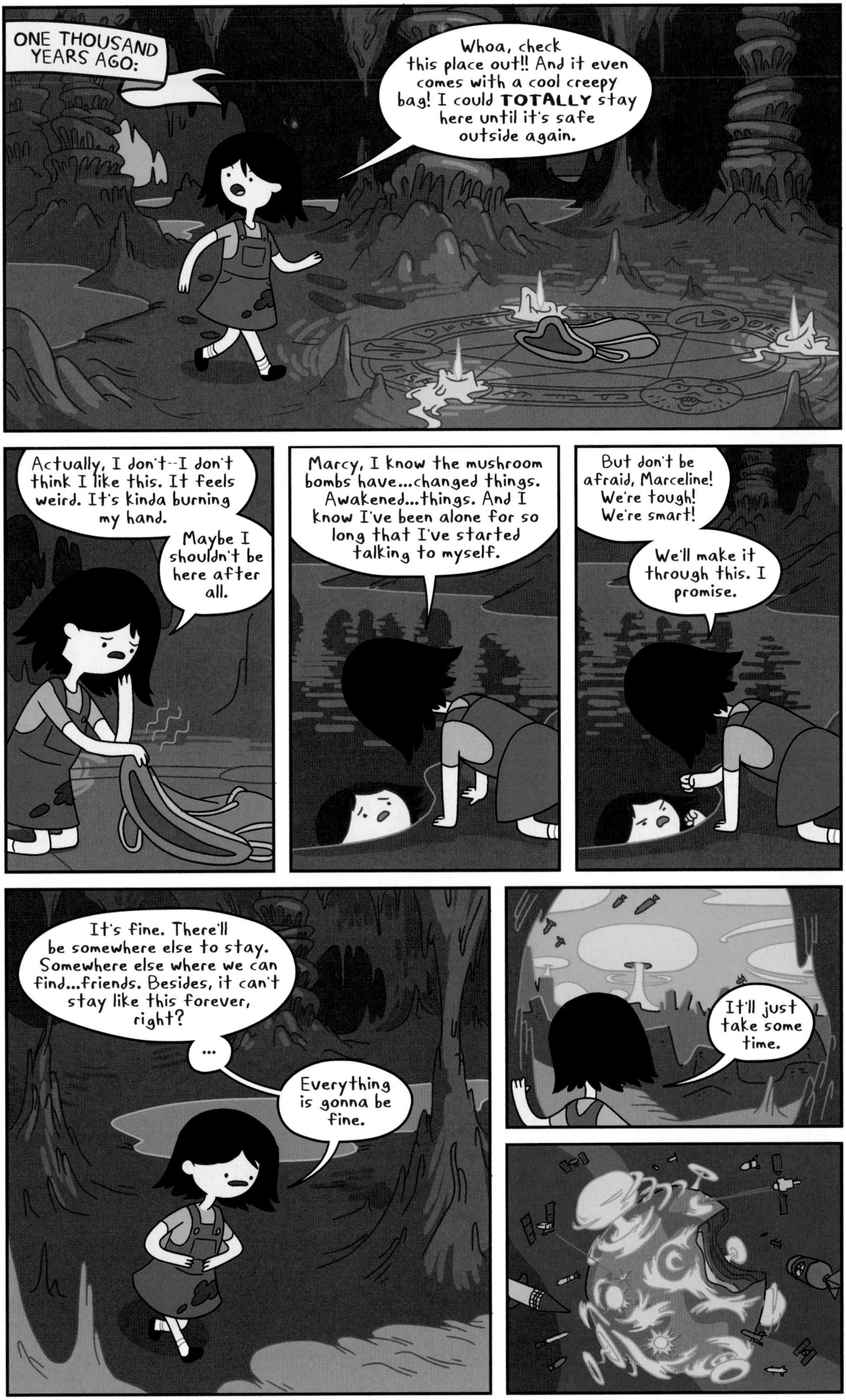
ONE THOUSAND YEARS AGO:
Whoa, check this place out!! And it even comes with a cool creepy bag! I could **TOTALLY** stay here until it's safe outside again.
Actually, I don't--I don't think I like this. It feels weird. It's kinda burning my hand.
Maybe I shouldn't be here after all.
Marcy, I know the mushroom bombs have...changed things. Awakened...things. And I know I've been alone for so long that I've started talking to myself.
But don't be afraid, Marceline! We're tough! We're smart!
We'll make it through this. I promise.
It's fine. There'll be somewhere else to stay. Somewhere else where we can find...friends. Besides, it can't stay like this forever, right?
...
Everything is gonna be fine.
It'll just take some time.

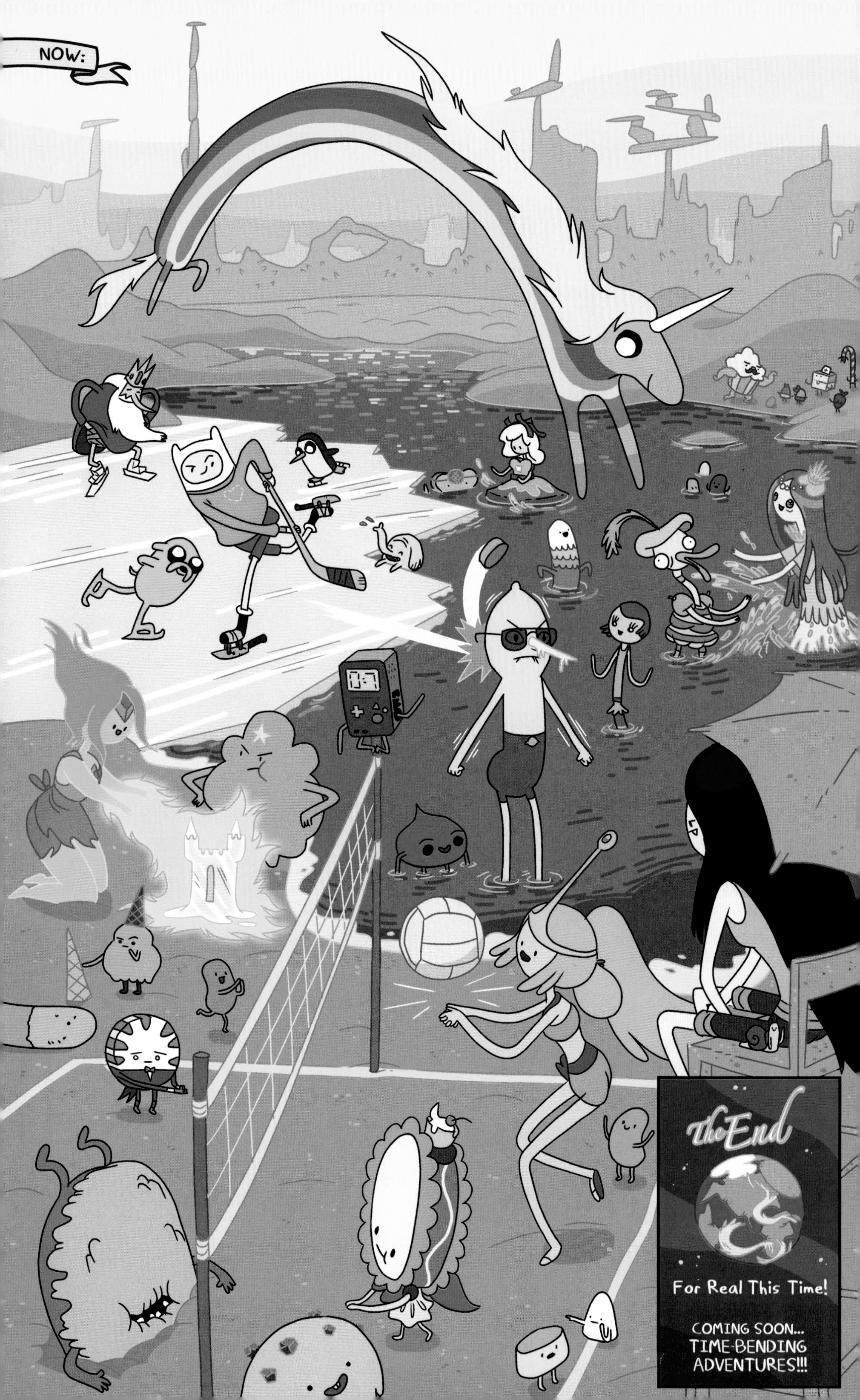
NOW:
The End
For Real This Time!
COMING SOON...
TIME-BENDING
ADVENTURES!!!

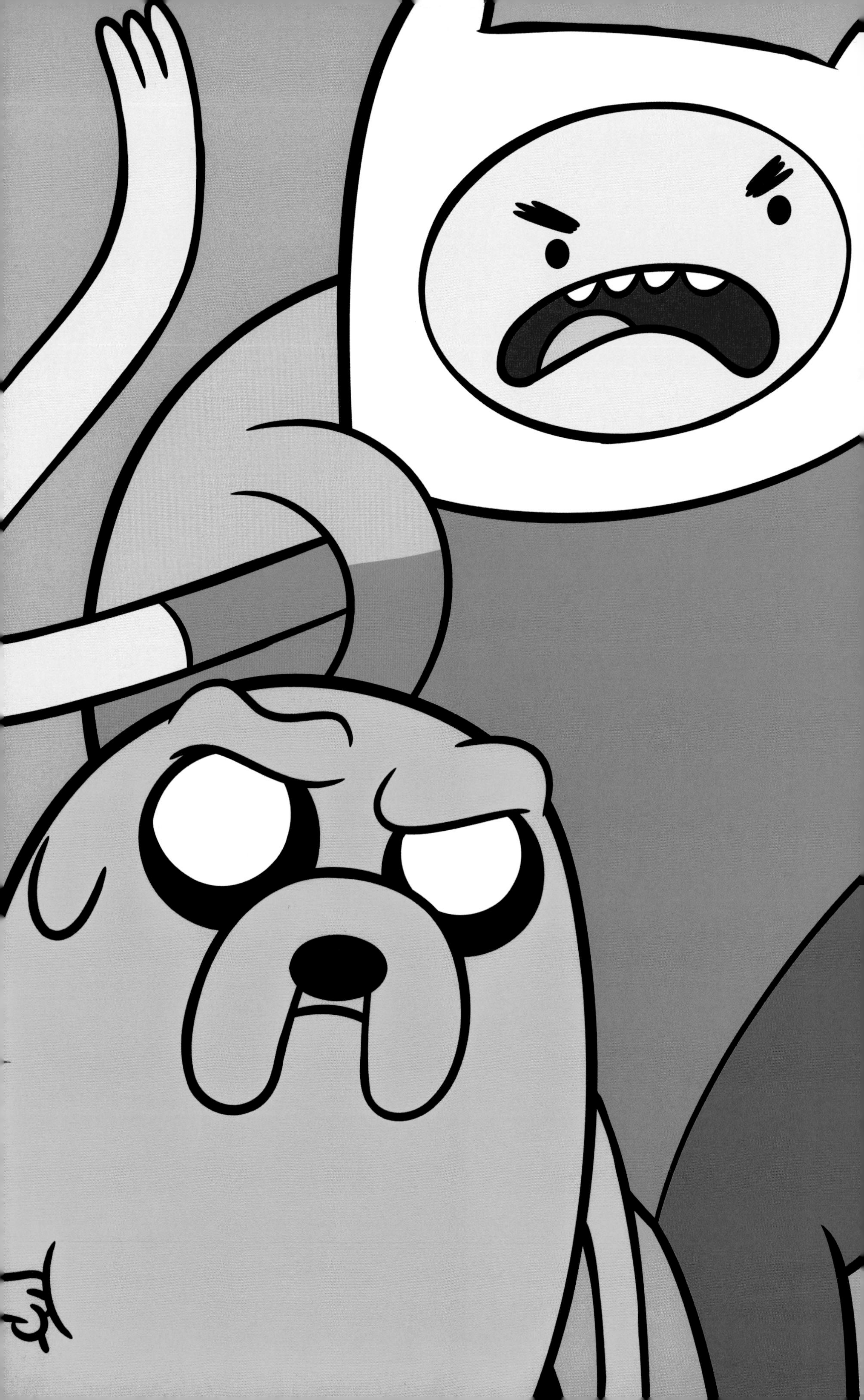

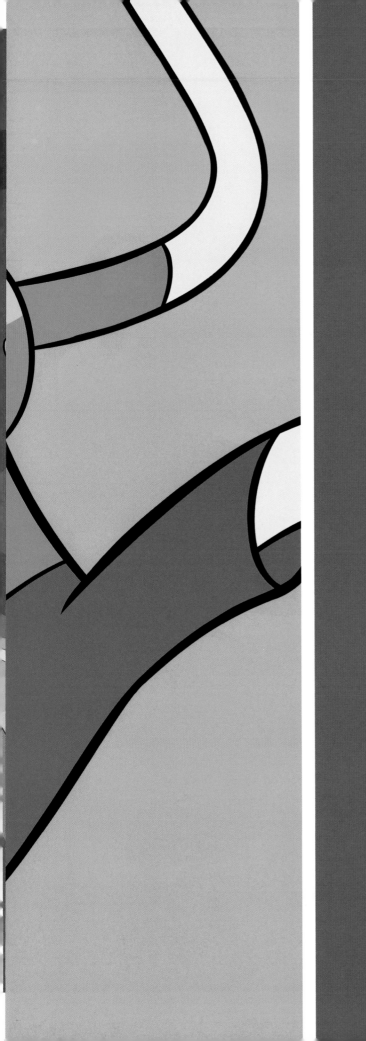

COVER GALLERY

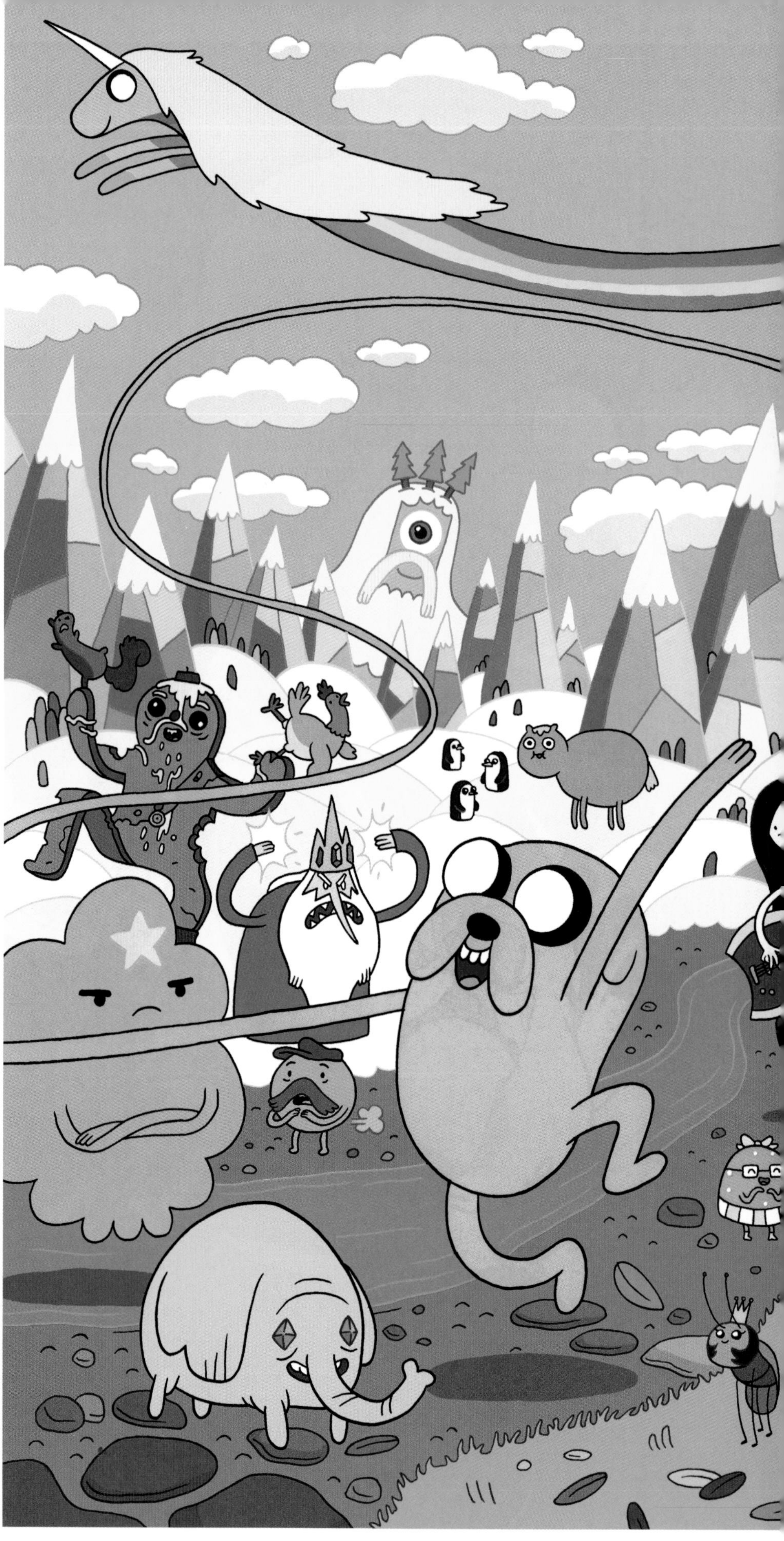

ISSUE ONE
CHRIS HOUGHTON
COLORS BY KASSANDRA HELLER

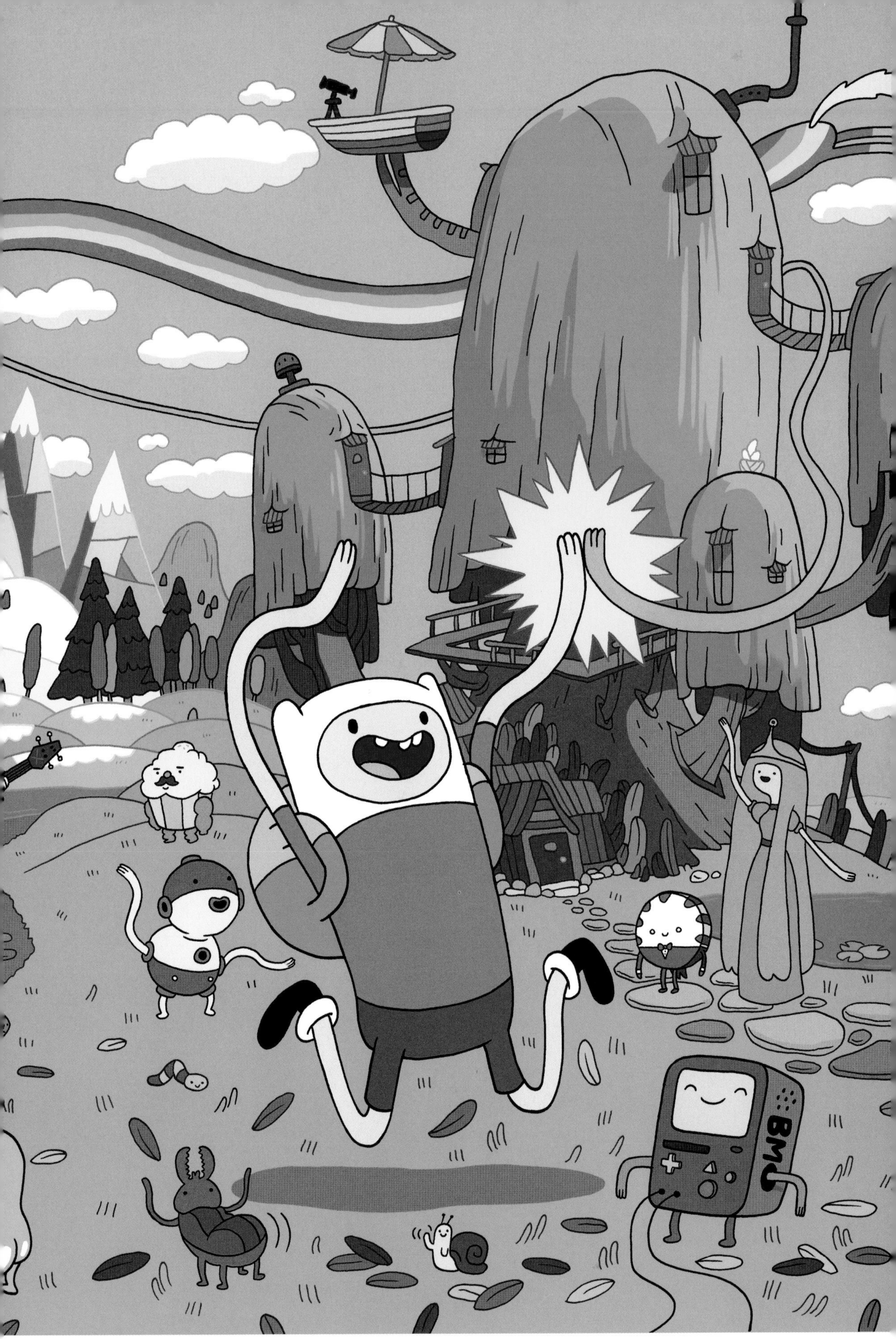
BMO

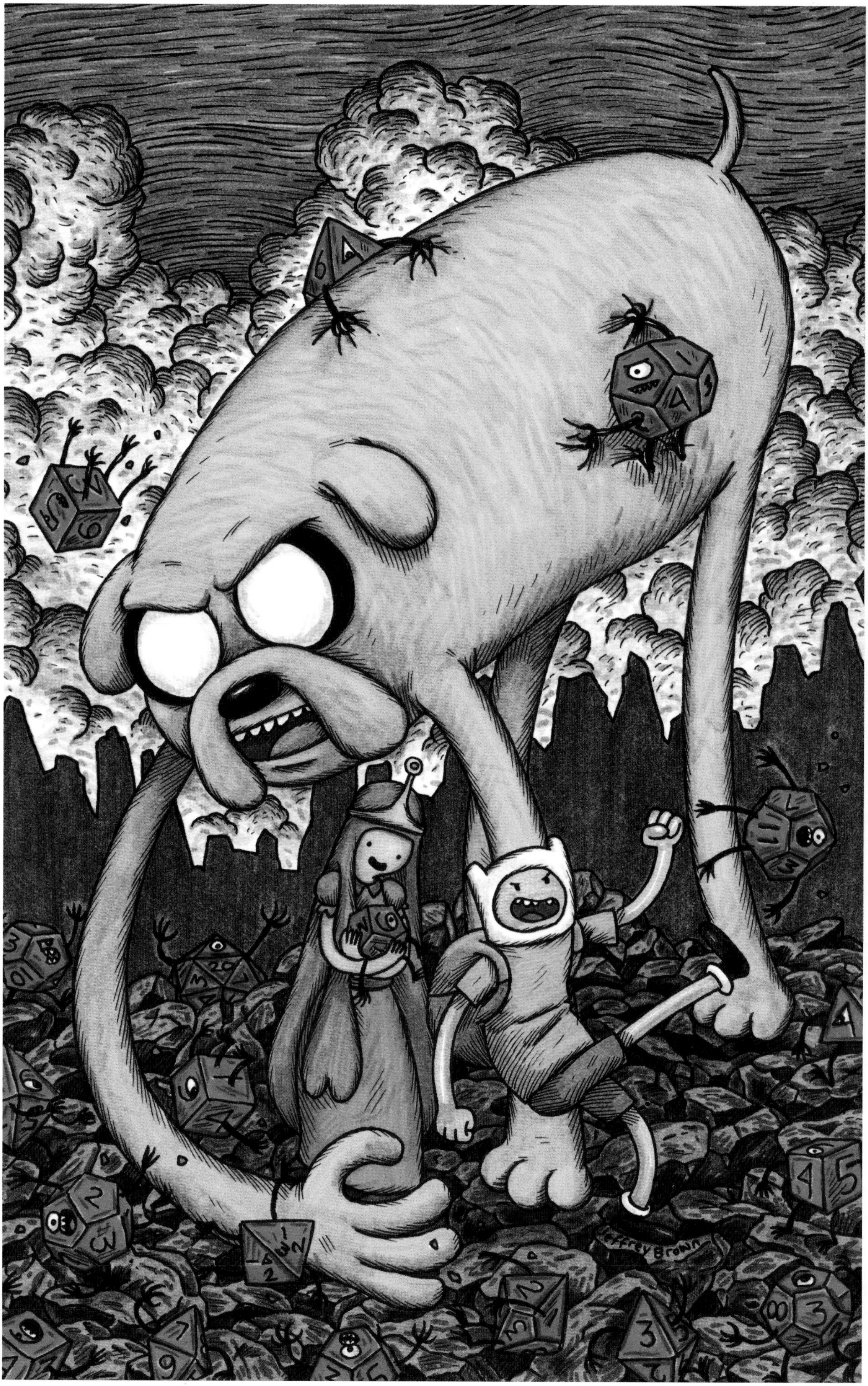
Jeffrey Brown

ISSUE ONE | JEFFREY BROWN

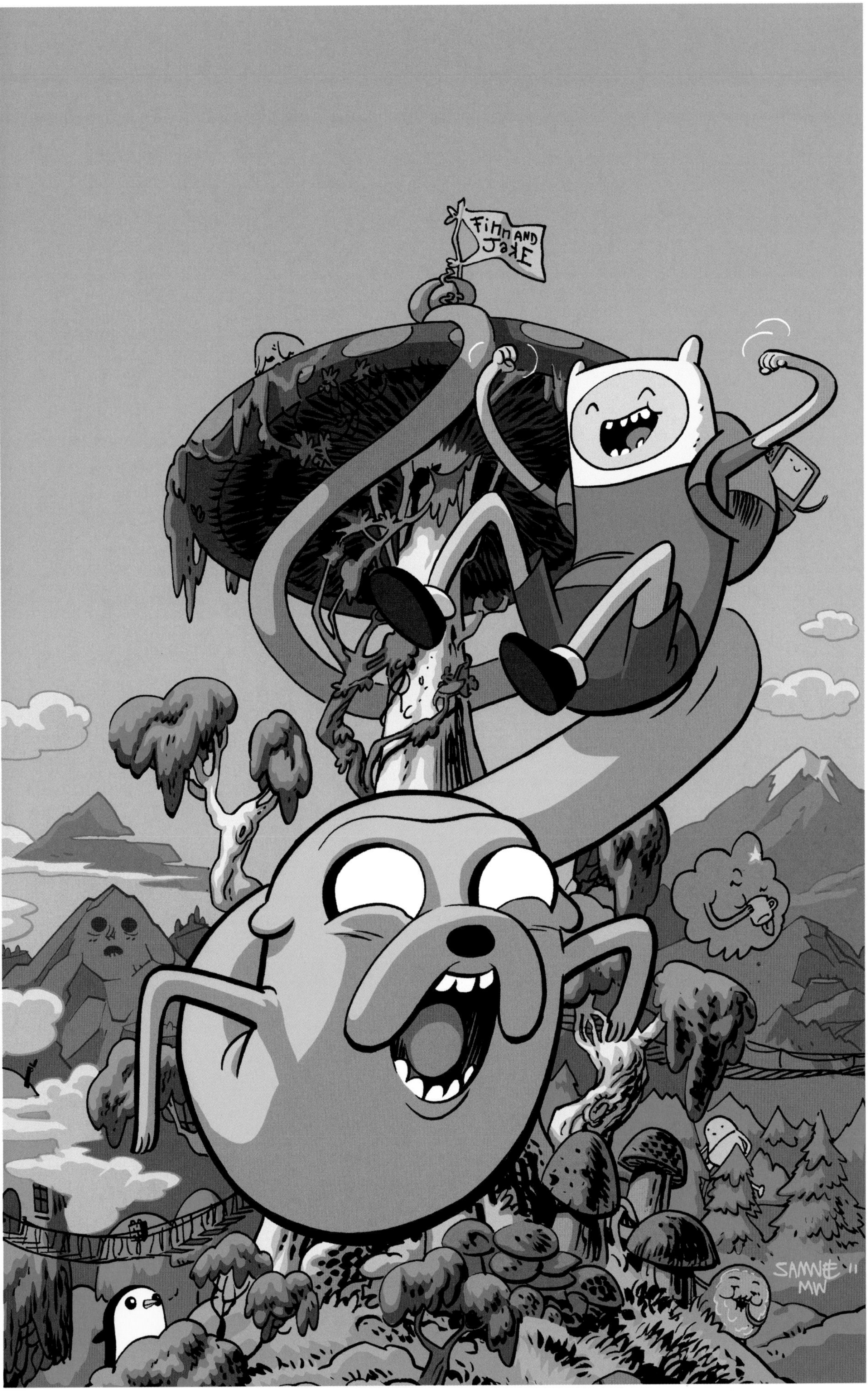
Finn AND JakE
SAMNEE '11
MW

EMERALD CITY COMICON ISSUE ONE EXCLUSIVE COVER | CHRIS SAMNEE | COLORS BY MATTHEW WILSON

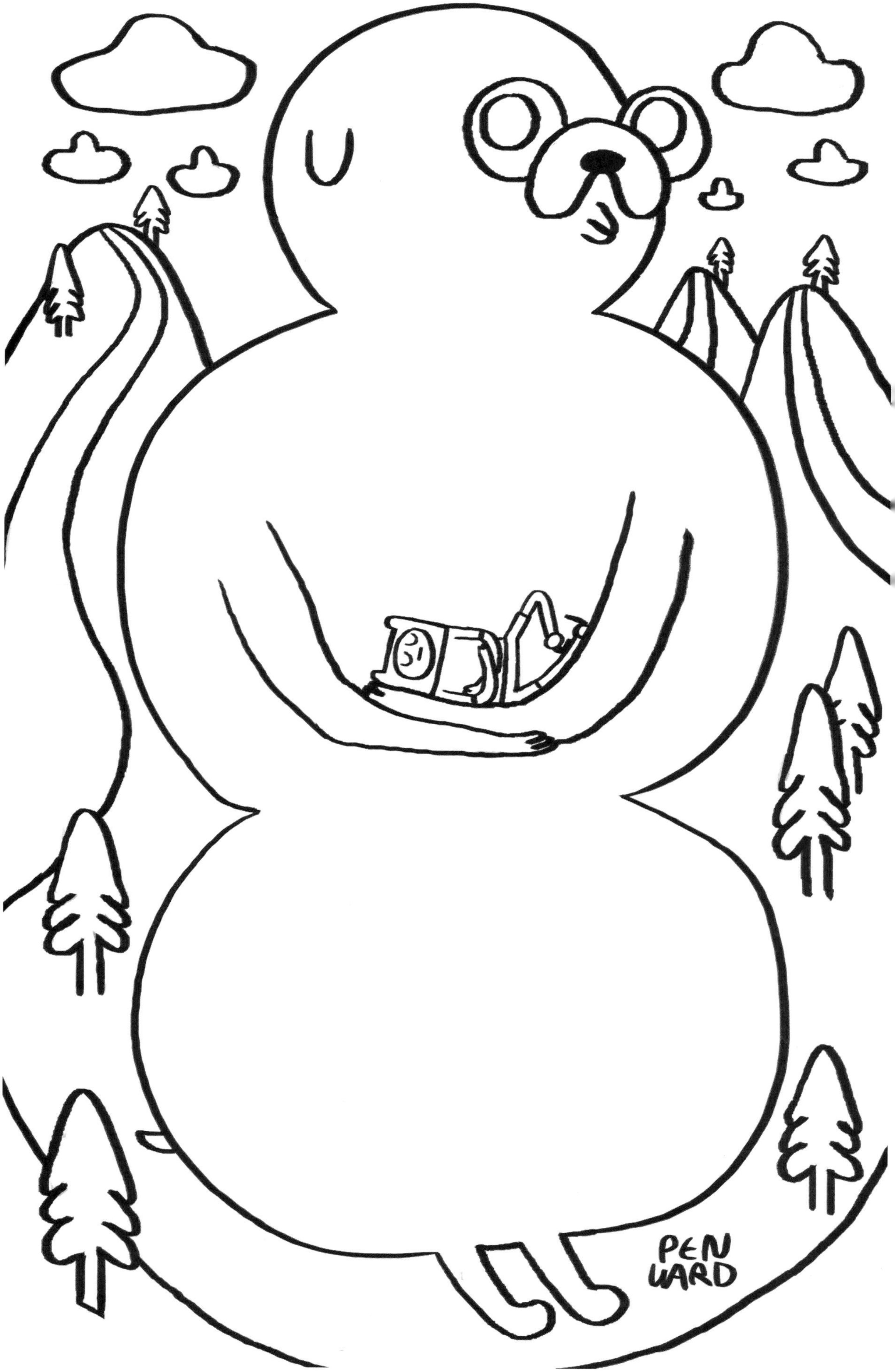
PEN
WARD

SAN DIEGO COMIC-CON ISSUE ONE EXCLUSIVE COVER | PENDLETON WARD

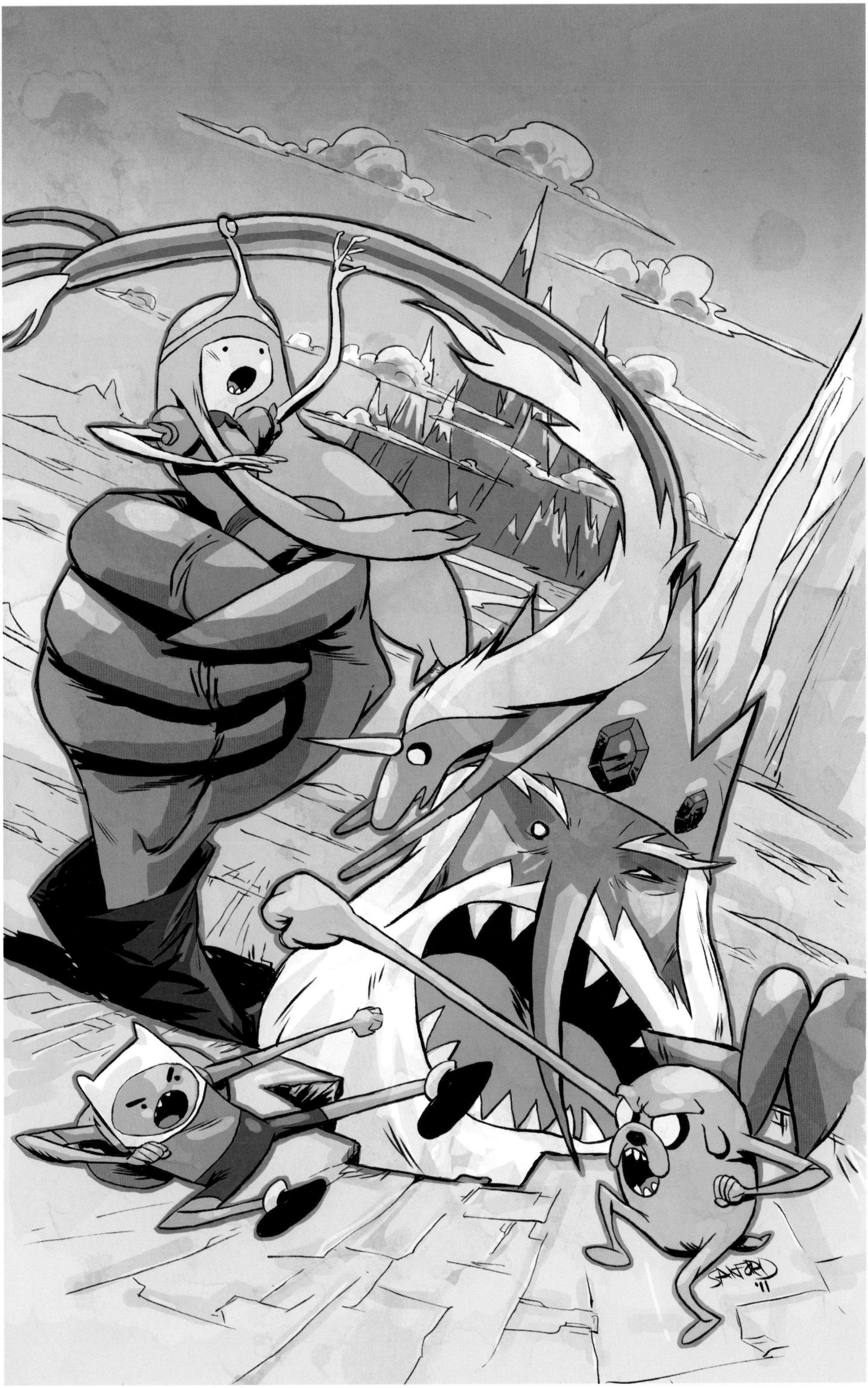

ANNAPOLIS COMIC-CON ISSUE ONE EXCLUSIVE COVER | SANFORD GREENE

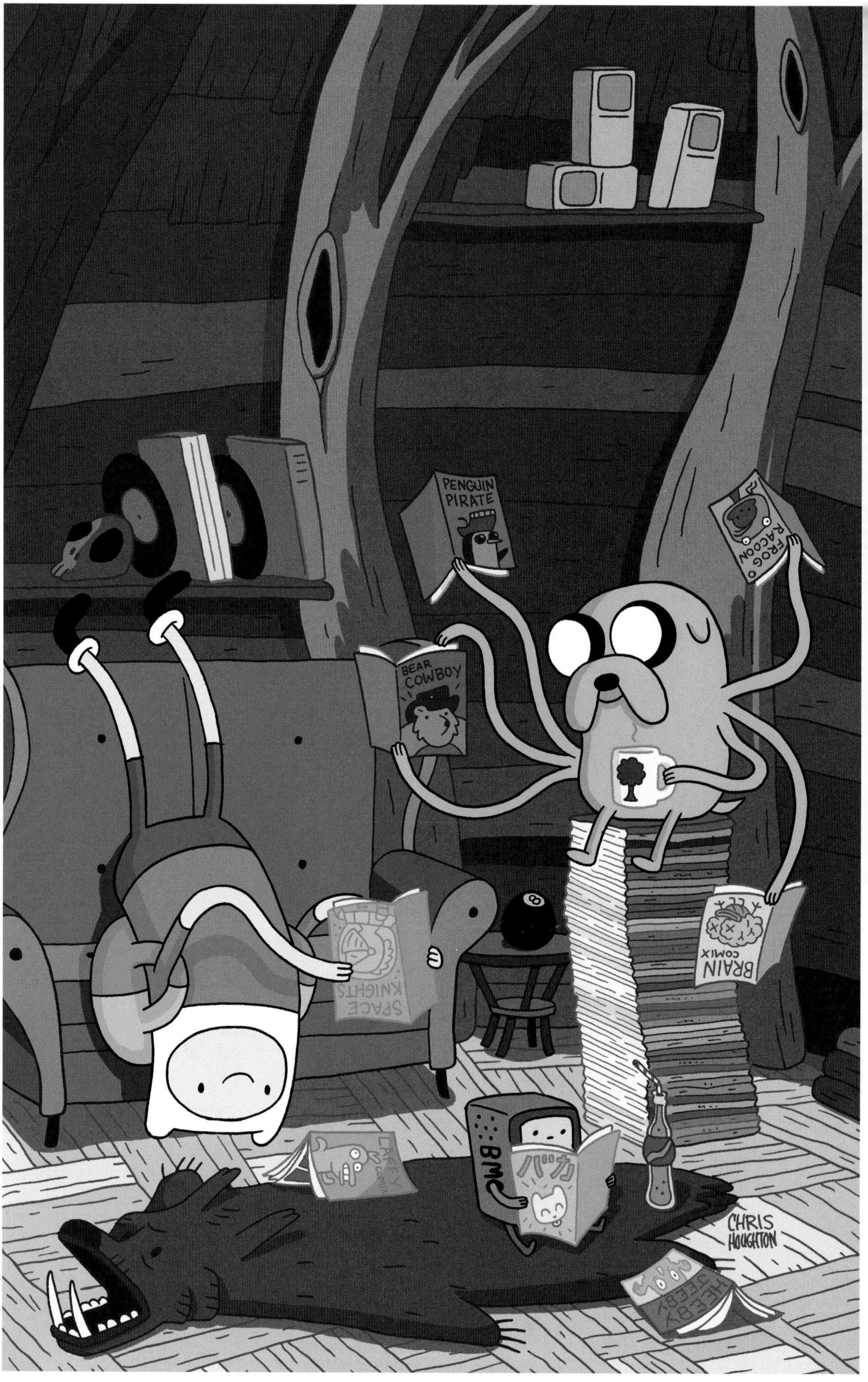
PENGUIN PIRATE
FROG RACOON
BEAR COWBOY
BRAIN COMIX
SPACE KNIGHTS
BMO
バカ
CHRIS HOUGHTON
HEEBY JEEBY

ISSUE ONE | CHRIS HOUGHTON | COLORS BY KASSANDRA HELLER

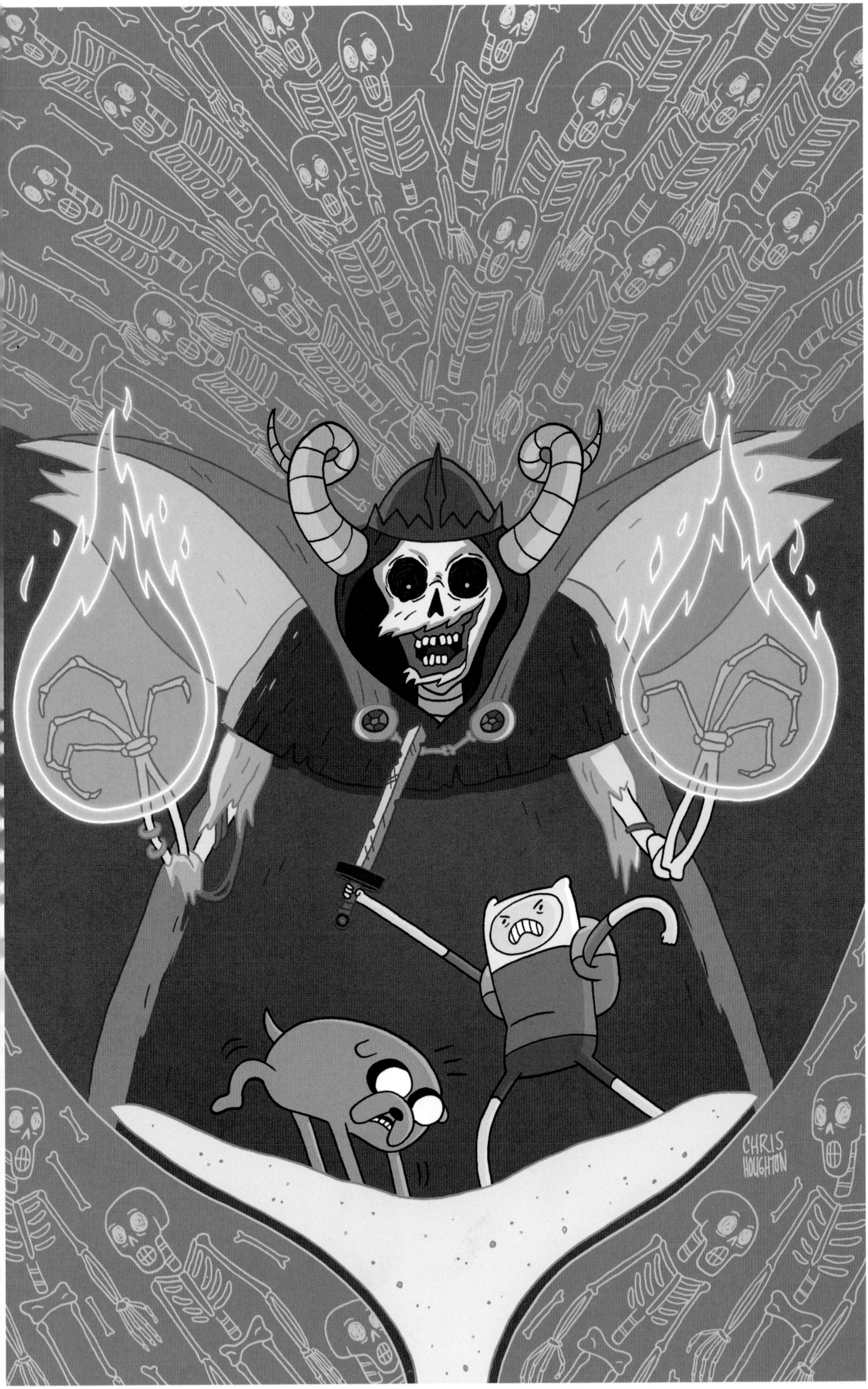
CHRIS
HOUGHTON

ISSUE ONE | CHRIS HOUGHTON | COLORS BY KASSANDRA HELLER

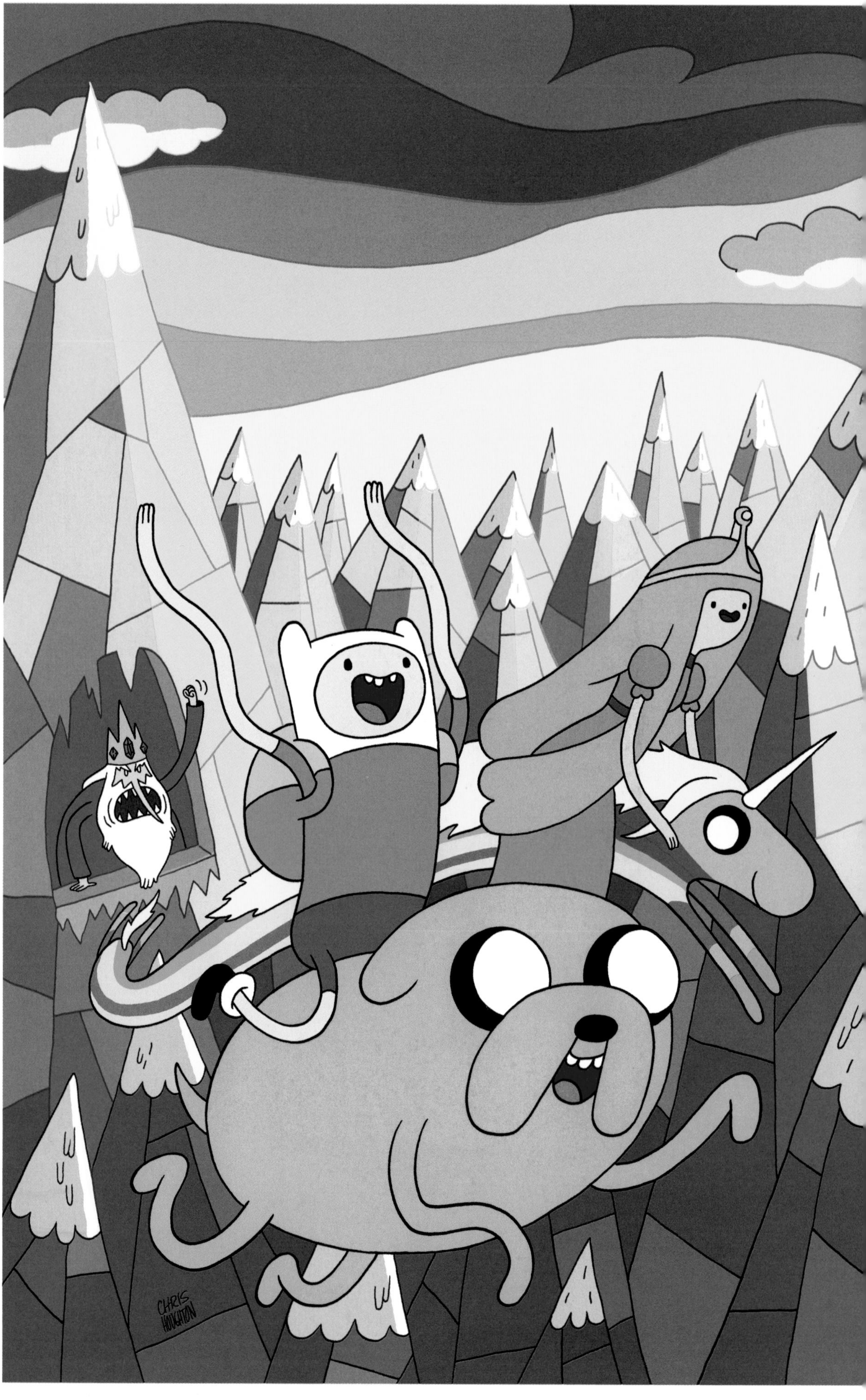
CHRIS HOUGHTON

ISSUE TWO | CHRIS HOUGHTON | COLORS BY KASSANDRA HELLER

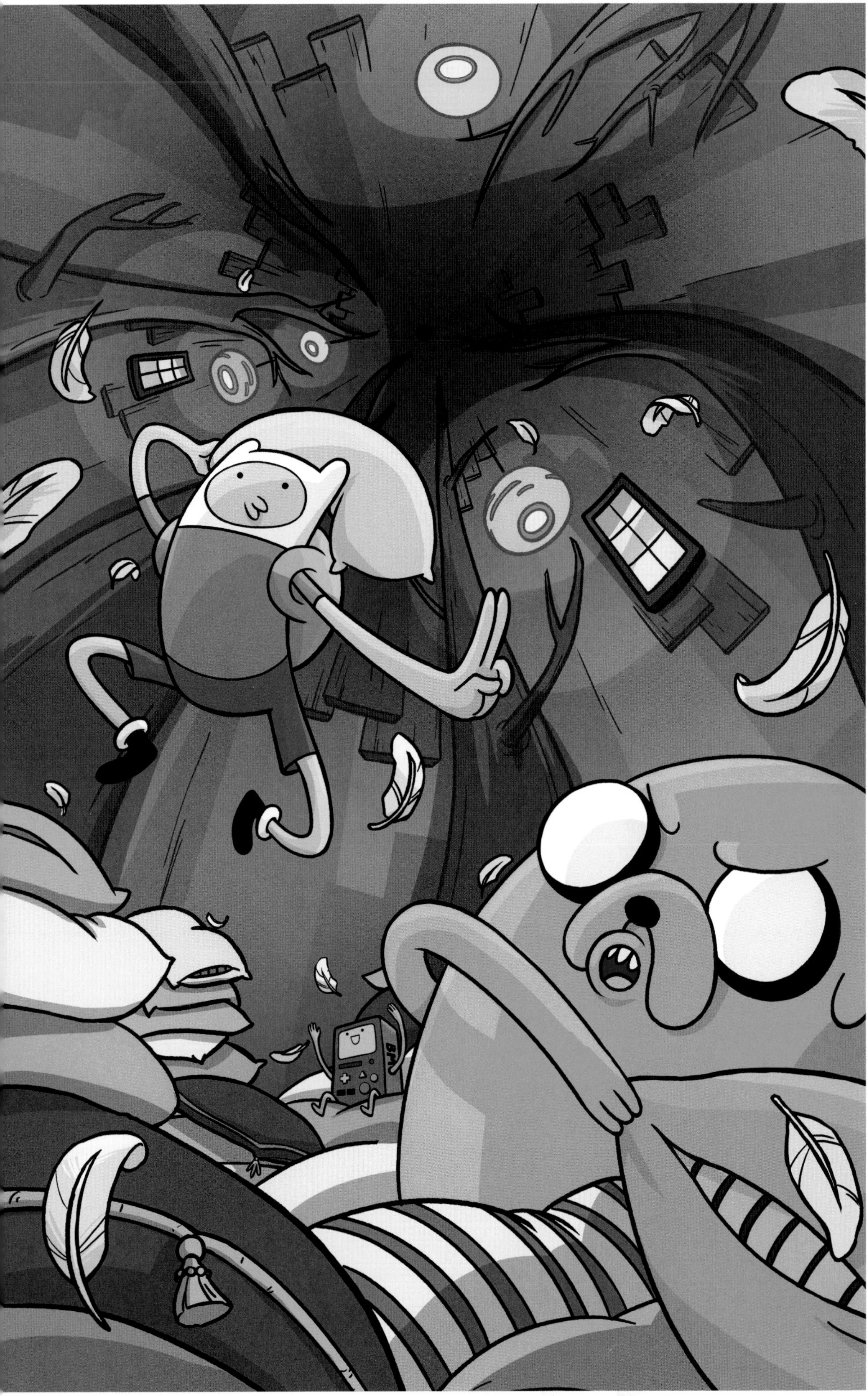

ISSUE TWO | JAB | COLORS BY BRADEN LAMB

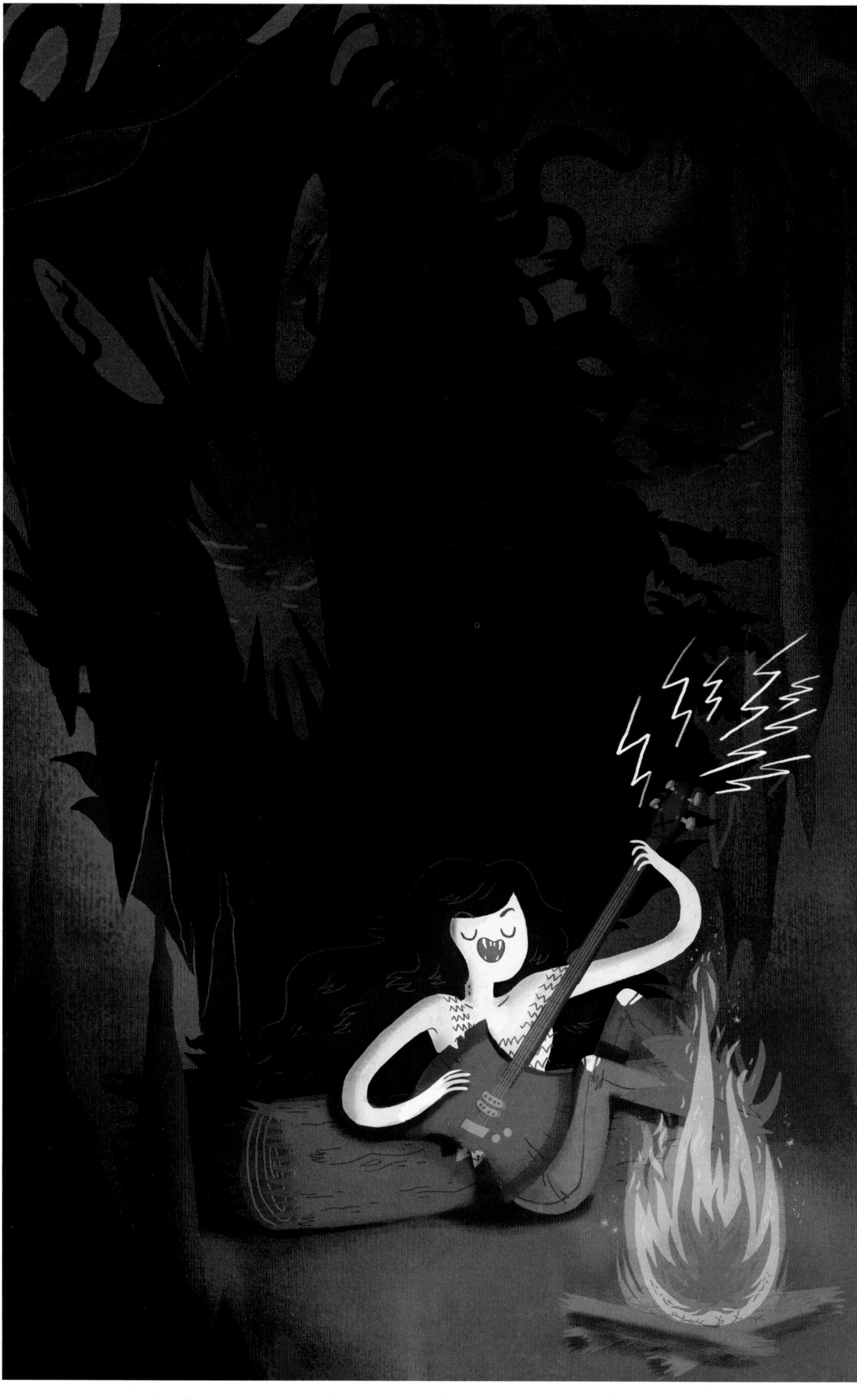

ISSUE TWO | EMILY CARROLL

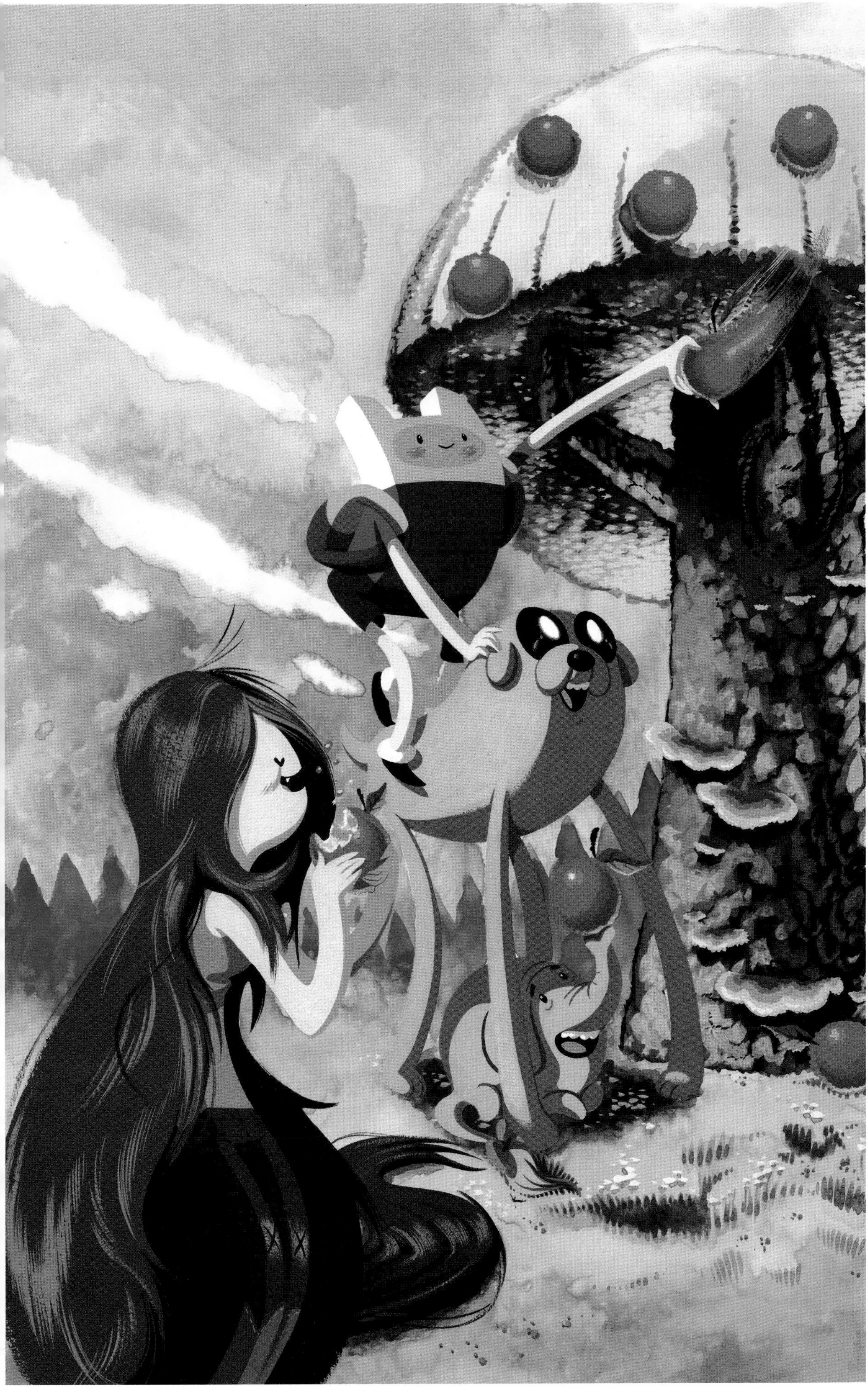

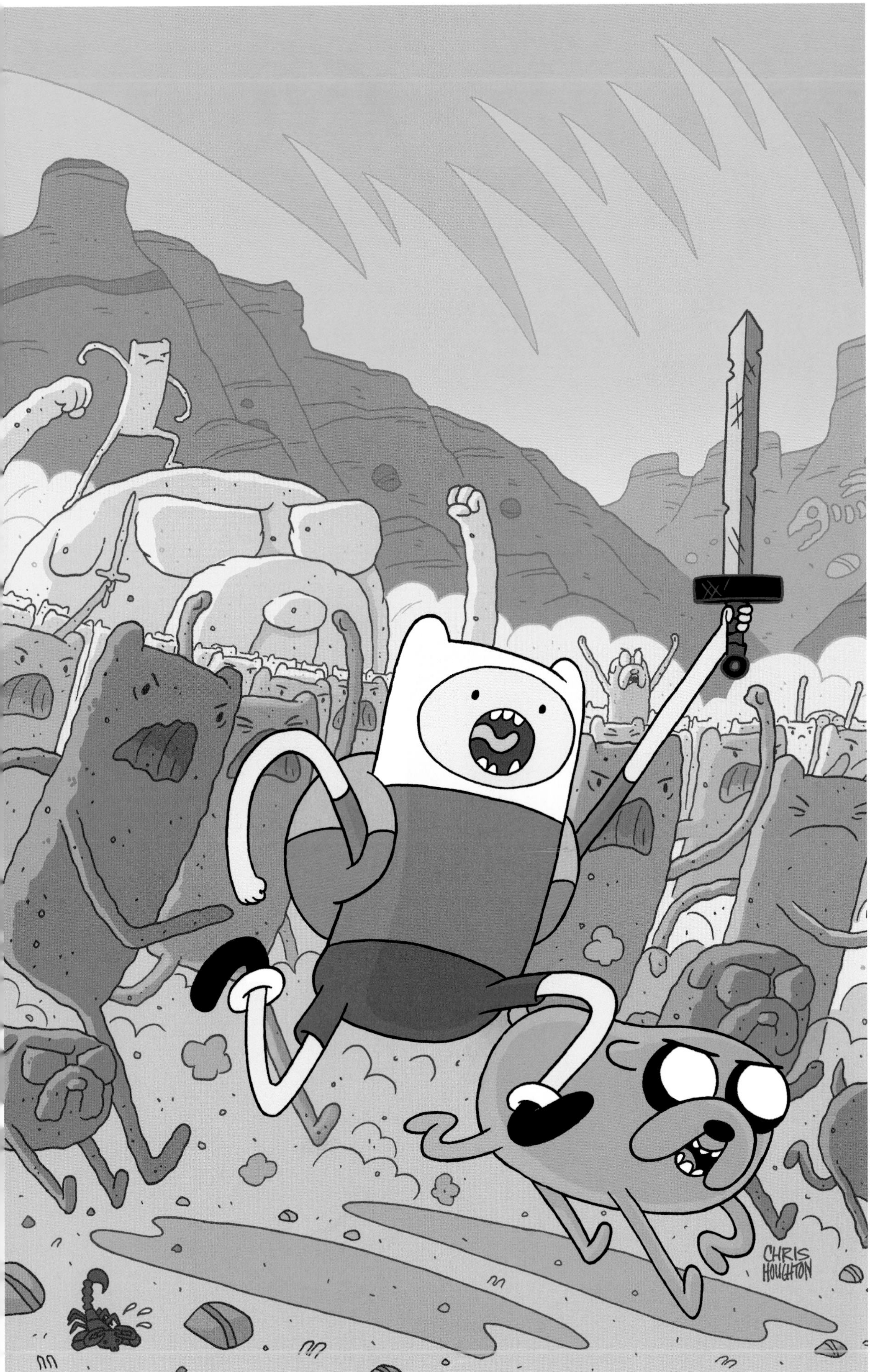
CHRIS
HOUGHTON

ISSUE THREE | CHRIS HOUGHTON | COLORS BY KASSANDRA HELLER

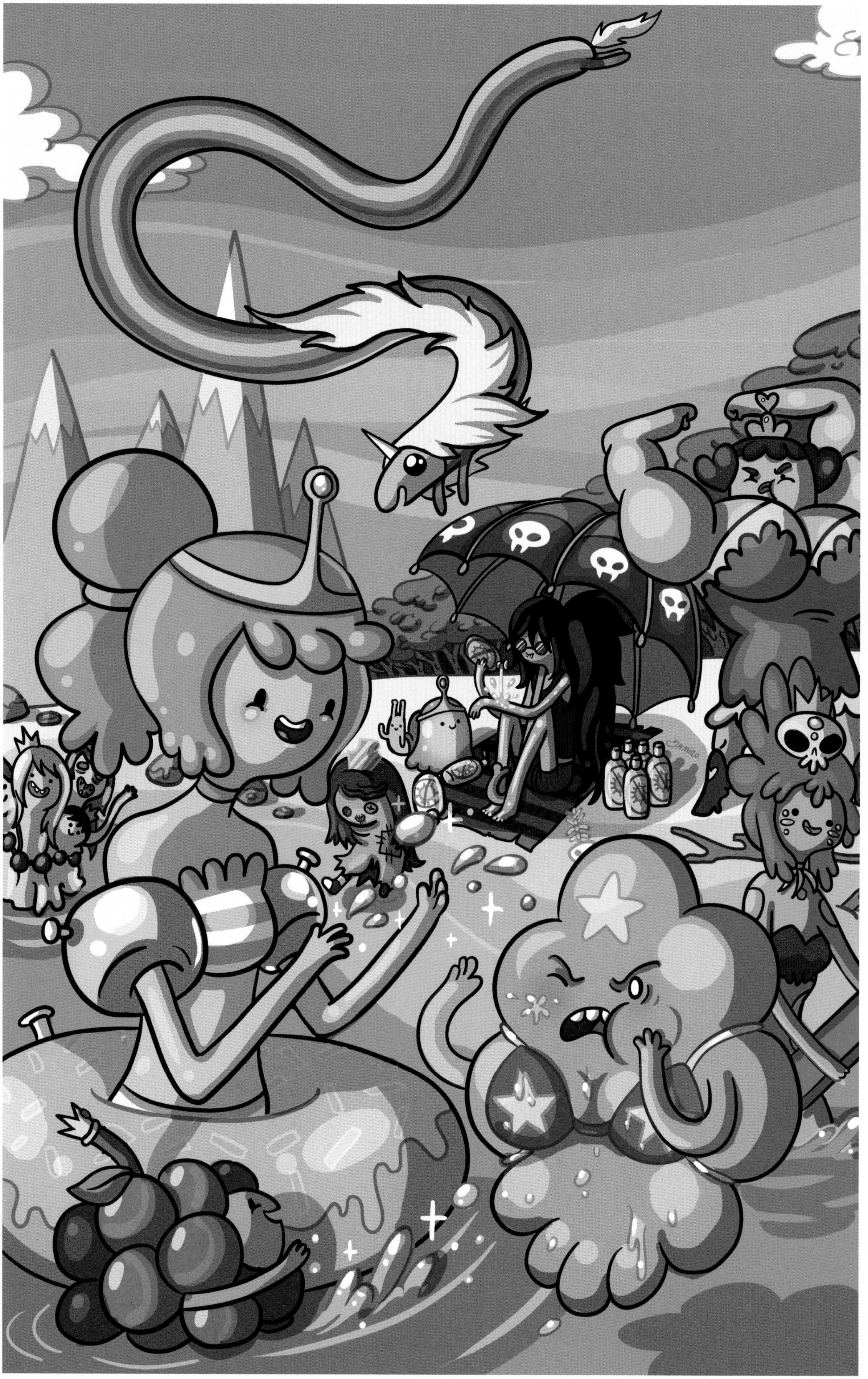

ISSUE THREE | ELENA BARBARICH

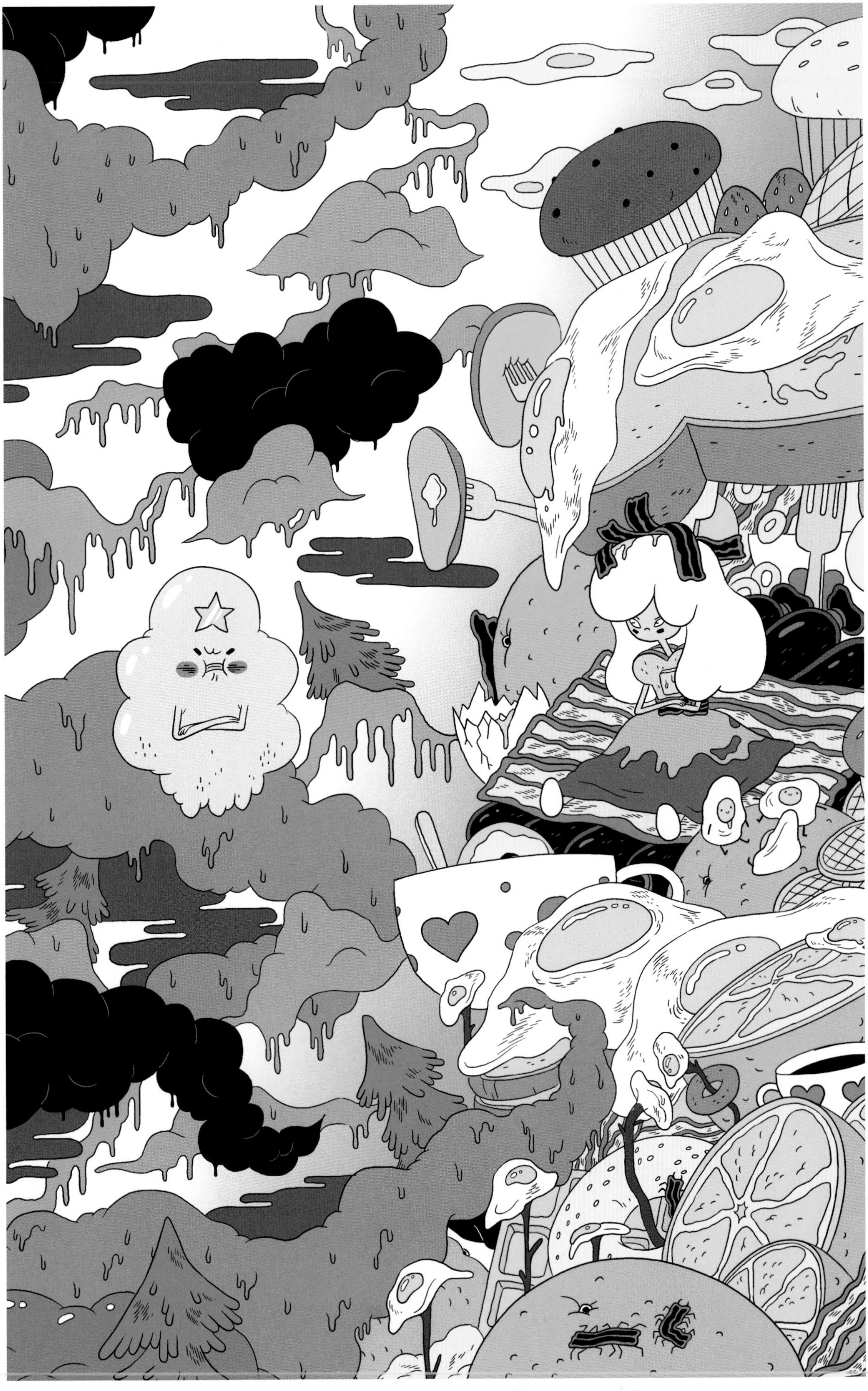

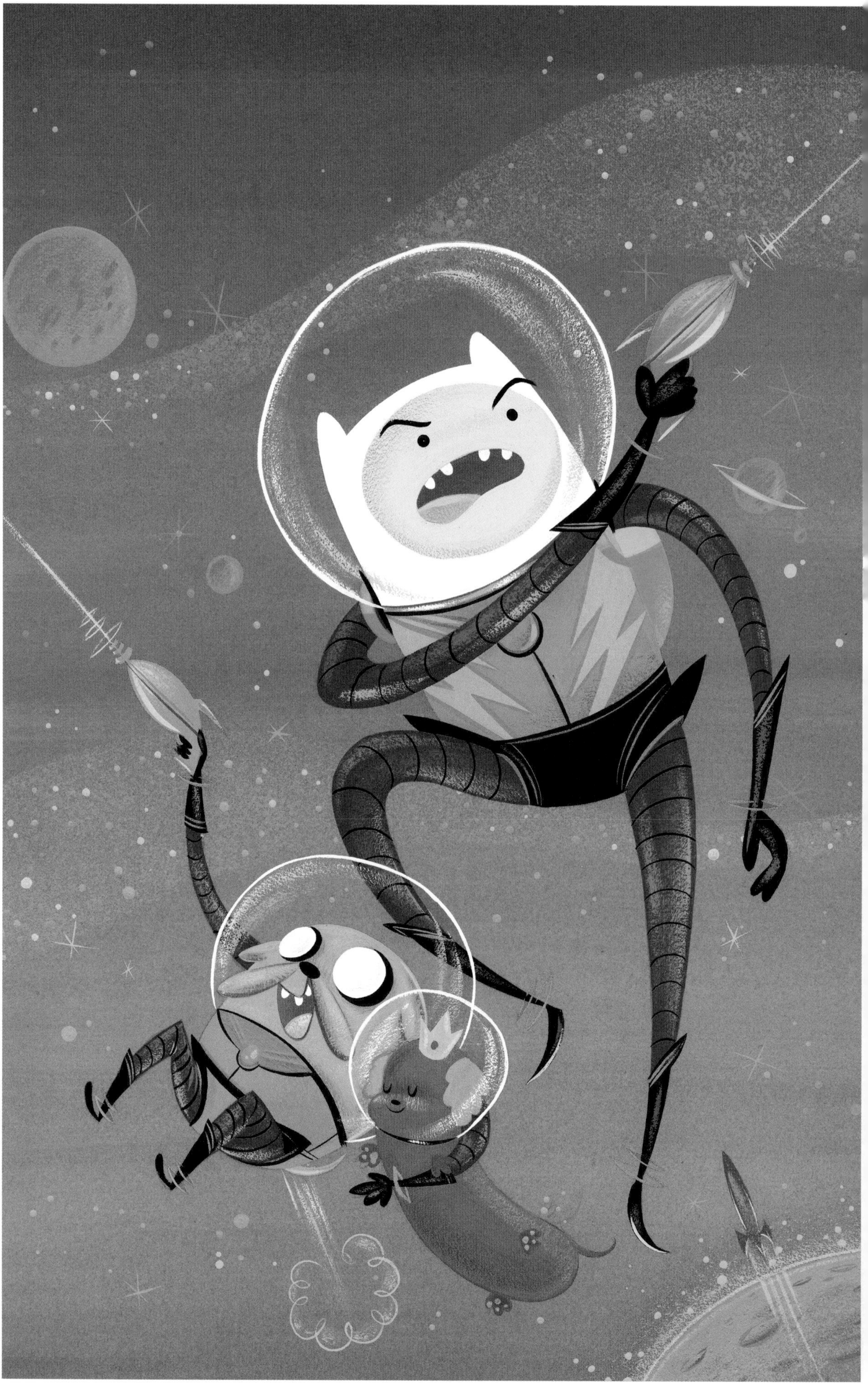

ISSUE THREE | STEPHANIE BUSCEMA

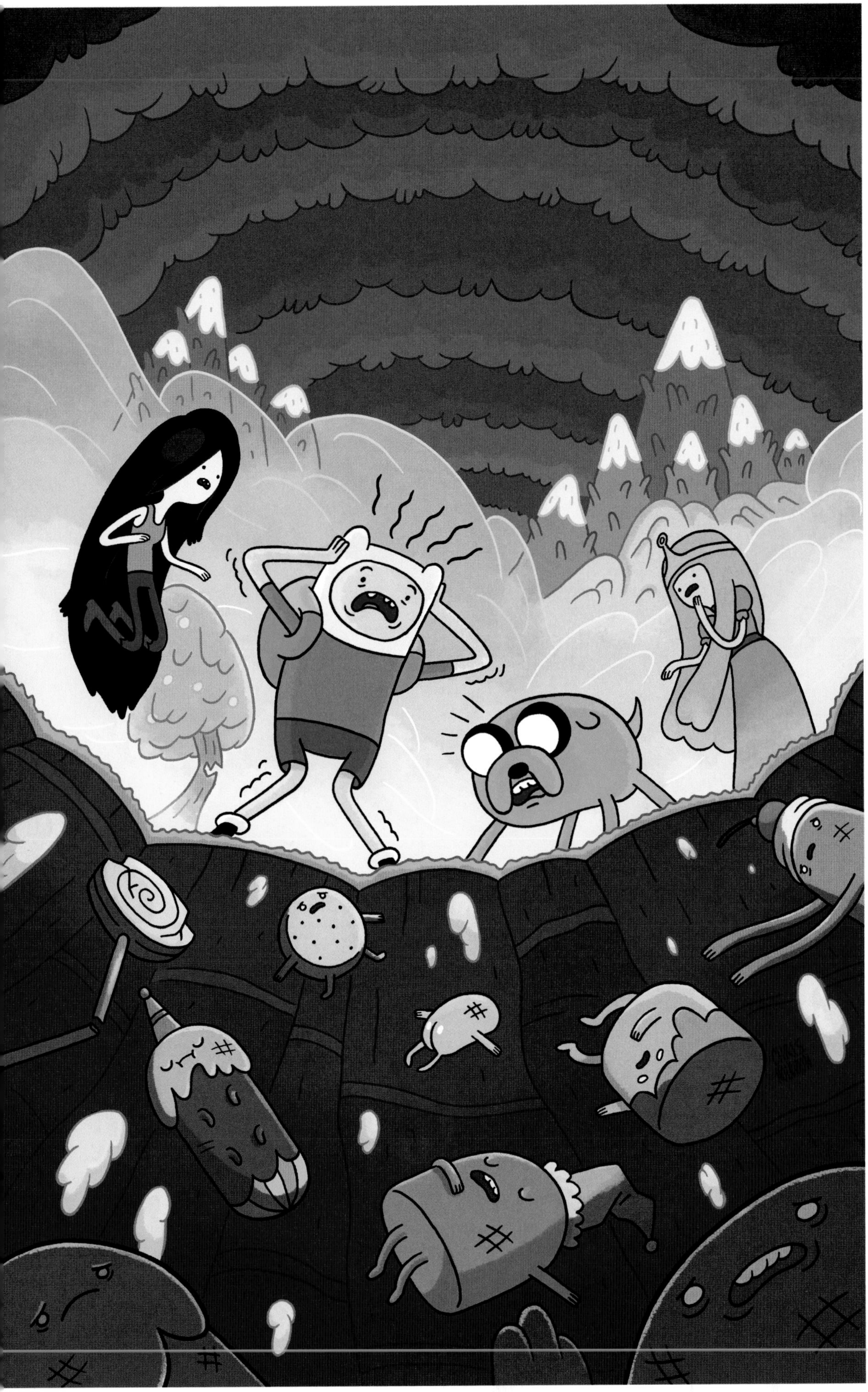

ISSUE FOUR | CHRIS HOUGHTON | COLORS BY KASSANDRA HELLER

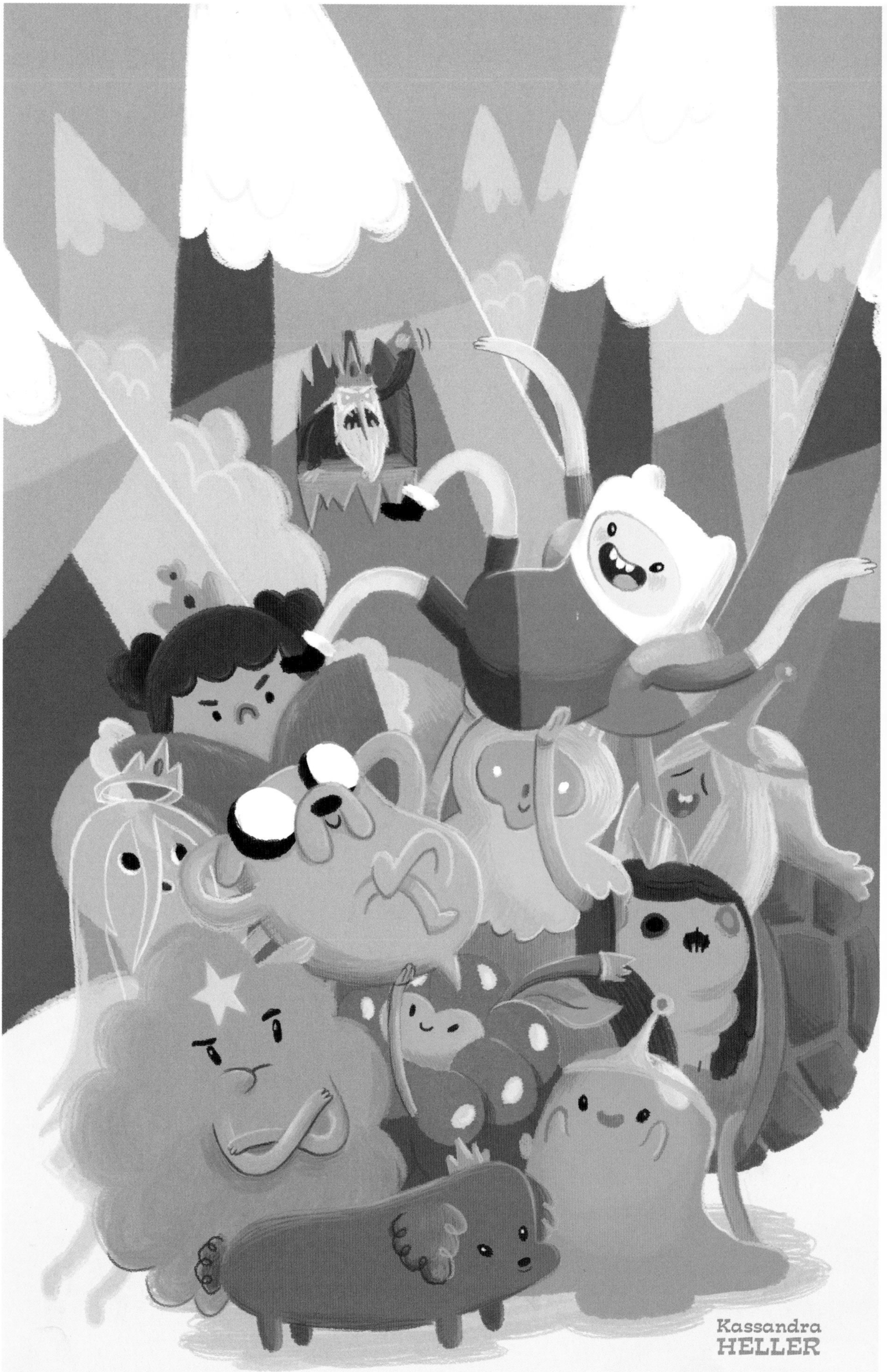
Kassandra
HELLER

ISSUE FOUR | KASSANDRA HELLER

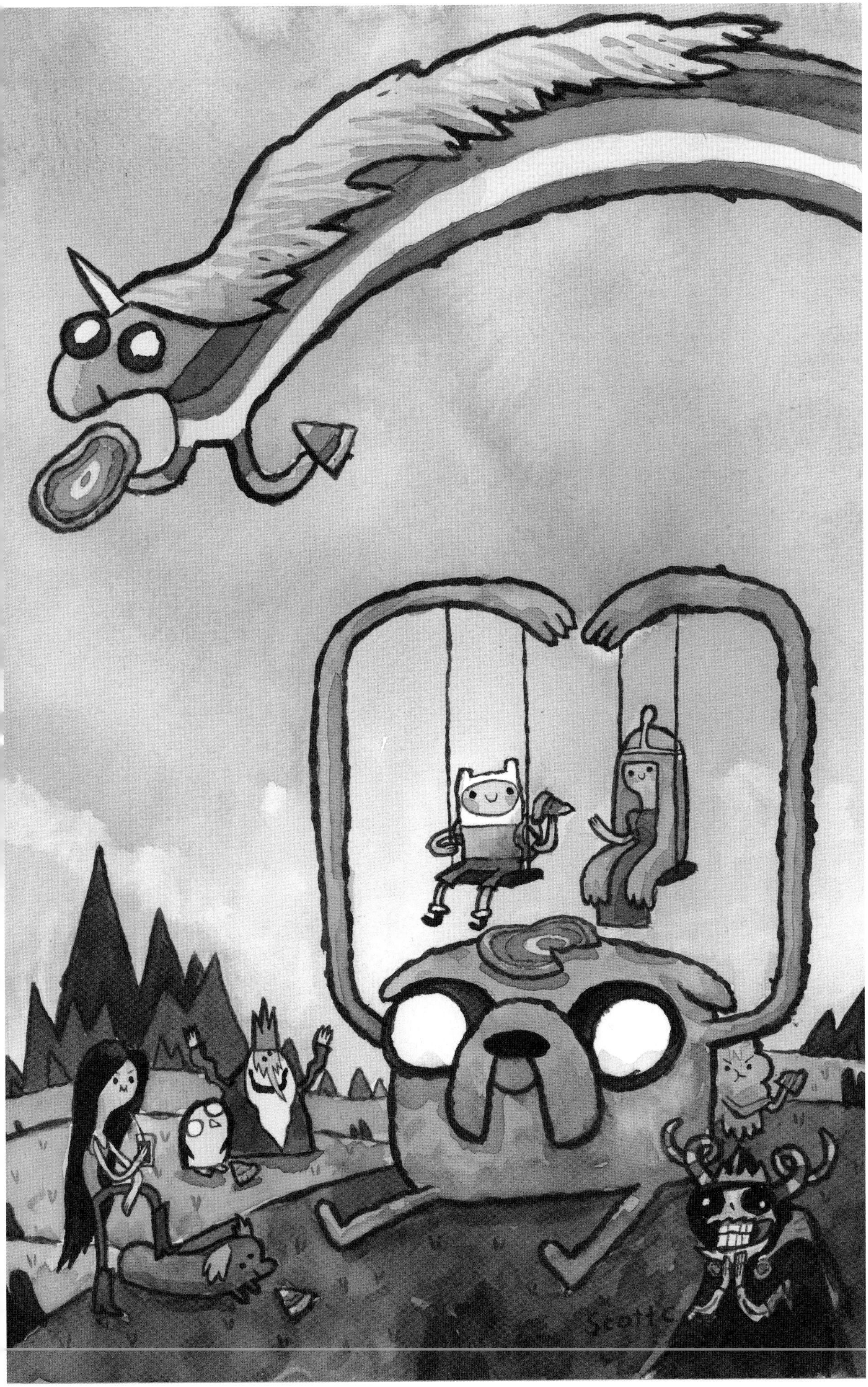
Scott C

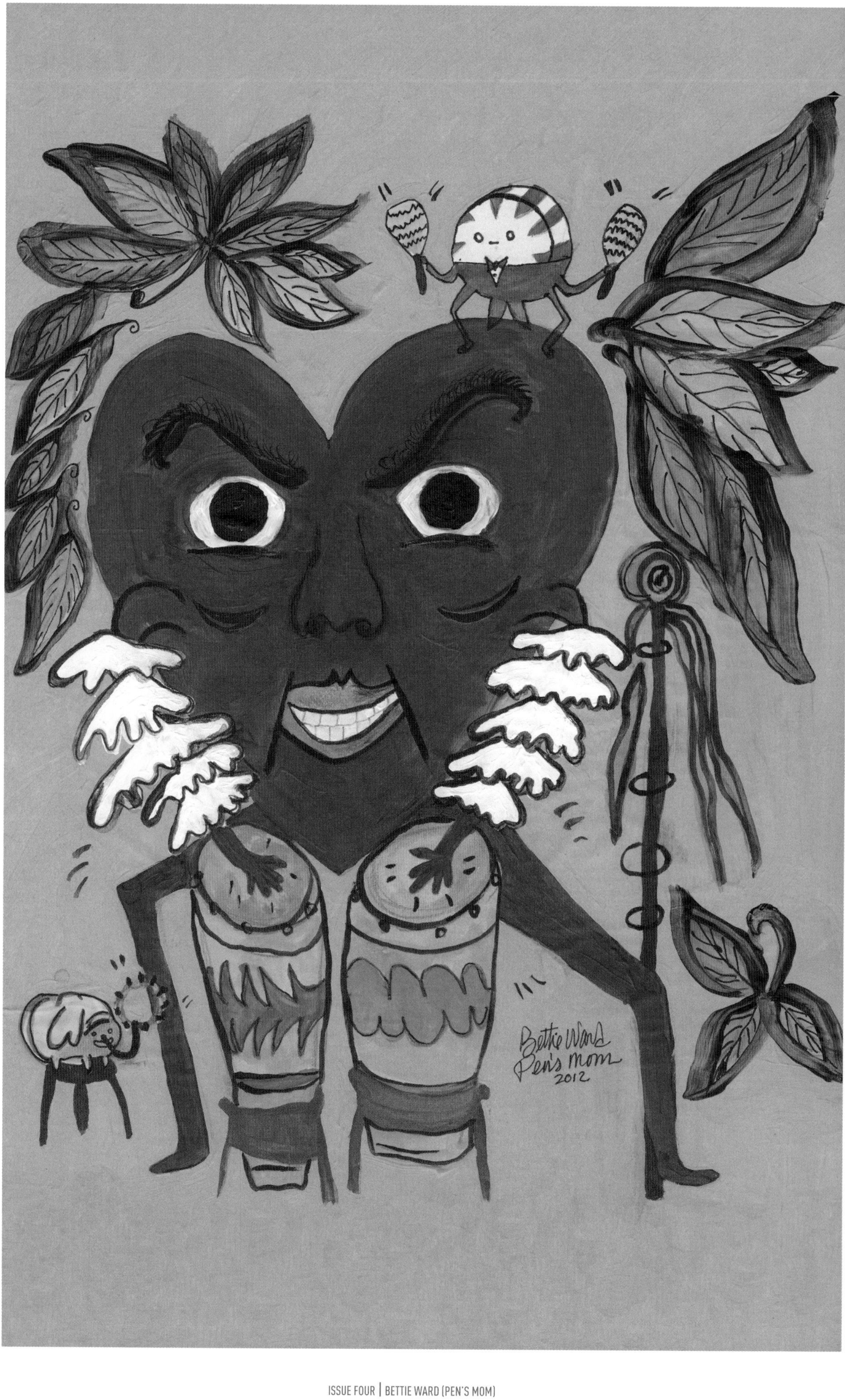
Bettie Ward
Pen's mom
2012

ISSUE FOUR | BETTIE WARD (PEN'S MOM)

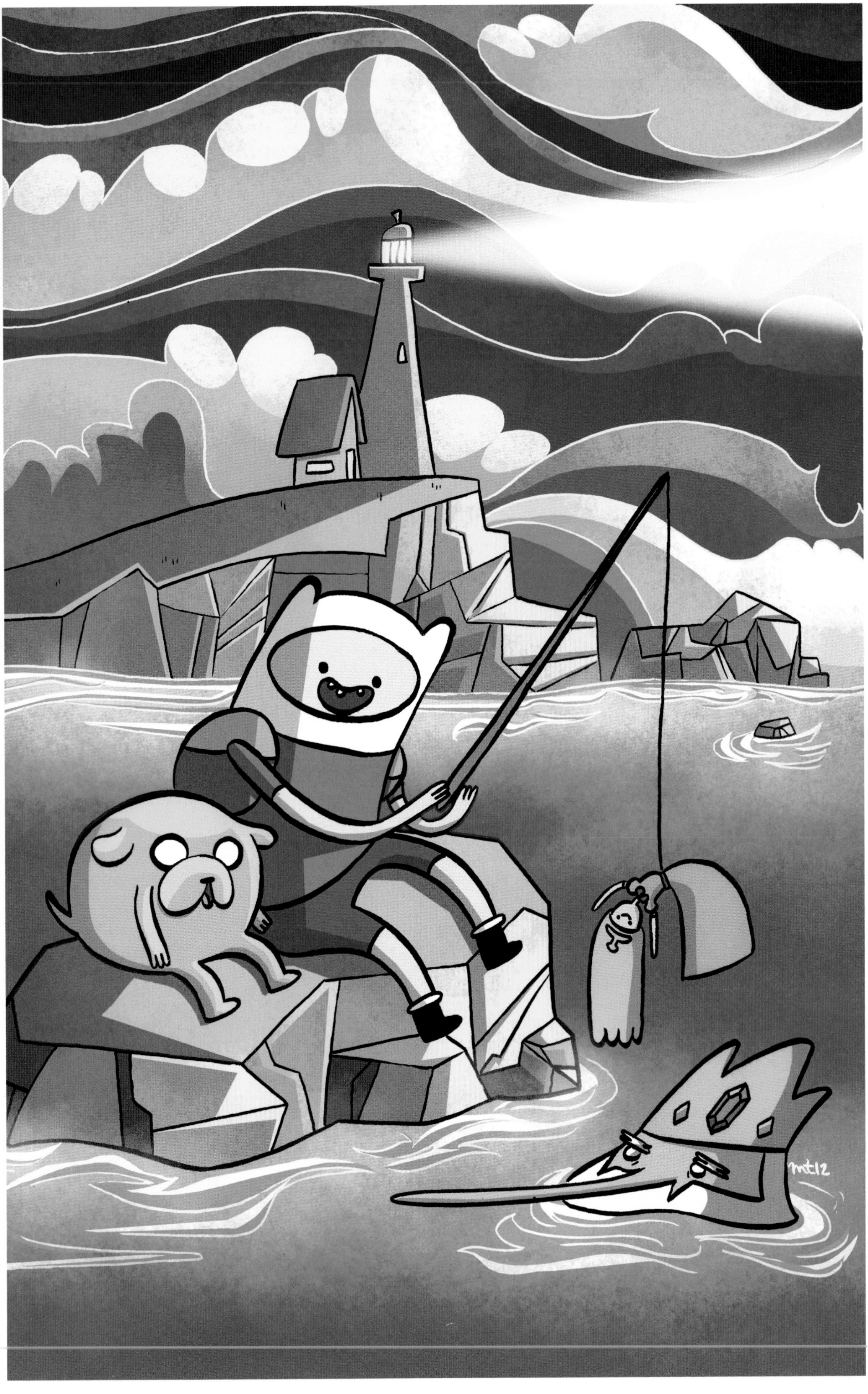
mt12

MAINE COMIC ARTS FESTIVAL ISSUE FOUR EXCLUSIVE | MELANIE TINGDAHL | COLORS BY LISA MOORE

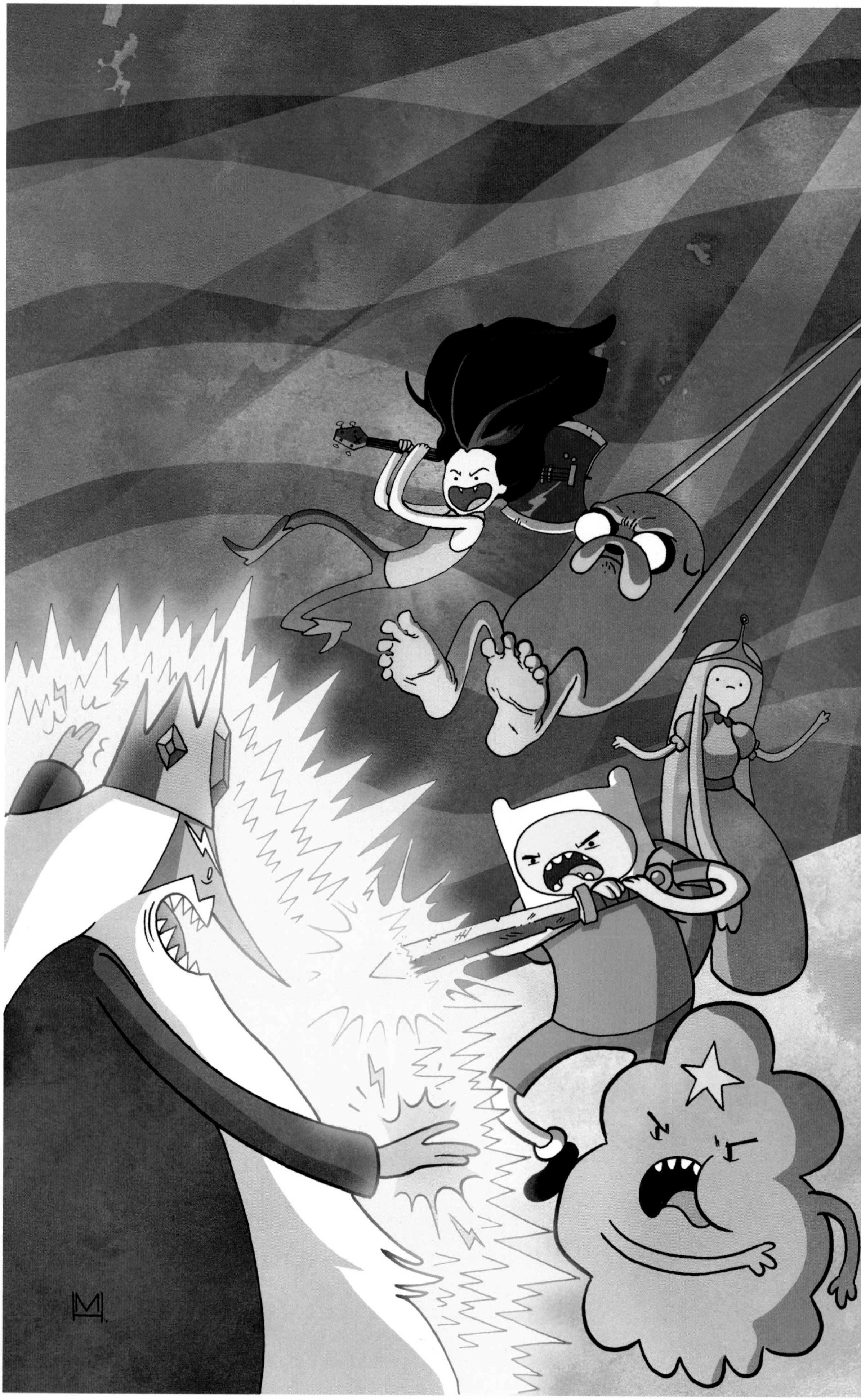

DOUBLE MIDNIGHT COMICS ISSUE FOUR EXCLUSIVE | MIKE HOLMES | COLORS BY LISA MOORE

BEHIND THE SCENES

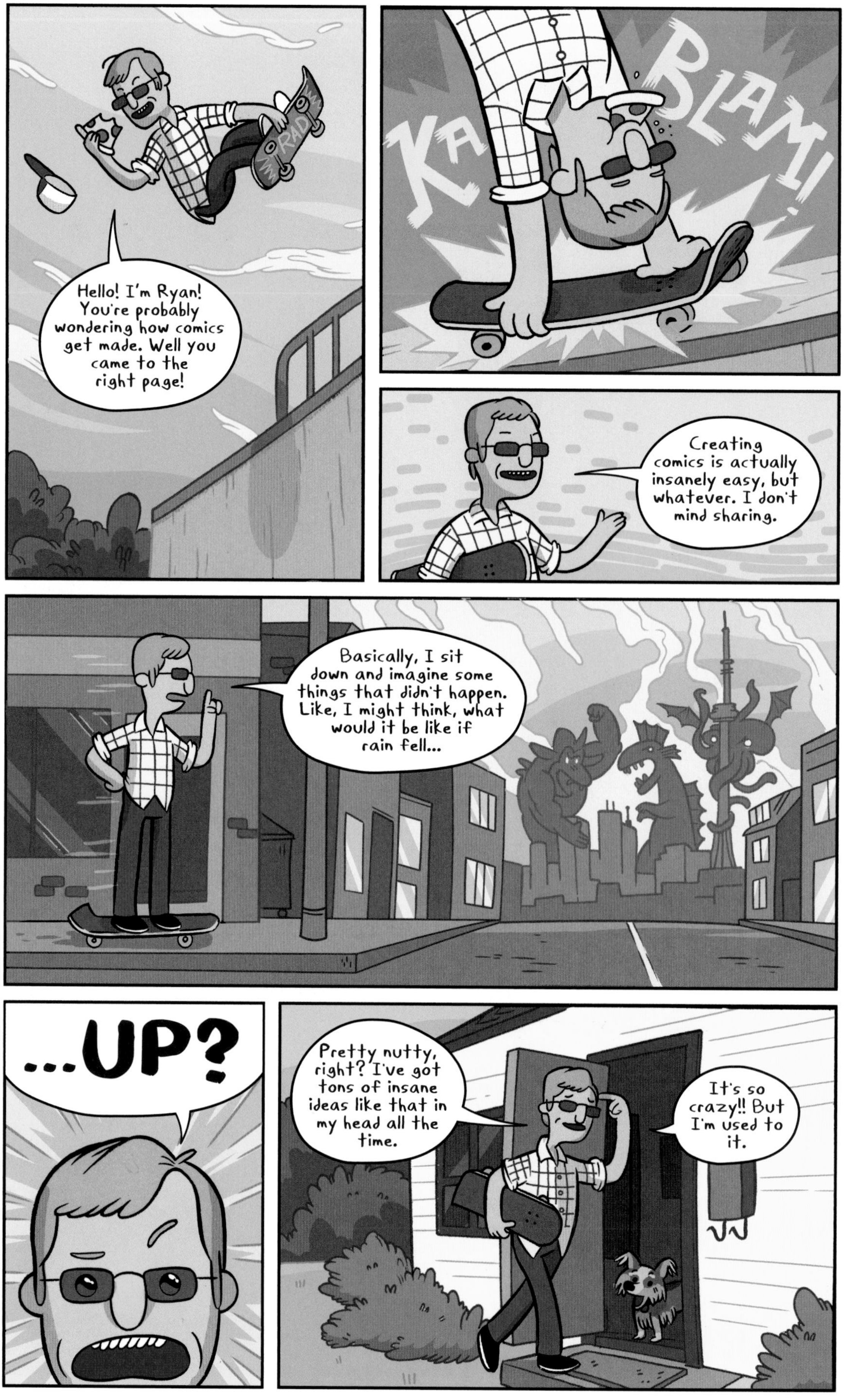
RAD
Hello! I'm Ryan! You're probably wondering how comics get made. Well you came to the right page!
KA BLAM!
Creating comics is actually insanely easy, but whatever. I don't mind sharing.
Basically, I sit down and imagine some things that didn't happen. Like, I might think, what would it be like if rain fell...
...UP?
Pretty nutty, right? I've got tons of insane ideas like that in my head all the time.
It's so crazy!! But I'm used to it.

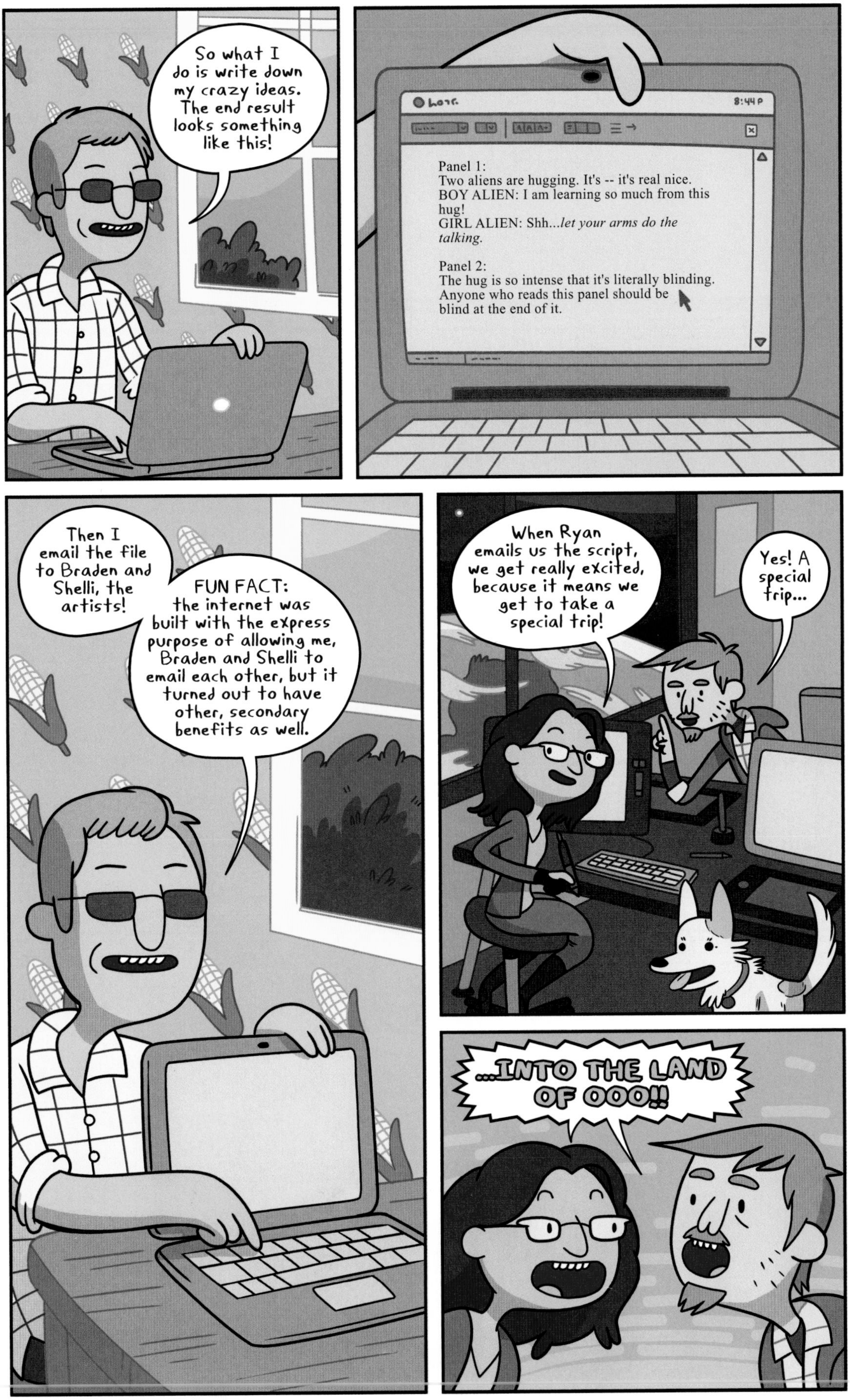
So what I do is write down my crazy ideas. The end result looks something like this!
8:44 P
Panel 1:
Two aliens are hugging. It's -- it's real nice.
BOY ALIEN: I am learning so much from this hug!
GIRL ALIEN: Shh...*let your arms do the talking.*
Panel 2:
The hug is so intense that it's literally blinding. Anyone who reads this panel should be blind at the end of it.
Then I email the file to Braden and Shelli, the artists!
FUN FACT: the internet was built with the express purpose of allowing me, Braden and Shelli to email each other, but it turned out to have other, secondary benefits as well.
When Ryan emails us the script, we get really excited, because it means we get to take a special trip!
Yes! A special trip...
...INTO THE LAND OF OOO!!

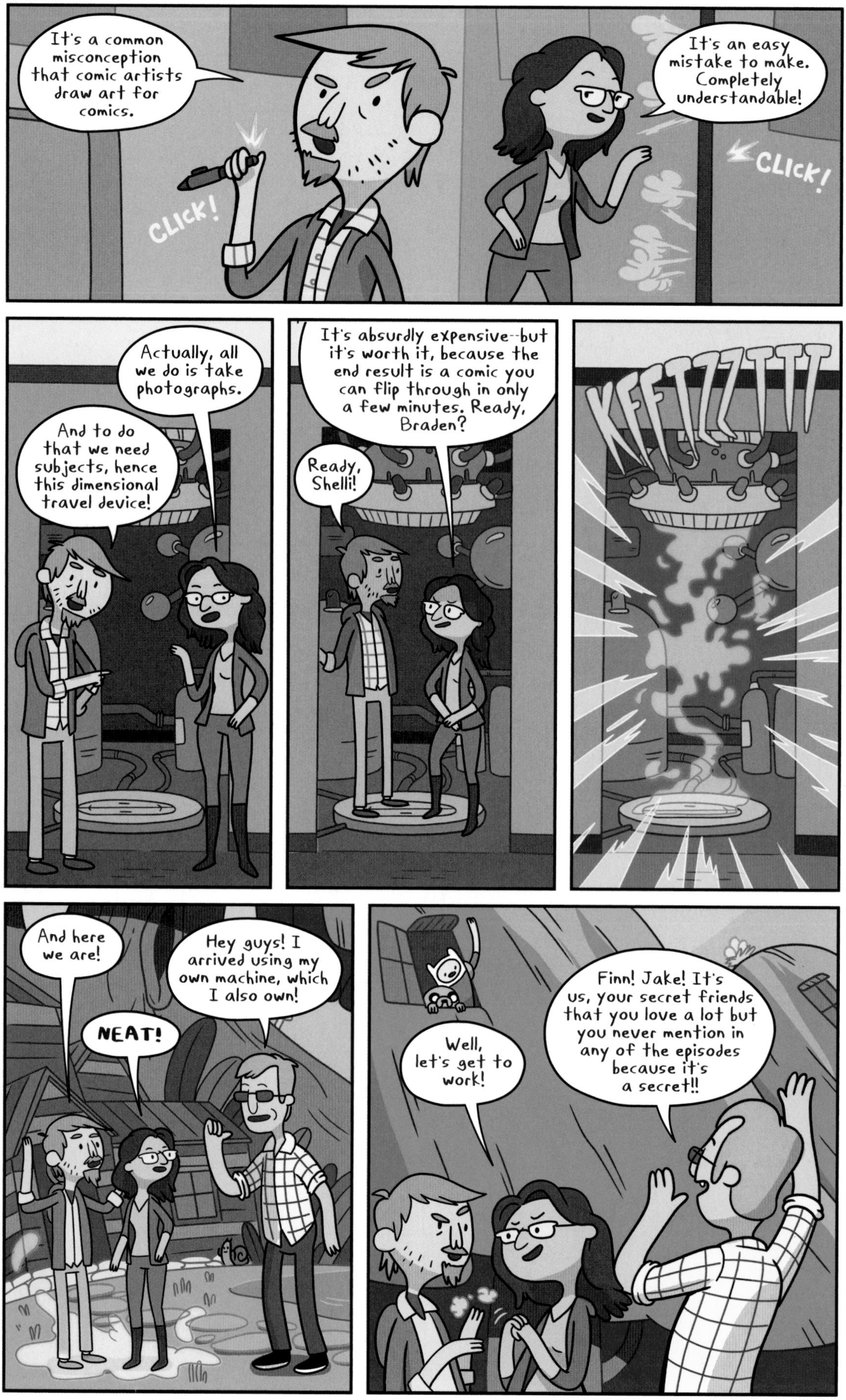
It's a common misconception that comic artists draw art for comics.
CLICK!
It's an easy mistake to make. Completely understandable!
CLICK!
Actually, all we do is take photographs.
And to do that we need subjects, hence this dimensional travel device!
It's absurdly expensive--but it's worth it, because the end result is a comic you can flip through in only a few minutes. Ready, Braden?
Ready, Shelli!
KFFTZZZTTT
And here we are!
Hey guys! I arrived using my own machine, which I also own!
NEAT!
Finn! Jake! It's us, your secret friends that you love a lot but you never mention in any of the episodes because it's a secret!!
Well, let's get to work!

SOON:

Okay, so LSP, if you could raise your arms a little?

My lumpin' arms are already lumpin' raised, Braden!

Just a li'l more, I promise.

Perfect.

CLICK!

Now all I do is paste some voice balloons on this that the letterer, Steve, has made, and we're done! It's so easy!

Yes, the art of comics is really just the art of photography!

Well, that and the art of owning a dimensional transport machine.

And now you know the 100% true facts of how comics like this are made!

It's lots of fun! Let's show everyone the final result, Ryan.

Comics! That's really all there is to it!!

Hats to meet you!

DAE JSR AFC SM M

THE END!

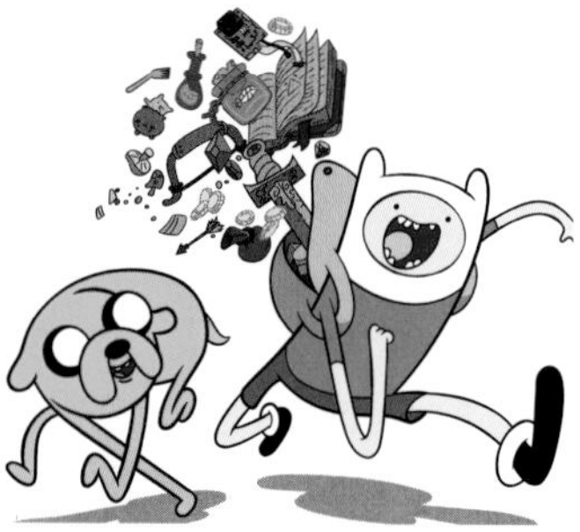

ADVENTURE TIME!

From Script to Page

by Ryan North

On the right, you can see the final page as it appears in ADVENTURE TIME Volume One. I thought I'd show how the script compares to the final page!

In issue one, I wrote out page layouts for Braden and Shelli, saying things like "we've got these panels 1x3 on the page, and then a splashy panel 4, and then panel 5 long and skinny beneath that." But then they surprised me with rough pencils that A) used my layouts in a few cases but B) came up with way better ones a ton of the time. So in this issue (and onwards!) I just said "hey, here are the panels with what's happening inside of them" and let Braden and Shelli do the layouts. They're awesome at it!

PAGE FIVE

Panel 1:
Jake (big) with Finn on his back and DP being pulled up by Finn, as he runs off at full speed. Finn is helping DP up by her hands.
FINN: If we just pick a direction and run, we're bound to hit the edge of the bag eventually!!
DP: Yes!
JAKE: SCIENCE.

Panel 2:
NARRATION: Twenty minutes later:
Jake, flopped out on the ground, exhausted, legs splayed, Finn standing beside him, DP is on her knees in the sand building something.
JAKE: Man, I'm pooped. I don't think running is the answer here, dudes. I think running--I think running might actually be the worst.

Panel 3:
DP has made three sand drinks with straws. She offers the extras to Finn and Jake.
DP: Gentlemen! Maybe we're thinking too two-dimensionally! Maybe we can escape...up?

Panel 4:
We see a low-angle looking up with Finn and DP as Jake spirals off into the sky, legs still on the ground. Finn and DP staring upwards. Finn is taking the offered drink absent-mindedly.
JAKE (words getting smaller as he blasts into the sky): Anything's better than runningggggggg

Panel 5:
Same angle, but now Finn and DP sip on their sand drinks while they stare at Jake going up into the sky.

Panel 6:
Same angle, but now Finn tastes what he's drinking and spits out sand while DP continues to sip and stare upwards at Jake.

ALT: a little tiny comic at the bottom of the page featuring Marceline, addressing the camera.
P1: Remember when the Lich was attacking me and my totally sweet house?
P2: Remember how instead of helping me out, you turned the page and read about Finn and Jake instead?
p3: Well I don't have to remember because he's still attacking me and IT'S HAPPENING RIGHT NOW!!

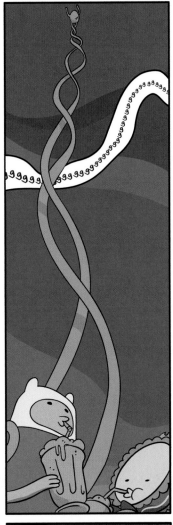

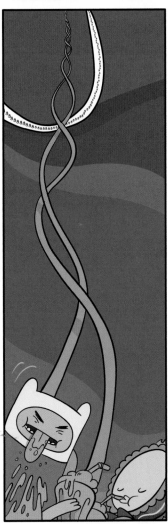

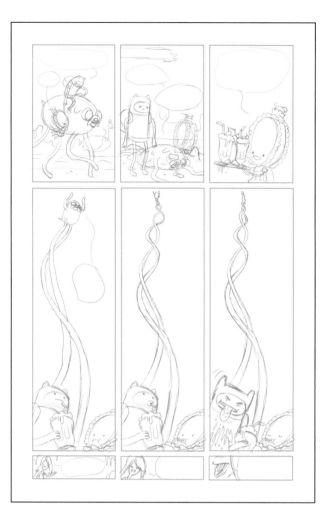

For example, check out the long, tall panels they drew on this page! They work SO WELL and communicate the heights that Jake's reaching up to in a really nice visual way. But it's not just layout: in the script I have Jake's "Anything's better than runninggggggg" line happen in panel 4, but here in the comic his dialogue is spread out across panels 5 and 6 too, being pulled up with Jake as he stretches himself higher. Nice! It makes the page more fun to look at (and read!) and we get the sense of Jake's words fading away as he gets higher up, which is exactly what I was going for. It's always awesome when you can translate vocal effects like this to a silent, visual medium, and still have them come through like I'm whispering into your ear!

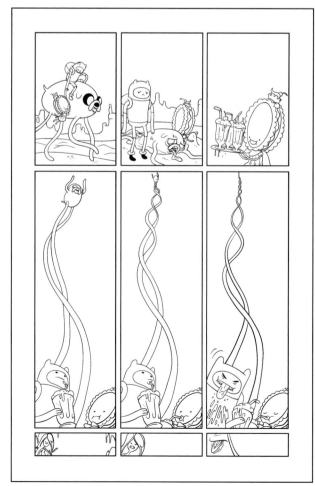

At this point I imagine writing this comic like a game of tennis: I send the ball over the net as hard as I can, confident that the other members of the team will be able to return it, and they do, but every single ball they hit returns as a hunk of solid gold.

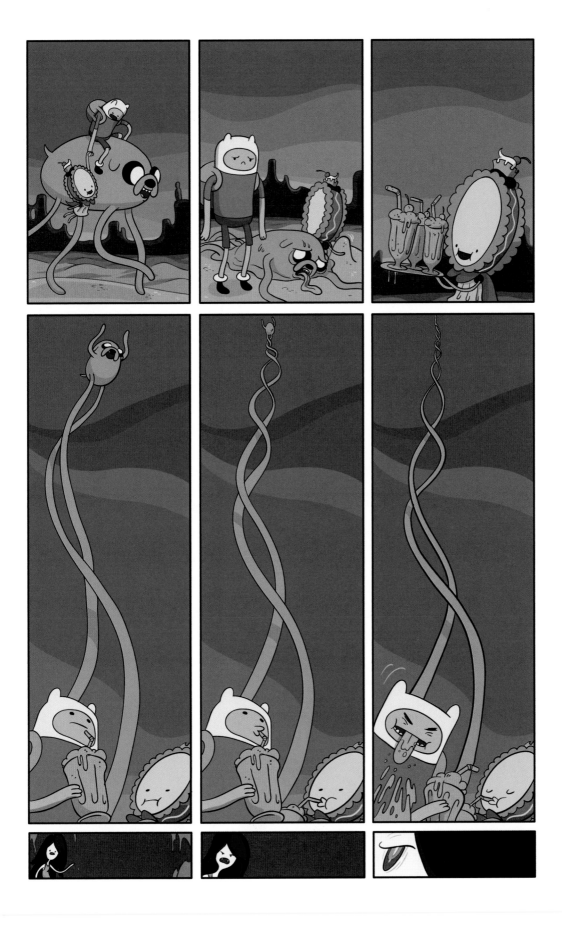

Dang. Teamwork, yo!

DESIGNING THE PRINCESSES

by Ryan North

The best part of ADVENTURE TIME is the princesses. Wait, actually -- maybe the best part of

ADVENTURE TIME is the adventures that happen all the time! But I also really like Finn and

Jake so yeah, they're probably the best part. But Marceline's amazing too, and the Ice King

is so great, and Lemongrab is unlike any other lemon I've ever known. And BMO's so good!

Okay, you know what? Among the best parts of ADVENTURE TIME, all of which are tied for

first place, are the princesses. And I got to invent some new ones for this comic!

Here's how you invent a princess.

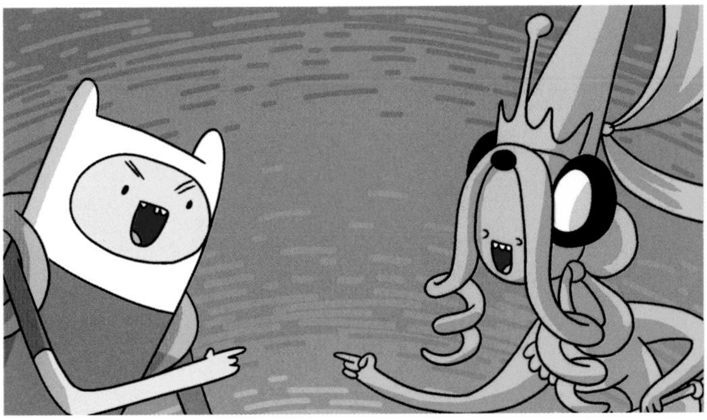

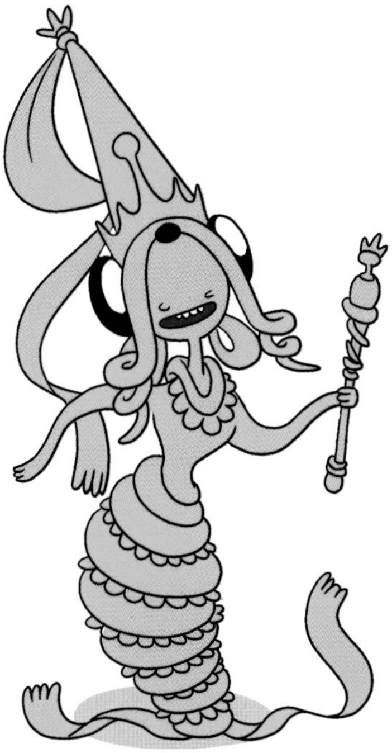

Jake Princess

Jake Princess was actually the easiest one: the idea was "What if Jake turned into a Princess?" I didn't have to give much direction to Braden and Shelli because they know Jake AND they're great at drawing cool things. Here's all I wrote in the script: "Jake turns into a beautiful princess. Princess Jake is the fanciest princess in the world: sceptre, crown: the works. I know she'll be awesome."

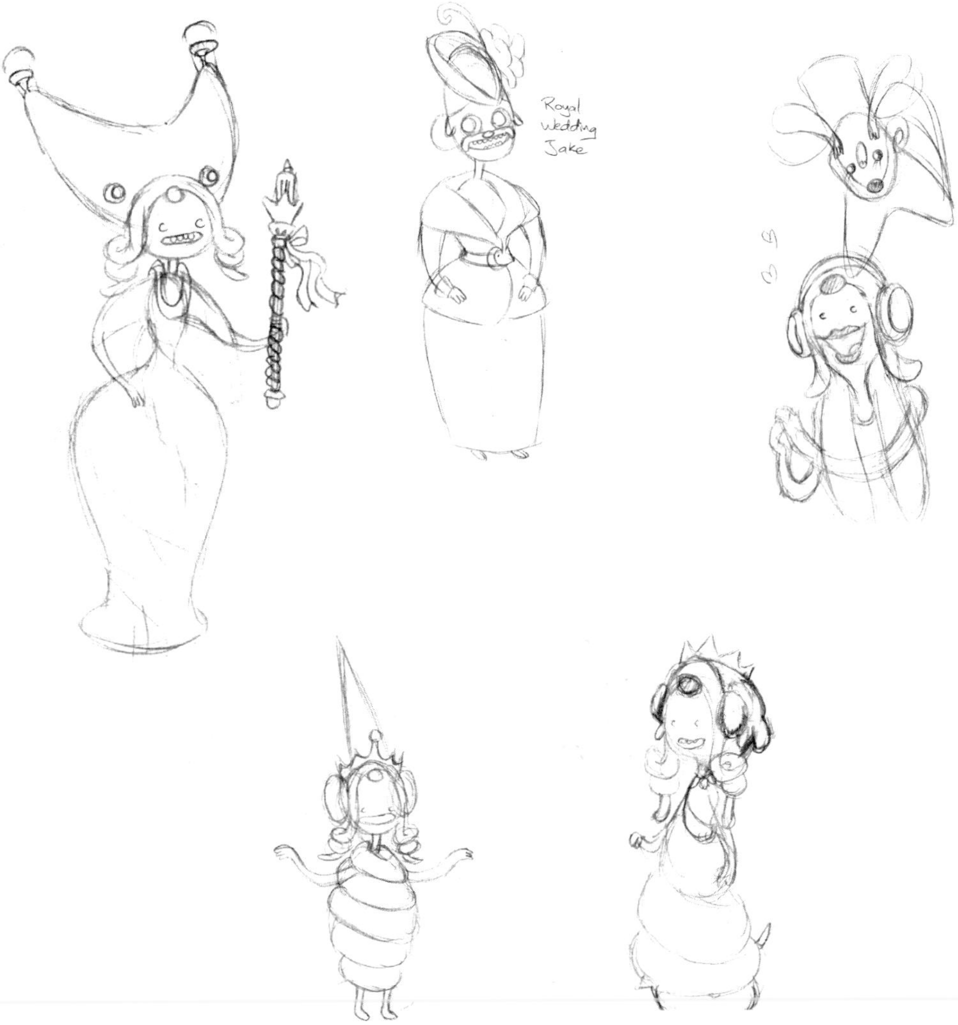
Royal Wedding Jake

Desert Princess

Desert Princess played an important role in the story, so she had to have the perfect design. Braden and Shelli did four very different ones and let me choose which one I liked best, which was amazing. To make that decision, I recalled the one piece of life advice that's never done me harm: "When in doubt, go for the giant cake."

Again, I just wrote a few words about her and let the artists fill in the rest: "She's made entirely out of different desserts. She's got a crown, so Jake can tell she's royalty." For Issue 1, Pendleton Ward had the idea to have her be made of mushed-together Candy Kingdom citizens, and I wrote that into the story the first chance I got.

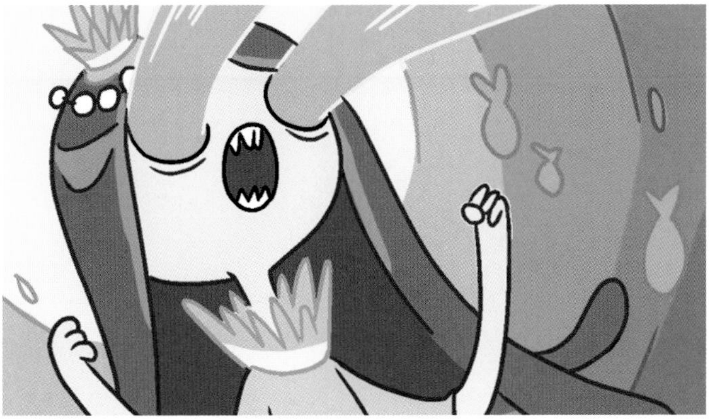

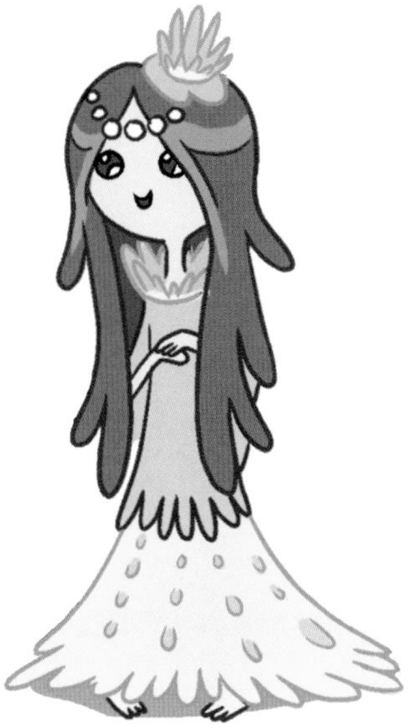

Water Princess

I felt bad about being such a lazy writer guy when it came to describing what these princesses looked like, so for Water Princess I sketched out a whole bunch of different options. You can see by this sketch the reason they asked me to write the comic and not to draw it. The good news is that Braden and Shelli ignored these sketches and made their own, way better design for her! But we all liked the woman with the mouth full of teeth, so I wrote her in as Lamprey Princess later on.

She is my favorite member of the nightmarish Lamprey Kingdom.

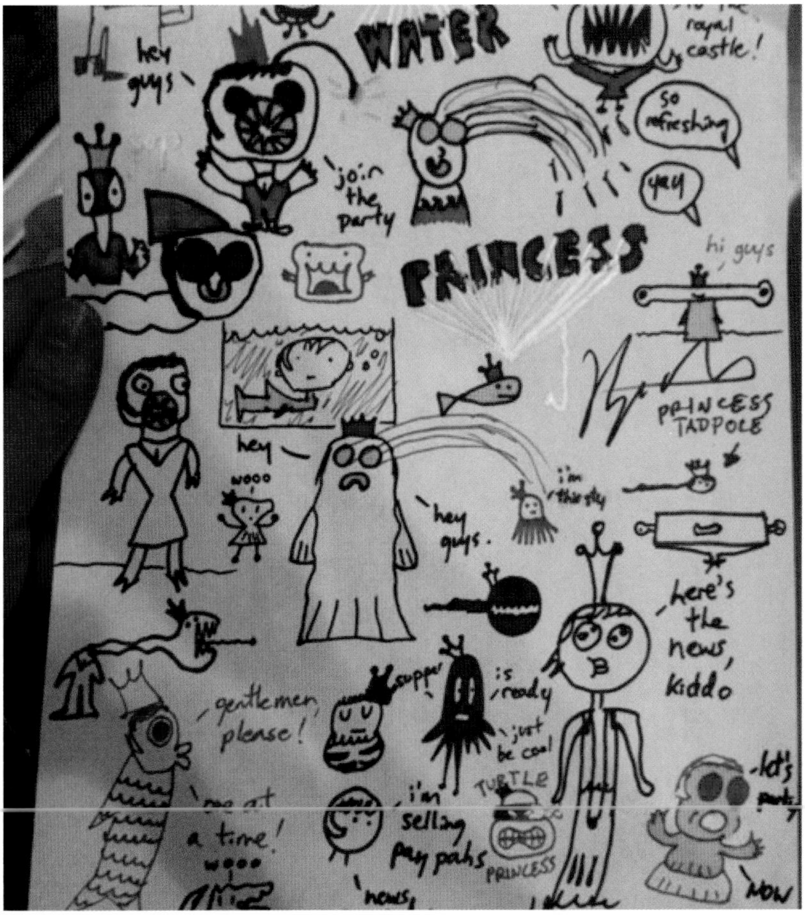
WATER
PRINCESS
hey guys
royal castle!
so refreshing
yay
join the party
hi guys
PRINCESS TADPOLE
hey
wooo
hey guys.
i'm thirsty
here's the news, kiddo
gentlemen, please!
supper is ready
just be cool
TURTLE
PRINCESS
NOW

COMING JULY 2013

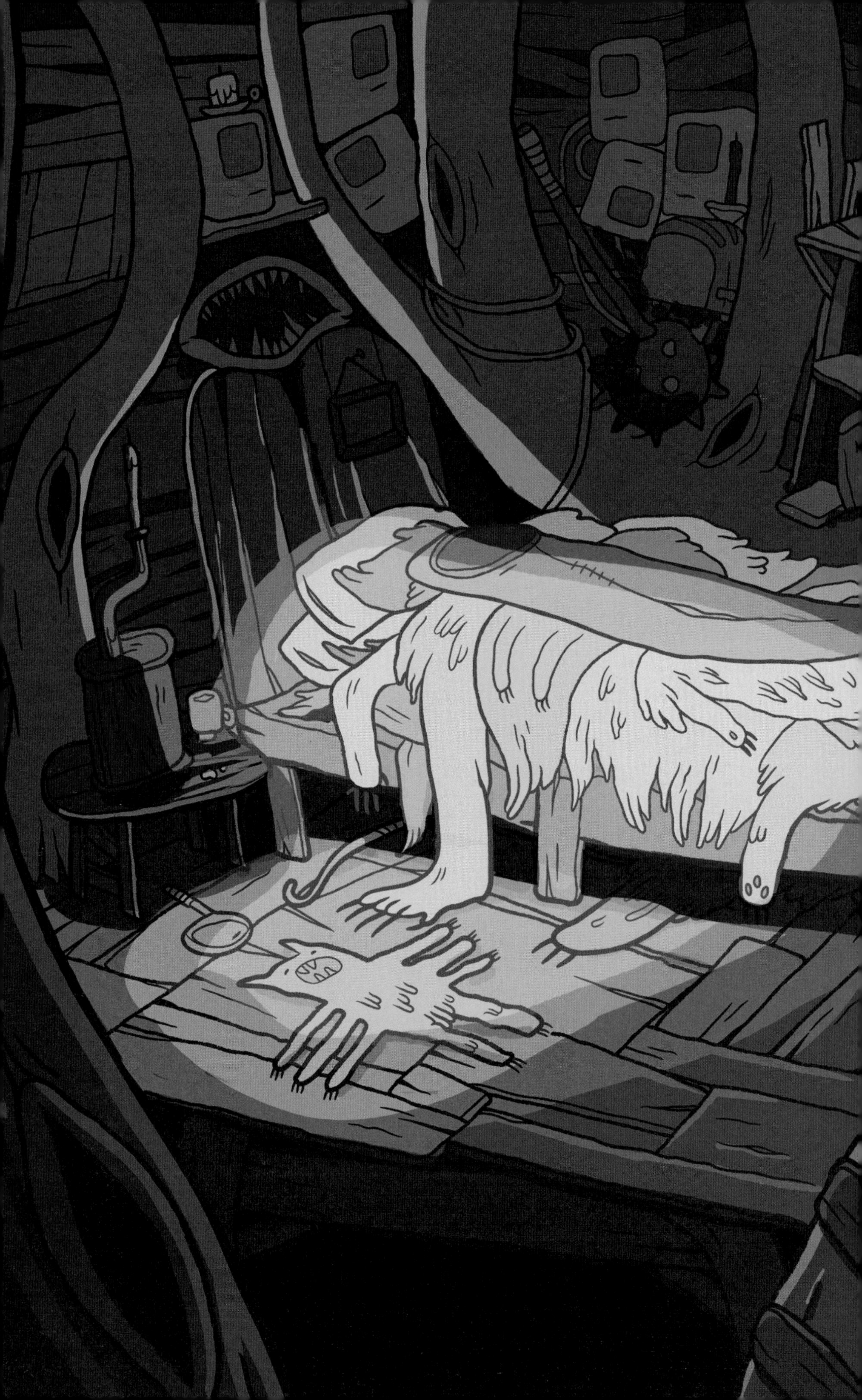

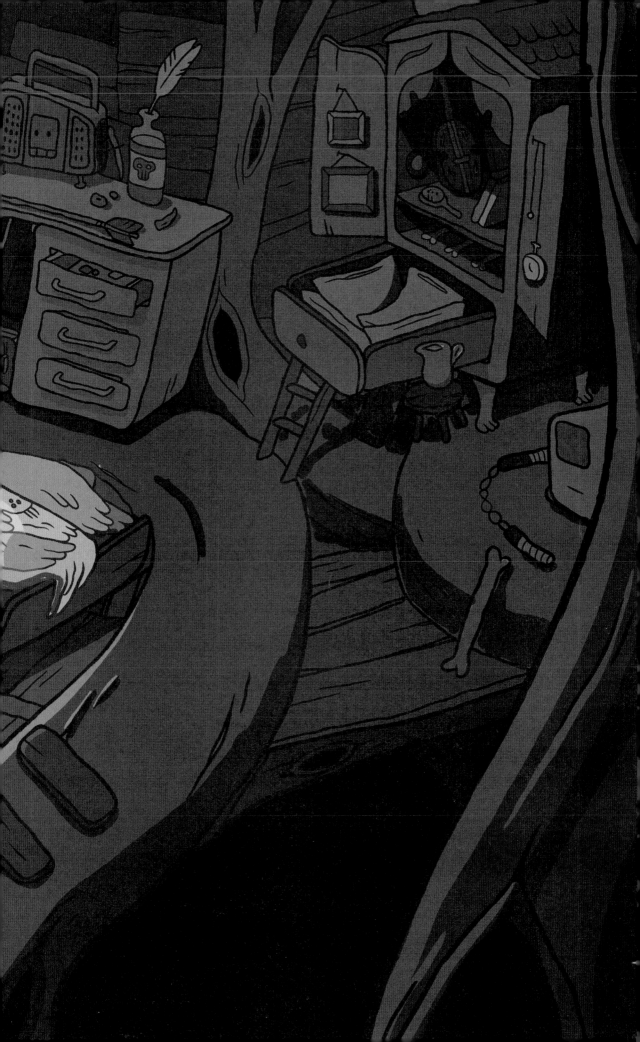

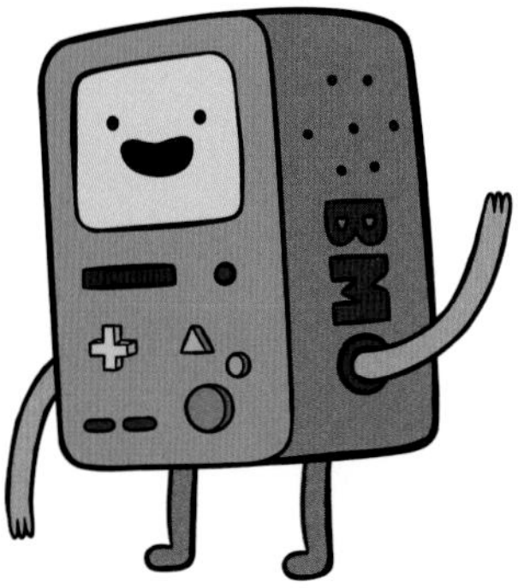
BM

Ryan North lives in Toronto with his rad wife and sweet dog. He writes comics at dinosaurcomics.com every day. His interests include skateboarding, being a good friend, and eating tasty things. He really hopes you like the comics!

Shelli Paroline escaped early on into the world of comics, cartoons, and science fiction. She has now returned to the Boston area, where she works as an unassuming illustrator and designer.

Braden Lamb grew up in Seattle, studied film in upstate New York, learned about vikings in Iceland and Norway, and established an art career in Boston. Now he draws and colors comics, and wouldn't have it any other way.

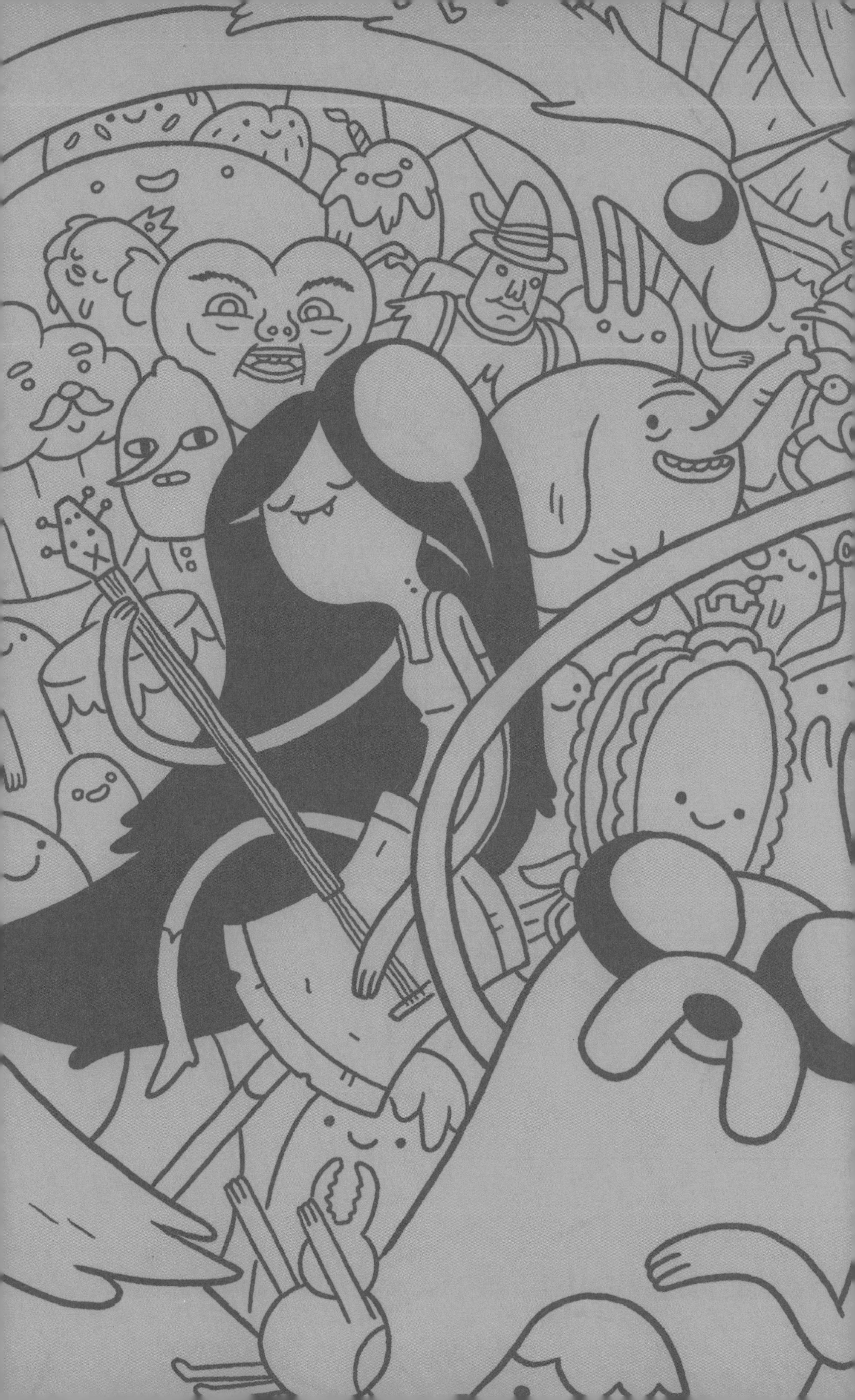